I FOUND YOU

BY TROY HARWOOD

Written by Troy Harwood

Edited by Joe Pierson

Cover art by Alejandro Colucci

Additional artwork by Bridgette Harwood

Contents

Prologue

JOURNAL

December 12, 1863

I don't know how much time I have, but I guess I'll start here. My name is Hughes Dumphree. I am twenty-nine years old, I'm looking for my family, and I'm afraid I am being hunted.

Writing this is likely more dangerous than not, but even if someone got their hands on it, I doubt they'd understand it. It's only for me. I just need some kind of comfort. Something to help me comprehend everything that's happened. Then, if I'm lucky, I can rid myself of this fear before it consumes me entirely.

~~It was only a few nights ago. That's when I saw him~~

It's been around a month since I arrived here. There were arguments almost immediately. Some even wanted to go back. Admittedly, I considered the same thing, but I didn't have the nerve to say it. I wasn't too close with any of them besides Connor, and after what he did, I knew he wouldn't budge. It was simply too late; we had to go ahead with it. So, they moved on, leaving me here just in time for winter. It was a thing of beauty at first, seeing so much snow. Despite it being almost always cold at home, snow had never fallen. I had only ever seen pictures of it. Unfortunately, only a few hours after arriving, it became abundantly clear that this constant snowfall was *not* a good thing. Just like home, I think everyone here has the same thought at least a dozen times a day; that it's '*bloody-well-freezing*'.

I'm actually rather surprised and disappointed that this isn't the only thing that relates me to these people. London is eerily similar to home. The streets are overstuffed, the air is dark, and too many people seem oblivious to it all. They slave away just the same, letting everything around them progressively rot. I don't know where they think they're heading, if they even are thinking like that.

I used to blame this ignorance on the alterations many had in their minds and bodies, but here they have no such changes. They're perfectly natural and pure. It's a depression that is all too familiar, but I suppose it's just another motivator for me to find the Dumphrees. Asking around, I've gathered they live outside the city, far from the smog and endless noise. Just the idea of their estate being so free from all of this rekindles my excitement and hope every time I think on it. Especially given my recent turn in luck.

About a week and a half ago, I was still living on the streets, alley to alley. Then, one night, in yet another overflowing alleyway, an elderly lady hobbled through. She was asking if anyone had seen her young daughter, and if there was any help one could offer. So many shrugged and shooed her away as they tried sleeping under their coats and atop their bags. I shamefully admit that I shook my head at first too. I mean, the chances of finding anyone in this dense and large a city are slim.

Yet, the further she walked away, the more I couldn't shake the irony that I too was looking for my people. And seeing no one offer a hand of help as she waddled away simply hurt to see. So, just before she left, I caught up to her and explained that, while I didn't know where her daughter was, I would help her look. In very few words, she introduced herself as Docie, and gave a brief description of her blonde-haired, twelve-year-old daughter, Abigail.

After we spent the next few hours searching the surrounding streets in vain, she offered me a place to stay. And that's where I am now. It's nothing like the Dumphree estate will surely be, but it is a roof over my head. A large apartment complex on the corner of yet another busy street. Every room is overstuffed with citizens living across the floor, and there's barely any light besides a handful of candles, but words cannot convey my thankfulness towards Docie. It seems many others here also hold the same gratitude for her hospitality. While she may not speak much, she makes up for it in what she gives. Many in the building have homemade scarves and jackets, all thanks to her constant knitting and sewing. She doesn't expect any help chipping in with rent either, but we all do it anyway.

Regrettably, though, we are still yet to find her daughter. It would've been defeating if she was missing for a day, let alone *weeks*. And while I still try to keep my hopes up, it is clear hers are fading. She's spoken less and less about her lately, which is usually the only time she does speak.

Thankfully, however, since I've been given this stable enough home, I've also been able to acquire a job at the nearby factory. George, one of my new living-mates, was able to introduce me to the place. Although it's not like I particularly needed him to. The factory seems to take anyone it can get, regardless of skill. So, hooray for me, I have no idea what I'm doing. I simply copy what everyone else does around me, banging away at metal until it resembles something recognisable. Then on to the next piece. Day in and day out. Not to mention the thick layer of black … dust? Ash? I don't even know what it is, but it always seems to cover the floor, walls, and even myself by the end of each day. At least back home, I had somewhat of a shower. Here, I have to wait for the rain if I'm in need of a good clean (which is all the time, really).

Regardless, this employment has allowed me to progress in my plan: that is to find out where the Dumphree estate is, make enough money to look the part, and finally, convince them that I am who I say I am.

None of this is going to be easy.

Firstly, I'm only earning what seems to be the equivalent of a few cents an hour. And, as I explained, I look terrible. Looking through a cake shop window the other day, I barely even recognised myself in the reflection. And that was before the shopkeeper shooed me away like a pest from the real potential customers!

Secondly, regarding the location of the estate, I've been sifting through discarded newspapers each day, scouring them for any details. The Dumphree name appears here and there due to their lucrative business dealings. I'm just hoping one day their estate will be mentioned too. It might be wishful thinking, but at this point, what else do I have?

Finally, there is the matter of convincing them of who I am. I have my story, and I've been able to practise retelling it to those around me, but that feels like the greatest risk of them all. Only time will tell, I suppose.

Anyway, in between the factory and my search for Abigail and the Dumphrees, I now have this journal to keep my thoughts occupied. I awoke the other morning to see the pale, lifeless eyes of an elderly man staring at me. He died in his sleep on the mattress beside me, and had this journal in his possession. Surprisingly, it was completely empty. Maybe the man didn't know how to write. Or he just had nothing *to* write. Either way, Docie being Docie, she gave it to me.

I didn't think I'd want to use it until the other night. I was sitting where I am now, in a quiet hallway near the summit of this complex, looking out a cracked window at the street below. And that's when I saw *him*. A man concealed by a dark hood walking the snowy streets below, carefully surveying every alley and building that he passed. I've tried convincing myself that my worries are mere baseless paranoia, but every time I tell myself it has nothing to do with me, it feels like a lie. I knew the moment I saw him that he was *looking*. That he was *different*. The way he held himself, eyed his surroundings, clung to the shadows …

I knew he didn't belong here. Just like me. And even though he never could've spotted me from down there, I still felt the pure compulsion to run. My mind has felt heavy with fear ever since. I'm sweating just at the thought of what is happening back home. I can only hope that writing this will help me lift that burden going forward.

Thankfully, looking back out the window now, I don't see him below.

VOLUME ONE

THE EAGLE

Chapter 1

'I'll find you.'

A woman's voice whispered from the darkness.

A deafening gunshot followed.

Hughes' eyes snapped open with a fright. It was another nightmare. Another memory. One that would not let him return to sleep.

He stared at the ceiling, fighting to clear his mind as a piercing chill hung in the air. Over a dozen other guests slept on the mattresses sprawled out across the floor while their snores and heavy breathing filled the room. Hughes turned his eyes towards the boarded-up windows. Only darkness seeped through the cracks.

The night wasn't yet over.

His gaze fell upon Docie. She lay alone on one of the few mattresses with a bedframe beneath it. Through the shadows, he couldn't make out if she was sleeping or not.

Surely she's awake, he thought. *If I can't sleep, how could she? Every night must be worse than the last. Maybe another search will do her good.*

But what if he's out there?

Just keep your head low and you'll be fine. He's not going to find you. You need the air anyway. And maybe we'll find another newspaper. Another clue.

Hughes nodded to himself with a hesitant conviction. At last, he pushed himself off the mattress and slid on his tattered woollen coat. With a nervous breath, he quietly crept around all the other mattresses. The wooden floorboards creaked and groaned beneath his feet. He finally reached the apartment door before a voice whispered out to him from behind.

'Psst. Hey.'

Hughes froze and turned around with surprise. He peered through the dark room, spotting the silhouette of one of his roommates half-sitting up on their mattress. From the large gut and deep voice, he knew it was George.

'*Where you off to?*'

Hughes glanced around, ensuring everyone else was undisturbed, before whispering back, '*Out for a walk. Another look for Abigail. You can go back to sleep.*'

George fell silent.

'*I'll see you later,*' Hughes continued, beginning to turn around before George let out a sigh.

'*All right, hold on, hold on, I'm comin',*' he groaned as he climbed to his feet, grabbing his coat.

After descending the long, creaky stairwell, the pair walked outside into the early morning fog. The street was quiet and difficult to see through, only illuminated by the warm glow of gas lamps lining the footpaths. They buried their hands in their pockets as they began strolling through the lonely streets.

'Couldn't sleep, ay?' George asked.

'No. Not quite,' Hughes replied with a shake of his head. 'You neither?'

'Well, I *was* fine till your big stomping feet woke me up.'

'Oh, it was my fault, was it?'

'Every bit of it. Don't know how Docie hasn't kicked you out yet, ya know? I would've.'

'Well, good thing you're not Docie, you … bloody … foozler,' he retorted, unable to keep a straight face.

George laughed. 'Oi, that's one of mine, you hornswoggler! Takin' my words now, are ya?'

'Maybe I'm catching on to some things.' He playfully shrugged.

'Can't get rid of your accent, though, can ya? What even is it, anyway? I ain't ever heard a voice like yours before.'

'It's a mixed accent. Father was British, mother was French. Pretty sure I told you this.'

George stared off blankly, trying to remember. 'May have been a bit wobbly that night.'

Hughes chuckled. 'You know, something tells me you're right about that.'

'What's a Dumphree been doing off in France, anyway? And shouldn't they know you're 'ere now?'

'I think I told you this one too, you know? It's a long story, but I grew up there, and I've never actually *met* Flavel Dumphree. I'm going to have to do some convincing.'

'And 'ow the bloody 'ell are you gonna do that?'

'Well, I do have this.' Hughes pulled out a small, crumpled, and discoloured old photo of an older gentleman with a thick beard and a brown suit. 'This is my father, Albert Dumphree. I'm sure Flavel will recognise the face. So, hopefully, in showing him this, I'll be able to convince him of who I am. But I have to find him first. You don't happen to know where he might live, do you?' he jokingly asked.

'Aw, I wish. I'd be bloody knocking on his door sayin' I'm a Dumphree too, if I did.'

Hughes chuckled again as a horse and carriage trotted out of the fog before them. The driver tipped his hat and nodded to them both as he passed by. 'Mornin'.'

'Mornin'.'

'Morning.'

Hughes smiled at the horses, admiring the sight of them. Just as they moved out of view, he caught a glimpse of something entering an alleyway across the street. It was a familiar silhouette drenched in black shadow.

A pain struck his heart, and his legs froze.

George glanced back at him, slowing down in place. 'You all right? Horses give ya a fright?'

'No, no, I just…' Hughes stared at the dark alleyway ahead. It was deathly quiet. He swallowed, desperately pulling his eyes away from it. 'How about we turn around – go another way? I think I've searched this way before.'

George curiously glanced around the street and shrugged, 'All right. Good by me.' He continued back the way they came as Hughes locked eyes with the alleyway once more.

The darkness peered back at him.

'Come on, then.' George called out, gesturing him along. Hughes nodded and nervously turned away, jogging to catch up to his friend.

Soon, the sun rose behind the endless dark clouds and black smoke. The sounds of shouting voices, ringing bells, and trotting horses grew by the minute throughout every street in the city.

Hughes and George trekked through yet another waking street. Blended with the crowds of citizens, they approached a nearby clearing.

'Do you know where we are?' Hughes asked, taking in their surroundings.

'I think so, I think so. I'm pretty sure I've been to a pub not far from 'ere once.'

'Oh, okay. *Great*.' Hughes replied, rolling his eyes.

As they reached the end of the street, a large factory grabbed Hughes' attention. Painted on its side were the words: *DUMPHREE LOCOMOTIVE FACTORY*.

Hughes paused in disbelief, nudging George's arm. 'George. Is this the Dumphree factory?'

George stopped and tilted his head, taking a moment to read the sign. 'D … um … ff … ree. Oh, what do ya know? I forgot it was around 'ere.'

Hughes' mouth fell agape. '*Now* you remember?'

'Well, I told ya, I was only around 'ere when I was at the pub.' He innocently replied, rubbing the back of his head.

Hughes shook his head, half-amused. He turned his gaze back to the factory, gesturing towards it. 'This is how I get to them! Flavel could be inside there right now!'

'Well, go on then. See if he is.'

'I can't meet him dressed like this. I need to get the right clothes — I need to *look* like a Dumphree if he's going to believe me.'

George patted his shoulder and looked him in the eye. 'If he's really family, he'll believe ya no matter 'ow you're dressed.'

Hughes stared back at him, taking in his words. Slowly, he nodded. 'You're right. I just need to meet him and tell him the truth. That should be enough.'

'Go on, then! Go get 'em!' George exclaimed with a pat on the back.

Hughes let out a sharp breath and straightened his coat. With an air of confidence, he marched across the clearing and straight towards the entrance. Workers poured inside as the factory manager stood at the front gate, checking each of them off as they entered.

Hughes approached the manager directly, eager and anxious. 'Good morning.'

'Mornin',' The manager replied in a drawn-out manner, eyeing him with suspicion as he waited for an explanation.

'I was – um – I was wondering if Flavel Dumphree works here?'

'Well, this *is* his factory.'

'So, he's here? He's inside?'

'What's it to ya?'

'I'm a family member of his. A cousin.'

'You? You're saying *you're* a Dumphree?'

'Yes.'

The manager looked him up and down before scoffing. 'Yeah, nice try, mate. Now, get lost.' He turned his focus back to his call sheet, signalling the line of workers to continue entering as he checked them off.

Hughes reluctantly watched him. He shuffled in place before speaking up once more. 'All right, I'll work here. I'll work in the factory.'

The manager rolled his eyes, continuing to tick off the names on his sheet. 'Are you askin' for a job now?'

'Yes. I already work at the Fitzgerald factory, but I'll leave and start here right now if you'll take me.'

The manager paused and eyed him up and down a second time, unconvinced.

'You can even cut my pay in half,' Hughes added.

The manager's eyebrows raised before he sighed. 'All right, then. You can start here next Monday. I don't wanna be hearin' any more of this Dumphree business, though. You're a factory worker, all right? Flavel's barely here as it is, anyway.'

Hughes smiled with relief. 'Thank you.'

'Yeah, all right. Go on, now.'

Hughes nodded and strolled back to George with a skip in his step.

George's shoulders fell with disappointment. 'They turned ya away?'

'Not exactly. I don't think Flavel's there now, but I got a job.'

'A job? In there? That bloody quick?!'

'Yep. Now it's only a matter of time before Flavel comes visiting and I get my chance.'

'Well, that's somethin' right there! I knew you'd get that step closer!' he exclaimed, gripping Hughes' shoulder. 'I reckon we oughta celebrate! How's about we go to that pub I been to nearby?'

'If you can actually find it, then I'm with ya.'

George stared off blankly again, 'Oh, yeah … Yeah, that might be a bit of trouble, won't it?'

Hughes chuckled and shook his head. 'George, your mind never fails to amaze me.'

'Imagine how *I* feel. Ah, we'll find somewhere! Come on, a bit more exploring won't do us any 'arm!' he proclaimed, throwing his arm around Hughes' shoulder as they walked down yet another city street.

* * *

The air turned colder, and the snow fell heavier as the sun drifted towards London's clouded horizon. Docie swung back and forth in her rocking chair. Her knitting needles clicked together as she worked away on a new scarf. She sat beside her boarded-up, broken windows, looking down on the street below.

The rest of the tenants sat on the floor throughout the room, scooping up beans with their small wooden spoons from their small tin bowls. George and Hughes sat closest to Docie, glancing at one another, determining the right moment to say something.

Eventually, Hughes settled his breath and gazed up at her. 'We covered quite a bit of ground in the East End today. There wasn't any sign of her, but at least it's another place we can check off the list.'

Docie's expression remained solemn, continuing to focus on her knitting. 'You don't have to keep looking so much.'

'Of course we do, Docie. We *want* to look. And there's still a lot of places we can.'

'Frenchie's right, Dose,' George added. 'If anything's true about London, it's that it's a bloody big place. Easy to get lost, but if ya look 'ard enough, you can find your way … You know, I once lost my favourite pub in the 'ole city?'

'Why am I not surprised?' Hughes remarked.

'Say what ya will, but I 'ad the best bloody drinks you could ever imagine there. The best pints you'd ever have, I tell ya. But then, the mornin' after, I couldn't bloody remember where in the hell it was. I coulda sworn it was somewhere in Camden, but nup, it weren't bloody there! No one ever even 'eard of it! And it was that way for *five years*. Five. Bloody. Years. Torture, I tell ya. And then, guess what? *I found it!* I bloody found it! I was out and about on the town, stumblin' about, and *there* it was. I never thought the day would come, but there ya go … it did!'

'Where was it?'

'Well, I don't bloody remember now, do I?'

'But it had the best drinks you've ever had?'

'Not when I tried 'em again, they didn't. They were the fuckin' worst drinks I ever 'ad. So, I didn't go back there. No bloody way.'

Hughes chuckled and shook his head at Docie. She smirked back at him.

'But you see what I mean?' George continued. 'Just cause she's been lost for a little while, don't mean it's forever.'

Docie gave him a small, thankful nod.

'Who's the new scarf for?' Hughes asked her, admiring her knitting.

'New customer. Down the street.'

Hughes smiled at the news before they went quiet for a time. Eventually, he spoke up again. 'I've been using that journal a lot lately. A lot more than I thought I would. It's been helpful. Keeps my mind in order, a bit.'

'Don't ya get tired of being inside ya own head all the time?' George interjected. 'Even if I could write, I wouldn't. Bloody boring work, I say.'

'Well, I don't know. There's not really a lot else for me to do, is there?'

Docie turned her eyes down towards him. 'I could teach you how to knit. And sew.'

'Really?'

She nodded and gently held out her knitting needles to him. 'Would you like to?'

'I'd love to. Thank you.'

'Make me a big fluffy coat when you're ready then, will ya?' George added, playfully tapping his arm.

'Sure … If you remember to remind me.'

George leant his head back and threw his hands in the air, 'Well, that just ain't fair now, is it?'

Hughes and Docie looked at one another again, beginning to quietly chuckle.

George cackled and slapped Hughes' shoulder, 'You bastard.'

* * *

Clangs of metal echoed throughout the Dumphree factory. Hughes stood amidst the heavy smoke and sweltering heat, hammering away at a piece of metal. Dozens upon dozens of other workers stood around him, doing the same.

Machinery pumped back and forth, liquid steel bubbled inside hanging tanks, and an endless line of metal materials were carried in and out of the factory. Black dust covered Hughes' face as his sweat dripped onto the workbench before him. He twisted around and peered through the smoke and steam, searching for any sign of Flavel.

There was none.

He turned to the worker beside him. 'Hey, have you ever seen Flavel Dumphree around here before?'

'Who?'

'Flavel Dumphree. Mr. Dumphree. He owns this factory.'

'Oh. Not that I know of, no. Sorry, mate.'

'That's all right. Thank you.' Hughes gave him a friendly nod before looking back down at his workbench, forcing himself to get a sturdier grip on his hammer.

At the end of the day, Hughes and the workers shuffled out of the factory in a long line. All of them were covered in black smoke and ash, their faces barely recognisable underneath it. The factory manager and his assistants handed out payment to each worker who passed them by. Eventually, Hughes reached the front of the line. The manager dropped two threepence coins into his hands and gave him a nod. Hughes drearily nodded back before continuing on his way.

The next day, Hughes marched back into the factory. Then the next. And the next. And the next. Over and over, he shook the sweat from his hands, banged away at metal, and strained to carry large industrial materials back and forth throughout the factory. And still, there was no sign of Flavel Dumphree.

By each sundown, Hughes sat with Docie, copying her knitting technique. The needles fumbled about in his hand as he fiddled with the positioning of his fingers. Docie leant over and gently adjusted them for him.

On other days, they both sat before her small sewing machine. Hughes watched closely as she gradually fed the edges of a new coat through the machine. As she finished sewing one side of the coat, Hughes noticed small purple ribbons pinned over different corners of the garment.

'What are these ribbons for?' he asked.

'Points of balance, they are.'

'Points of balance?'

'Every piece of clothing needs them. Don't wanna be wearing somethin' uneven, do ya? Wouldn't feel right. Nor could you hang it up without it tippin' over.'

'Yeah, of course ... I guess I never really thought about clothes in that way before.'

'Now ya will.'

'Now I will.'

By each nightfall, as the moon overtook the sky, Hughes wrote in his journal. In the highest and quietest hallway in the building, he sat on the frame of a cracked window, occasionally glancing away from his journal and down at the shadowy streets below.

* * *

After another day of work, Hughes dragged his feet back through the city streets. Gradually, he slowed down as a shop window caught his eye. Veering off the path, he approached the window, staring at a collection of fine suits on display. His gaze fell to their price tags. The cheapest was five pounds.

How much do I have? he thought. *Maybe ten, fifteen shillings? It'll probably take me months more time to afford one of these. When would I even wear it, anyway? If he comes into the factory, I'll be in my work uniform, not a suit. So, I shouldn't really bother.*

His eyes refocused on his own reflection in the window. Just like every other day, his face and clothes were overtaken by ash and dirt. His clothes were loose and drenched in sweat, carrying with it an overpowering smell of smoke and fire.

Would he even believe me? Looking like this? Not even the factory manager did.

The following week, Hughes dragged a large sheet of metal onto his workbench. He gripped the bench and leant forward a moment, catching his breath. Sweat dripped from his nose and thick beard. He watched as it bounced off the metal before noticing numerous cuts and scrapes across the back of his hands. He gently ran a finger across one of the fresh cuts, accidentally peeling back some of his skin. Recoiling in disgust, he quickly pulled his fingers away.

He shook his head, clenched his fists, and picked up his hammer. Placing one hand on the metal sheet to keep it steady, he banged away at each loose corner until they came off.

Beside Hughes, another worker noticed him. He casually surveyed his smoke-ridden surroundings before pretending to focus on the workbench in front of him. 'Heard you askin' people about Dumphree 'round here. You lookin' for him?'

Hughes' ears pricked up at the name. His eyes darted around them before quietly replying, 'I am, actually.'

'You got a problem with 'im?'

Hughes paused, eyeing the worker up and down. 'I might. I'm guessing you do?'

'I might … You enjoy workin' here?'

'As much as one can.'

The man looked at him and squinted. 'You speak funny. What's your accent?'

'It's mixed. French and British.'

'You not born 'ere then?'

'No. Born in France.'

'It like this there, too?'

'Even worse.'

The man stopped a moment as his expression died just a little bit more. 'You lookin' to change things around 'ere, then? Make 'em better? Would you want that?'

'Yeah. Of course.'

'Good.' The man nodded. 'Tonight at midnight. Paul's Walk. The bank of the Thames. Be there if you're still interested. And don't speak of it until then.'

'Okay. Thank you.'

* * *

Big Ben rang out across the darkness. Bellowing horns from incoming ships shouted back. Hughes donned his raggedy coat as he walked along the edge of the Thames, keeping a twitchy eye on his surroundings.

Black silhouettes occasionally strode past, coughing and murmuring. Hughes kept his arms close by his side and his head down as he walked past them. Eventually, he came upon Paul's Walk, a small walkway at the edge of the bank of the Thames.

The place was shrouded in shadow as a light mist hovered above the ground. He sniffled from the cold, inspecting the shadows around him.

Before long, he heard the crackling of a fire and an echoing voice from somewhere below. He approached the walkway's railing and peered over, spotting a group of twenty or so figures gathered around a fire on the small beach of the river. The voice of a man spoke to them, but he was impossible to make out behind the crowd.

Drawn by the sight and sound, Hughes sneaked down a set of stairs to the beach. He kept his feet light as he drew closer towards the rear of the group. The orange glow of the fire grew more intense and the voice clearer. It was a well-spoken one, with clarity and strength behind it.

As he joined them all, he recognised some of their faces. They were workers from the factory. The worker who spoke to him earlier in the day noticed him. He gave Hughes a nod of acknowledgement, and he gave one in return. Hughes finally peered beyond the small crowd and spotted the man speaking to them all. He was tall, had a slick black moustache, and as he spoke, he locked eyes with each and every one of them.

'Isn't that why we came here?' The man proposed. 'For a new life in a new world? One where we could grasp at that new chance? A fresh start where we could become *anything* we wanted? But that's not what's happened, is it? … No. We were tricked. We were lured into those factories with false hopes and shameless lies. We aren't here for *us,* we're here for *them,* for people like Flavel Dumphree. We're giving *them* the life that *we* were promised. And us? Look at us. It's sad. No man should treat another like this. No man should have what they have while *everyone* else suffers below them. There is no other word for it but cruelty. Unfair, unjust, cruelty.'

Hughes shuffled in place, subtly eyeing everyone else's reactions. Some nodded in agreement, others shook their heads in shared anger, and others were too ashamed to move much at all.

'But you've heard me say enough of this,' he continued. 'No amount of words can truly describe it. We all live it. We all feel it.' He gazed down upon the pebbles and rocks beneath his feet, remaining silent for a moment. Eventually, he pulled out a pistol from his coat pocket and cradled it in his hands. 'So, judging by his former appearances, I believe Dumphree will be inspecting the factory tomorrow or the next day. And that'll be our best opportunity. I'll do the deed. No one else has to. I just ask you to be ready to stand by my side when the time comes. We *have* to be united for any of this to work. They won't hear our voices unless we are many.' He nodded at the crowd as they nodded back. 'I won't keep you any longer, but be ready, stay vigilant, and never forget that we *deserve* the better lives we are asking for. Good night.'

The crowd began to disperse, some leaving and others chatting amongst themselves. The man strolled down to the edge of the water, inspecting the pistol in his hands. Hughes sifted through the crowds and walked up beside him.

The man looked at him and casually slid the gun back into his pocket. 'You're a new face. I don't believe I've seen you before.'

'Yes, I only started working at the factory a week or two back.'

'Well, I'm Cloyd,' he said, firmly shaking Hughes' hand.

'Hughes.'

'And what's brought you here, Hughes?'

'Well, one of your friends told me about this meeting. I thought I should come see what it's all about.'

'I'm hoping you agree with what I was saying, then. It would be a tad awkward if not,' he replied with a chuckle.

'Well, I didn't realise it was going to be so severe a movement. You're really going to use that?' Hughes asked, gesturing to the pistol in his pocket.

'I'm afraid so.'

'Why not speak to him instead? Try and work out some sort of deal or something?'

'It was like I said, Hughes, they won't hear our voices otherwise. If they even cared about our voices, we wouldn't be in this situation in the first place.'

'But if you're so united, why is murder the only option? Surely all of you speaking up will be enough.'

'It won't be. They'd throw us onto the streets if we just *said* we don't like the way things are. As much as I'd prefer a peaceful route, it would give them no incentive to change things. We got here because not caring about us is more beneficial to them. If we're just a replaceable machine, then it's much less complicated for them. It's much more … productive for their business. But if we *show* them that we are not just the machines they think we are, well, then they have to wake up a little, don't you think?'

'So, you'll kill him and then make a demand? They'll just send you to jail.'

'I know,' he replied, almost with a smile. 'They'll probably even execute me for it. But that's a sacrifice I have to make. It's the only way to spread the message. Dumphree's death and my words will be all over the papers. It'll be on the mind of every single factory owner and businessman in the country. They'll all be wondering if one of *their* own workers will do the same to them. And maybe they will. And that will gnaw at them. It'll create such a dread that the only way to subdue it is to make things better for the workers. To give them more pay, more rights, more respect, more of a voice. All of it.'

'That's very optimistic.'

Cloyd smiled and nodded. 'Someone's got to be. Someone's got to remember that this river here wasn't always like this.' He gestured to the Thames before them, black as the night. 'You really think it was always this bleak? … No. It would've been beautiful once … And besides, nothing ever changed because every man did the same as the other.' He turned around and glanced at Hughes once more. 'A few of us are going to the pub. Would you care to join us?'

'Uh – no, no, I'm all right, thank you.'

'Well, I'll see you tomorrow, then. If it's all too much for you, though, you don't have to come or you don't have to help. But if you do, every man and woman who benefits from this will be forever thankful that you did. Good night, Hughes.'

'Good night.'

Cloyd strolled off with a few of the other workers. One of them stomped out the fire and rushed off after them, leaving Hughes alone in the dark. He watched the group walk further and further away, chatting and laughing with one another.

Later, Hughes sat on the lonely window frame that he had every other night. His journal rested atop his lap as he stared out beyond the broken glass, tormented by his thoughts.

I should help Cloyd, he admitted to himself. *I know I should. After all, those were the same words that brought me here.*

But remember how truthful those words turned out? And you know, you know, this isn't going to change anything. You know where this will go. You know it won't matter.

So, I shouldn't. In fact, it's probably worse that I do, isn't it? And I came all this way for Flavel. You can't just let him die, especially for a man who's going to die anyway and a plan that isn't even going to work. And if I saved him, if I stopped this, that would finally give me the opportunity to speak to him. If I do this for him, he'd have to listen to me. He'd have to believe me. Then he can take me far away from here. Then I can finally be free.

But what about everyone else? Docie? George? Everyone in the factory? Hell, every factory.

That's not why you came here, though. Remember that.

But I know. I know what they're feeling. I know exactly what they're going through.

Hughes' eyes gradually fell upon the dark streets below.

The shadows stared back at him once more …

* * *

The following day, Hughes repeatedly bashed away at metal sheets with a hammer. Endless waves of smoke brushed past him, causing his eyes to water. He rubbed the tears away before noticing his hand was shaking uncontrollably. He quickly lowered it before glancing around the factory. Across the aisle, working beside some of the machinery, was Cloyd. His demeanour was entirely casual. Hughes looked towards the factory's entrance, waiting.

There was no sign of Flavel.

Feeling a rising sickness in his throat and stomach, he forced himself to lift the hammer and continue his work. The hours ticked by. The afternoon had arrived as Hughes checked the entrance for the hundredth time. Still, there was no Flavel. He turned around to check on Cloyd. He continued working away as usual, glancing at the entrance every minute or so.

Perhaps he was wrong, Hughes thought. *Perhaps he's not coming. Maybe it'll be tomorrow. Or maybe not for a long time. Let's just get this day over with and get out of here.*

He shook his head and turned back towards the workbench. After steadying the piece of metal before him, he lifted his hammer high above his head, yet before he could bring it down, he heard a pair of horses neigh outside the factory. His hands lowered and his eyes gradually turned towards the factory doors, hearing the clopping of hooves nearing closer and closer. His breath ceased and his chest began to tighten as he waited.

Finally, a black carriage, with strips of gold lining its edges, arrived outside the factory. Its door opened and out stepped Flavel Dumphree. His moustache was thick and grey, and he wore a long and sleek black coat, one that was cleaner than any piece of clothing or equipment around him. A handful of his aristocratic associates stepped out after him as they approached the factory in tow.

Hughes' gaze shot towards Cloyd, who pretended to work as he subtly eyed Flavel's every step. The owner proudly strolled through the factory, passing them by with his head held high. One by one, each worker stopped and gazed upon them as they strolled past. Any voices or shouting fizzled into silence. The only sounds that remained were the clanking machinery and bursting pipes of steam.

Hughes swallowed as he glanced back at Cloyd. He had now completely stopped working and was staring solely at Flavel's back.

Don't do it, Hughes thought to himself.

Please don't do it.

Cloyd reached into his pocket and stepped into the middle of the factory's aisle. Hughes froze in place as Cloyd pulled out the pistol from his pocket.

'Flavel!' Cloyd cried out.

Flavel and his associates stopped and turned around. Finally, they noticed that all the workers were no longer working. They were staring at *them*, and Cloyd was at their lead. He lifted his handgun and pulled back its hammer.

'*Oh my God!*' one of the associates gasped.

'*What is the meaning of this?*' another shouted.

'*How dare you point that at us!*' one more added, furiously pointing at Cloyd.

'Quiet, *quiet*!' Flavel ordered them before looking back at Cloyd. Ever so slowly, he lifted his hands and took a step forward. 'Please, sir, what is your name?'

Cloyd said nothing in return, continuing to hold his aim steady.

Hughes' eyes desperately bounced back and forth between the two of them.

'Whatever it is, I know we can work it out,' Flavel continued. 'All we need to do is talk. No violence is needed.'

Cloyd stood firm and motionless.

Hughes glanced down at his hammer.

'Please, put the gun down,' Flavel offered.

Cloyd shook his head, saying only two words. 'No more.'

Hughes closed his eyes in anguish and took hold of his hammer.

Cloyd tightened his grip and pressed his finger on the trigger. Then, a hammer came crashing across his head. He was thrown off balance and instinctively pulled the trigger. The bullet ripped into the concrete ground as he stumbled to his knees.

Blood oozed out of his head as he lifted the handgun once more, desperately attempting to aim at Flavel. Hughes, standing behind him, reluctantly lifted the hammer and smashed it across his skull once more. Cloyd collapsed to his side, his eyes twitching and blood pouring out of his head.

Hughes stared down at him as his hands shook and his skin turned pale. He glanced at the rest of the factory. Everyone stood in complete silence, staring at him in a speechless daze. The hammer slipped from his hands and bounced onto the floor with a clank. He stepped away from the body before his legs gave out beneath him. Stumbling to his hands and knees, he felt the urge to throw up. Tears began to fill his eyes as he leant over in pain.

Eventually, a hand rested on his shoulder and a comforting voice came with it. 'Here, boy. Let me help you.'

Hughes looked up to see Flavel pulling him to his feet. He placed his arm around Hughes' shoulder and carefully walked him towards the staircase at the rear of the factory.

'Let's get you upstairs,' Flavel said.

One of the associates turned towards the factory manager, whose mouth was still agape. *'Get the police, dammit! Now!'*

'Uh – yes – yes, sir,' the manager repeated, hurriedly rushing out of the factory.

Flavel walked Hughes into the small office overlooking the factory and sat him down on a chair. He hastily scanned the room, spotting a cup of water on the desk. 'Here, here, have some of this.' He took the water and placed it into Hughes' shaking hands.

Staring off into space, he quietly sipped the water.

Flavel knelt in front of him, attempting to meet his gaze, 'I can't thank you enough for what you just did for me. What is your name, sir?'

Hughes' focus steadily returned as his eyes looked into Flavel's. Gradually, he slipped his hand into his pocket and pulled out the photo of Albert Dumphree, passing it to him. 'Your – your father is John Dumphree, and your uncle is Albert Dumphree, yes?'

Flavel leant back a little, inspecting the photo. 'Yes … I believe this *is* my uncle. How did you get your hands on this?'

'I know we've never met, but Albert is my father. I am your cousin, and I have been looking for you for a long, long time, Flavel.'

'You – you know Albert? You're a Dumphree?'

'*Yes.* My name is Hughes Dumphree … and I need your help,' he said with a final breath.

Flavel stared into his eyes, taken aback for a moment.

Then, a smile came over him, and he pulled Hughes into a hug. 'Oh, my Lord, I never thought I would see the day! It is so good to finally meet another Dumphree!' He pulled away and gripped Hughes' shoulders, 'Don't you worry about a thing now. We're going to get you out of here in no time, and you'll be where you belong soon enough. I will sort this mess out, but for now, you stay here and rest. I'm sure you're in much need of it.' He smiled and patted his shoulder before swiftly exiting the office.

Hughes sat alone, staring into space once again. His eyes welled with tears as a smile overcame him. At last, he wept.

I made it. I finally made it.

Chapter 2

Through the cracked window, grim clouds loomed over the city. Small rays of the morning sun trickled through, but never enough to lighten the maze of streets below. Leant against the window frame, Hughes soaked in the view one last time. His eyes fell towards the streets drenched in shadow.

I'll be far away now, he thought. *Far away and safe. All the more reason I did what I did.*

Taking a small, stuttered breath, he placed his hand on the rugged wooden frame and straightened his posture. Returning to Docie's room a few floors below, he packed what few belongings he had into his bag. Most importantly, his journal.

'Got any room for me in that bag?' George's hearty voice asked from behind him.

Hughes couldn't help but smile as he stood up and turned around. 'Maybe lose a few pounds first.'

'Or you could just get a bigger bag?'

'I am gonna miss your bright ideas, George.'

'Mm, I *might* miss ya … we'll see,' George said before letting out a jolly laugh and wrestling Hughes into his arms, rubbing his head with his fist. 'Don't be gone too long, Frenchie!'

'All right, all right,' Hughes insisted as he pulled away with a chuckle, 'You've had your fun. Now go bully someone else, why don't you?'

George winked and waved as he left, 'I'll be at the pub if ya need me.'

Hughes smiled to himself, shaking his head as he turned towards Docie, who sat in her rocking chair beside the windows. 'I don't know how that man keeps his spirits up.'

'Probably something to do with the spirits at the pub, I would think.' She sighed.

'I would think you may be right.' Hughes smirked, approaching her as she climbed to her feet. 'I can't thank you enough, Docie. For everything you've done.'

'Ah, no, no need.' She waved away his thanks, twisting around and reaching for something behind her chair. 'But you can't go to that fancy-like place looking like ya are now.'

'What's that supposed to mean?'

'Ya looked in a mirror lately? I hope not.' With a raise of her eyebrows, she turned around to face him, holding out a newly sewn jacket.

Hughes paused, running his fingers along the black cotton. 'Thank you, Docie. Truly.' He stepped forth and gave her a delicate hug. 'I'm sorry I can't take you with me. But I will be back. I'll visit, I promise.'

With a small smile, she nodded, 'Just keep ya'self warm.'

Twirling the jacket around, Hughes slid his arms through both its sleeves.

It fit perfectly.

Of course, it does, he thought. *It smells like her too. It's nice.*

Before another thought could cross his mind, Docie's shaking hand held out a handful of knitting materials and tools. Even more gifts. Hughes' smile strained at the sight of them.

Should I say something about Abigail?

But what can I say? What is *there to say?*

With defeat, he carefully took her gifts, patted her shoulder, nodded in thanks, and left without another word.

Hughes' chilled breath escaped his lips as he stepped out onto the curb of a busy London street. Horses trotted by while workers shouted, chatted, and whistled. In the distance, the horns of trains screeched and blared.

Pulling his jacket around his chest, he turned and looked upon the corner building one last time as its frosted windows stared back at him.

* * *

Hot steam and dark smoke poured out from the Dumphree factory. A new day had begun as Hughes walked before the entrance, searching for any sign of Flavel's carriage.

It had yet to arrive.

With a heavy breath, he turned and peered inside the factory. A handful of workers stared at him with tired, helpless eyes.

I should apologise. I should invite them with me, give them a chance ... but I can't. Of course, I can't. Besides, it was either Cloyd or all of us. If anything, I saved these people from a pointless death. If only they knew where it would all end up. Then they'd understand.

Hughes felt the burn of their sorrowful eyes even as he turned his back on them. Each moment that passed, he only grew more desperate for the carriage's arrival.

Please take me away from this place, he repeated to himself. *Please.*

A quarter of an hour later, Flavel's golden-lined carriage arrived.

'You're Hughes?' the driver asked, pulling up before him.

'I am.'

'Good. Flavel isn't here, but I'll be taking you to his estate. Get in.'

Without daring another glance at the factory, Hughes climbed inside. He settled his breath as he shut the carriage door and sat down, free from the factory's gaze.

The city crawled by as the carriage rocked through the countless streets. Every corner was another variation of the last, lined with grey people and their endless chattering, barking, vomiting, coughing, and cursing. As the carriage approached the edges of the city, Hughes watched as families of farmers stumbled their way into the smog and unending noise. Even children were carrying their homes on their backs, with faces that seemed as though they'd lived a lifetime already.

And they call this a revolution.

Eventually, far enough along their journey, the smoke and voices began to fade. Leaning forward, Hughes' eyes were struck with awe as he looked out at the endless rolling hills. The grass was deep with green as it gently swayed in the wind. Shaking his head in disbelief, a childlike smile overcame him.

I can't believe how close I was to all of this.

Soon, when London was no longer in sight, the carriage stopped before the Dumphree estate. Hughes stepped outside. A rush of fresh, clean air filled his lungs. The birds chirped and the wind brushed against the surrounding trees. Everything was calm.

After giving his thanks to the driver, the carriage turned and trekked back the way it came. Hughes admired his surroundings as he strolled towards the two-story estate. Even the gravel beneath his feet was polished and clean. The maze-like garden to his right caught his attention.

So much greenery, he thought. *All of it alive and healthy.*

So, this is what the world is supposed to look like.

The front door opened, pulling his attention away from the garden as Mary Dumphree stepped outside. Her great white dress glowed in the same manner as the house, but her expression was one of grim concern. 'You're Hughes, I expect?' she presumed.

Hughes stuttered for a moment, trying to find his words. 'Uh – yes, yes I am.'

Disappointment and disapproval washed over Mary's eyes as a silence overcame them.

Hughes stepped forward and outstretched his hand. 'Pleased to meet you. You must be … Mary, yes?'

'How did you know that?'

'Well, it's difficult *not* to hear about the Dumphrees and your success back in London.'

Mary scanned him up and down before she led him inside. 'Please take off your shoes. And don't put anything of yours on the floor.'

'Oh, yes, of course.' Hughes obliged as he removed his shoes and stepped onto the shining marble floor. He paused at the sight of the lavish house.

It's so clean, as though no one has ever even lived here.

Before he could say a word, Mary ushered him upstairs and to his bedroom. 'You should find this all comfortable enough, and please take care of the bed. Flavel will be here soon.'

'This is more than I … ever expected. If there's anything you need – '

'There isn't,' she interrupted, 'and clean yourself up before dinner.'

With a slam of the door, Hughes was left in silence.

Well, she's going to take some work to win over.

Straightening his jacket, he strolled towards the polished window, greeted by the sight of lush gardens below and the endless hills and fields beyond them.

Then, at the bottom corner of his eye, he spotted Mary walking into the garden with a small pair of scissors in hand. With care and precision, she began trimming the hedges and tidying the flowers.

Huh. The garden looks perfect already. She must be a perfectionist.

* * *

Two hours had passed when Flavel arrived in his carriage.

'How are you, my darling?' he asked Mary as he stepped inside and kissed her cheek.

'Dinner is almost on the table.'

He nodded before noticing Hughes climb down the stairs. 'Ah, wonderful, you've come, Hughes!'

'Oh no, thank you for having *me*.'

'It's nothing,' he insisted, placing his hand on Hughes' shoulder. 'Let's eat. We have much to discuss.'

Soon, the housemaids placed the remaining food and drinks around the dining table as Hughes, Mary, and Flavel took their seats.

At the head of the table, Flavel tucked a napkin into his collar with a smile. 'Well, where do we even begin?' He chuckled.

'I want to know why you're here,' Mary began without delay.

Hughes noticed her unwavering eyes awaiting his response.

Flavel shuffled in his seat. 'Please, Mary, he is our guest. And family.'

'Then why has it taken him so long to even so much as visit us? Or write us?'

'Well, I imagine – '

'It's fine,' Hughes interjected. 'It's a fair question. I'm happy to explain.'

It's better we get all of this out of the way as soon as possible, he thought. *You knew this was coming, and you've prepared yourself. You know what to say.*

'For all my life, I've lived in France, you see. I'm not sure if you knew, Flavel, but your uncle, my father, moved to Rennes in 1825.'

'Yes, I was only a boy then. Can barely remember.'

'Well, he had a strong desire to see the Rennes Cathedral. Upon arriving, however, he found that the French Revolution and such had stalled its reconstruction. The architect at the time, Mr. Mathurin Crucy, was also unwell. So, one thing led to another, and my father took a role in overseeing its construction.'

'Fabulous. Just fabulous,' Flavel said proudly.

'He never sent any letters,' Mary noted.

Hughes shrugged. 'My father's choices were his own. But I do know that by the time I was born, he was entirely dedicated to not just the cathedral but the town *and* the country. It was his home. And mine. Until he passed away just a year or so ago.'

'I'm terribly sorry to hear,' Flavel said. 'My father passed about five years ago. Maybe more now. Since then, I've taken full charge of the Dumphree business.'

'I had heard. In fact, that's why I came looking for you. After my father's passing, I didn't … I didn't have anything left back there. No wealth, no family.' Hughes looked off, remembering. 'But I knew I had family here, and that's what I needed. I wanted to rekindle that. So, I came looking for you.'

'But you were on the streets, working in our factory. Why didn't you approach us sooner?' Mary asked.

'Well, I didn't know where your estate was, so I figured my best opportunity was to wait at the factory until I could speak to you personally. Considering how I looked, though, no one else believed me. I had spent the last of my money travelling to England in the first place, so I had no choice but to work just to keep myself alive. Then, before long, I heard about Cloyd's plan.'

'Fascinating. You should write a book or something about all of that,' Flavel suggested, raising his eyebrows. 'Wouldn't that be wonderful, Mary?'

'Yes. Wonderful.'

'*I* would certainly read it,' Flavel added, sipping his wine.

'Well, I'm just happy I finally found you. I wasn't sure if I ever would've.'

'We're glad to have you, Hughes. Now, eat. Lord knows I'm starving,' Flavel added with another smile, joyfully cutting into his food.

Hughes quietly glanced back at Mary, who continued to eye him with suspicion, before she turned her focus towards her plate.

* * *

Later that night, Flavel and Hughes strolled alongside the garden and towards the closest hill, taking in the cool air. The pale moonlight gazed upon them and bounced off each and every blade of grass. Hughes glanced into the garden as they passed it by, noticing Mary once again working on the plants, flowers, and hedges.

Again? he thought. *Even at this hour? So determinedly?*

'Did that man, Cloyd, say why he wanted me dead?' Flavel asked with a grave tone.

Hughes ceased his thoughts of the garden and nodded. 'Yes. In a way.'

'What was it? Money? Freedom?'

'All of it. Just a better life.'

'He could've negotiated. I would've given him more money if that's what he needed. Sometimes they don't even realise that's what they really need, though. That *that's* what will solve their problems. Instead, they get inside their heads too much; concoct notions of liberty and righteousness and sacrifice. That won't help them.'

'I did want to stop him from trying anything, but from what I could gather, he wouldn't have stepped down.'

'You would be surprised, but it doesn't matter now. You did something that I'm forever grateful for. Our name brings out a lot of rivals these days. If I was killed, I don't know who would've swept in and taken everything of mine.'

'Well, with our parents gone, I think it's more important than ever to keep the Dumphree name alive.'

'I couldn't agree more.'

Stopping atop the hill, Hughes gazed outward at the quiet, open land. 'You have a truly beautiful place here. I would … I would love to be a part of it. To have our family together again. But I can also tell Mary isn't exactly taking a liking to me. Do you know why?'

Flavel raised his eyebrows. 'Well, yes, she's not particularly subtle, is she? But I do have my suspicions as to why.'

'What are they?'

Flavel sighed. 'I don't know if it matters, Hughes. If she doesn't take a liking to you, I don't think you staying here for much longer will work. It will only raise a kind of hell I simply don't want in my home. And Lord knows I already have enough to deal with elsewhere.'

A nauseous feeling bubbled inside Hughes' throat.

I can't let them force me back there.

'Do *you* believe what I've told you?' Hughes asked. 'Do you trust me? I know it's all strange and asking a lot of you, but do you?'

'I certainly like to think so …'

Hughes took a quiet moment to think, before something came to him. 'Did your father ever tell you the irony of the eagle? It was a saying my father used to tell me, anyway. He said, "The greatest gift of the eagle was that it could see everything …'

'"… But the greatest curse of the eagle was that it could see everything."' Flavel continued in unison with Hughes, bringing them both a smile. 'I know it. My father told me that one too. They must've learnt it from our grandfather.'

'I think so … Flavel, the last thing I want to do is invade your home and make Mary uncomfortable, but can you give me some time? Some help? I want to convince her to let me stay, to let me help our family, but I can't do it alone.'

Flavel thought for a moment. Finally, he nodded as a reluctant tone overcame him. 'We've been trying to conceive a child. We haven't had any luck so far, though. My best guess is *that* has something to do with her uncertainty about you. Affecting her mood somehow … I respect your determination, Hughes, but I don't know what could change her opinion.'

'I'll figure that out. All I need is time and you on my side.'

Flavel smiled and patted his shoulder. 'For everything you've been through to get here, it's the least I could do.'

Later that night, Hughes walked through the Dumphree house before noticing a glow emanating from the lounge room. Silencing his footsteps, he peeked inside, finding an orange fireplace and Mary sitting alone before it, staring into the flames as her head rested on her hand.

She does seem downhearted, he thought. *But what can I do to help her?*

* * *

The following day, Hughes found Mary at work in the garden once again. She stood atop a stool, trimming a line of hedges. Her demeanour turned sour as she heard his approach.

'You must really love this garden, Mrs Dumphree,' he opened with a smile.

'What do you want, Hughes?'

'I just … wanted to see how you were.'

'I'm fine,' she replied, continuing her work.

Hughes stood in silence for a moment.

Come on, don't be an idiot and just stand there. Say something!

'I haven't seen such beautiful land since I was in France. Even then, I've never seen anything like this. You're very lucky.'

'Mm. You enjoyed living there?' she forced herself to ask.

'I did. It was a wonderful place to grow up.'

Mary barely nodded in reply, trimming off more leaves and shrubs.

'Do you have many guests come visit your garden?' Hughes continued, glancing at the greenery around him.

'From time to time.'

'What about friends? Do you have some you invite over?'

Mary paused for the briefest moment before resuming her work, this time slightly harsher in her movements.

'I was just wondering, is all,' he nervously added. 'You seem to be working so much on this garden. I mean, it already looks perfect to me. I thought maybe – '

'Look,' she interrupted, shooting him an upset glare, 'I know you may have won over Flavel, but I don't want to hear your stories. I don't want to hear your voice.' She stepped down from her stool. 'And I don't want you in our home. One way or another, you're going back to where you came from and leaving us in peace. Now, will you let me continue my work?'

Hughes nodded and bowed his head. 'I'm sorry. Of course.'

Returning to his bedroom, Hughes sat down at a small desk before the window. Her words repeated over and over in his head.

'One way or another, you're going back to where you came from.'

I can't go back, he thought. *I can't. Not after* everything. *But what does she want? Why can't she believe me? Or perhaps it's not a matter of belief. Maybe she just doesn't like me.*

The dark silhouette he once saw in London crept into the forefront of his mind. Searching for him. Stalking him. *Hunting* him.

What if I had to go back there?

What if that man finds me?

No. Stop it. It was just nerves, okay? No one's after you. No one can find you.

Hughes gazed out the window again, seeing Mary stroll through the garden. She stopped and admired some of the pink and purple flowers, petting them and smelling them. For once, she smiled, before a sadness washed over her and her hands rested themselves upon her flat stomach. Without a moment to linger, she returned to the house, out of sight.

The pregnancy, Hughes thought. *Why else would she be so determined to keep this place perfect?*

Turning around, Hughes glanced at his bag on the floor. With an air of promise, he lifted the bag onto his bed and unbuckled its straps to find Docie's knitting materials and tools. Reaching in, he pulled out a collection of pink wool, caressing it in his hand.

* * *

Later that night, after another quiet and uncomfortable dinner, Hughes approached the lounge room and peered inside. Mary sat where she had the night before, staring into the glowing fire, alone.

This is it ...

You can do it. This will work.

With a short swallow, he strolled inside. Mary gazed towards him, reluctantly watching as he sat down on the armchair beside her. The floorboards creaked and the flames crackled. With a humble smile, he handed out a small, soft, pink scarf for her.

Mary sat up in her seat, confused and hesitant.

'I know it's not a lot,' Hughes explained, 'but I wanted to give you something. Not just for you, though ... I haven't really mentioned her when I've talked about my home, but my mother used to be an artist of a kind. And some of my best memories of home and her were her gifts. She used to make me things. Little trinkets and pictures and the like. And I've always cherished them. So, you know, I know that stuff is important and ... I want to be honest with you. Flavel told me about you trying to have children.'

Mary's head bowed into the shadows, hiding her shame-filled eyes.

Hughes continued, 'But I understand what you're trying to do with the garden. I think it's a good sign you'll be a good mother. I know they'll love it. I know I do. And so anyway, I hope it's all right, but I made this for your child, or children, as an early gift. And I have other material as well. If you don't know, I can teach you how to make more for them. Keep them warm. 'Cause, yeah ... it does get bloody cold out there.' He said with a chuckle.

Mary remained silent, staring at the floor.

'And if you need any help with the garden,' he added, 'I'm more than happy to lend my hands there too.'

Gradually, her eyes returned to him, letting the light of the fire touch her face once more. Quietly, she took the scarf into her hands and ran her fingers through it.

As she took her time inspecting the scarf, Hughes bit his lip and turned his gaze towards the warm fire.

Just leave her. I should just leave her. Don't overstay yourself.

With a nod of assurance, he climbed to his feet and faced her. 'Well … good night.'

Mary paused, staring down at the scarf without a word.

Hughes gave himself another nod before walking towards the hallway.

'Thank you …' her timid voice finally said.

Hughes stopped before the exit.

'And I never said thank you for what you did for Flavel,' she continued. 'It meant … a lot … and I *would* like to learn.'

Hughes smiled as he turned back to face her. 'I would like to teach you. We can start tomorrow, if you'd like?'

She nodded, her face softening.

'Okay. Well, I look forward to it. Good night, Mary.'

'Good night,' she replied with a faint smile.

Chapter 3

Hughes, his face freshly shaven and wearing new clothes, pulled out weeds from the Dumphree garden. He paused for a moment, wiping sweat from his brow as he soaked in the glowing surroundings. The wind hummed, the birds sang, and rays of the sun broke through the clouds.

'How is it going?' Mary asked, walking up to the edge of the garden.

'Perfect, thank you. Almost done with this lot.'

'Good. Lunch will be ready soon. Don't take too long.'

'Don't worry, I won't. My stomach won't let me. It's practically talking to me.'

'Good to hear,' she said with a humoured smile. 'See you soon.'

'See you.' He nodded before looking back at the remaining weeds before him. 'All right, weedies, who's next?'

A little while later, before he finished removing the last weed, Flavel's carriage arrived at the estate.

Hughes slipped off his gloves and strolled over to Flavel as he stepped down from the cart. 'Back so soon?'

'Yes, yes. I wanted to have lunch with both of you today,' Flavel replied, shaking Hughes' hand and patting his shoulder. 'I wanted to talk to you about something.'

'Sure, whatever you need.'

Flavel turned back to the carriage driver. 'Thank you, Bill. Please, give yourself a break.'

Bill tipped his hat to him before riding off towards the edge of the estate.

Hughes and Flavel began walking towards the house as he continued, 'So, I thought now that you've been here a good month or so, it might be time you start joining me on my business ventures. Into the city and such.'

'Really? Are you sure?'

'Of course. I mean, you said yourself you wanted to help the family. I can't think of a better way.'

The two of them reached the front door as Hughes put on a false smile, unable to find any words.

'Don't worry,' Flavel continued, 'we'll discuss it over lunch, but I think you're a smart, capable man. And you've *worked* in the factories. You've experienced what it's like firsthand. There's not many people at our level that can say that.'

Hughes finally nodded. 'I hear what you're saying.'

'Excellent. Let's eat, and we'll talk *plans*!' Flavel exclaimed before entering the house.

Hughes paused for a moment, biting his lip with an uneasy breath, before following him.

* * *

What choice do I have? Hughes thought to himself. *I offered myself to them and they've taken me in. I can't refuse them now. And besides, what did you think was going to happen? I wasn't just going to get a free ride. This is the only way to truly live like this.*

Hughes inspected himself in his bedroom mirror, now wearing a dark grey suit with a pocket watch hanging by his side.

That man ... could he still be looking for me? Even now?

No. Surely not. He probably never even was.

No, you <u>know</u> he never was.

Either way, with everything I've done so far, I can't just give up.

Hughes inhaled through his nose, puffing up his chest and giving himself a small nod of confidence.

Out the front of the estate, Flavel and Hughes climbed into their carriage as Mary stood by the door, watching them.

'Good luck!' she called out, waving goodbye as the horses trotted off towards London.

Hughes watched the air darken outside his window as they drew closer. The grass faded into mud, and soon the sun was all but gone.

Was it always this grim? he asked himself. *Did I forget it so quickly?*

Over the course of the day, Flavel toured Hughes across the city, introducing him to various associates and staples of their industry. From one side of London to the next, endless machinery chugged away, casting a black shadow over the ocean of silhouettes working at their disposal. As the day neared its end, Hughes' face had turned grim. His eyes hung heavy as their cart arrived at its final destination, the Dumphree factory. Peeking out the window, he held his breath at the sight of it.

'Don't worry, the workers have left. It's just you and I,' Flavel reassured him before stepping out of the carriage.

Their footsteps echoed throughout the empty factory as they approached the rear office. Hughes kept his head down as he carefully glanced at the surrounding shadows, following Flavel with haste.

Once inside, Flavel circled the office's polished wooden desk, running his hand along its surface. 'I used to work here personally before my father passed.' He sighed, taking a seat behind it. 'Eventually, I had to get a manager for the place. Not enough time for me to look after it.'

'And he's not here now?'

'Most certainly not. I got rid of him.'

'Why?'

'I don't know if you forgot, but I almost got bloody *murdered* in here. Might've tripped your memory,' he replied, raising his bushy eyebrows almost with a chuckle. 'Anyway, that's why I brought you here. I think with some guidance and training, you'll be a perfect fit to take care of this place whilst I'm out and about.'

'What? Why *me*?' Hughes asked, leaning forward as his voice broke.

'Because, like I said, you already know how the place operates down *there*. Now it'll be even easier for you to learn how it works up *here*. And if I'm honest, I need someone who can bridge the gap between us and them. The tensions are high. You bashing someone's head in with a hammer should be a good enough sign of that, I'd think.'

Hughes turned away, gazing out the window at the factory below. 'I can't ease those tensions. Not after what I did. They'll hate me.'

'If one or two are like that, then we'll throw them back to the streets. That won't hurt us. We've got future workers lining up for days. Besides, we have such an influx of new people that I'm sure barely any of them would even know you at this point, let alone remember you.'

Maybe he's right, Hughes thought. *Maybe enough time has passed, and enough people have come and gone. But what about the man? Looking for me ...*

No. Just stop it. You'll be fine.

Flavel walked up by his side, looking out the window as he patted his shoulder. 'You're family, Hughes. Help me build this place to even greater heights.'

Soon enough, with a solemn breath, Hughes forced himself to nod. 'Okay ... okay.'

'I knew you'd come through!' Flavel exclaimed with a smile. 'This place has a bright future with you and I, Hughes. I don't doubt it.'

Hughes' eyes lingered on the shadows cast by the machinery below. They crept along the factory floor as the moon gradually shifted.

Eventually, the darkness was overpowered by the light of the morning sun. The Dumphree carriage trotted before the factory with Hughes ready for his first day. He waited a moment, strengthening his will, before stepping out and marching inside the factory.

The workers had already begun their tasks. Hammering, burning, melting. All the while, the assistant managers barked orders at them, their voices echoing through the smoke and steam. Walking straight towards his office, Hughes kept his head low and his eyes fixed on the floor. Then he came upon a familiar spot. A dark red stain. Amongst all of the commotion, there laid Cloyd's final mark on this factory.

The image of his lifeless body flooded Hughes' memory. The pool of blood beneath his head. The life fading from his eyes. The nausea and dizziness from that moment began to return. With worry, Hughes gazed at the workers banging away at the metal around him. A few of them passed him an indifferent glance before returning to the grind.

Do they know me?

Does it matter?

No. It doesn't.

You got yourself here. It can't be for nothing. Just keep going.

Hughes pushed his legs forward and climbed the stairs towards his office. With a swift shut of the door behind him, he rested his back against it and regained his breath.

Eventually, as he sat down at his desk, he noted the coolness of the room compared to the scorching heat of the workplace below. It gave him quick relief before he picked up his dip pen and began writing the day's reports. What comes in, what goes out, what gets done, what still needs to be done.

At last, his mind quietened.

Just like his first day, this was every day at the Dumphree locomotive factory. The next, and the next, and the next. The numbers and words on each report grew, as did the piles of paper on and around his desk. Yet, each time he entered the factory, he saw the stain. Whether he stopped in his tracks or merely gave it a glance, he could never not see it. Every time, Cloyd's body lay there as the hordes of workers crashed and smashed around them. Always the first and last man to greet him at work.

Two weeks later, Hughes had few remaining questions for Flavel and his assistant managers. He had learnt all he could. With his back straight and eyes concentrated on a report atop his desk, he wrote intently before a knock came at the door.

'Come in,' he said, continuing to write.

Patrick, one of his assistant managers, stepped inside, wiping the sweat from his brow. 'Your carriage has arrived.'

'Oh, thank you, Patrick. I should only be gone an hour or two,' he explained as he stood up and slipped on his coat. 'If that new shipment arrives for South Yorkshire, handle it for me. I know it's a while away, but we should start preparing. That merger will be finalised soon enough.'

'Of course, Hughes. Also, one of the workers wanted to speak to you.'

'What for?' He squinted, straightening his coat's collar.

'He says he knows you. An old friend. Do you want me to tell him – '

'No, no, let him in,' he interrupted, watching the door with caution as Patrick stepped back outside.

After a moment, George entered the office with his boisterous voice. 'Frenchie! Mate!'

A chuckle of relief came over Hughes as the two of them hugged. 'George! It's been far too long.'

'So long you've lost ya beard! I barely recognised ya. You look like you're off, though. Am I holding you up?'

'No, no, please, take a seat. I've got a moment,' he insisted as they sat across from one another. 'You're working here? I had no idea! How long?'

George's expression turned grave. 'Hughes, I said hi to you this morning. Don't you remember?'

Hughes looked at him in dismay.

Finally, George let out a hearty laugh. 'I'm just pulling ya leg, you tosser! Nah, only a couple days. Once I heard you were the *manager*, of all things, I thought to hell with it, why don't I come work for *you!* Ya couldn't have become *that* much of a bastard yet.'

'You never know. I might just be,' he joked with a shrug.

'How'd ya even manage this, hey? Gettin' to where you are now. That bloody seat.'

'I honestly don't know. Just … family.'

'Ah, that's the way, isn't it?'

'How are you finding the place? Is there anything I can do for you?'

'Nah, nah, it's about the same as everywhere else, ya know? But I actually wanted to warn ya about something, Hughes.' George's voice took a sobering turn.

'Warn me?'

'Yeah. You know that fella you told me about? The one ya whacked? Well, I've been listening a little to some of the folks here, and let me tell ya, they're not happy. They mean to do you some harm, Hughes. They're after ya.'

Hughes leant back in his chair, looking off.

To think I believed no one would remember.

'I wanted to give ya the heads up, so you've got your wits about ya when they come.'

'Thank you, George. Do you know their names?'

'I think the chief of 'em is called Earl, but I don't know the rest of 'em. I can try and point 'em out. Then ya can report 'em to the police or something?'

'The police can't do much if they haven't done anything to me. It'll just be our word against theirs …'

'Mmm.' George nodded along in thought for a moment. 'Ya know, I could do a little investigatin'. Like ya did with that other fella, ya know? Get in with 'em, find out what I can. I can tell ya everythin' I hear.'

'Are you sure about that, George? You really don't – '

'Nah, it's nothing. Anything to help ya out. The quicker we get rid of them, the better, I say.'

Hughes looked at his old friend for a time, worried and unconvinced.

He's skinnier than I remember. He looks weaker, dirtier, less colour in his face. But he's still just as jolly. Still the same old George, determined as ever. It's like he doesn't even realise he's wasting away. Yet, I could use his help. After all, learning even just a little about Cloyd allowed me to save Flavel. Perhaps George could do the same for me.

'All right,' Hughes finally said, 'but I want you to be careful, okay? If they really are out for me, they won't be playing nice.'

'I know. Don't you worry,' he assured him as the two of them stood up.

'If there's anything you find out that can help us settle this without violence, please tell me. I need to know.'

George gave a nod and a smile before shaking his hand. 'Of course. It was good to see ya again, mate.'

'Likewise, George,' Hughes replied as he walked him to the office door. Before opening it, he stopped and turned towards him. 'I almost forgot to ask. How's Docie? Everyone else?'

'Aw, you know, same old. Docie's still bringing people in, givin' 'em shelter.'

'Of course … And Abigail? Any luck?'

'Afraid not, afraid not. But some of us still try to keep an eye out when we can. You'll have to come around soon, though, bring us some of that fancy food you've no doubt been havin'.'

'That sounds like a plan. Hold me to that.'

'Ya bloody know I will!' George agreed, shaking his finger at him.

Hughes chuckled as he opened the door. 'I'll see you soon.'

'Have a good day, Frenchie,' George said as he walked out of the office and down into the smoky haze below.

Hughes squinted through the smoke, hearing only the clanking and moaning of endless contraptions. On occasion, a silhouette could be glimpsed moving through the steam, disappearing just as fast as they appeared.

Just walk straight through. Don't stop.

After shutting the door behind him, Hughes descended the stairs with caution. Upon his final steps, the thick cloud of vapour overwhelmed him. Without delay, he pushed through the smoke, machinery, and workers. Clearing some of the steam, he spotted his carriage waiting outside. He clenched his fists and quickened his step, nearing closer and closer. His ears flinched and head twitched at the noises around him, but he did not stop. He felt his heart rising up through his chest, about to burst out of his throat, before …

He stepped out from the smoke. Safe and sound. With a breath of relief, he climbed into the carriage, leaving no moment to linger. His eyes peered back into the black and orange interior of the factory as he rode away.

* * *

A series of horns roared across the polluted Thames as hundreds of ships were called into port. Meanwhile, the Dumphree carriage arrived at a street curb beside the river. Hughes climbed out and made his way straight over to Flavel and another man in a dark suit.

'I'm terribly sorry for the hold-up,' Hughes said as he shook both of their hands.

'No matter, Hughes,' Flavel assured him. 'This is Claude Lockhurt. He's a part of the Surrey Commercial Docks Company. He's going to help us merge with their new expansions.'

'A pleasure to meet you,' Claude said, bowing his head to Hughes.

'Likewise. I imagine the docks will be seeing quite the growth now.'

'Oh, indeed!' he exclaimed with pride. 'As I was just telling Flavel, we're soon approaching nine docks in the district, and the demand is only growing.'

'It's a graceful sight, seeing more and more ships coming into port every day,' Flavel added.

'Indeed. We've had a fantastic influx of traffic from Scandinavia, Canada ...' Claude continued on as his voice faded into a distant blur.

Hughes' own voice took hold of his focus.

What do I tell Flavel? Will his involvement only make matters worse? Perhaps these friends of Cloyd's can be reasoned with.

In the corner of his eye, something caught Hughes' attention. As Flavel and Claude continued their discussion, Hughes looked off across to the other side of the Thames. Between the gaps of the many passing vessels, a little girl with bright blonde hair stumbled along the muddy shore. Beside a handful of other children in rags, she carried boxes off a small docked boat.

An elderly man with a crooked nose stood over them, shouting orders that were impossible to hear. The children barely seemed to notice, going back and forth like clockwork. Any childlike qualities seemed completely lost behind their dead faces. The little girl tripped as she stepped off the boat, dropping her box onto the ground and smashing it open. Bottles and wrapped food spilled out everywhere as the man began shouting at her. He grabbed a hold of her neck as ...

'Hughes. Hughes, did you hear that?'

Hughes looked back at Flavel and Claude, finding them awaiting his response.

Flavel continued, 'With this new partnership we're going to be doubling our intake! You best get some good rest tonight; we've got a lot of work to do. This truly is an age to remember.'

'It most certainly is.' Hughes added, nodding to both.

That night, the Dumphree fireplace flickered a reddish flame. Its crimson waves danced across Hughes' face as he sat alone, writing in his journal.

The wooden floorboards in the hallway creaked as Mary walked past, noticing Hughes in the lounge room. 'Am I ever going to get to read that thing?' she asked with a smirk, walking in and sitting on the armchair beside him.

'Maybe one day. If you're lucky,' he chuckled.

'I look forward to it. Maybe it'll inspire *me* to write.'

'You should. It's good. It's like you're … talking with somebody even when there's no one there. You feel like you're actually making progress, in a way.'

'Well, lucky for you I'm an *actual* somebody. Talk with me. What's troubling you?'

Hughes gave her a small smile and shook his head. 'What makes you think I'm troubled?'

'Your very intense manner of writing gave it away just a little. Besides, you've taken on a lot these past few weeks. I wouldn't expect it to have been easy.'

Twisting the pen in his hand, Hughes nodded for a moment. 'I'm not exactly sure what to do.'

'About what?'

'I think I could be in danger. I think there's people that are out to get me in the factory.'

'I *knew* there would be!' she exclaimed, immediately standing up. 'Flavel! Get in here!'

Hughes opened his mouth to stop her, but it was too late. He rolled his eyes and shook his head.

Great. Now what?

'What is it?' Flavel asked, curiously walking inside, wearing his nightly gown and holding a glass of brandy.

'I told you you'd both be in danger in that damned city. I don't want you – '

'Hold on, hold on, what's happening?' Flavel interrupted.

Hughes stood up with a sigh. 'I don't know anything for certain, but from what I've heard, there's friends of Cloyd's working in the factory that are planning something against me.'

'Do you know their names?'

'One of them, but – '

'Then we throw them out, like I told you we would,' Flavel declared without hesitation.

'I don't think that's a good idea.'

'*Why not?*' Mary asked, anxiety tainting her voice.

'Because if they do mean to kill me, that won't stop them. If anything, that could make it worse. This is their dead *friend* we're talking about …'

Mary hesitated as his words struck her.

Hughes continued, 'If it comes down to it, I want to be able to negotiate with them.'

'Offer them money?' Flavel clarified.

'Potentially. I don't know. I'm still working it out. And it depends on what comes of it. I'm already working on finding out more.'

'Can't you just contact the police?' Mary pleaded to Flavel.

'We can't draw that sort of attention,' he said, shaking his head. 'You know that, dear. Especially with our new partnership with the Lockhurts. If the papers get a hold of that, then you can be bloody well sure my competitors will exploit it. The factory will be deemed "the worst place in London. Rampant anarchy of biblical proportions" or some such nonsense. The Surrey company won't want to use us, and then others won't, and then we'll lose *everything.* No police. We *can't.*'

'Then I think we wait,' Hughes stepped in. 'We can't act now anyway, they haven't even attempted anything yet.'

'Well, if you're playing the waiting game,' Mary sternly said, 'then you've got to be prepared, *that* I'm making sure of. Take a gun wherever you go in the city.' She turned to her husband. 'From your cabinet.'

Flavel nodded.

In their dining room, Flavel opened his hunting cabinet, revealing layers of rifles and pistols. From it, he took out the four-barrel Howdah pistol and carefully handed it to Hughes. 'This'll do more than enough damage when the time comes.'

Hughes reluctantly took the heavy pistol into his hands. '*If* the time comes.'

Taking out his own pistol from the cabinet, Flavel patted Hughes' shoulder and nodded. 'If.'

Chapter 4

Hughes' dip pen scratched across the page as he wrote away at dozens of more reports on his desk. Every now and again, his hand paused and flexed, fighting the pain from the pressure of the pen.

A knock at the door sharply drew his attention to it. 'Yes?'

'It's George!'

Hughes closed his eyes with relief. 'Come in.'

George entered at a leisurely pace, shutting the door and sitting down across the desk. He took a long breath as his shoulders sank into a comfortable position. 'I think I might have some good news for ya, mate.'

'Yeah?'

'I went to a pub with 'em last night. Eventually, most of 'em had passed out, and then it was just me and Earl. Finally got to have a good chat with 'im. Just the two of us.'

'What'd he say?'

'He told me he don't think he'll be able to go through with it. He wants to seem strong to the others, but he's got his doubts. Some common bloody sense seems to have knocked on his door. As ya do, he doesn't want them to all end up in a ditch by the end of it, like it all meant nothin'.'

Hughes nodded along, uncertain. 'Did he say anything else? Anything that I should worry about?'

George shook his head. 'He seemed like he really meant it. I think it might be over, mate.'

Hughes ran his fingers along his chin, staring down at his desk as if in a trance. 'It could've been the drink talking.'

'I don't know, he seemed to hold his drink pretty well. A lot more than the other lobcocks in the group, that's for sure.' George glanced around the room, noticing a freshly used pillow and blanket lying on the office couch. 'Barely seen you down in the factory these last couple weeks. You hidin' away?'

'I don't want to antagonise him. The less he sees of me, the better.'

'Well, you're gonna have to come out sometime. I think you're out of the fog.' George climbed to his feet before noticing Hughes' troubled stare. 'I'll keep an eye on him still, just in case. Don't ya worry.'

'Thanks, George.'

'I think it'll cheer you up to come visit us at the lodge too. We're all missing ya.'

'I know. I will, I will. I'm just … very busy.'

'Aren't we all?' George smirked. 'Well, don't want the machinery missin' me too much. Keep safe, mate.'

'You too.'

George exited the office, fading into the smoke and heat below.

Before any more thoughts could come to him, Hughes picked up his pen and continued writing. Soon enough, the moon had risen, and the factory was empty. Hughes' fingers shook profusely as he continued writing. More numbers, more imports, more exports, more revenue. Always growing.

He pushed himself to write one more number before he finally let go of the pen and gripped his hand, grimacing in silence. Clenching and unclenching his fist, he left his chair and approached the window at his side. He gazed upon the dark, empty streets below, surrounded by endless factories.

It still doesn't feel safe, he thought.

Something George told him the week prior had not yet left his mind. 'Earl knows you,' he had said. 'He was the one who introduced ya to Cloyd. Invited ya to that meeting. I think he just regrets ever trusting ya.'

I know that pain, Hughes admitted to himself. *That trust being broken. Inadvertently helping someone … murder another. Cloyd was his friend. Someone he looked up to, someone who was fighting for them. And now I'm here, keeping them trapped in this awful place.*

Maybe he really is too scared to do anything. After seeing what I did to Cloyd, seeing the position I'm in, it is possible he thinks it's too big of a risk.

But at the same time, it seems too easy that he would just give up. How could he ever forget what happened? How could he ever move on? Wouldn't he want to avenge his friend? Wouldn't he want to try and break free of his pain? After all, that's what I did. I couldn't stand it down there and back home. I still can't.

Maybe this is all <u>my</u> fault.

Maybe I just shouldn't be here …

A sickness began to rise in his throat.

Or maybe Flavel is right, he considered. *Money is ultimately what we're all after, isn't it? A better life is only possible because of it. If that's the heart of the issue, then maybe that's how I can solve it.*

Hughes turned and opened a desk drawer, finding his pistol sitting beside a small bag Flavel had given him, a bag filled with hundreds of shillings.

The money <u>has</u> to work. If what George said is true, if it comes down to it, Earl won't want violence any more than I do. He'll see reason.

* * *

The sun fell twice more. Church bells rang throughout the city as hundreds of streetlamps came to life one by one, emanating an orange glow across the streets of London. Far below the watchful moon and grey clouds, the Dumphree carriage trotted through one such street.

'Well, good to see you've gotten enough sleep lately,' Flavel remarked to Hughes, both dressed in fanciful suits and long coats.

Hughes looked back at him with dreary eyes and dark bags hanging beneath them.

'You've got to stop sleeping in that damned factory,' Mary added, sitting across from him in the carriage. 'It can't be any good for you, spending that much time there. Especially with the way things are.'

'Oh, he's not in any danger, Mary,' Flavel moaned. 'If they were going to do us any harm, they already would've tried.'

'You don't know that,' she replied with a soft concern in her voice.

'Well, *I* think I do. But regardless, all we need to worry about right now is impressing everyone tonight. All the members of the Surrey company will be here. I don't want any talk of this "danger". All right? Good.'

Shortly after, the Dumphree carriage arrived before a tall and glowing hotel. The family stepped outside and were met by a doorman who awaited them at the entrance. After being escorted to the top floor, the trio stepped inside a function room brimming with countless men in black suits and women in great dresses. An hour later, there was chatter, laughter, and boastfulness as food and drinks were served on platters. The candles cast warm shadows as the windows gazed out across a vast view of the city.

Amidst it all, Hughes was alone, leant against the bar counter, sipping a glass of wine. He gazed at the crowds of guests, Flavel and Mary among them, watching them take turns laughing, questioning, admiring.

How long can I sip at this before I have to go back over? he asked himself.

Turning back to the counter and placing his glass down, Hughes noticed a young woman approach the counter.

'A glass of sherry, please,' she asked the barman.

'You sure you can handle it, darling?' the man teased, not yet moving from his post.

'Quite,' she replied with an exaggerated smile.

The barman tilted his head and raised his eyebrows as he poured her a glass.

'Thank you,' she said, rolling her eyes as he turned away. Glancing to her right, she noticed Hughes watching their exchange. 'Who are you, then? I haven't seen your face before.'

'Oh – uh – my name is Hughes.'

'Hughes …?'

'Dumphree – Dumphree. We've just partnered with the company. You?'

'Claude Lockhurt is my father. I imagine you two have met.'

'We have. He seems like a fine man.'

She gave another hollow smile as she sipped from her glass.

'I asked for *your* name though, not your father's,' Hughes reiterated.

Her green eyes peered back at him, surprised and curious. 'Stella … What's your accent? I can't pick it.'

'It's a … blended one. I grew up in France.'

'France? What's that like?'

'It's surprisingly not too different from here.'

'You say that as if it's a bad thing.'

'Oh, I would never imply that.'

Stella skidded closer to him, quietening her voice with a smile. 'I find it hard to believe France could be just as miserable.'

Hughes quietly chuckled. 'Oh, you'd be surprised. I come from a very particular part of France.'

'Do tell.'

'Well,' he paused for a moment, considering, before taking a bigger sip of his drink. 'Believe it or not, there's actually more people where I come from. More in the streets, more buildings, more factories, more everything.'

'Are you playing tricks on me?'

'Not really.'

'Well, considering that, I guess you're glad you came somewhere a little quieter.'

'Not exactly quiet in any factory.'

'Oh, you're a factory man. I'm surprised you're not covered in all of that dust and dirt and … whatever else floats around in those places.'

'Despair. Loneliness. Dread. All the best stuff.'

'Oh, yes, we all need a good dose of that sometimes. Have you been here long?'

'I've lost track a little, but I think a few months. Maybe more.'

'So, I'm guessing you haven't gotten to see the whole city yet?' she asked, running her fingers along her shining black hair.

'Haven't had a lot of chances, really. Why? You want to show me around?'

'Oh no, I wouldn't want to pull you away from all of this important business and such.'

'Oh God, of course not. We wouldn't want that,' he remarked with another smile.

In a quiet cobblestone street, lit only by the streetlamps above, Hughes and Stella strolled alongside one another. They both dodged and skipped over puddles as they breathed in the cool air.

'I'll have to go to this place in France you're talking about it, you know?' she revealed, raising her eyebrows at him.

'And why would you want to do that?'

'It's the only way I'll be able to believe what you say about it.'

'My word isn't enough?'

'I'm afraid not, sir.'

'Well, good luck getting there. I'll send my regards.'

'You'll see. I'll find it. Eventually.'

'So eager to leave?'

'I've only ever known this place. I want new places to walk and see,' she explained, gazing at the clouded skies. 'Although you don't make travel sound *entirely* enticing, I must admit.'

Hughes laughed. 'I don't mean to. The Dumphree estate is beautiful. One of the most beautiful places I've ever seen, actually. Probably ever.'

'So, you *are* glad you left home?'

'Yeah, I guess so.'

'Well, that's that. I'm definitely going to France.'

Steadily, the moon trailed along the night sky as the pair continued to stroll through the fog.

Hughes glanced at their surroundings before finally coming to a stop. 'Are you sure we're not lost?'

'Yes, yes,' she said with a hand wave, continuing on her way.

'Shouldn't we start heading back?'

'We'll be back,' she explained, turning to face him. 'I'm just taking a different way.'

Hughes bit his lip as he continued to survey the street with uncertainty.

'Don't worry. *I'll* keep you safe,' she assured him before carrying on her way. 'You just have to keep up.'

Hughes jogged to catch up to her as he chuckled. 'You could just walk forever, couldn't you?'

'Maybe … probably. If only you didn't slow me down so much.'

'Yeah, you'd be bloody halfway across the world by now.'

She smiled before spotting a lively pub ahead. 'Oh, there's another good place to drink. It gets a bit rough, though, so don't go too late.'

'Right. Noted.' He nodded before hearing an eruption of voices from within the pub.

Suddenly, a bundle of men stumbled out of the door, clinging to each other as they fell to the ground. Hughes and Stella stopped dead in their tracks as the men drunkenly swung their arms and words at each other. As much as they tried, they could barely land a single hit on each other, let alone stand on their own two feet.

A grouchy-voiced bartender stormed out behind them, shaking his head. 'You bloody nobs. Get some sleep, will ya!'

'I got 'im, I got 'im, I'm gonna – ' one of the men mumbled as he stood up before falling back to the ground.

Hughes and Stella both laughed at the sight of them.

'See what I mean?' she said, nudging his arm.

'Yup,' he replied in amusement before noticing something beyond the scuffle. It was a figure. A hooded man approaching them from down the street, clinging to the shadows.

Hughes' smile fell away.

The way he walked, the clothes he wore, the bag on his back.

All of it sent a *shiver* down Hughes' spine.

'Come here, quick!' he exclaimed, grabbing Stella's arm and rushing her into the alleyway beside the pub.

'What – what are you doing?' she cried, breaking free from his grip and smacking his arm with her purse.

'Shhh – shhh!' he insisted before peeking out of the alleyway.

The dark figure approached the men on the ground, looking over them intently.

Stella's anger fell into confusion as she carefully peered into the street beside Hughes. They both watched the figure scan his eyes across the rest of the street. His face was impossible to make out beneath the shadow of his hood.

'Who is that?' she whispered.

The figure looked towards them just as Hughes pulled Stella back out of sight.

Hughes' heart pounded as he clung to the wall. He shot a glance towards the shadows deeper within the alleyway. With haste, he took Stella's hand and led her towards them. They both disappeared into the darkness as the figure walked before the alleyway. His long shadow stretched across the cobblestone ground. For a few moments, he stood entirely still, staring at the blackness that shrouded Hughes and Stella.

Breathing.

Waiting.

Hughes clenched his teeth and held his breath. Stella squinted, attempting to decipher the man's hidden face. Before she could grasp any features, the figure stepped out of sight.

Hughes' breath began to return as Stella smirked at him. 'What was *that* all about?' She chuckled and gently pushed him. 'You really looked scared there.'

Hughes stumbled to find his words. 'I thought he was – he was after me!'

She shook her head and laughed. 'If you lost your nerve about every strange man walking these streets at night, you'd *never* get home.'

'I'm serious!' he exclaimed, trying not to smile at her own enjoyment.

'You really are a strange man. What could anyone be after you for?' she asked, walking him back out of the alleyway.

'I – I don't know. I just thought I recognised him from somewhere.'

'Yeah, well, I recognise you get too easily spooked in the dark,' she noted, stopping as he continually checked their surroundings. 'Come on, *I'll* get you back safely.' She reached out her hand. 'Can't be cowering in fear forever.'

Hughes hesitated a moment, still looking for any sign of the figure, but he was nowhere to be seen. Finally, with a deep breath, he took Stella's hand, and she walked him back through the long, winding streets. Soon enough, the pair returned to the front of the bustling hotel. The guests were in the midst of departing, splitting off towards their respective carts.

'There you are, Stella!' Claude yelled out from across the street, standing beside his own horse and cart. 'Come along. We're leaving.'

'Okay! Just a moment!' Stella yelled out before turning back to Hughes. 'Feeling safe now, are we?'

'Never felt more so,' he replied with a reserved smile.

'Well, thank you for the walk, Hughes. And even with our strange detour, it was fun.'

'It was. Thank *you*.'

'Good night,' she said with a nod before turning and walking across the street towards her father.

Hughes hesitated as he watched her leave.

Should I say something? Are you really going to let her leave? Just like that?

'Wait, Stella,' he finally let out, walking a little closer as she stopped and turned around. 'I thought maybe … you could show me more of the city sometime. Or just go for more walks and things. I really did enjoy it.'

She beamed back, 'That sounds wonderful, Hughes. Write to me. I look forward to it.'

'Me too.' He smiled before she waved goodbye and climbed into her cart. Slipping his hands into his pockets, he watched as her cart trotted away, feeling a warmth enrapture his heart.

'You seem awfully giddy around her,' Mary said, startling Hughes as he suddenly turned to see her standing beside him.

'Whoa, *Mary!* – uh – I – I don't …'

Mary waved her hand. 'No need.' She leaned in with a childlike glee. 'I think she's *gorgeous*. Now, come along; let's head home.' She squealed in excitement as they walked towards the Dumphree cart.

* * *

Another week passed. George's visits had become less frequent, and Hughes' time with Stella only grew. Even when relegating himself to his office, he began writing her letters.

On another of their walks through the city, Hughes stopped before the gates of a cemetery. They were grey and weathered, and beyond them, countless tombstones stretched into the distance.

Stella slowed down as she noticed his intrigue. 'Someone you know in there?'

'No, I've just … never seen one of these places.'

'A cemetery? Surely, they have those where you're from.'

He looked at her, reluctant to elaborate. 'Well, not that I've ever seen. They usually have a different way of disposing of the dead.'

'Do you want to see it?'

Hughes couldn't help but nod as his eyes were drawn back towards the aisles of the dead.

'Come on,' she remarked, leading him beyond the gates.

The constant noise of the city seemed entirely distant as they stepped inside. There was nothing to hear but the wind and their footsteps. They passed by endless rows of new and old tombstones. Hughes noticed batches of fresh flowers, trinkets, and other gifts rested upon many of them. The grass was well-kept, and there were dedicated areas for trees to grow, giving shade to the rested.

Stella noticed the amazement and appreciation in Hughes' eyes.

What a wonder, she thought, *to see one so enamoured by such a place.*

Along their walk, Stella eventually brought him to one particular gravestone.

Irene Lockhurt

Stella looked upon the monument with grief.

'I'm sorry for your loss,' Hughes said with care. 'What was she like?'

'My father would say stubborn. But really it was an incredible strength she had. I wish I had half the fight she did.'

'You don't think you do?'

'I'm lucky I'm out here as it is. Lord knows my father doesn't like me going anywhere. He's got my whole life set out for me now. Without her, I don't think there's much I can say to him to change that anymore.'

Hughes squatted down before the grave, stretching out his hand and letting the grass feed between his fingers. 'I lost my father not that long ago too. But I didn't get to have a place like this for him. Can't visit him or talk to him or be close to him. You're really lucky to have this. She's still here, in a way.'

A teary-eyed smile came over Stella. She carefully sat down on the grave and patted the ground beside her, allowing Hughes to sit at her side. The trees softly swayed above them as the pair let the cool air brush against their skin.

Hughes nodded to himself as he took in their surroundings. 'This is a beautiful place.'

Stella smiled as she placed her hand on the earth next to his. 'It is.'

* * *

Alone, Mary and Flavel Dumphree sat at their candlelit dining table, finishing their food. Mary glanced at the empty seat across from her, before turning to her husband with concern.

'He'll be fine,' Flavel assured her, patting his lips with a napkin. 'He's just working late again.'

'You don't believe that. He's spending too much time out there, you know it.'

'He said the danger is gone, Mary. If they haven't done anything by now – '

'It's not good for him! He should be back here, not out *there*!'

Taking a sip of his wine, Flavel shrugged. 'What do you want me to do? He's a man. He does what he thinks is best. I can't change that.'

'You should go get him. Bring him back yourself.'

With a sigh, Flavel stood up and shook his head. 'At the end of the day, Mary, he's helping us. He probably feels he owes it to us. Leave him be.' Flavel pushed in his chair and walked towards the dining room door.

'*Please*, darling. Bring him back. He needs someone. He needs you.'

Flavel stopped before the hallway, taking a deep breath. Finally, he shook his head and left the room.

Back in London, rays of moonlight escaped through the cracks in the clouds. The hooting of owls and smashing of beer bottles echoed throughout the fog-ridden streets. An echo from within the factory awoke Hughes from his slumber. He groaned as he pulled his head off the table and wiped the dribble from his mouth. Checking his watch, he found it was almost midnight. With a deep sigh, he noticed the mountains of paperwork and files cluttering the office. Finally, his eyes fell upon a letter he was writing.

"To Stella"

He smiled, before another distorted echo cried from within the factory. Squinting at the door, Hughes stood up and slid on his jacket. He opened his desk drawer and gazed upon his pistol and a small bag of coins.

Do I really need these?

That's why they're here, though. Just in case.

With reluctance, Hughes slotted them into his pockets before carefully opening the office door and walking down into the heart of the factory. It was there he saw them. A collection of silhouettes standing in the shadows of the machinery.

'Who's there?' he asked, his voice beginning to tremble.

'Hughes! It's–!' George yelled out before a fist struck his cheek.

While still difficult to make out, Hughes could see George knelt before a group of men, bruised and beaten. They held him in place, pressing a rugged blade against his throat.

'What are you doing to him? *Let him go*,' Hughes demanded, stopping before getting any closer.

'We're just doing what we've been plannin',' one of the men said from the shadows.

'Who are you?' Hughes asked, his eyes darting between all of the figures.

'Don't act like you don't know. Your mate, George here, we've seen him. Going back and forth from your office. You might think us stupid, but we're smart enough to know a *rat* when we see one.'

Hughes' entire body began to shake as he felt the air leaving his lungs.

'Come on, fellas,' George's friendly voice interjected, 'we can work this one out. There's no – '

The man smacked the handle of his knife into the back of George's head. *'Shut up!'* He peered back at Hughes, who remained helplessly frozen. 'So, you're not gonna say anything?'

Gradually, Hughes raised his hands as a heavy desperation consumed his voice. 'I'm sorry … your name is Earl, isn't it? I know I can't ask for your forgiveness, but I'm just asking for you to let this man go.'

'Or what? You gonna kill us too?'

'I don't want anyone to die. Enough people have. I don't stop thinking about what I did. I can't … But I've thought about how to maybe help make things better.' With a steady, cautious motion, Hughes reached into his pocket, pulling out the bag of coins, 'I've got money, and I can get even more, for all of you. You don't have to fight or kill.'

Earl glanced at the others for a moment, his expression too difficult to see. Then, looking back at Hughes, he signalled with his hand. 'Toss it over.'

'Let him go first.'

'No. That ain't how this is workin'.' He pressed the blade an inch deeper against George's throat, 'Toss it *here. Now.*'

As George let out a whimper of pain, Hughes quickly nodded. 'Okay, okay.' He tossed the bag towards them. Upon hitting the ground, some of the coins spilled out. They spun and rolled around for a moment, tinging and ringing, before falling silent again.

Hughes' eyes strained to make out their expressions, waiting for any sort of reaction. After a moment of pure silence, he forced back the urge to vomit. '*Please*, will you let him go now?'

Earl softened his voice. 'Hughes … I know Cloyd made a mistake. He didn't have the best plan, and I can't see myself doing any better if I kill you. But all of this has only made it clearer how much you people really just don't *care* about us. We'd be hunted down like dogs if we hurt you, but people like Cloyd, like me, like George, if we die, we're just another name to cross off your lists.'

Hughes shook his head. 'No, no, when George was helping me learn more, I wanted to know how I could *help you*. How I could help all of us stop this, and even when I knew about what you were planning, I let you keep your jobs here. And you still can. You can be safe, you can work, you can earn a living. I know what it's like out there too.'

Earl sniggered under his breath, 'Nah. I think you've forgotten.'

'*Wait – no!*' Hughes yelled out as Earl ripped the knife across George's throat.

George gargled for air as blood poured out of his neck and mouth. He collapsed to the ground, choking.

Hughes froze, his mouth agape and eyes welling with tears. He forced himself to look away as George gripped at his throat, his thick, red blood consuming the coins on the floor.

Eventually, his breath faded.

Earl shook some of the blood off his knife. 'And to think that he thought we were becoming friends.' With the gesture of his head, Earl and the three figures turned and walked towards the factory's tall open entrance.

Hughes could barely see through his tears as he watched the men leaving. Then, at last, he felt the weight of the pistol in his pocket.

No.

You can't.

His eyes trailed down towards George, quietly lying in a puddle of his own blood.

A painful rage boiled inside him as he looked back at the men responsible. His breath fell silent as he pulled out his pistol and walked after them.

Earl turned and stopped, noticing Hughes' approach. His eyes widened as Hughes aimed at him and stopped in his tracks, his finger hesitating on the trigger. Sweat dripped from his palms as he gritted his teeth.

No. Don't.

Don't do it.

Earl's surprise gradually fell into a glare. After a moment of nothing more, he snickered again and turned around, continuing on his way.

Hughes' feet began moving after them. Without another moment to linger, he sucked in his breath and fired a bullet. Earl was knocked to his side as the bullet struck the back of his shoulder. The other men turned, ducked, and froze as the loud bang echoed behind them. Hughes continued walking forward, quickly aiming at another, firing a bullet into the side of his chest. The man cried out in pain as he collapsed to the floor.

Just as the others began running outside, Hughes fired another bullet into one of their backs, throwing him onto the floor. Earl and another man fled the factory. Hughes fired a fourth bullet, missing both of them.

If they escape, they could tell others, he immediately thought.

The police, the media, _everyone_.

Hughes ran out after them, aiming his pistol and pulling the trigger. The pistol clicked. There were no bullets left. The men turned the corner of the factory and disappeared from sight.

'Help! Help! Somebody!' he heard Earl screaming in the distance.

Hughes panted, fighting to catch up to them before …

'Wait – wait!' one of the men shouted before another gunshot rang out through the night air.

Just as Hughes turned the corner, he saw one of the men drop dead onto the ground. The Dumphree carriage and Flavel stood before them, aiming his pistol at Earl, who stood frightfully still. With another blast and flash of light, Flavel shot and killed him. Earl's body collapsed onto the ground next to the other man. Hughes finally stopped and caught his breath, bending over his knees.

All was silent again.

'Hughes! Are you all right?' Flavel yelled out as he ran up to him, grabbing and inspecting him for any wounds.

'I'm – yes ... No.' Hughes could not help but break down into more tears. 'They killed George.'

Flavel frowned and hugged him.

'We should just tell the police,' he continued in defeat. 'We need them, we need them ...'

'No, no, Hughes, we can't. No one can know of this. We'll be finished otherwise.'

Hughes fought to regain his breath and control himself. 'What can we do?'

Flavel looked back at the two bodies, contemplating for a moment. 'I know ... I know what to do, but we have to hurry.'

Chapter 5

The black water of the Thames brushed against the docks. Hughes stood at its edge, gazing down as Flavel swiftly walked up by his side.

'This'll do,' Flavel said, out of breath.

Hughes shook his head. 'How? Won't they be found?'

'Yes, but not for a while. Bodies wash up along the Thames all the time. By the time they're found, they'll have floated far from here, and probably be unrecognisable by then. Not that they'd likely be able to identify them anyway. Now come on, I need your help.'

Flavel hurried back to their carriage, dragging out one of the bodies. After making sure there was nothing in his pockets, he struggled to hold him up properly, 'Hughes! *Quick*!'

Hughes walked over with haste, helping him lift up the body and carry it to the dock's edge. They threw the man into the river, causing a great splash before he floated away.

As the moon faded in and out of sight behind the grey clouds above, the pair threw away the rest of the bodies until only George remained.

They laid him down at the edge of the dock, catching their breath for a moment. Hughes was struck with pain as he looked upon his once friend. 'I want to bury him.'

Flavel shook his head. 'We can't. It'd take too long, and if they ever found him … I'm sorry, Hughes.'

Hughes only gave Flavel a tired and defeated look in return, before helping him throw George into the river. The pair watched as he was taken away by the current, disappearing into the darkness.

Flavel patted Hughes' shoulder with a pitiful glance. 'We'll go clean up and then head home. We'll figure out the rest from there.'

Hughes looked down at the river one last time, his eyes and expression no more lively than the bodies themselves.

The following day, Hughes returned to the factory, walking past the same dark stain on the floor. He glanced at the workers around him as they carried on, paying no mind to him as he passed by. He felt not a single glance as he entered the office. His chair creaked as he sat down, still surrounded by paperwork.

He stared at it all. Endless numbers and words.

What do they all even mean? he pondered.

Soon enough, Patrick entered the office and handed him the roll call sheet. 'We have a few missing today. Might want to get some new ones in.'

Hughes' eyes scanned down the sheet, finding the names of Earl, George, and three others, all crossed out and unmarked for attendance. Hughes reached for his pen before noticing his hand was shaking. He clenched and unclenched his fist, steadying himself, before taking the pen and signing his name. 'Give them a day. If they don't show tomorrow, then hire some more.'

With a nod, Patrick took the sheet and left the room. Silence took hold once more as Hughes picked up his pen and returned to work.

Later that day, as Hughes continued to write in his office, the sounds of gunfire echoed in his ears. The louder they became, the harder and faster he wrote. His lips tightened as he fought to subdue the noises. George's writhing body flashed in his memory.

Suddenly, a loud metallic crash, followed by screams of pain and cries of panic, sounded from below. His head shot up with a fright, taking a moment to believe the sound was all too real, before he rushed out of his seat and down into the smoky haze of the factory, finding workers running to and fro.

'What's happening?' he cried out, pushing towards the source of the wailing. 'What's happening!'

Workers disappeared in and out of the smoke as he finally came upon the rear corner of the factory. A handful of workers lay across the concrete floor, their skin melting and burning from liquid steel that had poured out of a fallen tank. The injured workers rolled back and forth in pain as others struggled to stand, their screams piercing the air.

Hughes froze in place as he watched them in horror.

Other workers attempted to drag the burning bodies away from the molten metal.

What do I do?

What do I –?

How do I –?

'Back away, sir! Back away!' another assistant manager, Merritt, cried out, pushing him away from the scene.

'No – *no*, I need to help them!'

'No, sir! Don't!'

'I need to!' Hughes cried out, pushing Merritt aside and running back to the suffering workers. As he reached one of them, he looked over his half-melted face, realising it was Patrick. 'Oh God, Patrick. I've got you, I've got you.' Hughes wrapped his hands around Patrick's shoulders and began dragging him away from the hellscape.

Patrick groaned and sobbed as his head rolled side to side. Hughes pulled him out of the factory as numerous other workers fled the scene around them. Hughes knelt beside him, looking over his charred, red skin in disbelief. 'Patrick? Are you there, Patrick?'

He was no longer breathing.

Hughes stared down at his young, disfigured face.

Patrick?

You're gone too, aren't you?

The remaining workers were swiftly pulled out of the sweltering smoke as Hughes' breath settled and he sat down beside Patrick's body in defeat. The surrounding noises faded into the distant background as he stared at the glowing factory. Muffled voices and footsteps blurred by as firemen arrived to join the commotion.

What am I doing?

Merritt ran over and bent down beside him. 'Are you okay, sir?'

Hughes glanced at the assistant manager in a daze, before giving him a half-hearted nod.

'Don't worry, sir,' the manager nervously explained. 'This has happened plenty of times before. It'll be all cleaned up, and work will resume within the hour. And the men will stay an extra hour too, so we don't fall behind schedule. I'll make sure of it.'

Then, just as Merritt said, an hour passed, and Hughes once again sat at his desk. He blankly stared at the office door, hearing the clanking of metal and barking of orders echoing from below.

Steadily, his eyes trailed down towards the call sheet sitting atop his desk. As if it were instinct, he reached out for his pen. He stopped himself as he noticed his hand shaking once again. Taking a deep breath, he clenched his fist.

Finally, he grabbed the pen and slid the call sheet before him. With the flick of his wrist, he crossed out Patrick's name.

* * *

The night of George's murder, when Hughes and Flavel returned to the Dumphree estate, their story was prepared.

'If anyone ever draws attention to it or asks,' Flavel told Hughes, 'we were aware of some tensions between Earl, George, and some of the others working in the factory but knew nothing more than that. One day, they simply didn't return to work, and we put no mind to it because people phase in and out all the time. It's not unusual.'

Hughes could still hear the words in his head as he sat atop Irene's grave, leaning against her tombstone.

I'm used to the lies, he thought. *These shouldn't be any different.*

But look at where they have gotten you. Were they ever worth it? Is this life truly any better than the one before it?

Ever since I left, there's been blood on my hands. Now more than ever. George would be alive if I didn't let him get close to Earl. Hell, he would be alive if I didn't kill Cloyd. Not to mention Patrick and all of those other men working for me. And all because I wanted what? Money? My own comfort? A better life? What life is this?

68

Hughes looked upon the grass beneath him, feeling it pressed against the palm of his hand.

Mum, Dad ... 'Can't I just be with you?'

'Hughes?' A soft voice reached out.

Hughes glanced up to see Stella approaching him in the cemetery.

'I've been trying to find you. I thought you might be here,' she said with a small smile, kneeling beside him before noticing his bloodshot eyes. 'What is it? What's happened?'

'It's best no one else knows,' Flavel had told him. *'Especially your friend, Stella. I can't risk the Lockhurts finding out about this and severing our union.'*

Hughes stared into her eyes, on the verge of opening his mouth and explaining everything. With a tremble in his lips, he forced himself to look away. Before long, his shoulders began to shake, and he broke down into tears.

'Oh no, come here,' she said with care, sitting up against the tombstone and pulling him close. He rested his head on her breast as she wrapped her arms around him, stroking his hair. 'It's okay. It's all right. I'm here.'

Gradually, Hughes felt his breath return as she spoke her soothing words. Both of their hands met and held each other as he closed his eyes, listening to the sounds of the leaves and branches flowing in the wind above.

Over the coming days, their walks together became more frequent. Each time, they stood closer and closer to one another.

On one such day, strolling alongside the Thames, their shoulders were almost touching.

'The plants and such are actually keeping this year,' Stella said with a smile. 'After the last winter, I didn't think they'd have much in them.'

'How many do you have?'

'Oh, I don't know *exactly*, but a lot.'

'So, it's a garden? You have a garden?'

'Yes, I have a *garden*,' she teasingly replied.

'You'll have to show me.'

'Perhaps I shall. I would love to see some of them in France too, you know?'

'Well … don't expect much.'

'Oh, you've got to be kidding me. They don't have *gardens* either*?* What does your home *not* not have?'

'Oh, it's got a lot, it's just … all different.'

'It sounds like the *strangest* place. Almost as strange as you,' she said with amusement. 'Besides, don't you have a garden at your estate?'

'We do, yes. It's a wonderful one. That's why I want to see more.'

'Well, show me yours, and I'll show you mine; how's that for a deal?'

They stopped as Hughes nodded. 'Agreed. It's a deal … All right, I'd best head back to the factory.'

Stella's smile faded as she looked into his tired eyes. 'Do you really think you should?'

'I have to.'

'But look at you.' She placed her hand on his cheek. 'Ever since that accident, you've been fading away. From where I stand, it doesn't seem good for you. I think you know that too.'

Hughes shook his head, struggling to meet her gaze. 'It's not that.'

'Then what is it? What's happened? You know you can tell me. Lord knows I've told you enough about me and my silly life.'

His eyes returned to hers. 'I know. Thank you, Stella. I really do enjoy our time together.'

A little smile returned to her face as she caressed his cheek. 'I do too.'

Hughes felt the words building in his throat, before voices rose from behind him. 'Stay back! Stay back!' a police officer shouted at a growing crowd, waving them away from the edge of the Thames. 'Clear the way. Nothing to see here.'

Hughes and Stella turned around, both watching as a group of policemen pulled a body out of the water. Stella looked away as Hughes stepped closer.

Is it them? Hughes wondered. *George? Earl?*

They've finally been found?

As Hughes grasped a clearer view, he saw it was not George or Earl or any other man present that night. Instead, it was the body of a little girl with blonde hair that was dragged onto the rocky bay below. Her skin was grey, her clothes tattered and soaked, and her face swollen.

The officer who recovered her stood back, covering his mouth out of revulsion. The crowd gasped and murmured in shock while Hughes watched on in silence.

'I have to go back to work …' he told Stella, watching the officers pull an old rag over the body.

Later that night, Hughes returned to the Dumphree estate atop his horse. With a clumsy twist, he jumped off the saddle and smiled to himself, patting the horse's neck. 'Don't mind me. Still getting used to that.'

After locking up the stables and having dinner with the Dumphrees, Hughes stood before the gun cabinet alone. His eyes were transfixed on the spot where his pistol once sat, staring at the empty hooks.

Eventually, he took his rest before the fireplace. The flickering flames blurred into the rotting corpse of the little girl. The charred skin of Patrick. The blood-soaked remains of George. The lifeless eyes of Cloyd. The woman with a bullet through her forehead, lying on a sterile white floor.

Too many images for his mind to forget.

Outside the lounge room, Flavel rolled his shoulders and took a heavy breath. He turned, seeing Mary watching him with reluctance. Flavel frowned before entering the room and sitting on the couch across from Hughes. 'You're up late. Again.'

Hughes forced a small smile. 'Can't sleep. But I will. Don't wait up for me.'

'No, it's not really to do with that, Hughes. I just … I came to tell you something important.'

A wave of concern came over Hughes.

Flavel paused for another solemn breath. 'I know you've been seeing a lot of Claude's daughter lately. You two are getting along well, aren't you?'

'What is this about?'

Flavel leant back in his chair, taking no pleasure in his words. 'Claude spoke to me today. He knows about you two spending time together, and I'm not sure if you know, but Stella has a partner. A future husband.'

'What? That can't be right.'

'It is. She's arranged to get married in the coming months.'

'With who? How – how do I not know this?'

'I didn't either, and I don't know who it is, but it doesn't matter. You need to stay clear of her.'

Hughes almost snickered at the idea before recognising Flavel's grave manner. His heart sank.

'He's seen how close you two have become,' Flavel continued, 'and ... well, he can't have that. Especially with our deal with them, the last thing we need is you getting in the way of a Lockhurt marriage. If that happened, I doubt Claude would ever even speak to us again. We'd lose all of the work we've been dedicated to for the last few months. *Hundreds* of man-hours and *far* too much expense to lose.'

'So, what are you saying I do?'

'Stop seeing her.'

Silence filled the room as Hughes stared at Flavel. No words came to him. His muscles ached, and his eyes began to glisten. In time, his gaze fell upon the floor as he restrained his tears.

Flavel stood up and walked over to his side, stiffly patting his shoulder. 'I'm sorry, but it's for the best. I know you know it too.' Flavel gave him one last glance of sympathy before leaving the room.

A quick gasp escaped Hughes' mouth before he silenced himself and held in his pain. His fist pushed against his forehead as his gaze returned to the floor where the bodies of the dead lay before him.

* * *

The following day, Hughes leant against a tree in the heart of London Park. The branches danced above his head as he stared into the distance.

How could she not tell me? he asked himself. *She has so much to explain. So much I need to know ... I can't. Just say what needs to be said and be done with it. No questions. Don't drag it out. It'll only make it harder.*

As Hughes remained entrenched in thought, Stella, wearing a white flowery dress, approached him. He turned towards her as she gifted him a smile.

'Good morning, sir. Where shall we go today?' she asked with anticipation. 'You know, I could finally take you to that pub we saw when we first met.' Her words broke off upon noticing his confusion. 'What is it?'

Hughes struggled for a moment, his lips hesitating, before he finally asked, 'You're getting married?'

Stella's shoulders and cheerful demeanour fell as her eyes filled with heartache. 'Hughes – '

'Why didn't you tell me?'

She stepped closer and reached out to touch him before restraining herself, speaking with a fragile voice. 'I *wanted* to … I was going to. I was just waiting for the right time is all.'

'Who is he? How long have you known?'

'A few months,' she explained with a painful sigh. 'Maybe more, I don't know. And he's just some son of another business associate of my father's. I barely even know him.'

'Your father is choosing for you?'

'Of course. Maybe that's not a thing where you come from either, but it is here … but I don't *want* to marry him.' Stella took another step towards Hughes, looking up at him as she rested her hand on his chest. 'I've been loving our time together, Hughes. I want to see you more every day that passes. I was waiting for the right time because I was hoping you might feel the same. And if I had to marry anyone, I'd want it to be you.'

Hughes gazed upon her with tearful eyes. A small smile broke out across his face as he could not help but rest his hands on her waist. 'I want you too,' he admitted with relief, before his lips trembled, 'but I don't think it can work.'

Stella rested her hand on his cheek and desperately smiled as her own eyes began to well. 'Of course, it can. We can sort it out together. We'll find a way. Why does it have to end like this?'

Their heads met and gently pressed against each other. Hughes admired her soft face, feeling his heart swell before a sickness returned to his throat. The dark stain of the factory floor plagued his mind. The helpless final moments of his friend. The old rag consuming the mangled blonde hair. The darkened silhouette at the base of the alleyway. The empty hooks in the cabinet.

He swallowed and shook his head, almost unable to see through his tears. 'It can't … I can't … I'm – I'm sorry. Goodbye.' Hughes pulled away, holding Stella's hands for a final moment before letting go and leaving her presence.

She stood frozen in disbelief, watching him leave without so much as a glance in her direction. Bringing her hand to her mouth, Stella struggled to withhold her tears. With a quick glance at her surroundings, ensuring no one else was watching, she turned and left with haste in the opposite direction.

An hour later, Hughes sat behind his office desk. His pen hovered above the page as he stared at the paperwork, the numbers and words becoming an incomprehensible blur. Finally, he dropped the pen and leant back in his chair. His eyes trailed towards the empty seat across from him. With every second that passed, a greater pain weighed upon him.

A knock at the door drew his attention and lifted his heart. 'Come in.' He watched with hopeful curiosity as the door opened, only for Merritt to step inside.

'Just the call sheet for the day, sir,' Merritt said, placing the sheet of names before him.

Hughes inspected the names before landing on the empty space for his signature. The sight of it made him pause.

Merritt noticed his silence. 'Are you okay, sir?'

Hughes snapped out of his trance and glanced up at his assistant manager. Without another moment to linger, he stood up and grabbed his coat. 'Why don't you take over for the day, Merritt?' Hughes pulled out his pistol from the desk drawer and slipped it into his pocket.

'Wh-where are you going? I don't understand.'

Hughes slid on his coat as he walked around the desk and patted Merritt's shoulder. 'Yeah. Neither do I.' Hughes exited the office, leaving Merritt alone and confused, surrounded by paperwork.

Slouched over as if he were about to fall asleep, Hughes gradually rode his horse towards the Dumphree estate. He paused before the grand house, looking beyond the stables and towards the distant hills, where a collection of trees surrounded a small, natural pond.

It looks peaceful there, he thought. *That's a good place.*

Hughes took his time riding the horse past the estate and its garden, up the small hill and towards the trees. Before reaching the pond, he awkwardly jumped off the horse and dragged his feet towards the water's edge. There, he fell to his knees.

The trees shaded the quiet retreat from any sunlight. Nothing but the soft trickling water, singing crickets, and chirps of birds could be heard. Hughes closed his eyes and filled his lungs with the fresh air, revelling in the sounds of nature.

Opening his eyes, he removed the pistol from his coat and held it in his hands. With a painful reluctance, he pulled back the hammer.

Come on. Just do it.

His hands shook as he attempted to raise the weapon.

In an instant, using all of his strength, he lifted the gun and pressed the barrel against his temple.

'Hughes!' a horrified voice shouted from behind him. Hughes quickly lowered the gun and turned around, seeing Mary rushing towards him. 'What are you doing?'

'Mary, please,' he pleaded with tears running down his cheeks, 'just leave me.'

'I will *not*!' she said with a frantic determination, stopping a few feet away from him. 'Put that thing away!'

Hughes' eyes returned to the pistol as he shook his head. 'I can't.'

'Why?'

The sounds of nature returned as Hughes remained fixated on the weapon in his hands. 'All I've done since I've been here is get people hurt, or killed, or let them down, and what have I got to show for it? That I'm in charge of a *factory*? That place … that *damn* place. It is no place. The air, every day it smells more and more familiar.

It's destroying everything. And here I am … helping it along.' His fingers rubbed against the grip of the pistol. 'It's all my fault. All because I was too occupied with wanting some sort of stupid *"fair shot"*… I don't deserve it.'

Mary shook her head, stepping closer and kneeling beside him. 'I know what it's like out there, Hughes. I hate it too. I think, when you first came, that's why I was so afraid. I thought if you came from there, what were you really like? And that frightened me.'

Hughes scrunched up his face, fighting back his tears.

'But I've seen who you are,' she continued with hope. 'I know who you are.'

'You don't.'

'I know there's things I don't know about you, yes. But I don't need to know everything to know that you are a *good* man. I've seen how much you can help, how much you *feel*. Not everyone's like that … and I think Stella's good for you.'

Surprised, Hughes turned away from the pistol and looked at Mary.

She paused for a moment, hesitating to speak her next words. 'You know it wasn't my choice to marry Flavel? … It was arranged. Mostly business related. My parents chose for me.'

Hughes' expression turned pitiful.

'Don't be sorry or anything,' she added. 'I've learnt to love him over the years, in his own way … but, Hughes, you're *different.* You've always struck me as someone that knows *more.* That you're somehow smarter than whatever we're all doing here. When Flavel wanted to throw those men onto the street, you wanted to give them a *chance.* You wanted to *help them*, even after everything. You don't see anyone else doing *anything* like that here.' Mary smiled through her quiet tears. 'Don't break yourself for these ridiculous rules and arrangements now. If you want to be with Stella, *be* with her. *Go* to her. Lord knows, if I could, I would've done more of what I wanted when I was younger. There's still so much you can do.'

Mary outstretched her hand and rested it upon his shoulder. Hughes sniffled, gazing back at the pistol as his tears began to fade.

For a long time, the two remained in silence.

Eventually, Mary reached out her other hand. Hughes looked back and forth between his choices.

Finally, he rested the weapon in her hands.

'Thank you, Hughes.'

A small, trembling smile broke out across Hughes' face. 'Thank *you*.'

Mary pulled him into her arms and, at last, they embraced.

* * *

Stella's bedroom was quiet and still, while the cool morning air gave the room a bluish-grey tone. Stella lay awake in her bed, staring at the cracks of light between her window's curtains.

Soon, she forced herself out of bed and dressed for the day. Wearing a pinstriped grey dress, she finished tying up her hair as she stood before the bedroom mirror. She glanced at the drawer below, carefully picking out an old necklace with Irene's name engraved into it and an old picture of her enclosed within it. After holding the necklace in her hands and close to her chest she slid it around her neck.

The house was cold and sterile, decorated with many busts, sculptures, and intricate wallpaper. Stella walked downstairs and heard the voice of her father down the hall.

He must be talking to an associate or one of the housemaids, she thought to herself.

She quietened her step as she sneaked towards the front door and exited the house. As she turned around to face the waking London street, Hughes stood at the base of the stairs before her. He wore a fine suit and a sad smile.

'Hi,' he nervously greeted.

Stella turned to ensure the front door was closed before looking back at him with hesitation, 'What are you doing here?'

Hughes scaled a handful of steps before stopping. 'I wanted to say I made a mistake … a lot of them, actually. But I want to start making things right, in every way I can. And not just little things. I want to change … *everything*. But the first thing I want to fix is with you.' Hughes climbed the last step, standing on Stella's level as he looked upon her. 'When I do all of this, I want *you* by my side.'

'But the marriage … it's all – '

'I don't care about any of that. Just like you said, we can work it out together. We can make our own way … and I know I haven't told you everything about me, but I want you to know the truth. I want you to know me. *Everything* about me. I just want *you.*'

The two of them stared into one another, their eyes glowing and chests heaving.

'So, what do you say?' he asked, honest and hopeful. 'Are you with me?'

Stella smiled and took his hands into hers. 'I am.'

Hughes' face lit with joy as they pulled each other close and joined in a long, deep kiss.

Chapter 6

Three weeks had passed when a bundle of purple flowers was rested upon Irene's grave. Stella returned to her feet, standing beside Hughes. Their dark coats blew in the wind as their hands met and wrapped around one another.

A short while later, the pair strolled back through the quiet cemetery.

'Are you nervous?' Hughes asked.

'Well, maybe only a little.'

'Mary will be fine, trust me. It's Flavel I'm not too sure of.'

'He still hasn't spoken to you?'

'Not a word.'

'How did he even agree to have me over?'

'That's all Mary. I think she just pestered him endlessly until he gave in.'

Stella smirked. 'Reminds me of my mother. I just hope it's not too awkward.'

'Don't worry. It'll be fine … maybe just a little awkward.'

Stella shook her head and playfully elbowed Hughes' arm.

Eventually, their walk saw them through the bustling streets of London. Hughes stopped, inspecting their surroundings.

'What is it?' Stella asked.

'This is around where I used to live, before I found Mary and Flavel.' Hughes pointed down the street to their right, 'A couple streets that way, I think.' His tone turned solemn. 'I still need to visit.'

'Why would you?'

'I made a promise. Docie, she's the one who took me in. I told her I'd come back.'

'Well, you still can.'

'I know. There's things I need to tell her.'

Stella placed her hand on his chest and gazed into his eyes. 'Then tell her.'

Hughes glanced down the street, nodding with a silent breath.

'You should go before our dinner,' Stella continued. 'Don't let it weigh on you. Do you want me to come with you?'

Hughes rested his hand over hers. 'No, that's okay. I should do it alone. Then I'll tell you everything.'

Stella smiled and rested her other hand on his cheek. 'I look forward to it, sir.' She stood on her toes and softly kissed his lips.

As the day neared its end, the final glimpses of the sun were shrouded behind an endless wave of dark clouds. The streets began to quieten, and their lamps were lit. Atop his horse, Hughes trotted towards the old corner lodge. Its cracks, paint, and structure looked as though it had aged years since he had last left it. The entire complex was silent and infested with shadow. Hughes swallowed at the sight of it before sliding off his horse and tying it to a post at the edge of the street.

Stepping inside the building, Hughes heard only creaks, coughs, and broken whispers. With caution, he gripped the handrail and scaled the rickety flights of stairs. On each floor he climbed, he found ever more rooms littered with people sprawled across the floors. Almost all of them were silent, either asleep or in a daze that seemed like death. On occasion, one would turn their head, staring at him with empty eyes.

Eventually, Hughes came upon the second apartment on the sixth floor. His old home. He crept inside and discovered countless more tenants lying across the floor and sitting against the walls, rugged up in rags and handmade coats. Then, just as he thought he might, he spotted Docie sitting in a rocking chair at the end of the room, facing the window.

Hughes carefully approached her and knelt down at her side, hushing his voice. 'Docie, hi. It's me, Hughes.'

Docie slowly turned to face him. Her skin was paler than he remembered as she stared at him distantly for a time. Eventually, her expression lifted. 'Hughes.'

He smiled as she rested her hand over his. 'How are you, Doce? I'm so sorry it's been so long.'

'I didn't think you'd come back,' she replied with a quiet, raspy voice. 'You shouldn't have.'

'No, I *wanted* to. I made a promise to you. And to George.'

Docie shook her head. 'George left a while ago. I don't know where.'

Hughes bowed his head for a moment, fighting to maintain his composure. 'Well, that's also why I came. I wanted to make sure you knew the truth … George is dead, Docie … and it's because of me. I let him – '

'There's someone after you.'

Hughes froze and his voice stuttered, 'Wh – what?'

'You need to leave, Hughes.'

'No, I'm trying to explain to you what happened. There *were* people after me. At the factory. And I let George get in between us, and they got a hold of him and they – '

'He wasn't at no factory. This man was *here*.'

Hughes felt his chest tighten.

'He sounded a bit like ya, too,' she added. 'Had your funny accent.'

'*What did he say?*'

'He was asking all about you. Where you are, where you're going, what you're doing. I didn't let him onto anything, but I could tell he's no good. He's still out there looking for ya. He's been coming here a lot. Waitin'.'

Hughes glanced at the others sleeping in the room. '*Is he here now?*'

'I don't know. I don't think so. But you need to leave, Hughes, it's not safe.'

Hughes anxiously eyed the front door.

Surely, I would have seen him if he was here, he thought.

I would have noticed.

Overcoming his nerves, Hughes shook his head and turned back towards his friend. 'Thank you, Docie. It's okay, though. I'm going to be okay. I don't think it's anything to worry about.' Hughes surveyed the rest of the cold, decaying room. 'You don't deserve this. I'm working on getting my own place, and once I do, I'm coming back for you. You won't have to live here anymore. I'm going to take in as many people as I can. Things are going to change. I'm going to make them.'

Docie looked at him with pain before squeezing his hand. '*Go.*'

Hughes reluctantly nodded and climbed to his feet.

Abigail, he remembered.

Should she know? Would it only cause her pain?

Or would it give her closure? An answer.

I owe it to her, to tell the truth.

'Docie. Your daughter …'

'You don't need to. I already know.'

Hughes placed his hand on her shoulder. 'I'm sorry.'

Night had fallen, and the air was cool as Hughes exited the building and scanned his surroundings. The entire street was barren. All alone, he felt a chill tickle his skin as he returned to his horse. Climbing onto its saddle, he glanced at the street one last time.

Distant voices echoed through the fog.

Shadows shifted in the corners of his eyes.

Something's not right, he thought.

Come on. Let's just get out of here.

Hughes whipped the reins and dashed off into the fog, riding as fast as he could.

* * *

Church bells rang out through the night as Hughes helped Stella climb up onto his horse. She wrapped her arms around him as they rode out of the city together. After a long ride through the countryside, the pair approached the Dumphree estate.

Stella smiled at the sight of it. 'Wow, this place *is* beautiful.'

'Wait till you see it during the day. You'll get to see the sun rising just over there.' He pointed off to the distant hills.

After assisting her back onto the ground and tying up the horse in the stables, the two of them stopped before the front door.

'Ready?' Hughes asked.

'As much as I can be.'

Hughes smiled and extended his hand for her to take.

Sometime later, Hughes, Stella, Mary, and Flavel all sat around the dining table, quietly eating. Hughes caught a glimpse of Flavel, who only met him with an unfavourable glance.

Hughes returned to his food before Mary broke the silence. 'Well, I think it's lovely you've come, Stella. I must show you the garden tomorrow.'

'Oh, yes, please. I've already heard much about it.'

'I can imagine. Hughes has done his own work on the garden with me from time to time. He's quite good. Not as good as me, but quite good.'

The three of them chuckled while Flavel sipped his wine, unimpressed. Mary noticed his sour expression before she turned her attention back towards the others. 'Well, I suppose there's no point in waiting any longer. I have some exciting news to tell you.'

Hughes and Stella listened closely.

'I'm pregnant!' she gleefully revealed.

A great smile came over the two of them.

'Congratulations, Mary!' Stella exclaimed.

Hughes stood up and walked over to her. 'Come here.'

Mary chuckled and climbed to her feet, hugging him. 'Thank you, darling. Thank you.'

'I knew it'd happen one day,' Hughes remarked. 'They're going to love it here. I know it.'

Even Flavel could not help but smile for just a moment.

After the dinner, Mary and Stella chatted by the fireplace. Meanwhile, Hughes stood on the back porch, admiring the dark hills and fields before him. Flavel stepped outside beside him.

'Congratulations,' Hughes said.

Flavel nodded in return, keeping his eyes firmly on the view before them. 'Thank you …'

The two of them stood in silence for a time.

'I don't know how many there'll be,' Flavel began again, 'but regardless, with children on the way, we're going to need more room here.'

'I know. I've already begun looking for a place.'

Flavel looked down at his feet, allowing another silence to consume both of them. 'I know some fine places that should suit … I'll help you settle them.'

Hughes turned to him with surprise.

Flavel glanced back, unable to meet his gaze for too long a time.

'Thank you, Flavel.'

'Yes, well … good night.' With a light pat on Hughes' shoulder, Flavel strolled inside.

Hughes' gaze returned to the horizon as he smiled to himself.

* * *

Later that same night, Hughes' room glowed a dark blue tone as he climbed into bed with Stella, both of them giggling and shushing each other.

'Do you really think this is appropriate? They might hear us,' Stella asked with an anxious yet excited whisper.

'Oh, I think we're well past being appropriate to most. Does it bother you?'

Stella shook her head, smiled, and swung her arms around him as he snuggled up to her, their noses almost touching.

'The night wasn't too awkward, was it?' he asked.

'No, it was lovely.'

Hughes nodded and leant closer, kissing her lips. 'Tomorrow. I'll tell you.'

'Are you sure?'

'I am. Everything about me.'

'Well, I look forward to getting to know you then, sir.'

Hughes smiled and rolled on top of her, kissing her lips and then down to her neck. She moaned and wrapped her legs around him.

Hours later, Hughes awoke.

The clock ticked.

The wind softly howled.

The moonlight shone through the window.

Hughes looked beside him, finding Stella fast asleep. He smiled before glancing at his bedside table. His glass of water was empty.

With a sigh, Hughes slid out of bed and took his glass. He stopped beside his wooden drawer, taking a moment to open it. Inside was his journal. He briefly flipped through the pages, looking over all of the writing he had practised. Everything he was to tell her.

After returning the journal and shutting the drawer, Hughes walked downstairs and into the kitchen. His mind began to awaken with thoughts.

No matter how many times I write it, I still don't know how to say it to her. How will I explain it all? What should I start with? Will she even believe me? Maybe she'll just think I'm mad ...

But I need someone on my side here. Someone to understand. It'll make it so much easier. Although, it's not like anything has been easy so far. This won't be any different.

Hughes refilled his glass at the sink and took a sip before a floorboard creaked outside the back door. Hughes' ears pricked up as he turned around, peering outside the window.

Gradually, a dark, hooded silhouette revealed itself, staring at him from the porch.

Hughes' heart froze and his breath shook.

Is that ...?

Oh God, it is. It really is him ...

After all of this time ...

Okay, no. It's okay. You can do this.

It'll be all right. You know what to say. Just tell him the truth.

Gathering his nerves, Hughes walked towards the back door and quietly opened it. The cool breeze brushed against his skin as he stepped outside.

The figure stood beside him. He wore a heavy, dark green coat, a multi-layered backpack, and fashioned a large, unkempt beard.

Hughes eyed him up and down, helplessly shaking.

Oh no, I should have grabbed my gun. I should have just ... no!

No more of that. Just _talk_ to him, dammit ...

'How long have you been looking?' Hughes asked.

The man said nothing in return.

'This is about what happened? When we left?'

'What do you think?' his deep voice replied at last.

'That wasn't supposed to happen.'

After the click of a hammer, the man lifted a silenced handgun and pointed it at Hughes' head. Yet this handgun bore no resemblance to any of this time period. It was slick, light, and jet-black.

Hughes lifted his hands a little, fighting to remain calm. 'It wasn't! The only reason I was there was because I was promised no one was going to get hurt. *Connor lied to me.*'

'Then why didn't you stop him?'

Hughes paused, unable to find his words.

'You just let him do it and then went off with him,' the man continued, shaking his head and tightening his grip. 'You're just like him. *You don't care.*'

'I *do.* Not a day has gone by that I haven't thought about that ... I wish it never happened, but – but we have a gift now, don't we? An opportunity to *change everything.* Nothing has to end up like it was. We can fix it all before it ever even happens.'

'If that was how it worked, I wouldn't be here right now.'

Isn't it still worth trying? Hughes thought.

Just as he was about to speak his mind, the gun fired, and a bullet ripped through his head. He collapsed to the floor, lifeless, as his glass smashed onto the ground with him, shattering into pieces.

The man lowered his gun, staring down at Hughes' body. As voices awoke from inside the house, the man stepped back into the shadows, disappearing from sight.

* * *

Thin trees, almost eighty metres high, marked a dense hillside forest. The sun barely broke through the leaves and branches above as the birds chirped and the wind whistled.

This man, this hunter, trekked down through the forest. The dirt, sticks, and bark cracked beneath his boots.

Eventually, he came upon a clearing. Off in the distance stood a large city surrounded by thick walls and wide-open fields. The inside was populated with houses and temples distinguished by their curved hip roofs. Floods of people entered the city on foot and with carts. The wind carried with it the faint whisper of a hundred thousand bustling citizens.

This was...

Beijing, China, 1410 CE

VOLUME TWO

THE HUNTER

Chapter 7

The hunter approached the outer walls of Beijing, trekking through green, swampy fields. His boots squelched on the muddy grass as he studied the countless citizens walking in and out of the city's entrance.

Almost a dozen guards stood at both sides of the front gate. They held spears by their sides and wore silver brigandine armour over their red robes. The hunter stopped in the field, spotting even more guards pacing back and forth atop the outer walls.

They'll stop me if I just walk past them, he thought. *But they'll probably close the gate by nightfall. And I can't risk porting in if I can't see inside. I have to get in before the day is up.*

The hunter gazed at the trail leading into the city. Using the tall grass as cover, he walked back alongside the path and sat down beside it. Sparse silhouettes marked the horizon, carrying supplies and equipment to bring into the city. He squinted, carefully watching the long gravel road. Waiting.

Soon, a faraway cart appeared, pulled along by a horse and its rider. The cart was significant and concealed by a fabric roof.

Perfect.

The man stood up and sneaked along the path towards the cart, shrouded by the tall grass and shrubbery. As he grew close enough, he knelt down and unholstered his silenced handgun. He lined up his aim at the gravel track, waiting for the horse and cart to reach his position.

Finally, just as the horse began to pass by, he fired a single suppressed shot into the ground next to the horse's hooves. Dirt flew up into the air as the horse panicked, neighing and standing back on its hind legs.

'Whoa, whoa!' the rider yelled out, desperately attempting to control the horse.

Amidst the distraction, the hunter rushed around to the rear of the cart and climbed inside, hiding himself amongst numerous bags of grain and rice.

The driver felt no change in weight as he fought to pull back the reins of the horse. After finding its footing again, the horse worryingly trotted side to side for a moment before finally settling down.

The driver, confused, patted its neck, speaking in his native Mandarin tongue, 'You all right, girl? Don't go crazy on me, now. We're almost there.' He raised his eyebrows at the animal, completely puzzled, before he urged his horse forward with the click of his tongue. 'All right, come on. Let's go.'

The horse trotted towards the large gates of Beijing. The frenzied sounds from the city only grew greater.

Upon reaching the city gates, a guard lifted his hand. 'Stop there,' he ordered, before gesturing to two other guards.

The guards walked to the rear of the cart, peering inside. The hunter hid behind the supplies, keeping completely still as he listened to their movement. After a few more glances, the guards nodded to each other and walked back to their posts.

The front guard waved the cart inside.

'Thank you,' the driver said, clicking and driving the horse forward.

The man peeked out from behind the cart's supplies as they rode through the gates. Once they were far enough away, he crept to the edge of the cart, watching them trot past others entering and leaving the city. Looking to his left, he gazed upon a series of trees lining the long stone path beneath them. Beyond the trees was the tall, spiralling Temple of Heaven, still in the midst of construction, yet standing taller than anything else in the city.

At last, they entered the central district of the outer city. They were quickly surrounded by swarms of citizens going about their day. Many of them wore simple grey and white robes, while others stood out with brighter colours and intricate designs sewn into them.

Once the crowd was dense enough, the hunter jumped out from the cart and slid in amongst the people. The driver felt the slight shift in weight and glanced back, seeing nothing but the endless droves of citizens. Dismissing the feeling, he continued riding off through the city.

With his hood concealing his face, the hunter watched the vibrant street around him. Families walked through the markets. Workers carried supplies of food and equipment in every direction. Merchants traded and conversed with patrons. Children ran by as they played and laughed. The steam and smoke of cooking food wafted through the air. The man could not help but smile, just a little, at the sight of everything around him. A feeling of excitement bubbled inside his stomach.

Soon, a line of soldiers appeared, marching straight through the crowd. The man's smile faded as they caught his eye. The citizens were quick to shuffle out of their way. They wore tall, round black caps, distinct red robes with the images of dragons embroidered into them, and were each equipped with a long sword attached to their belt.

These were no mere guards.

The hunter concealed himself amongst the crowd as they marched past. Their leader, the captain, maintained a sharp eye on his surroundings. No citizen dared meet his gaze.

Once in the clear, the hunter turned and disappeared in between the buildings and houses, moving towards the edge of the city.

All right, it's time to find Issa, he reminded himself. *This city is large, but it's neatly structured. The outer city is rectangular, while the inner city is just a large square. Trailing the perimeter and pushing inwards with each rotation will be the most efficient way I can cover the most ground in the city.*

* * *

Several weeks had passed by when the man sat rested in a tight alleyway between two houses. The city was quiet as the moon shone upon the pointy, red-tiled rooftops. His beard had grown, and his eyes were less lively than when he had first arrived.

Can't you just sleep? he asked himself.

Just for a moment ...

He closed his eyes.

Distant voices inside his head began to rise, forever crawling closer towards him.

Before long, his eyes opened again, and the noises ceased. Instinctively, he reached under his shirt and pulled out a necklace. It was a small silver sculpture of a long, pointy seashell. He ran his fingers along its bumps, cradling it with care. Eventually, he pulled the necklace close to his chest and closed his eyes, holding it tightly. For a moment, there was peace … before the pain returned.

After opening his eyes again, he slid the necklace back under his shirt and unzipped his backpack. Inside were countless plastic containers of drugs. He shook three pills into his hand and threw his head back, swallowing them all at once. With a sigh, he zipped the backpack up again and rested his head against the wall behind him.

It won't be long, then you can move on to the inner city.

I just hope she's there …

She will be. You found Hughes, you can find her, and you can find the rest. There'll only be four more once you find her. Then–

His thoughts were stifled as a woman's scream pierced the city's silence. The hunter shot to his feet and slid on his bag, cautiously stepping out of the alleyway. Hearing more cries, he rushed towards the source and entered another alleyway. Sliding on his hood, he peeked into the next street.

There he spotted a handful of dragon-robed soldiers surrounding the front of a house. A helpless mother wailed in fear as she was forced onto her knees. A father and his teenage son were dragged out of the house and thrown onto the ground before the captain, who stared at them with stern, unwavering eyes.

'Please! We haven't done anything!' the father cried.

'Enough!' the captain shouted.

One soldier placed his sword against the mother's neck, forcing her to restrain her tears as she shook in fear.

'You are still supporters of Zhu Yunwen,' the captain continued.

The father, on his hands and knees, shook his head. 'No, we – we are proud followers of the Yongle Emperor. We are loyal.'

The captain looked at the son beside him, whose eyes burned with hatred. 'You, boy, is what your father says true?'

The boy continued to glare at the captain.

His father turned, desperate for him to relent.

Finally, the boy spat at the captain's feet.

'No!' The mother howled.

The captain smirked, almost impressed, before swiftly pulling out his sword and cutting down across the boy's throat. The father looked on in horror as the mother screamed in agony.

The hunter almost pulled away before stopping himself. A contemplation to help yearned within him, yet he remained still. His heart wrenched at the sound of the mother's cries as he continued to watch the rest of their nightmare unfold.

The captain pointed his blade towards the father as it dripped with blood. 'In the name of the Yongle Emperor, you are sentenced to death for treason.' In one stroke, the captain cut down the father. His body collapsed next to his son's while the mother cried in pain. 'Burn the bodies and take her to the palace,' he ordered.

The mother was pulled to her feet by two soldiers and pushed towards the inner city as the pair of bodies were dragged away into another street. The captain shook the blood off his blade and sheathed it through his belt.

The hunter began stepping back into the alleyway just as the captain glanced in his direction, catching sight of him. The hunter immediately retreated into the shadows, gritting his teeth.

'There's someone watching!' the captain shouted, pointing towards the alleyway. 'Arrest him!'

'Shit!' the hunter muttered under his breath, running back the way he came.

Seconds later, a pack of dragon soldiers ran into the alleyway after him. The hunter almost tumbled over as he turned out of the alley and sprinted through the connecting street. Barking orders echoed in the distance, alongside the footsteps of more and more soldiers in pursuit.

The hunter's eyes desperately scanned the street ahead, trying to find his next path. Turning off into another street, three more dragon soldiers appeared ahead of him, blocking his way. One soldier, with a bow and arrow, lifted his weapon and fired. The hunter ducked and slid along the ground as the arrow flew over his head.

Quickly turning around, he crawled and stumbled back into the previous street. He glanced behind him, finding almost a dozen soldiers chasing after him. He sharply diverted through another alleyway and into the next street. Slinging his backpack in front of him, he rustled through it with haste. As he neared the next alleyway, he pulled out a small metallic ball.

Clicking a button on the circular device, he threw it off to his right and rushed into the alleyway. The soldiers entered the street not far behind him just as the ball began to shoot off loud, bright sparks. The soldiers jumped back in fright, amazed by the sight of it.

Continuing down the next alleyway, the hunter almost reached the other side before a soldier appeared in front of him. The dragon swung his bladed spear right towards his neck. The hunter ducked and dodged the blade as it crashed into the wall behind him. Immediately, he pulled out his handgun and smacked the base of the grip into the soldier's nose.

With a yelp of pain, the soldier's nose cracked and bled as he fell to the ground. The hunter glanced back down the alleyway, seeing no more soldiers and only hearing the sparks continue to pop and crackle in the distance. Taking this chance, he sprinted into another street and spun around, looking for somewhere, *anywhere* to hide. He panted and wavered before a strong feminine voice called out to him.

'*Hey, you!*'

The hunter stopped and turned to see a woman standing before a two-story house, wearing a silky white dress, hair done up in a bun, and her face doused in white makeup.

'Those dragons are after you?' she hurriedly asked.

With his face still concealed by the shadow of his hood, the man nodded, speaking in her tongue. 'Yes.'

She eyed him up and down for a moment, contemplating. The distant sound of sparks began to fade. They both glanced down the street, hearing the soldiers grow closer.

'Come on, then. In here,' she said at last.

Hesitating, the man gazed back and forth between her and the sound of the nearing soldiers.

'It's either in here or you're running all night,' she explained.

Tilting his head in frustration, he rushed into her home. Just as she shut the door behind them, half a dozen soldiers ran into the street, confused and splitting off in every direction.

The hunter stepped into the foyer, engulfed by the glowing warmth of red and orange lanterns. He inspected the paper walls around him, decorated with images of flowers and trees. Various pillows and blankets were laid about his feet while moans of pleasure and intimacy reverberated through the walls.

The man paused, hearing the noises. 'This isn't just your home, is it?'

'Surely you knew.'

He glanced back at her from under his hood before continuing to survey the room in silence.

'Remove your hood,' she requested, attempting to catch a glimpse of his face.

'I'm okay, thanks.'

'If you're going to stay here, I need to know my girls are safe. I can't do that if I don't even know your face.'

'Then I'll leave.' He walked back towards the door.

She quickly put her hand on his chest, stopping him. *'One way or another, they will catch you out there.'*

He stood still for a moment.

At last, he pulled back his hood, revealing his white skin, thick beard, and watchful eyes, which bore the weight of thirty-seven years. His gaze fell to the floor, refraining from meeting hers.

The woman was almost speechless at the sight of him. 'You're not from *anywhere* around here, are you?'

He said nothing in return.

'How long have you been here?' she continued.

'A few weeks. More or less.'

'And the soldiers, why are they after you?'

'I saw something I wasn't supposed to. They were killing a family.'

Her expression turned grim, yet unsurprised. 'Yes, well, I can say you picked the *wrong* time to come to Beijing.'

'Why?'

'If you came a few years ago, you wouldn't have had a problem. But it's the Yongle Emperor who has no tolerance for outsiders or those out of line.'

'But you still helped me,' he noted, looking into her eyes.

Her own gaze broke away. '…What brings you here, then?'

'I'm looking for someone.'

'What for?'

The man settled his breath and stepped closer to her. 'You're not in any danger from me; that you can trust me on. As soon as those soldiers have cleared, I'll leave.'

The woman swallowed before meeting his gaze, scrutinising his features. His intentions. 'Those soldiers will be searching the streets all night. Even in the day, they'll be out there.' She eyed the front door, considering, before turning back to him. 'You'd be best staying here. You look like you could use the sleep anyway.'

'Are you sure?'

'People stay here all the time. It's no difference to me. Frankly, the more rooms filled, the better.'

'I don't have money.'

'And I don't expect any. Come on.' She gestured with her head, leading him into another warm hallway with dozens of bedrooms on either side. Moans and giggles could be heard from some of them as she slid open a door and revealed to him an empty bedroom. 'You can rest here for the night.'

He peered inside before returning to her with appreciation. 'Thank you.'

'My name is Lu Zhi.' She introduced herself with a nod, waiting expectedly.

'I'm Ryder.'

Stepping closer to him, she hushed her voice and sharpened her tone. 'You try anything, *Ryder*, I'll make sure the dragons find you.'

He stared into her eyes as she met him in equal measure, unrelenting.

Finally, he nodded in accord.

Once sliding the door shut, he slung his bag off his back and sat on the edge of the large, cushioned bed. He pulled out his handgun and rested it on his lap as he watched the door carefully.

Outside the room, Lu Zhi sat on a chair at the end of the hallway. A knife rested in her hands as she watched his bedroom door with a rival caution.

* * *

The following morning, Ryder lay on his bed, his eyes still open and his pistol rested beside him. Wrapped between his fingers was his seashell necklace.

Eventually, he sat up on the edge of the bed. His head felt dizzy and his heart weak. With the rub of his chest, he took a few deep breaths.

You'll be fine. Just find her and get out of here.

Ryder reached into his bag, pulling out some pills and quickly swallowing them. Immediately, he felt his body begin to realign and his energy restore.

Sliding open the bedroom door, he stepped outside, finding Lu Zhi sitting and watching him at the end of the hallway. She climbed to her feet upon his approach.

'Sleep well?' she asked.

'Probably as well as you.' He turned to see a handful of courtesans walking in and out of their rooms, preparing themselves for the day. 'Well, thank you again,' he said with a farewell nod, walking towards the front door.

'You won't be back?' she asked, following him closely behind.

He rested his hand on the door and stopped. 'Don't count on it.'

'If you do, though, I expect some more answers.'

He gave her a final glance before sliding on his hood and stepping outside into the busy street. She slid the door shut and took a long breath. The voices of the other courtesans grew as more of them awoke. Lifting her shoulders and straightening her gown, Lu Zhi returned to the hallway.

Slipping through the sea of citizens, Ryder's eyes scanned every person, building, and market stall that he passed by. Just like every day before, he thought of

Issa's black hair and Chinese descent allowing her to smoothly blend into the environment. She could stroll right by him at any moment, entirely unseen.

Hell, maybe she already has, he thought to himself. *It's the scar across her lips and her one yellow-tinted eye that will give her away, though. That's how I'll find her, even amongst all of this.*

Ryder took extra care to inspect everyone's eyes as he moved past, all of them shades of brown and hazel.

In the midst of thousands of voices and people, Ryder felt something bump against his foot. He looked down at his boot, discovering a lone passionfruit lying before him. He squatted down and gazed ahead, spotting a little girl, only six years old, nervously staring at him from a distance. Amidst the flowing crowd around them, he lifted his hand and signalled her to come over.

Hesitantly, she walked towards him, holding her hands together and bowing her head. As she approached him, he picked up the fruit and offered it back to her. The girl looked at him, a little unsure, before he smiled and nodded from under his hood.

Slowly, she reached out her small hands and took the fruit from his grasp. Seeing more of his face under the hood, the little girl's eyes filled with wonder, and her jaw dropped. He brought his finger up to his mouth, gesturing for her to remain quiet. She nodded along in disbelief, unable to take her eyes off him.

'Bai! Bai!' a woman's worried voice called out from the crowd.

The little girl turned and saw her mother standing by one of the market stalls, looking for her. Without a second's hesitation, she ran back into the arms of her mother.

Ryder's smile faded as he watched the mother holding her daughter close. He gazed at the ground beneath him, suppressing his memories.

Keep going.

Gathering his strength, Ryder returned to his feet. Behind him, growing murmurs arose from the crowd. With a turn, he caught a glimpse of the dragon-robed soldiers marching through the street, searching. Immediately, Ryder twisted around and sifted through the crowd in the opposite direction.

In the final hours of daylight, Ryder came upon the eastern edge of the outer city. His tired eyes trailed over the countless citizens who passed by in the crowded street. Still, there was no sign of yellow eyes or distinctive scars. He sighed and slowed to a halt.

She must be in the inner city.

Casually, he turned his gaze towards an alleyway beside him and noticed a trail of blood leading through it and into the next street. His fists clenched and eyes focused.

This better be you.

With care and caution, he followed the trail through the alleyway and into the next street. The thousands of voices and footsteps suddenly seemed distant. Many of the houses and buildings that lined this street were yet to be completed.

At one end, he spotted a handful of construction workers packing up for the day. Meanwhile, the trail of blood led him in the opposite direction, towards an incomplete house across the street. With a subtle motion, he lifted his handgun out from its holster and crept towards the house.

Stepping inside, he found the trail leading to the rear of the building, where muffled voices bickered back and forth. Before he could follow it any further, footsteps approached from the back room.

Ryder's eyes darted to a staircase leading to the second story. Remaining light on his feet, he rushed up the stairs as a dragon soldier walked out of the room and outside the house, oblivious to his presence.

Ryder quietened his breath as he squatted low, sneaking past piles of construction supplies. Towards the end of the room was a missing section of the floor, one that looked down upon the room beneath it. Warily, he peeked through the opening, finding a handful of soldiers surrounding a beaten and bloody workman on his knees.

The captain circled him, resting his hand on his hilt. 'Don't deny it. You are still a supporter of Zhu Yunwen.'

The workman shook his head, speaking with what little energy he had left. 'No, you're mistaken. I promise. I have gladly served the emperor.'

'Then why did I hear whispers of your discontent? From other traitors, no less.' the captain said as he stopped behind him.

'They're liars! I have never said such things!'

'Well, if this is true, then I'm sure you'd be happy for us to question you further in the Imperial City.'

The workman nodded with a breath of hope. 'Of course.'

The captain bent down beside him and smiled. 'Good. We have ways I'm certain will pull the truth from you.'

'What? No – no! I promise! I *am* telling the truth!'

The captain gestured to the other soldiers, who grabbed the workman and dragged him out of the room. He kicked and screamed for his life, to no avail.

The captain stood alone for a moment. His smile faded as he shook his head and sighed. Eventually, he walked out after them, leaving the building in silence.

Ryder pulled away from the gap in the floor and sat down against the supplies behind him, deflated.

More of these soldiers again, he thought.

Where aren't they stalking?

He closed his eyes, taking a moment to rest.

This is going to take a while, isn't it? At least there were places I knew Hughes would go, but here? I've got nothing. I just have to keep looking through this whole damn city.

At least I can assume she's found a way off the streets. No one would last long out here if they tried. Maybe she's with a distant family of some kind, like Hughes. I mean, why else would she come here? It's not like it's any safer than her last home. Not that it really matters now, anyway.

Eventually, Ryder opened his eyes and climbed to his feet. He readjusted the straps on his backpack and walked towards the stairs before he heard a creak on the floorboards below.

He froze in place, listening out.

All was silent.

Ryder glanced down at his arm, noticing his hair sticking up as the temperature began to drop. It was as though a cool breeze was blowing through the house, yet there was no wind.

Then there was another creak below. Then another. And another. More and more footsteps split off throughout the house. Ryder cautiously stepped backwards and crouched behind the supplies again. Confused, he peered back through the opening in the floor.

There was no one there, yet he could still hear them.

His eyes squinted.

Where are they?

Heavy footsteps steadily creaked up the stairs towards him. He pressed his back up against the supplies and peeked out at the staircase.

The footsteps abruptly ceased.

Ryder's heart pounded as he stared at the top of the stairs. Ever so slowly, he reached his hand towards his holster. His fingers wrapped around the handgun's grip, carefully unholstering it.

The silence was almost deafening, before it was shattered by the sound of heavy footsteps barging up the stairs towards him. For the briefest of moments, it was as though the wall beside the stairs became distorted, as if an invisible shadow was passing over it.

Ryder's heart skipped a beat. Out of pure instinct, he lifted his handgun and fired multiple silenced rounds at the blank space at the top of the stairs before turning and clambering to his feet. He sprinted towards the back window as silenced bullets whizzed past him and ripped into the walls. He felt something strike his back and take his breath away before he vaulted over the windowsill and out of the house. Roughly landing on his feet below, he stumbled against the wall beside him.

Letting out a groan of pain, he forced himself to sprint along the narrow trail behind the incomplete houses. More silenced shots whipped past him and kicked up the dirt around his feet. He almost tumbled over as he turned and ran back into the empty street, rushing towards the alleyway he first came through.

Another bullet hit the ground beside him, flinging up dirt. Just as he reached the alleyway, a second bullet ripped right through the top of his backpack, narrowly missing his neck. He ducked his head and sprinted behind cover.

Staggering out the other side of the alleyway, Ryder pushed through the busy crowds, gaining as much distance as possible. Surrounding citizens stopped and stared at him, confused and frightened as he ran by.

Feeling something in his stomach, he looked down to find a bullet had flown right through him. Blood poured out of his stomach as he quickly held his hand over the wound. His face began to lose colour as he continued pushing through the crowds, leaving a trail of blood behind him.

Chapter 8

The sky shattered into shades of orange and pink as the sun set on Beijing. Ryder clenched his teeth as he limped through the dissipating city crowds. He glanced behind him, searching for any sign of the invisible spectres. There were too many people, too much movement.

He soon noticed the trail of blood following him closely behind. Glancing through the swarms of people for somewhere to rest, he spotted a clear space beside a house. He pushed to the edge of the crowd and leant against the wall, panting in pain as he rummaged through his bag. After pulling out a roll of bandages, he wrapped it around his stomach.

His hands shook uncontrollably as he tore the bandage from the rest of the roll and tied it off. Blood seeped through the white fabric, drenching it in red. He pushed himself off the wall and continued onwards, swinging the bag onto his back before glancing behind him again. No more blood was dripping from his wound.

He continued forward, slipping through the crowds until finally spotting Lu Zhi's brothel ahead.

Would they know I've been there? he asked himself. *Surely not. If they did, they would've killed me last night. And either way, it's better to be in there than out here.*

Ryder stumbled up the front steps and slid open the brothel's door. Once inside, he pulled the door shut and leant his shoulder against it. He fought to gather his breath before noticing a handful of young courtesans frozen at the opposite end of the foyer, staring at him with wide eyes and at a loss for words.

Ryder almost sighed. '*I need a room ... Please.*'

In the same bedroom he had the night prior, Ryder sat down on the edge of the bed. He grunted as he slid off his bag and coat.

One of the girls stood by the entrance, watching him through a small crack in the door. 'Was it the Jinyiwei?' she nervously asked.

He looked up at her, confused by her words.

'Were they after you?' she continued. 'Did you *fight them*?'

He shook his head, 'I don't – just – just leave me be.'

The girl nodded and hurried away as Ryder reluctantly lifted the bandage and pulled up his shirt, inspecting the rugged, flesh-torn bullet wound. Blood oozed out from it.

The bedroom door suddenly slid open. He immediately grabbed the handgun sitting beside him as his eyes darted towards the entrance, finding Lu Zhi standing before him. *'What's going on?'* She demanded.

Ryder settled his nerves, letting go of the handgun and looking back down at his wound.

She shut the door behind her and hastily walked over to him, seeing the blood around his stomach. 'Let me see,' she said, bending down before him.

Ryder watched her with great caution as she gently lifted his shirt, seeing his broken skin and bloody wound.

Her eyes were overcome with concern. 'What happened?'

'People after me. That's all.'

'That's all? Looks like more than you can handle.' She raised her eyebrows at him before looking back at the wound. 'Stay here. I've got some things to clean it up and seal it.'

Before Ryder could say anything, she had already left the room. Holding in his pain, he pulled his bag closer and rustled through its contents. While being careful not to twist his body too much, he was quick to pull out a blue container and chug down two capsules. Taking a deep breath, he leant his head back and closed his eyes. Only a second later, he could feel his body beginning to repair.

Not long after, he lay down at the head of the bed as Lu Zhi knelt beside him, wiping off the blood around his wound with a wet towel. Every now and then, her eyes glanced at a strange metallic device clamped around his wrist.

Ryder noticed her curious gazes. 'It's just a weapon,' he explained.

She looked at him, unconvinced. 'It doesn't look like one.'

'It's not from around here.'

'Nothing about you is.' She glanced back at the device. It had a weathered metal exterior alongside several small screens with glowing red, digital numbers on them. The mere sight of it made her shiver uncontrollably. She forced herself to look away, before noticing the blood stains on his shirt. 'Looks like you're going to need new clothes.'

'These are the only ones I've got.'

'Well, I hope this is an important lesson for you.'

'Yeah. Don't get shot.'

She smirked a little before grabbing her sewing needle. 'I'm going to close up the wound. It may hurt.'

He nodded before closing his eyes. Piercing his skin, she began feeding the needle around the edges of his wound. After a few minutes, she finally tied off the last stitch and ensured it was secure. 'It should hold.'

Ryder looked down and trailed his fingers around the stitches. 'Thank you … You're pretty good at this.'

'Lots of practice,' she said before picking up his jacket, rubbing it between her fingers. 'Do you want me to wash these?'

'No. Thank you, though.'

'I've never seen clothes like this before either,' she continued, inspecting the jacket and its fabric. 'They feel so different.'

'Yeah, well, don't worry. I won't be here long,' he replied, sitting up on the edge of the bed.

'Your wound will take a while to heal. Are you sure that's wise?'

'I'll be fine.'

'Join us for dinner. You'll need the food.'

'Really, I'm okay.'

She raised her eyebrows at him again and tightened her lips, refusing to budge. He looked back at her, realising her stubbornness.

Eventually, he sighed. 'Is this just an excuse for you to ask me more questions?'

Letting out a small smile, Lu Zhi stood up and collected everything she brought in. 'I'll let you know when it's ready,' she said, leaving the room and sliding the door shut behind her.

Ryder sat in silence once again.

After a moment, he shook his head and chuckled, letting the humour of the situation best him for just a moment.

* * *

As night fell on Beijing, Lu Zhi led Ryder into a narrow dining room. A series of candles cast warm shadows on the walls, while all of the courtesans sat around a long dining table, some still wearing their pale white makeup.

Lu Zhi stood before them, gesturing to Ryder. 'Girls, this is our guest. His name is Ryder.'

The girls looked at him sheepishly, saying nothing.

Ryder stood in an uncomfortable silence for a moment.

Okay, then, he thought to himself before nodding to them all and carefully sitting down across from Lu Zhi.

The wooden table was lined with steaming bowls of fresh rice, vegetables, fish, and meat. Ryder felt a sudden bout of hunger strike his stomach as he looked upon the food. The girls began passing around the bowls, each taking what they needed in as quiet a manner as possible.

'You look like you've never eaten before,' Lu Zhi noted with a smirk.

Ryder awkwardly nodded in thanks as the girl beside him passed over a bowl of rice, bowing her head so their eyes could not meet. 'It's been some time since I've had proper food like this.' Taking some of the rice, he then passed it along to the next girl, who also timidly nodded in thanks.

Finally, he took a bite of the food. A wave of relief came over him as his shoulders sank and his eyes closed.

For a time, they all ate in silence. Only the sounds of their chewing, clicking chopsticks, and creaking chairs filled the room. Ryder glanced around the table, noticing some of the girls looking back down at their food as their eyes met.

Lu Zhi also noticed their apprehension, nodding to one of them encouragingly.

After amassing the courage, the girl turned to Ryder, her voice hushed and head low. 'Uh – Ryder … we were wondering … where did you come from?'

He glanced at Lu Zhi, reluctant yet unsurprised.

She shrugged at his expression. 'It's a fair question, is it not?'

Ryder sighed and placed down his chopsticks, attempting to find his words. 'I – uh … I come from a place far away. Very far.'

'What's it like there?' one of the other girls asked.

'It's … well, it's much bigger than here.'

The girls whispered and murmured to each other in disbelief.

'It's bigger than Beijing?' Lu Zhi asked.

'Tell us about it!' another girl shouted before covering her mouth with her hands, taken aback by her own excitement.

Ryder paused for another moment, biting his bottom lip before he finally nodded to himself. 'The cities … the cities stretch for as far as you can see. And the buildings, they touch the clouds, and … there's more people than you can imagine.'

'And you're looking for someone that came from there too?' Lu Zhi asked.

'Yeah …'

'Why?'

Ryder glanced around the table as all the girls listened intently. 'I'm looking for a group of them, actually. But I think one of them's here in this city. They're dangerous. And they've come to places that they shouldn't have. They're putting everyone and everywhere they go at risk. So … I'm trying to stop them.'

The table remained heavy in silence.

Finally, one of the girls handed out another bowl of rice to him. 'Well, you better eat up.'

Lu Zhi smiled as the rest of the girls giggled.

A small smile almost broke out on Ryder's face too as he nodded in thanks and accepted her offering.

Later, after they had eaten, Ryder returned to his bedroom door as Lu Zhi stopped beside him. 'I hope you enjoyed the food.'

'I did. Thank you.'

A pause lingered between them before Lu Zhi's expression turned grave. 'Will you be staying much longer?'

'No. I don't think so.'

'I noticed you didn't mention to the girls the people that are after *you*. Are they from your home too?'

'I don't know who they are, but yes.'

'And why are they after you?' she asked, clinging on to every one of his words.

'Some other people just want to handle things themselves. But they seem to forget about everyone else.'

Lu Zhi nodded along with his words. 'Well, you are welcome here. Whenever you need it.'

Ryder turned to face her as he tilted his head. 'Why are you helping me? You've done so much already.'

She glanced around them, ensuring no one else was in sight. After a tentative moment, she stepped closer and hushed her voice. 'It's the Yongle Emperor … he controls *everything*. Those dragons, the Jinyiwei, they march the streets with his eyes. They kill for him. They take girls from their homes and disappear into the Forbidden City, never to be seen again. They even come *here* for them sometimes, but I try to keep the girls together. I bring them off the streets. I watch them, make sure they're safe … but I have an awful feeling we're running out of time. There's nothing to stop the emperor from taking all of us eventually.'

Ryder was overcome with pity.

A hint of desperation slipped through Lu Zhi's voice. 'I suppose I was hoping … if there are more people like you against the emperor, we could do something. We could keep my girls safe for good.'

A heavy sigh grew inside Ryder. 'I'm sorry … I can't do that.'

The light in Lu Zhi's eyes dimmed as she bowed her head, accepting his words.

'My best advice?' he added. 'Get the hell away from the city.'

'There's nowhere to go. And if we left, we'd only become more of a target.'

'But at least you'd be further away.'

'I know. Thank you for your honesty … You'd best get some *real* sleep tonight, then. I think you'll need it.'

'You and me both.'

'Good night,' she said with a small smile before leaving back the way they came.

Ryder shut his bedroom door and sat down at the end of his bed. Like clockwork, he removed his necklace and rested it in his palm. As he caressed the seashell between his fingers, he took notice of his backpack sitting beside the bed. Lifting it onto his lap, he inspected the bullet hole that tore through the top of it. His finger trailed the circular tear.

I don't have much time before I'm tracked to this place. I need to find her, quick.

As Ryder's mind ticked over, one thing Lu Zhi said repeated over and over in his head.

'I keep the girls together. I bring them off the streets.'

* * *

In the dead of night, the hunter carefully slid open his bedroom door. Peering outside, he found the hallway silent and still.

Holding his handgun by his side and wearing his bag on his back, Ryder sneaked out of his room and crept deeper into the brothel. Silently, he slid open each bedroom door and looked over the sleeping girls for any scars across their lips. There was no sign of them.

At the end of the hallway, he came upon a stairway leading to the second story. He glanced at his surroundings, ensuring the coast was clear. Gripping his gun tighter, he began sneaking up the stairs before the floorboards creaked under his boots. He came to a sudden pause, holding himself completely still.

There was only silence.

No one awoke.

Ever so slowly, he continued to scale the stairs. Upon reaching the second-story hallway, he slid open the first bedroom door.

The sleeping girl had no scar.

He shut the door and moved to the next room, sliding it open just the same. Through the shadows, he was unable to make out who was sleeping under the blanket. Creeping towards the bed, he began to notice that the shape atop the bed was abnormal. There was no movement. No head on the pillow.

Confused and cautious, his eyes scanned the dark room, seeing no one else. Looking back at the bed, he pulled the blanket away, discovering a stack of pillows underneath it.

Ryder rested both of his hands on his pistol as his eyes darted around the room, listening for any sounds of life.

There was nothing. Only silence.

Discreetly, he knelt on the floor and peered under the bed.

Only darkness stared back at him.

'Can I help you?' a girl's voice asked.

Ryder jumped to his feet, finding a girl in a red robe standing in the doorway. She had long, dark hair, hanging over and concealing her face almost as much as her bright white makeup.

Ryder peered into her wide eyes, noting that they were brown. 'Sorry, I was just looking for something,' he explained. 'I thought I had misplaced it.'

The girl's eyebrows dipped, unconvinced, before she turned around. 'I'm getting Lu Zhi.'

'Wait, wait, hold on,' he said, stepping forward to grab her arm.

Just as he reached her, the girl twisted around and smacked the handle of a knife into his face. Ryder groaned in pain before she kicked his chest, sending him stumbling backwards onto the bed. His stomach wound reopened, and he dropped his handgun onto the floor. He groaned in pain as the ceiling turned unsteady in the midst of his concussion.

The girl swiftly and quietly sat over his waist, pressing the edge of the knife's cold blade against his throat. His vision began to re-centre as the girl glared down at him, beginning to speak in English. '*I've already told Lu Zhi about you. She's gone to get the Jinyiwei, and they'll be here any minute now. So, who the fuck are you?*'

'*You don't know?*' he growled through his teeth as blood trickled out of his nose.

'*Answer,*' she hissed, pressing the blade deeper into his skin.

'Even if I told you, you wouldn't have any *idea*.'

She clenched her teeth in frustration before noticing the metallic gauntlet around his wrist. '*Take it off,*' she demanded.

'*Why?* You wanna leave now, do you?'

'I thought it'd be different, *but this place is just as fucked as home.*'

'So where are you gonna go? You really think anywhere's gonna be any different?'

She hesitated a moment before gripping her knife tighter. 'I might as well try.'

His tone grew more civil. '*Or* I can take you back home. Simple as that.'

'Why would I do that?'

'Because you have *much* bigger problems than me. There are already others in the city and if they've tracked you to here, they'll track you to wherever you go next … *but* … if you let me, I can help you, and you can help me.'

'What do you want?'

'Anything you know about where the others went. Make it easier for me.'

She stared down at him, breathing heavily as her demeanour gradually softened. Once more, she tightened her grip and pressed the blade against him. 'If you fuck me over, I'll *kill you*.'

He nodded, showing her his bare hands. 'Okay.'

Her eyes glared into his for a short time longer before she pulled the knife away from his throat.

Before another word could be spoken, the sound of marching footsteps and shouting soldiers echoed from below.

Issa's eyes widened as she snapped back at the door, hearing the soldiers searching every room. *'Shit.'* She turned back to Ryder and his gauntlet, instinctively reaching for it. *'Give it to me!'* she cried as she fought to pull the device off him.

Without delay, he grabbed her wrist and ripped off his necklace. Clamping the seashell's pointy end in between his fingers, he stabbed the trinket up into her neck. Blood poured out onto his hands and face as she helplessly choked. He finally overpowered her, twisting her onto her back as he climbed on top of her.

She helplessly gripped her knife as he held her wrist down and the necklace inside her throat. Blood soaked her clothes and the bed as her other hand attempted to grab at his face. After a few more seconds of gurgling for air, her writhing ceased, her hand let go of the knife, and her eyes turned cold, left staring up at the ceiling.

Ryder's breath shook as he pulled the seashell out from her neck, letting more darkened blood ooze out of the wound. Without rest, the sounds of the soldiers drew closer.

Sliding off the bed, Ryder picked up his handgun and turned towards the door. There he found Lu Zhi standing by the entrance, haunted by the sight of their blood-soaked ordeal.

Ryder froze, and the room turned deathly still.

Tears filled her eyes as she stared at Issa's body, before turning them towards the hunter. With no time to waste, Ryder refused to meet her gaze as he pushed past her and stepped out of the room, spotting a line of soldiers climbing the stairs.

'There he is!' the front soldier shouted, pointing at him.

Ryder turned and sprinted down the hallway as the soldiers set after him. Slinging his bag around to his chest, he pulled out another small silver ball. He activated the device and tossed it behind him. A second later, the ball exploded into a loud frenzy of sparks in the middle of the hallway. The soldiers halted in place and held their arms before their faces, attempting to cover their eyes as they bumped into one another.

Ryder rushed down another flight of stairs and spotted an open exit at the opposite end of the hallway. He sprinted towards it before the Jinyiwei captain stepped out from one of the bedrooms, blocking his path.

The captain noticed his fast approach and unsheathed his sword. Ryder yelled out and ran his shoulder into his chest, knocking both of them onto the floor. They scurried to their knees before Ryder grabbed his red collar and threw a punch across his face. The captain spat out blood as Ryder hurried to his feet.

Without looking, the captain swung his sword and sliced Ryder's hip. He yelped in pain and stumbled against the wall, gripping the wound.

As the captain climbed to his feet, he paused at Ryder's appearance. *'Who are you?'*

The hunter grunted as he lifted his leg and kicked the captain right through the paper wall behind him. As he collapsed onto the bedroom floor, Ryder sprinted out through the exit and into the surrounding streets.

Hearing more soldiers shouting in the distance, he narrowly slid into an alleyway between two houses. He pulled back his coat's sleeve and began pressing buttons on the gauntlet, changing the coordinates, days, months, and lastly, the year from 1410 to 1348. His finger hovered over the central *T-PORT* button, shaking and uncertain.

After inhaling a deep breath and gritting his teeth, he finally held down the button for five seconds. With each second, a tiny red light flickered. After the fifth second, the red light flashed blue, and with a strange thump, as though all of the air around him sucked in and popped, Ryder disappeared into thin air.

Chapter 9

Water trickled over the rocks of a river. Ryder knelt beside a small stream, buried deep in the heart of an old forest. Morning dew covered the grass and moss. A thick fog hovered between the trees. His hands and face were covered in Issa's dried blood as he stared into the flowing water.

What am I doing? he asked himself.

I couldn't even look her in the eyes.

He gazed upon his crimson hands, remembering …

* * *

In a lonely apartment, pieces of brain and skull were scattered across the wall. A man sat in a chair with a gaping hole in his head and a gun in his hand.

In a pitch-black warehouse, a handful of naked bodies were entangled in lines of barbed wire that hung from the ceiling. Large gashes ran through their skin as their lifeless eyes stared at the floor below.

A low-lit alleyway was lined with homeless people who were either dead or dying.

Gunshots rang out in a nightclub.

A factory collapsed in flames.

Gangsters opened fire.

Needles pierced arms.

Bodies glitched.

Blood dripped.

Bullets hit.

Ryder's eyes opened with a fright.

He lay alone in his bed, quietly catching his breath. He was fresh faced, only twenty-eight years old.

The air was still. His apartment, small and grey.

Ryder glanced at his bedside table. His electronic clock read: *3:04 a.m. – 15/04/2250.* His eyes trailed beside it, where his Victorian Police Department badge sat. He stared at it for a time, feeling his heart sink deeper and deeper.

Eventually, he slipped out of bed and onto the cold tiles. Entering his kitchen, he grabbed a glass of water and took a sip. From it, he felt nothing at all. Putting the glass down, he opened the fridge and inspected a handful of beer bottles.

He paused, contemplating.

Finally, he took out a bottle and cracked it open. Walking back through the chilly apartment, he stopped before a line of windows that looked out across the vast, never-ending city of Melbourne. Thousands of lights and holographic advertisements glowed against the night sky. Numerous skyscrapers towered over all else. Sparse vehicles flew through the air.

His tired eyes stared out, watching it all pass by, before he sculled down his drink.

At sunrise, Ryder walked through the central district of the city, wearing a long coat and his badge slung around his neck.

The air was marred by a greyish smog that dimmed the sunlight. Vehicles flew overhead as hundreds upon thousands of citizens walked to and fro. Some wore striking fluorescent colours while others were muted. Their clothes ranged from leather to denim to synthetic materials. Many of their bodies were distinguished by plastic, metal, and cybernetic augmentations.

Shining skyscrapers with reflective windows lined the street side. Railway pillars shook and rumbled as magnetic hover-trains shot by. Meanwhile, neon-lit advertisements covered the many stalls and sides of buildings, their speakers tirelessly humming about what to buy and how to look.

Hector, a grey-haired, round-faced man, also wearing a long coat, waited outside a half-constructed skyscraper. The left side of the top of his head had been reconstructed with wire-infused metallic plating long ago. Taking one big mouthful at a time, he indulged his way through a breakfast muffin.

'Morning,' Ryder said as he approached him, keeping his hands in his pockets and his coat wrapped around himself.

Hector waved his hand to excuse himself, mumbling through a mouthful of food, 'Morbbing! Sobby!'

Ryder smiled, gesturing to the muffin. 'I could use one of those. Next time let me know, and I'll come get one with you.'

Hector nodded, still unable to speak with the food in his mouth.

Ryder looked up at the tower before them, the new home of Forward Industries. 'You really think the rumours are true? The commissioner seemed pretty serious about it.'

Hector finally finished off his muffin, sucking the crumbs off his fingers. 'Eh, I find it hard to believe, personally. But, that said, my great-great-grandfather used to find teleporting hard to believe, so what do I know?'

Ryder took a long, nervous breath.

Hector chuckled and patted his shoulder. 'You'll be all right. Just try to act at least *somewhat* professional. We're only asking questions, nothing more.'

'They're some pretty damn big questions.'

'Well, let's go find out the damn big answers,' he remarked with an encouraging nod.

Together, the pair pushed open the glass doors and entered the skyscraper. The foyer was mostly complete. The bright white floors were polished, the air was clean, and at its centre sat a tall, reflective silver statue.

They were scanned through the security checkpoint before strolling through the foyer. Their footsteps echoed across the floor as they approached the silver statue towering over them. It depicted a naked woman leaning forward, with trails of silver stretching out from behind her arms and legs. Above the statue was an open void, looking up hundreds of floors to the top of the building.

Ryder whistled. 'Wow ... you think these guys are strapped for cash after building all this?'

Hector smirked and shook his head. 'That'll be the day.'

'Gentlemen,' a loud, warm voice called out to them.

The partners turned to see Miles Forder approaching them. With a tidy black beard, he wore a shimmering dark-blue suit and a belt over which his gut hung.

'You're the VPD representatives, yes?' he presumed, outstretching his hand.

'Indeed we are. I'm Chief Inspector Longs, and this is Inspector Mason,' Hector explained, shaking Miles's hand.

'It's a real pleasure to meet you, sir,' Ryder added, enthusiastically shaking his hand.

'No, no, the pleasure's all mine. Helms has spoken highly of you both for many years. You do *great* work.'

'Well, flattery is always appreciated but I know if he didn't have to, the commissioner would be here in our place in a heartbeat.' Miles replied. 'He does send his apologies again for being unable to attend today.'

'Oh, don't worry, I know once he hears from you two, he'll come running.' Miles said with a jolly grin. 'Besides, the more of you involved, the better the process will be for all of us. But, before we get to that, please allow me to show you around,' he insisted, gesturing them to follow.

'This place is really coming along,' Ryder commented, gazing at the high ceilings and the many reflective surfaces.

'Oh yes, it's been a long time coming, but considering our expansions as of late, it suits us just perfectly,' he explained with another smile, strolling through the gleaming foyer.

'I'm surprised you haven't situated yourself off-planet,' Hector added.

Miles chuckled and nodded. 'Ah, yes. Trust me, I've heard *no* shortage of people expressing that opinion. But what can I say? I was born and raised on this planet, made my living here, built this company here; I think it's only right to give something back. The bigger we are, the more we strengthen the economy. Really, it's the least I could do for my home world.' He paused, turning to the two inspectors. 'Also ... I like my comforts. I haven't moved house in almost thirty years – changing planets seems like a bit much.'

'I hear you there,' Hector agreed.

Later along their tour, the trio entered one of the building's elevators. The door closed behind them as Miles stood before an eye-scanner. The device scanned his retina before beeping and sending the elevator underground.

'So, as I'm sure you've noticed in recent years,' Miles noted, 'we've reached a point where it's rather difficult to improve upon Kiddler's original teleportation device. We will continue to release new models, of course, but ... the innovation is stagnating. So, with all of our resources, we decided to move into more experimental areas. Expand the bounds of technology. Find the *next* milestone of the industry.'

Ryder and Hector briefly glanced at one another.

Miles continued, 'And I presume you've already heard the rumours of what we may be working on here?'

'It's hard to miss them,' Hector admitted.

'Yes, much to my disdain. No matter how hard you try to keep something a surprise, someone always has to ruin it for everyone else. Anyway, thankfully it's something not a lot of people believe is actually possible.'

Ryder smirked at Hector.

Hector rolled his eyes a little. 'Are you saying the rumours are true, then?'

Miles smiled at them both before the elevator doors opened to reveal a long, stark hallway. Bright white floors and walls beamed a heavenly light. Awaiting them was Dr. Alice Locke, only twenty-five years of age, with long black hair and wearing a spotless white lab coat.

'Good morning, Alice,' Miles greeted her. 'This is Chief Inspector Longs and Inspector Mason, here to see what we've been working on.'

Alice gave them a distant smile behind her glasses as she shook their hands. 'I'm Dr. Locke. Pleased to meet you both. If you'll follow me.' She turned and led them through the hallway, passing by windows that peered into an array of advanced laboratories. Dozens of scientists worked across each of the rooms. Mechanical arms, chemicals, and test tubes lined the desks and walls.

'How long has this new research been going on?' Hector asked, his eyes scanning each lab they passed.

'We've been at work on this particular project for the past five years. Although plenty of research had been done in the decades before my time,' she explained, leading them towards the central laboratory.

Upon reaching an electronic door, Alice scanned her eye beside it. After a moment, the first door unlocked and slid open. The four of them entered the contained space, standing before another locked door. Alice checked to see they had all entered before pressing another button, shutting the door behind them. The air was swiftly pressurised, completely sealing them off from the outside hallway.

Ryder nodded, impressed, as Alice placed her eye before another scanner. Her retina was authenticated, and three beeps sounded inside the room. Finally, the second door unlocked and opened before them. The group entered the central laboratory as Dr. Deisy Forder, also wearing a lab coat and only a few years older than Alice, approached them with an infectious smile.

'This is my daughter,' Miles revealed, gesturing towards her, 'She is heading the project.'

Deisy shook both of their hands. 'Good morning. I'm Deisy.'

'Hector.'

'Ryder.'

Almost immediately, the inspectors' attention was pulled towards the centre of the room. There, a large see-through dome enclosed an almost incomprehensible sight: an utter darkness surrounded by a hovering purple ring. An endlessly generating array of small yellow lights floated through the black hole, continually sucked in and out of it. An endless loop. Always moving, yet never changing.

'What *is* that?' Ryder breathlessly asked.

'See for yourself,' Deisy replied.

Ryder and Hector slowly approached the dome as their eyes remained transfixed. Deisy turned and smiled at her father, amused. He smiled back and proudly patted her shoulder before she approached the two inspectors and stood by their side.

Together, Ryder and Hector stared at the floating anomaly. The closer they came, the greater power they could feel, the more their eyes were pulled deeper into the black hole. Their vision began to lose all sight of its surroundings, as though they too were about to be pulled into it. All that was stopping its grasp was the transparent, glasslike material between them and it.

Deisy held a touchpad close to her chest as she admired the creation. 'We call it the Core. It's what allows us to do what we've been doing.'

'And that is?' Hector asked.

'Time travel.'

They both looked at Deisy in disbelief.

She smiled at them. 'Yeah, *I know*. I'm not joking. We figured that even attempting such a thing would require a new power source. Something as strong as a black hole to physically allow us to move through time without ourselves ageing. And this was that answer.'

'Am I stupid in asking what *exactly* it is?' Ryder asked, reluctantly looking back at it.

'It's no easy concept to explain. It's a self-perpetuating power that seems to exist out of time and space. Its strength is … immense. The only thing we can compare it to *is* a miniaturised black hole. That's what we treat it as, anyway.'

'How did you do it?'

Miles stepped forward. 'Unless you're prepared to sign a lot of paperwork, I'm sure you'd understand that that's something we'd rather keep to ourselves. We wouldn't want this sort of information getting out there. But I promise you, every step of the way has been taken with as much caution and safety as humanly possible. We know the gravity of such a creation … no pun intended.'

Hector nodded. 'Something tells me I wouldn't understand it even if you did tell me … but you're saying you've succeeded? It actually works?'

'No physical human has tested it as of yet,' Deisy replied, 'but Marty has.'

'Marty?' Ryder asked.

Deisy waved them over to a desk housing a collection of computer screens. She opened security footage of an empty, condensed concrete room. 'What you're seeing is footage from our port test room. This was two months ago.'

The footage revealed Deisy and Alice entering the room with a cage. Inside it was a little white mouse, frightfully looking at its surroundings.

Deisy pointed at the rodent on the screen. 'That's Marty, one of our test mice. We placed him in there on the fourteenth of February, 10:30 a.m. Our time machinery was built into his cage. Then, we just chose a date and sent him into the future.'

On the screen, Deisy and Alice left the room. Marty looked around as his cage sat still for a moment. Suddenly, the cage evaporated and disappeared from sight.

Deisy pulled up another video file of the same empty room. 'Now, this was one month later, the fourteenth of March, 10:30 a.m. The date and time we sent him to.'

Ryder and Hector leant in closer, captivated.

With a little rattle, the cage appeared from nowhere, in the exact same spot it had left. Marty was still inside, unharmed and unchanged. Deisy and Alice entered the room and cautiously checked the cage. They smiled as the mouse looked at them, confused and curious.

'We tested his blood for ageing,' Alice continued, 'comparing it to a sample from right before we had sent him away. Despite it being one month later, he hadn't aged a single day. Marty was the first creature on Earth to successfully travel into the future.'

Ryder chuckled in amazement as Hector stood upright, attempting to comprehend the sight of it. 'Were there any side effects? Was the mouse all right?'

Deisy nodded with a smile. 'He was more than okay.'

Alice walked over with Marty in his metal cage, showing the two inspectors. They both looked at the mouse as he looked back up at them, his nose twitching and eyes blinking.

Ryder gently touched the small bars between him and Marty. 'You're one lucky little guy, you know that?'

'I imagine you'll be testing humans soon, then?' Hector presumed.

'The plans are in place, yes,' Deisy replied. 'But we're taking our time. It's not a matter we wish to rush.'

Later in their visit, Alice showed Hector the prototype wrist gauntlet she was developing. Meanwhile, Deisy walked with Ryder around the circular Core.

'If this really works,' Ryder said, 'it could definitely help out the police force. The number of things we could stop from happening. The people we could save.'

'That's a nice thought, but unfortunately as helpful as something like that may be, it could be equally harmful.'

'So you're not showing us this for us to use it?'

The two of them stopped to face one another. The purple lights of the Core danced across their faces as Deisy shook her head. 'I'm afraid not. My father brought you here to *alleviate* any fears you might have. He just wants you to understand what we're doing here, and to trust us in that.'

'Well, what are you going to do with it then? You're not going to share it at all?'

'No, it's not like teleportation. I mean, the public distribution of that has already drawn its fair share of criticism, but this is on a *whole* other level. There's no way we can just hand it around like candy. We haven't even dared go *back* in time. Hopefully, we never do.'

'Really? Isn't that half the point of this?'

'Initially, yes, but the closer we got to making it a reality, the more real the consequences seemed to us. Imagine if you went back and stopped us from inventing this device. If there was no time machine invented and you never received it, how would you have ever gotten there? Would you simply cease to exist? Would an entire timeline disappear forever? Would you ever be able to return to your original timeline? Those paradoxes run so deep, it's just … dangerous.'

'But now you could get the answers to those questions.'

'At what cost, though? Would *you* want to go back and find out? You'd be potentially losing everything and everyone you've ever known. Let alone everyone else's fates potentially being at risk. Even as a scientist, I will admit that some things just hold too high of a risk to be answered.'

Ryder nodded, glancing back to the Core. 'I didn't think about that … There's nothing you'd want to go back and see again, though?'

Deisy smiled at the thought. 'Of course. My mother … to hear her voice, and to talk to her, and feel her presence again. She left too soon.'

'I'm sorry to hear.'

She shrugged. 'We make do. Still got my silly father around to make me laugh. What about you?'

'There's a lot. Most days I see things I wish I didn't.'

'I can imagine it's not an easy job,' Deisy remarked, noticing a heavy weight scarring his eyes.

'Ah, you find ways to deal with it.'

'Alcohol, perhaps?'

His eyes shot back at her, completely staggered.

'You may want to smell yourself,' she suggested with a smirk.

He hurriedly sniffed his coat's shoulder, smelling the previous night's drinks. 'Okay, scratch that, I would go back in time and wash my clothes.'

'Well, that's *exactly* the sort of thing we built this for.'

'Perfect, it's about time you got your priorities straight around here.'

They quietly laughed and caught each other's reflective, starry eyes for a moment.

'Well, if you're not going back,' he continued, 'what *do* you plan to do with it?'

She took a long, thoughtful breath. 'Maybe contact the future. Learn things that could help the world now, you know? Save species, preserve environments, subvert disasters. We may not be able to change what's already happened, but we could make a lot of things better for the future.'

'Well, that doesn't sound too bad. I hope it works.'

'Me too.'

'You prepared for what's to come?'

She chuckled. 'Which part of it?'

'The number of questions you're gonna get. I know you guys are starting to open up to us now, but as soon as it goes public, you're going to have every layman, journalist, and government official breathing down your neck.' He gestured to the Core. 'This is a lot of power for *one* company to have. It's gonna scare them.'

'I know, and that's why we're going to be up-front and honest about it to everybody, just like we are with you. Because regardless of people's opinions, I think they deserve to know. Then, I have hope they'll see our intentions for what they are.'

Ryder gradually nodded at her words. 'Well, I like to think we'll have your back in that. But … if you ever wanna air your grievances, give me a call.'

'Are you giving me your number now?' she asked, raising her eyebrows.

'If you'll take it.'

Deisy twisted her lips, contemplating. She glanced around the laboratory, pushing her blonde hair back behind her ear, before discreetly handing him her phone.

He smiled and typed his phone number into her device.

'This is *very* professional of you,' she added.

'That's what I'm famous for,' he replied, handing back her phone. 'I look forward to having a drink together. Purely as a coping mechanism, of course.'

'Oh, of course.'

'Thank you for your time, Deisy. And your honesty. *Brutal* honesty,' he said, reaching out and shaking her hand.

'Likewise.' She smiled back.

Shortly after their tour, Ryder and Hector walked through the foyer towards the building's entrance.

'I don't know about you,' Ryder began, 'but if anyone's going to have this thing in their hands, they seem like decent enough people for it.'

Hector tilted his head from side to side. 'Well, one thing's for certain – as soon as this hits the public, they'll be fighting for the rest of their days. Probably only a matter of time before they break; having to hand it over or somehow doing something they shouldn't.'

'You really think they would abuse it?' Ryder asked, stopping at the security checkout.

'That's the thing, Ryder, it can be all too easy for people to have a different definition of what abuse is. Especially with something like this.'

The pair were scanned through the checkpoint and walked outside into the sea of bustling citizens.

Hector's digital watch beeped as an automated emergency message came through, drawing his attention. 'Ah, looks like we've got a situation going on in Garra Street. Let's just swing by, see if they need a hand, then we'll report to Helms. He'll definitely want to see it for himself. Come on.'

Hector continued on his way as Ryder sighed. He gave Forward Industries one more glance before following his partner and disappearing into the crowd.

* * *

Beside the river in the forest, Ryder washed his bloody hands in the cold stream. He splashed water across his neck and face, rubbing the red stains off his skin.

Deisy's face smiled at him in his memory. Their glasses of wine clinked together as they sat amongst the yellow glow of the restaurant lights. She told stories, pulled comical expressions, and laughed throughout the night.

Amidst the soft rain, they walked side by side in a neon-drenched street. Ryder's watch beeped. Another police notification.

Deisy watched as his expression turned grave at the sight of it. 'You know, you could always just leave.' Her voice echoed.

Blinding muzzles flashed explosions of light in dark rooms. Blood drops flew through the air. Red and blue lights circled. Voices screamed in pain.

Ryder struggled to open his eyes. His head moved about aimlessly as he groaned, sitting against the wall of a dark, wet alleyway. Saliva dripped out from his mouth as an empty beer bottle fell from his hand and rolled along the ground. His phone rested in the opposite hand.

Soon, a dark silhouette appeared at the end of the alleyway. The figure peered in from the shadows before approaching him. Eventually, the darkness passed, and a light shone upon the figure.

It was Deisy.

She knelt and placed her hand on his cheek. 'Oh God. Ryder? Ryder, can you hear me?' She gently slapped his cheek.

He groaned as his head drooped onto his chest.

'Come on. Let's get you out of here, into bed,' she said, placing his arm around her shoulder. She grunted as she helped him stand up. His weight almost made her tumble over before she grabbed onto the wall with one hand. After steadying herself, she helped him walk back out of the alleyway.

The river reflected in his teary eyes.

He sat in bed, under his blanket, as she handed him a glass of water. She sat beside him with a sad smile, gently fixing his hair.

'Why are you helping me?' he asked, his voice tired and slurred.

'Because you need help.'

The small waves of the river brushed against the forest dirt.

* * *

Melbourne, Australia, 2253 CE

The bright blue waves of the ocean crashed onto the golden shore before being pulled back by its current. Seashells of all kinds rocked back and forth with the ocean's own ebb and flow. Under the warm sun and clear skies, Ryder and Deisy walked along the ocean's edge together, hand in hand.

She pointed at the far end of the beach. 'Just beyond that rock face there is where it starts to get bad. I used to remember the good part stretched out all the way along this side of the peninsula. You know, I've even started to see rubbish washing up on the sand around this part?'

Ryder shook his head, disappointed. 'I haven't seen that.'

'I'm afraid we're going to be seeing a lot more of it soon enough. I'm just glad there's at least a *couple* of organisations looking after the remaining few beaches.'

'Has your dad considered helping them out?'

'I want him to, but I don't know. He's *way* too busy at the moment. Especially with the unveiling.'

'How nervous are you? On a scale of one to ten?'

'Oh, you know, probably ... one hundred. Thousand. Something like that.'

'Yeah. That seems reasonable.'

'Yep.' She anxiously nodded. 'Definitely didn't think I would be feeling like this when we started. I still hope they understand it, but ... they're just going to expect so much. We haven't even confirmed anything, and they're already going crazy about it. They're going to want to know everything, about the future *and* the past.'

'Ah, it doesn't matter what *they* want. It's not your job to give everyone the answers they're after.'

'But the fact that we've made it and are keeping it … I don't know. Maybe we do have a responsibility to answer those questions.'

'No, you're the expert on this. *You* made it, not them. If there's anyone who knows what's safe and what's not, it's you. You know the limits of this stuff.'

She gazed down at the sand and shook her head. 'It's hard to know. And I feel like it's getting harder.'

'Well, before that happens, and before you change the world tomorrow, I've got a couple of surprises for you,' he said as they stopped beside the shoreline.

'Really?' she replied, curious and excited.

Ryder took her hands into his and gazed upon her deep green eyes as she stared back up at him.

They smiled at one another.

'What is it?!' she eagerly asked.

Finally, he pulled out his police badge from his pocket, looking at it one last time.

Her eyes widened before she placed her hand over his. 'Are you sure? You're not out in the field so much these days. You don't need to.'

He gazed back into her eyes and nodded. 'I need to move on.' He looked out at the ocean, contemplating. 'You know, I was actually planning on throwing this into the sea but … *probably* not a great idea for the environment, right?'

She chuckled. 'Yeeaah, I think that's the right call.'

'It won't be as dramatic, but … I'll throw it out later. You get the idea.'

'I do,' she said with a smile, resting her hands on his shoulders.

He slid the badge back into his pocket before he got down on one knee. 'Deisy,' he said, pulling out a small, glass box and opening it to reveal a silver ring. Its edges curved up and down like the waves themselves. 'Things *are* going to get harder, but I want to make them easier together. Will you marry me?'

Her eyes glistened as she nodded and broke out into a bright smile. *'Yes, of course!'*

His eyes welled up as he smiled with her. They clung to one another, embracing under the bright sun as they kissed, cried, and laughed. The cold water brushed past their ankles, leaving dozens of seashells around them.

That night, the two of them lay together in bed, holding each other close. She turned around, letting him hold her from behind as he stroked her light, messy hair and kissed her cheek good night.

* * *

Melbourne, Australia, 2255 CE

In a bright talk show studio, Deisy sat on a curved couch across from popular news interviewer Maggie Filling.

'It's good to have you again, Deisy,' Maggie said with a smile. 'How are you doing?'

'Thank you, Maggie. I'm doing well.'

'I'm sure "doing well" is a bit of an oversimplification, right?' Maggie laughed.

Deisy forced a smile and nodded. 'You may be on to something there.'

'Now, what I wanted to talk to you about today is something a lot of people have been wondering lately: the government. They obviously have an itch that Forward Industries just isn't scratching.'

Deisy was unsurprised by the question, speaking familiarly. 'All people need to remember is that it's been two years that the public, and even longer for the government, have known about our invention. And in those two years, *nothing* of the disastrous consequences some are afraid of have come to pass.'

'Yet, they *are* two years of what, to a lot of people's frustration, doesn't seem to be much progress. When are we going to be finding out *more* about our pasts and futures? I see a lot of people asking why you haven't sent anyone to the far future, or even why you haven't travelled back in time on one of the star colony planets?'

Deisy chuckled and shook her head.

'Doesn't that pique your interest even in the slightest though, Deisy?' Maggie continued. 'Could we find life on other planets in the distant past? Could we answer the questions historians have had for centuries about our own past? Could we find out exactly what our future entails?'

'Well, one thing I've learnt since all of this has started is that there aren't many people whose interest *isn't* piqued by those questions. Of course, we all want to know those things, but as we've promised since day one, we are treating this with the utmost caution. Anything we do is planned out for months on end. Even years, sometimes. And people know that we *have* taken little steps forward. We have a couple of people that have gone, say, two months ahead of our time and then come back.'

'And I'll try my luck. What have you learned from those little expeditions?'

'Thankfully, I've learned nothing that would concern anyone else,' she said with a smile. 'Those trips are purely contained, experimental ones. We're certainly not letting people roam around freely in the future. They're not even allowed to leave a single room. We also keep what they learn entirely restricted to mundane things, like what the weather will be. And as to not complicate things, no more than a few of us are involved in those experiments. The last thing we want to do is attempt to tamper with time.'

'Wouldn't you say, though, Deisy, that there's a point where your caution overrides any true progress? What exactly do you think this invention has accomplished in the last two years? Because, to a lot of disappointed people, it doesn't seem like nearly enough to even warrant its *very* expensive existence.'

Deisy paused for a moment, fighting to shield her doubts as the automated cameras focused on her. 'We are as … excited and thrilled and wondered as anyone else is about this invention, but all we're trying to do is help us move forward and do it in the safest way possible. We're trying to understand how this works, dipping our toes into every area imaginable, and there are *a lot* of areas to cover, and they require *a lot* of thought and *a lot* of time. And if that means people are going to have to wait, then so be it. The last thing we need is us making matters worse by rushing this process. I refuse to do it. And honestly, to me, there's a lot more immediate issues we need to be focusing on in the world right now.'

'Those are certainly some powerful words.' Maggie said, turning and smiling at one of the cameras. 'Join us after the break for more of our discussion with the world's leading physicist and inventor, Deisy Forder.'

Ryder sat at the kitchen bench of his new high-level apartment. He watched the TV interview before it transitioned into vibrant advertisements. Twisting around in his chair, he returned to a thin laptop and continued his work.

Deisy opened the front door of their apartment and shut it behind her. She pressed her head against it as she dropped her handbag to the floor. With a heavy sigh, she wiped away a handful of tears and closed her eyes.

'Busy day, eh?' Ryder asked from the kitchen, continuing to type on his computer.

Forcing her eyes open, she walked down their front hallway. 'When isn't it?' She slid off her coat and tossed it onto the couch as she walked straight for the crib sitting at the edge of the room. 'How has she been?'

'Quiet, but I think she's been missing you.'

'Are you sure that's not just you?'

'Maybe a little.'

Deisy peered into the crib with a smile, finding their three-month-old daughter, Rose. 'Hey there, beautiful. How are you?' she said with a soft voice, picking up her baby and holding her close.

Rose's eyes opened before she let out a small smile.

'Hey. Hey there,' Deisy said to her as she sat on the chair beside Ryder. 'Look, it's your daddy.'

He turned and felt Rose's tiny foot. 'Hello, little miss. You're probably sick of seeing my face all day, aren't you?'

Rose giggled and stuck her tongue between her lips, making a farting noise as her parents chuckled.

'I missed you so much,' Deisy told her, gently poking her nose.

'We both missed *you*,' Ryder said, kissing Deisy's cheek.

She turned and smiled, kissing him back.

* * *

That night, before being placed in her crib, Rose fell asleep in between Deisy and Ryder in their bed. They both admired her in silence, listening to her gentle and faint breathing.

'I saw you on TV again today,' Ryder quietly began. 'Some rough questions in there.'

Deisy barely acknowledged his words, continuing to stroke Rose's little arm.

'Hopefully the next one isn't too bad,' he continued. 'They'll wear out eventually.'

'You know, I was thinking we should take her on a trip soon. Go back to the beach somewhere. It's been way too long since we've been there. And I don't know how much longer they're going to be around for.'

Ryder smiled and nodded, 'That sounds like a good idea. We'll do it.' He reached out and rested his hand on Deisy's arm as the three of them lay close together, keeping each other warm, safe, and loved.

Chapter 10

With great care, Ryder removed the bloodstained necklace from around his neck. He pushed his thumb back and forth against it, to no avail. Finally, he dipped the seashell into the river, attempting to clean it amongst the flowing water.

* * *

Melbourne, Australia, 2257 CE

In the bright, quiet central laboratory of Forward Industries, Deisy presented Alice with the new, shiny, pointed seashell necklace. 'It's for Rose,' she explained, looking over it with joy.

Alice squinted at the necklace. 'You're not giving it to her now, are you? She's not old enough for that.'

'No, yeah, she'll have it when she's old enough,' she clarified, her smile fading as she placed the silver seashell back into its little jewellery box.

Alice continued tinkering with a time gauntlet at their desk as Deisy looked at her, wavering.

Eventually, Alice noticed her indecisive gaze. 'Are you okay?'

Deisy hesitated a few moments longer. '… Are you all right here alone?'

'You're leaving early again?'

'I just want to get back to Rosy is all. I miss her a lot, and I just … feel like I should be there for her more.'

'This is going to be a regular thing, isn't it?'

Deisy's shoulders dropped as she leant against the desk. 'Would you mind if it was?'

'Well, we only got this far because of you.'

'That's not true. I couldn't have done it without you. And you're much better with this stuff than I am these days. You don't need me.'

'You're the face of the company. If anything, it's everybody *ever* that needs you,' Alice replied with a smirk.

Deisy snickered and shook her head. 'No, I'm just … I think it'd be better for me to, you know, step away a bit.'

'You've heard one too many questions from the press. You're putting too much mind to what other people think, Deis.'

'No, I really don't think I can give anything more. Not to them, or to all of this,' she explained, gazing at the surrounding lab. 'They keep asking for more and more, and I don't … I don't know *what* to answer, I don't know *how* … I don't know what to do anymore.'

'You keep doing what *you* want. We always knew there was going to be unreasonable demands from the public.'

'But they're right, A. Every time I think of how we might travel into the future there's a million different ways I imagine it going wrong. I *am* too scared to push this any further.' She looked at the Core as it stared back at her. 'Either that or I just don't have the mind for it anymore. The only place I know I can make an impact now is with Rose. I want to take her to the last beaches and forests before they die out. I want her to learn about the planet. I want her to see it and …' She paused for a moment, sighing. 'Everyone else is so obsessed with what's going to happen with the future travel and the company and what we're going to do next but … I just want a good future for Rose. That's all.' Her eyes fell upon the gauntlet that rested on the desk. 'Sometimes I wonder …'

Her words trailed off.

'Wonder what?' Alice asked.

Deisy looked back at her, noticing her confusion, before she forced a smile and shook her head. 'Nothing. Are you sure it's okay if I leave?'

'*Of course,*' Alice said as if it were obvious.

Deisy opened her arms and embraced her friend. 'Good night, A. Thanks for this.'

'That's all right. I'll see you tomorrow – or … whenever. Good night.'

Deisy walked towards the laboratory's exit as she removed her coat.

'And, Deis,' Alice said, stopping her before the exit. 'The necklace is pretty. I'm sure she'll like it.'

Deisy's face lit up once more, 'Thanks, A.'

With her satchel bag hung over her shoulder, she exited the central laboratory through its two sealed doors. Her footsteps echoed along the hallway floor as she approached the elevator.

Then, out of the silence came a confused and faded voice from behind her.

'Hello?'

Confused, Deisy paused and turned around. After a short moment of processing what stood before her, her mouth dropped and her eyes filled with horror, '*Alice? What happened? Are you okay?*'

Meanwhile, down the opposite end of the hallway, the elevator dinged, and its doors slid open, revealing a group of masked figures inside it. A Forward Industries security guard, Connor, stood at their lead. Deisy turned towards the elevator, about to call for help before she spotted Connor approaching. She noticed the group at his rear, all of them wearing black masks. Disoriented, she glanced behind her at the source of the voice again.

There was nobody there.

Connor hurriedly walked towards her as he unholstered his gun.

Deisy turned to face them, frazzled and almost speechless, 'Connor? What are you doing?'

Without wasting a moment more time, Connor pointed his handgun at her head, 'Take us to the gauntlets.'

Deisy clenched her fists, standing firm and defiant. Before she could speak a word, Connor smacked the grip of his handgun across her face. She yelped and collapsed to her knees. Her cheek was sliced open and began to bleed onto the white floor.

'*You need to listen to me,*' he demanded through his teeth, roughly grabbing her collar, pulling her to her feet, and pushing her back down the hall.

The masked assailants followed closely behind as they peered into each room they passed, searching for any sign of the time gauntlets. Two of them jogged ahead towards the central laboratory. They stopped as they spotted Alice working on one gauntlet through the window.

'Over here! There's one in here!' a follower called out.

Alice looked out the window, noticing their approach.

'*Open it,*' Connor ordered Deisy as they reached the first door.

She said nothing, merely staring at the ground and maintaining her composure.

Connor holstered his handgun as he gestured to his followers. A handful of them grabbed Deisy's shoulders and legs, holding her still while Connor gripped the back of her head, making her look up into the eye-scanner. She shut her eyes as tightly as she could as he used his fingers to force her eyelid open. Groaning and shaking her limbs, she desperately fought to break free.

Their grip was too strong.

The device scanned her retina.

The lock beeped and the door opened before them. Connor pulled Deisy inside as they all entered the room. He pressed a button, sealing the first door behind them and pressurising the air.

Alice bolted over to a keypad inside the central laboratory, immediately locking the second door. The second eye-scanner shut off before it could be used.

Connor pulled out his handgun as he looked at Alice through the see-through door. He pressed his handgun against the back of Deisy's head, 'Let us through or *she dies!*'

Alice stared at them, shaking and hesitating before the keypad.

'Don't do it, A! Don't let them – !' Deisy called out before Connor smacked the handgun into the back of her head. She yelled in pain, almost falling to her knees again as he held her up by her collar.

'Let us in, *now!*'

Alice gasped as her eyes watered.

Blood trailed down Deisy's face as Connor gripped his handgun tighter.

'I *will* do it,' he threatened.

With pain, Alice bit her lip and unlocked the second door.

Connor pulled Deisy into the laboratory as the five masked assailants trailed in behind them. They all froze in place as an emergency siren blared through the facility speakers. Red lights turned on and flashed in circles, dousing the laboratory in a crimson shade.

Deisy stumbled down to her knees, dizzy from her concussion. Connor pressed his pistol into the back of her head again as he barked at Alice, '*Seal the doors!*'

Alice swallowed and reluctantly used the keypad to seal the central laboratory doors shut.

Connor gestured his head towards the gauntlet on Alice's workbench. One of the masked female followers ran over to the device and began fiddling with it.

'Where are the other ones?' he asked Alice.

'They're not *here*,' she replied with a glare.

'*Where?*'

'Even if you had them, they're *not* operational!'

'And this one?' he asked, gesturing to the workbench gauntlet.

The female follower turned on the gauntlet, seeing its small screen light up with dates, times, and coordinates. 'Got it! It's working!'

'Good. Enter everything,' he ordered.

The follower began entering times and dates into the device as Deisy lazily shook her head, speaking with thin breath. 'Don't do this. It's too dangerous.'

'It's no less dangerous than any other way,' Connor retorted.

'You don't know what it'll do.'

'*You* made it. Didn't you figure you'd find out these answers one day?'

The elevator doors opened. Armed security guards rushed through the facility hallways towards the central laboratory. Connor looked back at the sealed doors, seeing the guards frantically attempting to open them.

'We're done – it's all in!' the female follower shouted, rushing up to Connor and handing him the gauntlet.

'Good.' He slid the gauntlet around his wrist and stepped away from the two scientists.

The first sealed door slid open. The guards rushed towards the second.

Connor inspected the gauntlet, seeing a line of coordinates beneath the first set of times and dates: *16:30 - 20/11/1863*. 'Come on, stand with me. Get a good grip.' He instructed his followers, who took hold of each other's hands and arms.

Deisy gradually climbed to her feet, blood trickling down her face as she eyed him with disgust. *'I'll find you.'*

Connor paused as he looked back at her. A brief flash of fear overcame him.

Then, determination. In an instant, he lifted his handgun.

Fear struck Deisy's heart as she froze in place.

Connor's gun flashed, and a bullet flew through her forehead. Her head flung backwards, spraying blood across the bright white walls and floor of the laboratory. Alice froze in fright as she watched Deisy collapse to the floor.

The security forces opened the second sealed door just as Connor activated the gauntlet. Within a split second, he and his masked followers disappeared into thin air. The oxygen pulled in and dispersed from where they had stood.

Alice stood helplessly still, feeling every ache and shiver in her body as she stared at Deisy, watching as a pool of blood grew beneath her head. The security guards rushed over to her side, all too late.

In the corner of the laboratory, a security camera looked down upon the scene. Hours later, in the Forward Industries control room, Ryder and Miles finished watching the grey-tinted footage in silence. A dozen screens sat before them, looping the footage of paramedics inspecting Deisy's body.

Miles, his face grim and lifeless, glanced at Ryder. Eventually, he shook his head. 'No one can know. It was just a laboratory accident … nothing more.'

Ryder returned a look of equal pain.

After a few more solemn moments without words, Miles left the dark room. Ryder brought his hand to his mouth, fighting to hold back his tears as he stared at the image of Deisy lying on the floor.

No more than an hour later, Ryder strolled through the lonely Forward Industries foyer. His footsteps echoed throughout the quiet building.

Alice met him halfway. They stood in silence for a time, unable to speak.

Alice cleared her throat. 'This was for Rose,' she said, handing out the small jewellery box. 'She was going to give it to her sometime, when she was ready for it.'

Ryder gently took the box from her hands. Opening it, he found the silver seashell necklace neatly folded inside it. He closed the box and looked at her, barely holding himself together. 'Thank you.'

Alice gave a half-nod back before they finally hugged. Their eyes welled up as they held each other tight. Then, they left their separate ways.

That night, Ryder sneaked into Rose's colourful bedroom. Glow-in-the-dark paintings and pictures of flowers and trees decorated the walls. He approached her crib and looked over her as she slept soundly. In the last two years, she had begun to grow wavy blonde hair, just like her mother's.

Ryder pulled the jewellery box out from his pocket and looked at it with heartache.

'Hi, Daddy,' her little voice said.

Ryder looked down at her with some surprise. 'Oh – hi there, baby. You're supposed to be asleep.'

'Where's Mummy?' she asked, rustling in her crib.

He froze, almost unable to breathe. 'Your mum – uh … she's … she's just …' He forced himself to smile at his daughter. 'She's just gone away for a little while.'

'I want Mummy.'

His smile trembled. 'I know. I do too. Come here, come lay with me for a while.' He reached inside and picked her up out of her crib.

Later that same night, Rose slept beside him in his bed. He watched over her, softly holding her hand as his lips quivered, feeling the weight of the silence and emptiness beside him smother his heart.

* * *

The silver seashell flowed through the river water as Ryder held its chain. He stared at it as it drifted in place, calmly floating amidst the current.

Maybe I should just go back, he thought.

Maybe she needs me ...

* * *

Melbourne, Australia, 2258 CE

A casket gradually lowered into the floor of a cemetery facility. Around it were physical and holographic images of Miles Forder.

Miles Forder
Loving Father, Husband, and Leader
March 4, 2189 – November 7, 2258

Numerous guests, all dressed in black, stood before the grave. They were gathered inside a large rectangular room. The walls and floor were covered in screens that projected moving images of a bright, clean outdoor graveyard, as if it were a sunny day.

Once the casket was lowered deep enough into the floor, another tile slid back over the grave and sealed shut.

One by one, the guests left the room.

Eventually, only two remained.

Ryder stood closest to the grave, looking at the photos sitting across the floor. He focused on a looping photo of Deisy and Miles together, smiling.

'How is Rose?' a voice asked from behind him.

He turned to see Alice dressed in a black coat.

The graveyard projections ceased. The floors and walls lit up the room in a bright, sterile white.

Returning to his apartment, Ryder gestured Alice towards the dining table. 'Would you like a drink?'

She shook her head as she sat down. 'No. Thank you.'

He walked into the kitchen, pouring himself a glass of whiskey.

Alice noticed numerous bottles sitting on the kitchen bench, some of them full, many empty. 'Did you talk much with Miles in his last few months?' she asked.

Ryder twisted the lid back onto one of the bottles. 'Yeah, he would come often, actually. Especially to see Rose … I didn't know about the disease, though.'

'Neither did I.'

'I heard rumours it was exposure to the Core for too long. Any truth to that?'

'Not that I'm aware. Where'd you hear that?'

'I don't know. Maybe the news,' he said as he sat down across from her, sculling half of his glass.

'Sounds like they're just trying to find a connection between Deisy's accident and Miles's … They haven't pestered you too much?'

'Honestly, I haven't seen them in months. I imagine they haven't spared you, though.'

'If it's not them, it's the government. There's not a lot we do without them looking over our shoulders now. They couldn't be more desperate to have the devices in their hands.'

'Can you blame them? I'm surprised they haven't already torn the company to the ground. National security concerns and whatnot.' He paused, quietening his voice. 'Do any of them know?'

'No. The board's been very thorough and consistent in their story. Eventually, they'll assign a new CEO too. Someone young, I suspect. A major reform will keep everything at bay eventually.'

Ryder nodded. 'Maybe, then, they'll finally do more.'

'Maybe … but not soon enough.'

'What are you saying?'

Alice's expression fell grim. 'We figured out the identities of the other five.'

Ryder reluctantly watched as Alice pulled out her touchpad and handed it to him from across the table.

'Tracking Connor's history, interactions, social circles and who's been missing since, we were able to figure out who it was,' she explained.

Ryder took the screen and looked over it. He swiped through each page, finding the photos and IDs of all five masked culprits.

Hughes Avil

Issa Lionel

Ode Scarlett

Grey Pines

Ian Russ

Finally, at the end, their leader.

Connor Mavire

He stared down at Connor's photo; a man in his mid-forties, most distinguished by his grey stubble. His face on the laboratory security footage still plagued Ryder's mind.

Before long, he forced himself to hand the touchpad back to Alice. 'Why are you showing me this?'

'You know why.'

He shook his head. 'She never wanted people to go back. There's a reason it's disallowed. You're just gonna trample on that?'

'It already has been, Ryder. None of that mattered the moment *they* took it and went back. And we're still here. It's not like more people going back is going to change that. We know that it's possible to go back and keep our reality intact.'

Ryder refrained from so much as looking at her.

'You remember her last words just as much as I do,' she continued in pain. 'These people have taken our creation and *perverted* it for their own use, and they continue to get away with it. It's *our* responsibility to fix that.'

'Why? Why are you asking *me?* Why can't you and Forward Industries just do it?'

'Because I don't know how long that'll take. Probably years. Maybe never. They just *barely* managed enough resources to discover these identities at all. They're walking on thin glass with the press, the public, *and* the government. *Every* world is watching them. One slip-up and the truth could come out. They can't afford that. *That* is their priority, not finding these people.'

'And you think me going back is going to make things *better*?'

'It'll probably set them back even further, yes, but at least then someone will be doing right by Deisy and her life's work. *We're* the only people that can do this. She knew the responsibility we had when we created such a thing. We *have* to live up to that for her. We *can't* let her down now. We can't just *let them* get away with this.'

'If we even were to do such a thing, why wouldn't we just go back and save *her* then? Not go looking for *them*, just save *her*, bring *her* back here.'

Alice's shoulders dropped as her voice softened. 'You know she would never let us do something like that. And that's different than going after Connor's people. If we went back and tried to save her, then it could have untold impacts on the future. You *know* the paradoxes it could create. But Connor's people are where they don't belong. Taking them out theoretically wouldn't change anything if we did it right.'

Ryder stared at his drink.

'I trust you, Ryder,' she insisted. 'You have *years* of experience dealing with the worst of the worst out there. You know what to do and how to do it. Deisy is – … That's set in stone. I'm just proposing something that we *can* do …'

Ryder closed his eyes and sighed a long breath, before finally returning to Alice's gaze. 'Alice … I can't leave Rose.'

Alice's determination shattered as soon as his words struck her. She closed her eyes and took a silent breath of her own. At last, she nodded and returned to her feet. 'I'm sorry … Keep well, Ryder.'

With nothing more said between them, Alice walked towards the front door, leaving the touchpad on the table. Stopping before Rose's bedroom, she quietly peeked inside. Rose was fast asleep in her crib. Alice smiled for just a moment before another wave of sorrow overshadowed her and she left the apartment.

Ryder sat in silence.

His eyes welled with tears as his body began to shake. After forcing the rest of the glass down, he marched back into the kitchen and yanked the lid off the whiskey bottle. Sculling it, he stumbled against the wall, drinking until there was nothing left.

Tears streamed down his cheeks as he returned to the hallway. The front door caught his eye, staring back at him. He gritted his teeth and threw the bottle at the door, smashing it to pieces. Fighting the urge to scream, he slid down against the wall and onto the floor.

Unable to hold himself together any longer, he broke down and cried into his arms.

* * *

Lights violently flickered at the end of the laboratory hallway. With each flash, a group of six silhouettes appeared, drawing closer and closer.

At the opposite end of the hallway, lying in a never-ending pool of blood, was Deisy. She forced her eyes open as blood continually seeped out of the bullet hole in her forehead.

Blood rippled beneath each step the followers took. All of them gripped a handgun by their side as they marched straight towards her. Deisy groaned as she fought to pull herself up, but it was impossible.

Finally, the silhouettes stopped before her, pointing their handguns down at her as she tried to speak, yet she had no voice.

They opened fire. Deisy twisted and writhed in the blood as she was riddled with bullets. More blood burst out of her chest and legs and mouth. Their guns continued, over and over, never ceasing.

The gunshots echoed further and further away, until …

Ryder's eyes slowly opened as he lay on his couch. The sun shone through the apartment windows. Half a dozen empty bottles laid across the living room floor as he groaned and forced himself to sit up. Upon leaning forward, he felt sick to his stomach.

'Ah, fuck,' he mumbled.

Pulling himself to his feet, he wobbled towards the kitchen. As he passed the front hallway, he noticed Rose was there, sitting on the floor beside dozens of pieces of broken glass, her arms sliced open and bleeding.

His heart skipped a beat as she looked up at him, confused. 'Oh – oh, Rosy, Rosy, Rosy – get away from that.' He rushed over and picked her up.

'What happened, Daddy? It hurts,' she said as she looked at her bleeding arms.

'It's okay, it's okay, you're just – you're just …' He panicked as he carried her back towards the kitchen. Sitting her on the bench, he scoured through the drawers and pulled out bandages before desperately patching them over her cuts.

'Daddy, what's happened?'

'I – I …' He looked at her as she stared back at him with a puzzled gaze. His focus returned to her arms, trying to rub off the blood around her bandages. The blood smeared across his fingers as his lips quivered uncontrollably. He rested his head against the corner of the bench, fighting to contain himself one last time before he finally burst into tears. 'I'm so sorry … I'm so sorry, Rosy.'

Seeing her father in tears, Rose began to cry with him.

'Oh no, baby,' he gasped as he picked her up and carried her out of the kitchen. Holding her tight, he attempted to restrain his tears again. 'I'm sorry … I'm sorry.' He stroked her hair and cradled her up and down. 'It's okay, it's going to be okay.' He walked through the apartment as she continued crying into his shoulder. Gradually, he noticed Alice's touchpad still sitting and waiting atop the dining table. The images of each culprit returned to him, burning themselves into his memory before a thought came to him.

What if I did find them?

With that single thought, came something Ryder had not felt in a long, long time.

Relief.

* * *

Night had fallen across the outer city as Ryder walked along a lonely sidewalk. A soft layer of mist hung in the air. His breath was visible, and his shoes squelched on the wet pavement. He held an electronic basket by his side as he looked across the street towards a tall, narrow building. At its front was an electronic sign reading *Tallgate Orphanage.*

He scanned both sides of the shadowy street, seeing only a few distant citizens walking to and fro. Taking a heavy breath, he marched across the street and climbed the front steps. Upon reaching the entrance to the orphanage, he was consumed by a sickly, yellow light that hummed overhead. The basket's handle stabilised as he gently rested it before the front door.

He knelt down beside it and quietly opened the lid. Rose slept soundly inside under a small blanket. The blood had been washed off her and fresh bandages covered her arms. Carefully reaching out his hand, he stroked her cheek and smiled through his tears. '*I love you.*'

From his pocket, he pulled out a folded note. After resting it on the blanket, he pulled out the small jewellery box and opened it, staring at the seashell necklace inside.

His eyes returned to Rose, hesitating.

She shouldn't have it, he thought. *She can't.*

Closing the jewellery box, he bent down and kissed her forehead. He closed the basket and buzzed the front door. Immediately, he turned and walked halfway down the steps before stopping in his tracks. He turned back, reluctant to take another step.

Voices rose from inside the building.

He stared at the crib sitting all on its own.

Footsteps approached the door.

Ryder inhaled a sharp breath, almost ready to lunge back up the stairs, before he suddenly forced himself the other way and walked into the mist. As he pushed himself further and further away, he pulled the necklace out from its box and placed it around his neck. He clasped the seashell tightly in his hand as he swiftly disappeared into the shadows.

* * *

Later that same night, Alice slipped into her pyjamas in her compact, high-rise apartment bathroom. She gazed at herself in the mirror, noticing her dark skin was turning pale before a knock came at her front door.

She paused for a moment, confused as to who would come at such an hour. Keeping her feet light, she approached the entrance and peered through the peephole. Her eyes widened at the sight of what she found, before she opened the door. 'Ryder?'

He looked at her with sleepless eyes, his hands buried in his pockets. 'Hey … may I?'

She stared at him for a moment, worried, before stepping aside.

'Thank you.' He nodded, entering the apartment with a bowed head.

'Would you like a drink?' she asked, closing the door behind him.

'Just some water, thank you.'

Still tentative, she walked into the kitchen and filled a glass of water for him. He approached the tall windows, staring out at the dark city. Taking it in.

'Here,' she said, walking up behind him and holding out his glass.

He turned and took it from her as his hands shook. 'Thank you.'

She noticed the seashell hanging from his neck. 'Is Rosy being looked after?'

He gazed back out of the window as he sipped the water. 'She's safe.'

'At your apartment?'

He shook his head. 'She can't be around me anymore, Alice. Not any of it.'

'What did you *do?*'

'*She's safe, all right? Trust me,*' he snapped, his voice almost shattering. 'She's far away from here and won't ever have to remember any of this.'

Alice's shoulders fell as she realised. 'You're going to do it?'

'Yeah.'

'You're not coming back for her?'

'You really think I can? I go and that's *it*. Even if I do survive, which I won't, I can't come back. And what, are you gonna raise her? Do you want that?'

Alice's eyes trailed to the floor, saying nothing.

'No. The further away she is, the better,' he continued before settling his nerves. 'I'm going to need to train for a while. Study everything I can. Prepare myself. It's been a long time since I've done anything like this.'

'I'll help you,' she assured him. 'I've already started working out the dates they travelled to. Decoding signals from the Core is complicated; the readings are rough and not exact, but it's enough to go off of. Then we can figure out a plan. I can get you into a gauntlet, but we'll have to make it look like you're working alone. It's not going to be easy.'

'I know.' He nodded, staring at the reflection of the seashell dangling around his neck.

* * *

Ryder pulled the necklace out of the chilled water. Its curves were still stained with blood. He looked at it with defeat before a croaking voice whispered from the misty woods around him.

'I'll find you.'

His head shot up, and he twisted around, seeing no one.

'Not soon enough,' another voice said.

His eyes widened as he peered in between the trees. The voices sounded distant, yet close. Still, there was no one else in sight.

Remaining cautious, Ryder pulled his bag up to his side. After dusting away small fractures of ice, he zipped it open and removed a small bottle of pills. He threw his head back, swallowing two of them. Finally, he closed his bag and gazed upon the necklace in his hand.

Come on. You know why you're here. Don't make it all for nothing now.

She doesn't need you. Deisy does.

Ryder clenched his fist around the seashell, before sliding it back over his head. Standing up, he swung the bag onto his back and began his trek through the old forest.

Far above the trees, the circular lookout towers of a mediaeval castle distinguished the horizon.

Chapter 11

Warwickshire, England, 1348 CE

Rays of light beamed through the branches and leaves above, shining upon Ryder as he approached the edge of the forest. Soon, a line of rudimentary houses became visible between the trees. Yet, there were no sounds of life.

He paused at the end of the forest, using a tree as cover as he listened out for any voices or movement. Still, there was nothing.

Ryder cautioned his step as he exited the forest. Entering the muddy street of the village, two rows of wattle and daub houses surrounded him. They were all small, roughly assembled and crooked. The wind howled through the street as one of the house's doors slowly opened and closed on its own, repeatedly banging on its frame.

Where the hell is everyone? he wondered.

Keeping his hand beside his holster, the hunter wandered through the empty village. There were clothes hanging from the windowsills and tools lying beside the doors. He turned his gaze ahead, beyond the houses, where he spotted the circular towers of Warwick Castle. After another glance at his surroundings, he followed the street in the castle's direction.

Soon, the sounds of clapping, cheering, and laughter neared. The smell of cooking meat wafted by with the wind. Ryder's pace quickened, curiously listening to the festive sounds. Upon reaching the end of the village, he found himself standing before a bright green field covered in colourful tents, flags, and countless villagers enjoying a boisterous festival. The women wore a mixture of green and brown smocks, as well as dresses with bonnets. Meanwhile, the men donned tunics, trousers, and leggings.

Ryder slipped in amongst the crowds and smiled at the sight of it all. The strings of lutes and high notes of flutes whistled through the air. He strolled by archery contests, groups of dancers bouncing up and down on their toes, tents filled with fresh meat and mead, and performers juggling sticks of fire. Yet, the further he walked, the more his eyes sharpened. He monitored every tent and festivalgoer that he passed by.

This is certainly a hot spot, he thought. *A good chance whoever fled here will be close by. Hopefully, that makes this search much easier than the last.*

Suddenly, Ryder felt a tap on his shoulder. He spun around, subtly grabbing his holster before finding a jester standing in his way, wearing a feathered hat and flamboyantly puffy clothes.

Mesmerised, the jester reached out towards his coat.

Ryder stepped back as they stared at each other in silence.

Maintaining eye contact, the jester continued to ever so slowly extend his hand. Finally, he felt the coat's material in between his fingers. 'What *strange* clothes you wear, sir. May I inquire as to how you made these? I have never felt anything quite like it.'

Ryder almost chuckled as he brushed his hand off him. 'I didn't make them.'

The jester tilted his head. 'Then wherever did you get them?'

'You wouldn't know it.'

The jester paused for a moment, staring at him with an inquisitive gaze. Before long, he let out a playful smile and lifted up one of Ryder's circular distraction grenades, 'Why, another *even stranger* object in your bag. Whatever does it do?'

Ryder's eyes widened before he snatched the device back. '*Don't touch that.*'

''Twas but a jest,' he said with an apologetic bow. 'What does bring you to Warwickshire then, good sir?'

Ryder hesitated a moment, studying his mannerisms. Eventually, his gaze drifted back towards the surrounding crowds, continuing to scan them for his next target, 'I'm looking for someone. Has anyone new or unusual passed through here in recent months?'

'New faces come and go from these parts quite regularly. Is there someone of a specific description you search for?'

'There's a few people actually, but I don't know which one is here. Do the names Connor, Ode, Grey, or Ian mean anything to you?'

The jester thought for a moment. 'Hm. I don't believe so. Where might they have come from?'

'They may sound similar to me. Or look ... different to your usual people.'

'Like you?'

'Yeah.'

The jester's eyes fell into greater reflection. 'I will put some thought to it. The festival will be running for another two days. Will you be here till the end?'

'I might be.'

'Then if I have news, I will find you.'

'Thank you ... and next time, a simple "Hello" will do.'

'Of course, I'm afraid my curiosity got the best of me. I do apologise,' he assured him with another bow. 'My name is Hamo.'

'Ryder.'

'Welcome to Warwickshire, O good Ryder,' he said with the shake of his hand.

A bell rang in the distance, drawing all of the townsfolk in its direction.

'What's that?' Ryder asked.

'Only the highlight of the festival, of course! I must be quick, but please, enjoy the show.' He smiled before scurrying off through the crowd.

Ryder shook his head and almost chuckled once more, beginning to follow the villagers. As the crowd cleared the last line of tents, a long rectangular stadium appeared behind them. It was surrounded by four sides of multileveled seating, where everyone was gathering to watch a spectacle below.

Amidst the shuffling crowd, Ryder approached the stands and leant against one of the wooden rails between him and a dirt track. Excited chatter filled the air as he scanned the crowds around him, searching for any familiar faces.

Hamo and two other performers entered the arena, juggling sticks of fire. They continually spun them high into the air before twisting around each other and catching them. In one final trick, Hamo caught all four sticks and blew on the flames, producing a spectacular burst of fire.

The crowd clapped and oohed at the sight.

Ryder nodded to himself. *Not bad, Hamo. Not bad.*

His eyes trailed upwards and caught sight of who he assumed was Warwick's very own ruler, on the opposite side of the arena. The figure sat down in his reserved royal seating, shaded by a pitched roof. His face was lean and pale, while his blue cape and engraved armour glimmered amidst the crowd. He was surrounded by his own personal guard of knights, each of them fully armoured and helmeted, maintaining a stern eye on everything and everyone.

As the entertainers cleared the arena, an announcer stepped out before the people. 'Hear ye, hear ye!' he cried out, silencing the crowd. 'Despite his many obligations, and much of his family abroad, our great earl, Thomas Beauchamp, has put time aside to grace us with his presence and spectate our festival's wondrous jousting games!'

The crowd clapped as the earl raised his hand, nodding and waving to those around him.

'Today,' the announcer continued, 'Our games shall commence with two most famous of jousters! On my right, Wilmot the Second of Lincoln!'

The audience gave a sobered applause for Wilmot as he rode into the arena, donning silver armour that shimmered in the sun. Attached to his breastplate was a layer of blue fabric with the symbol of a lion sewn into its centre. Holding his lance by his side, he steadied his horse at one end of the track.

'And on my left, our famous traveller from a land *far away!* A man Wilmot has been brave enough to challenge! Arnest Ansel, the *undefeated!*' he shouted, sending the crowd into a frenzy as they stood up and roared with excitement.

Ryder's eyes focused on the revered jouster.

Red stripes distinguished Arnest's armour, while a horned helmet concealed his face. He rode past the crowds and thrust his joust into the air. The villagers clapped, cheered, and whistled with all of their might.

The digital images of a handsome man with a defined jaw, blue eyes, and silver hair bled into Ryder's mind.

Tall. Strong. Loving the attention. And from a "far away land"? Ryder thought.

Grey Pines. It might just be him. He fits the description too well. A conman through and through, and what better way to use his skills than to trick a whole village into treating him like a hero? Typical.

Arnest flipped the lance around in his hand as he rode towards the opposite end of the arena.

'Let the games *begin*!' the announcer cried out before stepping off the tracks.

A royal musician stepped forth, lifting a golden trumpet to his mouth. The crowd fell silent. Arnest and Wilmot steadied their horses at both ends of the arena. They aimed their lances at one another, gripping them tightly, waiting.

Finally, the musician blew a short, loud note. The jousters whipped the reins of their horses. Their hooves kicked up dirt and rode straight towards one another. The men bounced up and down on their saddles, having mere seconds to aim their lances correctly.

Just as they were about to pass each other, Arnest thrust his lance forward, smacking it into Wilmot's chest. His breastplate caved in as he flew off his horse and crashed onto the ground. His horse skidded to a stop while his own lance bounced onto the dirt beside him.

The crowd erupted into an ecstatic roar. Arnest, having barely broken a sweat, thrust his lance into the air once again.

Wilmot groaned in pain as he rolled onto his chest and fought to push himself up. As his arms extended, they gave out beneath him, and he collapsed back onto the ground. A handful of royal assistants rushed over to help him.

The announcer stepped back onto the tracks with open arms. 'Arnest the Undefeated earns his title once more! What a glorious beginning! With more royal guests joining us, the games shall continue shortly. And any of those wishing to challenge Arnest themselves, step up, and pray that God may be on your side!'

The audience laughed as Wilmot was dragged off the track. Arnest strolled his horse back towards the arena's exit, waving to the crowd. Ryder kept his eyes locked on him as he sifted through the crowd. He followed him out of the arena and watched as he rode across the field, heading towards a large red-and-white-striped tent.

Ryder glanced at the surrounding festival. Only a few villagers remained, tending to their own business. Free from prying eyes, he continued forth, keeping his distance as Arnest stopped before the striped tent. He jumped off his horse and patted its neck. Two stableboys congratulated him before walking the horse away.

Ryder watched as Arnest disappeared inside the tent. He swiftly neared the entrance and stopped beside it. His eyes scoured behind him again, ensuring no one was watching. He pulled back the side of his coat, readying his hand beside his holster.

In and out, he told himself. *Just be quick.*

Ryder tightened his lips and sucked in his breath before pushing open the tent's flaps and stepping inside. There were three rows of tables and chairs, all covered with equipment and tools for the jousting games. Meanwhile, Arnest sat alone, facing away from Ryder as he removed his helmet. He placed it down on the wooden table with an exhausted breath.

Ryder paused, seeing that this man did not have Grey's distinctive silver hair. It was black. Arnest turned his head, revealing his dark stubble and brown eyes.

Shit. It's not him.

'Who are you?' Arnest asked in a thick German accent.

'Sorry. Wrong tent.' Ryder pulled his coat back over his holster and turned around. He walked straight for the exit before the flaps opened before him.

Sir Terric, the general of the knights, stepped inside, blocking his path. They both froze in place, staring at one another.

'I don't know who this man is,' Arnest said, looking at Ryder with caution.

Ryder lifted his hands. 'It's just a misunderstanding. I walked into the wrong tent, that's all.'

'Who in God's name are you?' Terric asked, his gaze turning hostile.

'I'm just passing through and visiting the festival. I'm sorry, I'll get out of your way.' He took another step towards the exit.

Terric unsheathed his sword. 'Guards!'

Ryder reached for his holster before Terric stepped forward, grabbed his collar and pressed his blade against his throat. *'Ah-ah. Don't move.'*

Two armoured and helmeted knights pushed open the tent's flaps. Without hesitation, they unsheathed their swords and pointed them at Ryder.

'State your business, stranger,' Terric demanded.

'I told you, I entered the wrong tent. This was just a mistake.'

Terric's eyes sharpened. 'Your accent. Where are you from?'

'A place far from here. You wouldn't know it, but I can tell you about it if you lower your sword.'

'You think you're in a position to *barter*? I don't know about where you're from, but here we don't take kindly to strangers prying about in other people's business.' He gestured to the two knights. 'Take his things.'

One knight pulled Ryder's handgun out from his holster, while the other stripped his bag off his back. The first knight held his handgun upside down, drawing everyone's curious eyes.

Terric gazed back at Ryder, increasingly suspicious. His eyes fell towards the hunter's sleeve, noticing a peculiar shape underneath it. He pulled back the sleeve, revealing his metallic gauntlet and its beeping lights. His eyes returned to Ryder, almost frightened. 'Remove this … *thing*.'

The second knight reached for the gauntlet. Ryder hesitated and pulled it away.

'Nuh-uh-uh,' Terric repeated, pressing his blade deeper into his neck.

Ryder forced himself to remain still, glaring at the general. Meanwhile, the knight tugged at the gauntlet, but it did not come off. He spent a short time fiddling with it from all sides, but still, it would not budge. "

Terric impatiently watched as the knight continued to fumble about with the device. 'Go on, I say! *Remove it.*'

'I'm trying, sir. I just … I don't know how this works. I've never seen armour like this.'

'There's got to be a way. *Find it.*'

The knight awkwardly bent down, inspecting the gauntlet closer as he squinted at it through his helmet.

In an instant, Ryder gritted his teeth and smacked the gauntlet up into the knight's head. His helmet rattled back and forth, disorienting him as he stumbled backwards. Ryder kicked Terric away before the first knight swung his sword at him. He ducked and dodged the blade, thrusting his shoulder into the knight's chest, knocking him onto one of the tables.

He turned and reached for his handgun before Arnest tackled him to the ground. Ryder attempted to grab at his face as the jouster sat atop his chest and pinned his arms beneath his knees. Terric and the first knight swiftly returned and pointed their swords at the hunter.

Meanwhile, the second knight stumbled to his feet, struggling to readjust his crooked helmet.

Terric shot a frustrated glare towards him. *'Idiot!'*

Arnest curiously inspected the gauntlet. He slid his finger alongside it before finding a small hole. Poking his finger inside it, he pressed a button and unclamped the device from Ryder's wrist. He smiled with wonder. 'I think I did it.'

The first knight reached for the device. Ryder grunted and pulled his arm away. Terric placed a boot on his arm, keeping it in place as the knight slid the gauntlet off his wrist. Ryder's chest heaved as he watched the knight hand the device to Terric, who carefully inspected its form.

'Excellent find, Arnest. I will ensure the earl sees these strange contraptions.' The general glanced back at Ryder and smirked. 'As for you, stranger, I think we just found our next challenger.'

A short time later, Ryder was marched across the field and towards the arena by Terric and a handful of knights. Ryder gazed at the gauntlet in Terric's hand. He clenched his fists as sweat dripped from his palms and his breath began to shorten.

Come on, Ryder, what have you done? This is ridiculous. It's <u>insane</u>.

You just have to get it back. You <u>have</u> to.

Another knight jogged up beside the general, handing him a thin and crippled leather breastplate. 'As you requested, sir.'

'Perfect. Thank you, Gregory.' Terric took the armour and passed it to Ryder. 'Here you are, stranger.'

Ryder looked at the breastplate, barely held together by string. '*This* is my armour?'

'Be grateful you're getting any.'

Ryder tilted his head in frustration before he was escorted into the busy arena. Musicians played cheerful music while entertainers continued their synchronised acts in front of the crowd. Hamo juggled sticks of fire as Ryder and the knights passed them by.

The jester's smile faded as he noticed them. 'Oh, no.'

Ryder spotted a horse further ahead, held steady by one of the stableboys. He stopped and reluctantly slid the flimsy armour over his head. Before he could finish putting it on, Terric pushed him towards the horse. Ryder almost fell over before he regained his footing and scowled at Terric, who gestured back towards the steed.

The announcer stepped onto the arena track as a trumpet blast silenced the music and crowd. 'Welcome again, ladies and gentlemen!' he shouted. 'It seems, in this short time, that the impossible has come true! A challenger has volunteered himself against Arnest the Undefeated! I best hope he went to church and prayed to God all day and night before this!'

The crowd laughed, and the earl smirked with them, curiously eyeing Ryder from his royal seating.

Ryder bit his tongue and held his head low, attempting to conceal his face from the crowd. He turned and looked back at the horse as it restlessly huffed and puffed.

How the hell do I even ride this thing?

Gradually, he approached the horse, holding up his hands and speaking to it under his breath, 'Okay, it's okay. It's okay. Sorry, buddy, I'm just … I'm just gonna get on top of you now. I guess.' Ryder gripped the top of the saddle and slid his foot through the stirrup. Bouncing himself up and down, he attempted to pull himself up. Without enough force, he put his foot back down on the ground and straightened his foot in the stirrup again.

'Perhaps there should be a challenge to see who can mount their horse the fastest!' the announcer cried.

The audience roared with laughter.

Ryder gritted his teeth. '*Fuckin' hell.*' He let out a nervous smile and snickered at himself, 'Come on. *Just do it.*' Giving himself more momentum, he finally pulled himself up onto the saddle. He almost slid off the other side before he gripped the horse's neck and straightened his stance. Shaking the sweat from his hands, he noticed the crowd pointing at him and murmuring to each other.

'Well, it's about time,' the announcer remarked, entertaining the crowd once more.

A knight approached Ryder and handed him a three-metre-long lance. Unable to mask his annoyance, the hunter yanked the lance out of his hands.

The general entered the stands, standing behind the earl as he crossed his arms and smiled in amusement.

'Returning to the arena, our most skilled jouster, Arnest the Undefeated!' the announcer howled.

The crowd flew into an infectious cheer as Arnest rode into the opposite end of the arena. He donned his horned helmet and thrust his lance into the air.

Amidst the fanfare, Hamo hurriedly walked up beside Ryder. '*What are you doing up there?*'

'Trust me, this *wasn't* my idea.'

'Whatever did you do?'

'Made a mistake,' Ryder explained as he eyed the exits of the arena. All of them were blocked by rows of knights.

'By the looks of you getting on the horse, it's as if you've never even ridden one before.'

Ryder looked back down at him, silent.

A great worry came over Hamo's face. 'Oh, a big mistake, indeed.'

'Can you get me out of here?'

'I could offer a word to the earl, but it seems a little late for that and unlikely he would even listen to me on such a trivial matter.'

'*Trivial matter?*'

'Well, in the grand scheme of things, yes. You are just *one man* on a horse. Despite my attire and skills in entertainment, my voice is usually needed for much more indispensable political matt – '

'All right, I get it, I get it!' Ryder bit his lips as his chest tightened. 'Got any tips for me, then?'

'Just squeeze your legs in to get the horse moving, whip the reins to make it go faster, pull them to stop it, and whatever you do, *don't get hit by his lance.*'

'How do I hit *him*?'

'You won't, so don't worry about that. Just focus on not getting yourself hit.'

Ryder nodded along with his words, taking a moment to process them. 'All right, then. I'm sure that'll be … easy enough.'

'Good luck,' Hamo uttered, anxiously patting the horse and walking back behind the rails.

Ryder gazed at Terric in the stands, cringing at the sight of the gauntlet in his hand.

The announcer called out once more, 'To grace our presence in watching the next match, please welcome our earl's lovely daughter, Margaret de Beauchamp, and her new husband, and son-in-law to the earl himself, Guy de Montfort!'

The crowd clapped and whistled. All eyes turned towards the eighteen-year-old Lady Margaret, and the tall, silver-haired Lord Guy as they entered the stands, waving and bowing to the villagers.

Ryder gradually sat up as his eyes widened, recognising Guy's blue eyes, chiselled jaw, and smug grin.

Oh, you gotta be kidding me.

Grey Pines is fucking royalty.

Chapter 12

The arena crowd was lively with chatter. Meanwhile, the earl was silent, continuing to watch Ryder from afar. He leant back in his chair, half-turning to Terric. 'Sir Terric, who is this jouster?'

'We caught him sneaking about in the entertainers' tent, my lord.' Terric held out his hand to a knight beside him. The knight handed him Ryder's backpack before he passed it to the earl. 'These are his belongings. They are unusual, to say the least.'

Margaret, sitting beside the earl, gazed at the backpack. 'Why, what a peculiar-looking bag.' She glanced at Grey beside her, who was busy smiling and waving to the crowd. 'Don't you think, my love?'

'I'm sorry?' he replied, turning his head and pausing at the sight of Ryder's bag.

The earl opened it, discovering an array of pills and supplies. A moment later, Terric handed him Ryder's handgun, and finally, his gauntlet.

Grey's eyes bulged open before darting towards Ryder, who was already staring back at him from atop his horse.

'If I was to guess,' Terric added, 'they seem like some forms of advanced weaponry and armour.'

'They look more like witchcraft to me,' Margaret said.

The earl looked over the gauntlet's glowing lights and numbers, unsettled and amazed. His fingers almost shook as he felt its cold exterior. 'I have never seen anything like it.'

'Nor I,' Terric agreed.

'Do you know what his intention was?' Grey hastily asked. 'What was he doing when you found him?'

'I'm unsure. He was in the tent with Arnest, the jouster. I suspect he may have been there to harm him.'

'The man can barely ride a horse,' the earl countered.

The crowd began to quieten.

Margaret nudged Grey's arm and hushed her voice. 'It's your turn to speak, my love.'

Grey hesitated, glancing back at the hunter. After clearing his throat, he climbed to his feet and put on a smile. 'Good morning, all! I am joyous to see you gathered here on … on such a fine day. Shall it be a riveting and unforgettable festival! Cheer and be merry, and let us see Arnest earn his title once more! Let the games *begin*!'

The crowd cheered as the royal musician stepped forth, preparing his golden trumpet. Grey sat back down and gazed at Ryder, whose eyes continued to burn through him.

Eventually, Ryder turned back to his opponent, readjusting his grip on the lance. Meanwhile, Arnest let out a calm, deep breath.

They waited in a heavy silence.

At last, the trumpet blasted.

Arnest squeezed his legs and eased his horse forward. In an attempt to copy his movement, Ryder squeezed his own legs inwards, yet nothing happened. His horse remained completely still.

Dammit. Come on, move!

Ryder awkwardly whipped the reins and squeezed his legs tighter.

At last, the horse began trotting forward.

Thank you, he thought, sighing with relief.

Gradually, both horses quickened their pace.

All right, come on, Ryder told himself. *We might as well try and hit him.*

Leaning forward on his saddle, Ryder beckoned the horse to move faster. In his closing window of time, he attempted to turn his lance towards his opponent. Arnest began straightening his own aim as they grew closer and closer.

Within moments their horses had broken into a sprint, racing towards one another as Ryder's lance was aimed too wide, while Arnest's was pointed directly at his chest.

'*Shit!*' Ryder ducked and pulled at the reins, yanking his horse to its side and narrowly dodging Arnest's lance as he rode past.

The crowd oohed and aahed, while others moaned with disappointment. The horses slowed down and rode towards opposite ends of the arena. Arnest gripped his lance tighter and cracked his head side to side. Ryder clumsily pulled at the reins again to turn his horse around and face his opponent.

Ryder glanced at the royal stands as Grey eyed him back with nervous anticipation.

Come on, you can do this. You can do this.

Ryder tensed his arm and turned his focus back to Arnest. Without warning, Arnest whipped the reins on his horse harder and faster than before. Ryder's heart jumped in his chest. He followed suit and fought to correct his lance's aim. Arnest gritted his teeth and aimed his lance straight towards Ryder, about to strike him.

At the last second, Ryder swung his lance like a sword, smacking his opponent's lance out of the way just before contact.

The earl raised his eyebrows, Hamo bit his bottom lip, Terric chuckled, Grey shuffled in his seat, Arnest groaned, and Ryder caught his breath.

Once again, the combatants rode to opposite ends of the arena and turned around. Ryder felt the muscles in his arm burning as he lifted the lance.

I'm going to get too tired for this. I just need to hit him while I can still lift this damn thing.

Arnest grunted and squeezed his legs in. His horse bolted forward as he aimed his lance at Ryder. Leaning forward on his own saddle, Ryder urged his horse forward. He glanced upon his lance, noticing his aim was off-centre once again.

Just hold it like a knife, he thought to himself.

With little time left, Ryder flipped the lance around in his hand.

The crowd held their breath.

Just as the jousters came upon one another, Ryder lifted his lance into the air and stabbed it down in between Arnest's shoulder guard, ripping it clean off as Arnest's own pole smacked into Ryder's chest. Instantly, the hunter lost his breath and was flung off the side of his horse, crashing onto the ground.

With a striking pain in his shoulder, Arnest dropped his lance and gripped the saddle to keep himself from falling off.

The crowd were stunned into silence.

Margaret's eyes widened as she leant forward in her seat. 'Arnest has *never* been struck before! I never thought it possible, especially in such a manner as that!'

'Yes … remarkable,' Terric muttered.

Ryder lay face down on the arena tracks. Hamo watched him from the stands, his eyes filled with disappointment. Arnest's right arm drooped in pain as he slowed his horse to a halt and glanced at Ryder, who remained silent and motionless.

The crowd began to murmur and whisper.

Eventually, Grey's shoulders settled in relief as a smile grew across his face. 'Well, he sure put up a fight, didn't he? 'Tis a shame he didn't make it.'

Then … *Ryder's fingers twitched.* Hamo's eyes lit with hope.

His arms began to bend. Arnest removed his helmet in disbelief.

His eyes flickered open. Grey's smile began to fade.

He placed his hands on the ground. The earl sat upright in his chair.

He gritted his teeth. Margaret's jaw dropped.

Saliva dripped from his mouth. Terric rested his hand on his hilt.

At last, Ryder pushed himself to his feet, straightened his shoulders, and laid his eyes upon one man. *Grey Pines.*

Grey anxiously peeked at the others beside him, ensuring they did not notice where the hunter's fury was pointed.

The announcer stood frozen for a moment. He blinked and regained his focus before stepping forward. 'Wh – what a battle, ladies and gentlemen! *What a battle!* Give your applause to our brave challenger, and Arnest the Undefeated!'

The crowd cheered, clapped, and whistled.

All the while, Ryder's deathly gaze remained unbroken.

Arnest's curiosity grew as he noticed his opponent's glare towards Lord Guy.

'The games shall continue tomorrow!' the announcer said. 'May you all enjoy the rest of the day's festivities!'

The crowds began to disperse from the arena as Margaret spoke to her father. 'He may not be able to ride a horse very well, but he was certainly able to hold his own against Arnest, better than most other jousters I've seen.'

'Yes, that is indeed so, my dear,' the earl replied. 'I wish to know who he is and why he is here.'

Grey gulped at the sight of Ryder before he turned to the earl. 'Allow *me* to talk to him, my lord. I'll discern if he's a danger and act accordingly.'

The earl eyed his son-in-law up and down, remaining silent for a time. 'So be it. I want to hear of your findings tonight.'

'Of course, my lord.'

'Margaret, we shall return to the castle. We must prepare for the feast,' the earl said, standing up.

Margaret nodded and kissed Grey's cheek. 'You must tell me all about him when you return. Be careful, my love.'

Grey forced a smile and patted her leg. 'I will.'

Terric turned to one of his knights. 'Remain here under Lord Guy's command.'

'Yes, sir.'

Terric escorted the earl and Margaret out of the stands as Grey sat still. He gazed back at Ryder, whose skin was turning pale and his eyes bloodshot. His broken armour hung from his shoulders as blood began to seep through his shirt. Even still, he remained resolute.

After a long breath, Grey exited the stands and entered the arena. Ryder clenched his fists and scanned his surroundings, noting the dozens of knights watching them from a distance.

Before long, Grey stood before him, face to face. He glanced around the arena, ensuring nobody was within earshot, before speaking in a manner that no longer held any royal flair. 'Well, you're not exactly very subtle, are you?'

'And you are?' Ryder retorted.

'Subtlety was never the aim. Skulking in the shadows was never going to get me to where I am now. Regardless, I can only assume you're here for me.'

Ryder remained silent.

'Wow.' Grey chuckled. 'I'm flattered … Ryder, isn't it?'

Ryder lifted his head with some surprise.

'I never do a job without knowing all of the players,' Grey boasted.

'But you didn't know Connor would kill her, did you?'

Grey's lips faltered. 'You've already spoken to one of the others?'

'Hughes. And Issa.'

'And what? They're dead?'

'What do *you* think?'

'I think they were young and stupid. They didn't know what they were getting themselves into.'

'Did *you?*'

Grey laughed. 'I could ask you the same thing. How long has this taken you already? You look like you've aged as many years as you've travelled, old man.'

'Well, lucky for me, it barely took me an hour to find you.'

'Yes, I am working on that front.'

'If you give me back my things and tell me what you know about Connor and the others, I'll leave.'

'What makes you think you have any power here?'

'I'm not the only one after you. I can tell you what I know.'

'I told you, *I'm* working on that front. And besides, you didn't come all this way just to let me go. I may not be subtle, but I'm not stupid.' He gestured his hand to the surrounding knights. 'I do appreciate your visit, though. The effort is admirable. And best of all, we're in this together now. Isn't that wonderful?' The knights marched over and grabbed hold of Ryder's arms. 'Take him to the dungeon.'

'Yes, my lord,' one of the knights replied with a nod.

Too weak to resist, the knights pulled Ryder along and escorted him out of the arena.

Grey watched on, contemplating, before turning and noticing Arnest atop his horse, eyeing him from further along the track. 'Oh, congratulations today, Arnest! You truly put on an excellent show. I imagine the people enjoyed it very much.'

'Come visit us and ask them yourself.'

'Yes, of course. One day … as soon as I have a chance.'

A silence befell them.

Grey continued nodding, thinking of what to say. 'Will – you and Lena be joining us for the feast tonight?'

'We will.'

'Excellent. You have certainly earned it. I shall see you both then, friend! Good day, now!' Grey exclaimed with a jolly chuckle.

Arnest forced a smile and nodded, turning his horse around and riding out of the arena. Immediately, Grey's chuckle dissipated as his focus returned to the castle.

* * *

Arnest's shoes squelched on the mud and dirt as he trekked through the now-vibrant village. His arm remained slumped by his side and his belongings slung over his shoulder as he passed the local pub and dozens of houses. Villagers walked their animals to and fro, while others gathered their clothes that hung outside. Arnest waved to each of them.

'Close one there today, ay, Arnest!' a villager called out.

Arnest smiled and nodded. 'Indeed it was.'

'Congratulations, Arnest!' another one shouted.

Then another.

And another.

One villager, with dark rings hanging under his eyes and a matted black beard, approached the jouster. 'Hello there, Arnest. I heard you almost lost today.'

'You weren't there?'

'I've been busy, I'm afraid. Roof is caving in again. Trying to gather the right materials for it.'

'I am sorry to hear it. When was the last time you slept, Osbert?'

'I wouldn't know. Wouldn't know.'

'Here.' Reaching into his bag, Arnest pulled out a handful of shillings and placed them into Osbert's hand. 'Put it to good use.'

'Ah, Arnest, you needn't do this. Are you sure?'

'Wouldn't have done it if I wasn't,' he said with a smile, patting Osbert's shoulder and continuing on his way.

Soon, he noticed another villager wheeling a barrow in his direction. Inside was a dead pig, partially covered by a grey blanket.

'You already went out today, Hopkin?' Arnest asked.

'Aye, needed at least *some* food for tonight,' Hopkin replied with a nod.

'Tell me next time. I'll give you a hand.'

'No need. This one's the last of them.'

'What?' Arnest stopped in his tracks.

'Yeah, she's the last. Something sick passed through the others. They're all gone, no good to eat.'

'Even your ones out back?'

'Come take a look,' he said, gesturing his head towards his decrepit home.

The two of them walked around to the rear of the house. Inside a small enclosure, a handful of pigs lay dead, covered in mud and swarmed by flies.

Arnest shook his head at the sight of it. 'Sickness got these ones too?'

'That's my guess. Don't know how it got them all, though. Ain't seen anything like it.'

'Mm.' Arnest nodded. 'We'll have to go hunting soon, then.'

'Aye. Make sure you steal me some food from the castle tonight while you're at it. Wouldn't mind some leftovers,' he added with a laugh.

Arnest chuckled and nodded. 'I'll see what I can do. Good day, Hopkin.'

'Good day … oh, and I'm bloody kicking myself I didn't see you get bested today! Make sure you lose next time I'm there, so I can see it for myself!'

Arnest smiled and waved away his remarks as he returned to the main street. Upon reaching the village's centre, Arnest was consumed by the looming shadow of St. Mary's Church. He gazed upwards, spotting a handful of builders extending portions of the gothic structure. Meanwhile, a large Christian cross stared down at him. He eyed it back, unimpressed.

Eventually, Arnest arrived at the outskirts of the village. He strolled over a small green hill and approached his home; the last house before nothing but vast stretches of green and brown fields. It was small and wooden, with a brown curved roof made of twigs and sticks.

Lena stood outside it, removing their dried clothes from the windowsills and folding them. Her golden-brown hair was long, and her smock was grey. She turned to see her husband returning over the hill before her smile faded. 'Oh my God, *you're hurt?*' she exclaimed with an accent almost as strong as his own.

Arnest shook his head and kissed her forehead. 'It's nothing, darling, it's nothing,' he assured her before approaching their front door. As he opened it, the door bent off its hinges and began to fall over. He leant forward and caught it before it fell too far.

Lena rushed over to the other side and helped him hold it in place. 'Come on, come inside. I've got it.'

He awkwardly stepped inside and took hold of the door for her. After loosely resting it on its frame, they both stepped back and caught their breath.

Shortly thereafter, she looked at him with disappointment. 'Nothing?' she continued, grabbing a wet cloth. 'Says the one who apparently "never" gets harmed.'

He smirked at her words, biting his tongue he slid his bag off his wounded shoulder. 'Well, to be fair, I haven't until now … and I still won.' He sat down beside their small, circular dining table.

'Really? You call this winning?' she remarked, sitting on his lap and sliding back his sleeve. Underneath she discovered a large red bruise across his shoulder. She shook her head and carefully dabbed her cloth on it. 'I'm glad I didn't see this one.'

'It was a good match, actually. You should have.'

'Who were you up against? Who did this?'

'I don't really know, actually. It was strange. He entered the jousting tent like he was looking for someone.'

She glanced at him with worry. 'Was it you?'

'No … well, I don't think so. He was leaving when he was caught by the earl's men. Then they forced him to joust against me. It was for their own amusement, I suppose. He doesn't look like any man I've ever seen before, though. Strange clothes, strange voice … and even stranger, he seemed to know Guy.'

'Really? How?'

'I don't know. Yet, after the match, with barely any words spoken between them, Guy had him taken to the dungeons.'

'Guy's ordering arrests now?'

'It seems so.'

Lena twisted her lips before resting the cloth over his shoulder. 'He's up to something. By God, they probably all are up in that castle.'

'Well, either way, we're still expected at their dinner tonight.'

Her shoulders dropped. 'Must we go?'

'Yes. I want you to have a decent meal for once. Hopkin was just telling me much of the livestock has died out.'

'Died out? *How?*'

'Some sort of sickness …'

'You don't think it's …?'

'I don't know. I just know you need to eat. And I want to talk to Guy. Perhaps he can help our troubles. Especially if things get worse.'

She sighed. 'Well, I tell you, they best be ready, then. I'm not going to hold back on their food.'

'Oh, they definitely won't be ready. And neither will this one,' he noted with a smile, placing his hand on her stomach.

The two of them chuckled and wrapped their arms around each other, falling into a passionate kiss.

* * *

Night swept across Warwick. Arnest and Lena walked towards the castle gates, arm in arm. Arnest wore a puffy shirt and leggings, while Lena donned an overgarment gown she had sewn herself.

'What do you think it's like in there?' she asked, gazing up at the approaching castle walls.

'Very clean, I'd say. And probably smells rather pleasant.'

'Well, that sounds nice, at least.'

They stopped before the tall gates as Arnest rolled his shoulder, wincing.

'Still feeling the pain?' she asked.

'No, no. I never feel pain.'

'Oh, yes, of course. How could I forget?' she remarked before poking his shoulder. He flinched as she giggled.

'You're dastardly!' he said with a playful smile.

At last, the castle gates opened before them, revealing the expansive grounds inside. The grass was finely cut, the gardens were lush, and the footpaths perfectly curved. General Terric and two of his knights stood at the entrance, awaiting them.

'Arnest,' Terric greeted with a small bow, 'it is an honour to welcome your presence here tonight. Anyone who delivers such rigorous performance in jousting certainly deserves a place within these walls.'

'No, please. We're immensely thankful for your invitation. This is much more of an honour for *us*,' he replied, shaking Terric's hand.

Terric turned to Lena and took her hand. 'And you must be …?'

'Lena.'

'Lena. It is a pleasure, milady,' Terric said, kissing her hand. 'Now, if you'll follow me.' With the turn of his heel, the general led the couple through the castle grounds.

Warm, glowing candles lit their path towards the inside of the castle as the gates creaked shut behind them.

Lena leant in close to her husband's ear and whispered, 'You're right. It *does* smell very nice here!'

Before the hour was over, the couple were seated at a long table in the dining hall, surrounded by dozens of other royal guests from throughout the country. The earl sat at the head of the table, with Grey and Margaret by his sides.

'I would like to commemorate this dinner to the first day of our wondrous festivities,' the earl announced to them all, 'and please, welcome our *special* guest and jousting victor of the day, Arnest the Undefeated.'

The guests broke into a round of applause as Arnest raised his hand and nodded, thankful.

'Enjoy the feast,' the earl concluded with a small smile.

The guests broke into discussion with one another as glorious servings of meat, fish, cheese, bread, and vegetables were placed before them. Lena and Arnest's eyes widened at the sight of it all.

He tapped his elbow against her with excitement. 'Go on. Dig in.'

'No arguments from me,' she replied, already piling the food onto her plate.

An hour later, the guests were scattered about the room. Some remained at the table, others stood and chatted with each other, and a small group were entertained by Hamo's card tricks.

Arnest spotted Grey on the opposite side of the room as he conversed with a handful of guests. He turned to Lena. 'I'm going to talk to Guy.'

'Do you want me to come?'

'No, no, you enjoy this. Just save my spot.'

'Okay. More food for me, then.' She shrugged, happily taking another bite of chicken from her fork.

Arnest smiled and patted her leg before standing up and sifting through the busy room. He waved and greeted those he passed, before finally coming to Grey. 'Lord Guy.'

Grey turned to him as the other guests cleared away. 'Ah! It's excellent to see you could join us, Arnest.'

'It is truly a gift to be welcomed into these halls. I can only imagine what it's like to live here.'

'Well, yes, it certainly beats the days living in the village.' Grey chuckled. 'Meaning no offence, of course.'

'No, no. I wouldn't doubt it. You earned yourself an impressive opportunity with all of this.'

Grey looked over at Margaret, smiling as she chatted with the earl. 'Well, when you fall in love with one as beautiful as her, there's not much of a choice in the matter.'

'Of course. You are a lucky man.' He nodded. 'But I did want to ask you of something, and I hope it's not out of place. It's just, considering we know each other, that we've both lived in the village, I can't help but think your position here can help us greatly.'

'How do you mean?'

While Hamo continued to entertain others with his tricks, he turned a subtle eye towards their conversation.

Arnest quietened his voice. 'There's only so many ways to put it, but ... we're struggling, Guy. Much worse than when you left. Weather has deteriorated the houses, our food is running dangerously short, and now a sickness is beginning to ravage through the livestock. They won't all admit it, but *we need help*.'

'Well, that's why we're holding this festival, of course. Give you all a bit of a boost. Many outside resources have been brought into the region for this occasion.'

'I know, and we all appreciate it very much, but it's ... it's not a permanent solution. We're burning through more food than usual *because* of the festival, even with the extra hands. And this sickness ... I do not know if it is what I fear it is, but if it is, then we are mere days or weeks away from a horrible fate. I do not want to panic anyone now but, if we are prepared, then much misery can be avoided. And now that you have such a strong voice, you could help us do just that.'

'I may not have the sway you are presuming, Arnest.'

'But surely you could at least have a word with the earl? Anything to lend us a hand. We would be forever thankful for it. If you join us down at the pub one night, all of us in the village, we'll show you our gratitude. I know it won't be the same as what you have here, but it will be something.'

Grey nodded in thought. 'Yes, yes, I see what you mean. I'll put some thought into it and ... see what I can do. For the time being, though, just keep carrying on as you do. You've survived much worse before, and your hard work *will* pay off, I know it. It did for me.' He smiled and patted Arnest's shoulder. 'We're also rebuilding St. Mary's Church for a reason. I know your thoughts on such matters, but perhaps a visit to the Lord is in order. Now, I have other guests to attend to. Do enjoy the rest of your night.'

Grey turned away as Arnest hesitated. After a short breath, he stepped forth and spoke up once more. 'Also, my lord … if you don't mind me asking, the man I jousted against today, what are you planning to do with him?'

Grey paused with a smirk. 'I think execution in the morning will be most likely.'

Arnest hid his confusion with a nod as Grey approached another group of guests.

Execution? Arnest thought to himself. *What in the world for?*

Arnest turned his gaze towards the dining hall's exit. It was open. He glanced at his surroundings before swiftly making his way through the crowds towards it.

Meanwhile, Hamo held up a card to his fellow spectators, finishing his card trick. They giggled and clapped for him as he bowed. Once they stepped away, Hamo approached the earl at the head of the table. Kneeling at his side, he whispered into his ear, 'My Lord, I have news of Lord Guy.'

Further along the table, Lena glanced around the room. She spotted Arnest as he stopped before the exit and looked back at her. She squinted at him and shook her head, confused. He nodded reassuringly before exiting the room.

Lena went to stand up before Lady Margaret sat down beside her, speaking with an untainted youthfulness. 'Hello there! You are Arnest's wife, aren't you?'

Lena paused and nodded with some surprise. 'I am, milady. It – it is an honour to be graced by your presence,' she said, bowing to her.

'Oh, no, I could say likewise! Your husband always puts on an amazing show when he jousts. I don't know how he does it.'

'I wish I knew, milady.'

'It's funny, though. I don't think I've ever seen you at his games. Were you there today?'

'Oh, no, I can't watch them.'

'Why not? You're certainly missing out.'

'I … I've seen him go through enough battle in my time, I'm afraid. I don't wish to see any more.'

'He's seen combat?'

'Back home, yes. Our old home, I mean. And on our travels here.'

'I'm terribly sorry to hear. Where was it you come from again?'

'Germania.'

'Ah, of course. Silly me. I should know my accents better! Whatever happened to drive you all the way here?'

'It was … the Black Death. Have you heard of it?'

Margaret pulled herself closer and hushed her voice. '*The Black Death?* I have heard whispers of it, but my father refuses to tell me anything. Is it true? *Is it real?*'

'I'm afraid it is, milady.'

'*What happened?*'

'I … have trouble comprehending it, even now. One day, people suddenly fell ill, and there was simply no cure for them. None at all. Almost everyone who had it died a *terrible* death. And it only spread more from there.'

'Your leaders, your overseers, what did they do?'

'They shut their doors. We were left to fend for ourselves, and that is when people … they weren't the same as they once were. Just as the land died, so did their souls. For something even as simple as a loaf of bread, they were willing to do things to each other that I still cannot bear to recall. It was as though a curse had stolen them. As though the devil itself walked across the land. Families and friends did things to each other, such awful things, their histories and relations be damned.'

'That is horrible.' She gasped, feeling goosebumps beginning to climb up her skin.

'It is. And it was a long journey to escape it. Everywhere we went was consumed by it. Even the skies were black. Arnest fought greatly to get us out. I thank God every day he led us here. A place we can call home again.'

Margaret rested her hand over Lena's. 'I'm glad to have you here in our home … Do you think it will reach England? Could it come all the way here?'

Lena swallowed as she glanced back at the dining hall's exit. Finally, she nodded. 'Truth be told, milady, I fear it may be here already.'

'*What?*'

'Our livestock are dying. I do not know if it is of the same cause, but I do believe it to be a bad omen; a sign of the devil's coming. If we do not prepare ourselves now, we will be consumed by the same darkness that Germania was. Our people are not ready, and I have a child on the way that I pray will not see such suffering. We need your help, milady.'

Margaret nodded without hesitation. 'Of course. *Of course.*'

Elsewhere in the hall, the earl approached Grey and a handful of his guests. The guests nodded and greeted him before respectfully stepping aside, leaving the two of them in private.

'My lord! How are you enjoying the night?' Grey asked.

'Well enough, thank you. And you?'

'How could I not relish it? It truly is a fine time to be alive, is it not?'

'Yes, indeed. I wanted to speak to you about our prisoner, though. From what I hear, you're planning an execution.'

'Wh – ' Grey paused, completely caught off guard and unable to find his words. After a moment, he forced a humoured smile. *'Where did you hear that, my Lord?'*

The earl stared at Grey, unwavering.

Grey stumbled with his words again. 'I was – well, I – I was considering it, yes. As well as other things, of course. I merely did not want to concern you with it until I was sure it was the right decision.'

'And what would make it a *right* decision, Lord Guy? What do you know of this man that makes him worthy of such a punishment?'

'Well, he … those *things*, that equipment he was carrying around, I have a grave feeling about them. I think he is here to harm one of us.'

'For what purpose?'

'For what purpose? Well, my lord, who knows what motives commoners give themselves when setting out to *assassinate* royalty? Perhaps he was sent by another or has a grievance with your rule.'

'None of this he has confirmed to you?'

'He won't budge, but to me, that's a telltale sign of his malice. If he were innocent, would he not deny it?'

'Innocent or not, I would like some proof of his intent. And just so you do not forget your place, *I* will judge his fate. I will question him tomorrow. Then we shall see if we can claw something out of him. Is that understood?'

Grey hesitated a moment before nodding. 'Of course, my lord.'

'Good. Now, you may carry on with your night.'

Outside, Arnest walked through the castle grounds. The air was cool, and the crickets hummed. He approached two knights standing guard at a locked gate. Beyond it was a stairwell leading down into the dungeon.

'Knights,' Arnest greeted them with a nod.

'Arnest!' the first knight exclaimed. 'You put on a valiant show today.'

'I wish *I* could ride that bloody well,' the second knight added.

'Perhaps I can give you some lessons. Although, I think my opponent might need a few more. I hear you're holding him down there.'

'We are,' the first knight replied. 'Word is the fool will be executed tomorrow.'

'I heard such as well. Just when you thought his day couldn't get any worse.' Arnest joked.

'Too right,' the first knight muttered.

'Poor idiot,' the second knight said, shaking his head.

'I hope you don't mind if I go down and visit him, then? I'm in need of a good laugh before his head goes flying tomorrow.'

The knights chuckled.

'Of course, Arnest. If I wasn't on guard duty, I'd do the same,' the first knight admitted as he unlocked the gate.

'Thank you, lads.' Arnest patted their shoulders before stepping into the darkness.

The singing crickets and muffled voices faded away as he trekked deeper and deeper into the dungeon. The temperature grew colder. The light grew thinner. The hairs on his arms stood up.

He reached the bottom of the stairs and found himself standing in a long and cold dungeon corridor. Both sides were lined with numerous empty cells. Drips and drops of water echoed. Heavy shadows shrouded the walls and cells around him. At the very end of the hallway, a glow emitted from a single candle, flickering from inside the last cell.

Curious and cautious, Arnest walked towards it. Upon reaching the end of the hallway, he gazed through the bars.

There, Ryder laid upon a thin bed of hay, staring at the empty space beside him. Steadily, he turned and looked beyond the bars, finding Arnest on the opposite side. He sat up from the floor, revealing his pale face in the orange light of the candle.

Arnest wrapped his hands around the bars and leant closer. *'Who are you?'*

VOLUME THREE

THE GHOSTS

Chapter 13

A dark living room rested in silence. The cold night's dew shrouded the windows. Patches of carpet had been torn away. The fireplace was lifeless. Graffiti stained the walls, and there was no furniture. It was entirely empty.

Except, there was a shadow.

Buried in the far corner of the room, curled up against the wall, was a fifteen-year-old girl, Alexia. She held her knees close to her chest as she stared at the floor of the front hallway. One by one, small tears ran down her cheeks. She sniffled and wiped her wrist across her nose. Gradually, her gaze fell upon her matted shoes as she twiddled her fingers.

Before long, the headlights of a car beamed past the front windows. She glanced at the window with a fright, hearing the car come to a stop. Its door opened, and a set of footsteps neared the entrance. She let her long blonde hair hang over her eyes as she concealed herself in the darkness.

You're safe in the shadows, she told herself. *They won't see you.*

The front door unlocked, and a tall man wearing a long coat stepped inside. His face was too difficult to make out amidst the heavy gloom. Alexia remained completely still, glaring at the figure before a flashlight clicked on. The man shone the light onto the hallway floor. A portion of the carpet had been torn away, leaving an old, discoloured bloodstain underneath it.

He lifted the torch and scanned the light across the living room, illuminating Alexia in the corner. She wore an oversized hoodie and torn tracksuit pants. He sighed and walked over to the corner, kneeling down before her, revealing his black-grey beard and brown eyes.

Alexia recognised his face. It was Detective Marlo.

'Alexia … come on, I've told you,' he said, his voice deep and smooth. 'You can't keep coming here. You know it's going to be sold soon. It won't be yours anymore.'

Alexia shook her head as she stared at the floor.

'And you know it's dangerous running out alone like this,' he continued. 'The streets aren't safe.'

'Did you find who did it yet?' she asked with a quiet, timid voice.

'Hey, we're not talking about that. We're talking about you putting yourself in danger. You need to stay with Rebecca and the rest of your carers. They worry about you.'

'No, they don't. They'll kick me out soon. I've seen them do it.'

'No – *no*. They'll find you a family long before then.'

'I don't *want* another family. I want *my* family. Did you find who did it yet?'

Marlo sighed and bowed his head.

Alexia's lips trembled. 'Why can't you just find them?'

'Because it's impossible, Lex …'

'What?'

Marlo shook his head and sighed again. 'If I could've, I would've caught him a long time ago … but the man who did this, he stole something that allowed him to … run away from everyone … forever.' The detective paused for a time before he continued with reluctance. 'I'm so sorry, Lex, but it's out of my hands. And you can't burden yourself with something you can't change.'

'I don't understand,' she replied, losing her breath.

'I don't really grasp all of it either, to be honest.'

'What's his name?'

'It doesn't matter, Lex. He's gone. *Completely*.'

She glared back at him through her green, teary eyes, unrelenting. '*What's his name?*'

* * *

Melbourne, Australia, 2279 CE

Purple raindrops fell from the darkness above. Glowing neon signs and advertisements plastered both sides of a smoky alleyway, casting purple and blue shadows everywhere. The same pair of young green eyes stared up at the night sky. Drops of rain and blood trickled down her bruised face.

Now twenty-four years of age, hazel streaks ran through her short blonde hair. Everything from her purple leather jacket to her black shirt and jeans was soaking wet.

Standing over her, a pair of gloved hands opened a metallic briefcase. A green light shone within the case, illuminating a collection of small oxygen capsules. Alexia stared at the sky as the briefcase was locked shut again, and a low voice spoke over her.

'I appreciate you coming through in the end. But I don't wanna see your face again. Our business is *done*.'

A handful of gangsters, wearing leather jackets and cloaks, decorated with chains and cybernetic trinkets, filed out of the alleyway.

Alexia closed her eyes as she lay on the wet pavement, alone. With the rise and fall of her chest, her breath was visible in the cold air.

Just sleep, she thought. *I just want to sleep.*

She remained silent for a time, ignoring the rain that flicked against her skin. Then, the darkness behind her eyelids was overtaken. A bright white light shined across her pale face.

An energetic female voice faded in through a speaker. 'Nowhere else is the future brighter than with Forward Industries. If you're in need of instantaneous overseas travel, your own personal porter, or want to join Forward Industries' exclusive membership program, scan here to begin planning your better tomorrow. The future is in *your* hands.'

Alexia forced her eyes open and turned her head, finding a long electronic wallpaper spread across the wall of the alleyway. The Forward Industries logo appeared on the screen before a white background.

The sound of heavy rumbling boomed above. A flying spacecraft, with flames shooting out from its four engines, flew over the alleyway. The buildings rattled as the craft hovered overhead and out of sight. The humming drone of the busy city streets and their spacecraft, hover trains, and endless electronic beeps and twinks returned to Alexia's ears.

Finally, she sat up and pressed her hands against the reflective pavement. Pushing herself to her feet, a stabbing pain struck her ribs. She groaned and gritted her teeth, resting her hand over her wound. Her eyes returned to the glowing advertisement one last time.

Soon, the Forward Industries logo faded away, and a new advertisement for interplanetary travel replaced it. Alexia carefully turned away and limped into a bustling city street, disappearing into the endless neon-drenched crowds.

An hour later, Alexia entered a narrow street, surrounded by unkempt apartment complexes. Limping towards the entrance of one such building, she held her wrist up to her nose. With her other hand, she scanned the top of her wrist against the front door's ID reader. The door unlocked and began to open automatically.

After a short moment, it malfunctioned and stopped halfway. She sighed and repeatedly thrust her shoulder against the door, opening it just enough so that she could slip through. After squeezing inside, she kicked the door back into place behind her.

Climbing up flights of stairs and past numerous hallways lined with small apartments, she came to her own. The digital number encoded onto the door was *278*. She scanned her wrist against the door handle. A small light on the handle flashed red, and a low beep sounded from its speaker.

It was locked.

Without an ounce of motivation left, she scanned her wrist again. This time the light turned green, and there was a high-pitched beep. The door unlocked. She sniffled and opened it before heated voices and yelling arose from the apartment across the hall. Pausing, she glanced at the opposite apartment's door. Another wave of sorrow overcame her.

She shook her head and stepped into her apartment, shutting the door behind her. The minuscule home consisted of a small kitchen and bathroom openly connected to her bedroom. Her belongings were strung across the floor and chairs. Numerous plants rested alongside the windowsill, gazing out at the surrounding apartment rooftops.

Alexia hobbled over to her kitchen bench, still holding her wrist up to her nose as she filled up a jug with green-tinted water from the tap. Once it was full, she approached her plants and watered each of them generously.

The plants were halfway dead. Some parts lively and green, other parts faded and collapsed.

Without a moment to linger, she chucked the jug back into the sink and soaked a small towel under the tap. Holding it in her hand, she limped over to her armchair couch and fell into it with a long sigh.

After pressing the towel up against her nose, Alexia finally rested her head back and sat in silence. The glowing lights of her lava lamps cast deep, colourful shadows across her face as she stared at the ceiling, watching the colours fade from one to the next.

* * *

Flashing red and blue lights reflected off wet concrete. Police officers walked to and fro across a mundane suburban street. Holographic police tape surrounded one household in particular.

Sitting at the rear end of an ambulance, thirteen-year-old Alexia was wrapped in a blanket. She shivered as her eyes remained frozen in fear.

Eventually, Detective Marlo knelt before her with a comforting smile. 'Hey there. You hungry?'

Alexia shook her head, continuing to stare into space.

'Thirsty?'

She shook her head again.

'Okay, well you let me know if you need anything, okay? My name's Marlo. Me and everyone here are gonna take care of you. We'll make sure you find a safe place to live.'

Alexia, back in her apartment, twenty-four years of age, opened her eyes. She lay in her double bed, alone, doused in strips of neon light that shone through her venetian blinds. Just like the hour before this, and the hour before that, their colour faded from one to the next. Advertisements echoed on repeat outside, blended with the never-ending sounds of spacecraft and sirens. She flinched at the sound of the occasional gunshot and distorted scream, and her eyes darted towards the handgun resting on her bedside table.

Yeah, okay. I'm not getting any sleep, she thought to herself.

Tossing her blanket aside, Alexia pulled herself out of bed. She slid on another pair of jeans and her purple leather jacket and picked up her handgun. Unloading its magazine, she found it was half-full. She reloaded the clip and firmly tucked the weapon into the back belt of her pants.

Stepping out of the apartment, she shut the door behind her and paused, finding her eleven-year-old neighbour, Lay, sitting against the wall beside her. An electronic reading pad rested on her lap, while her black, braided hair dangled over her shoulders.

She was attempting to read a picture book before she glanced up at Alexia, 'Oh, hey, A.' Her smile faded upon noticing Alexia's bruises. '*Oh no, what happened to your face? Are you okay? Do you need a helper-bot? I can go get one for you! I know where one is!*' she exclaimed, ready to jump into action.

Alexia waved her back down as she smiled and shook her head. 'No, no, I'm all right, Lay. It's nothing.'

'It looks like it hurts, though!'

'It'll heal, it'll heal, don't worry.'

'Where's Jemma and Chris? Are they taking care of you?'

'No, they're not coming around anymore, I'm afraid. They've moved.'

'Oh.' Lay's shoulders dropped. 'They didn't even say goodbye.'

'Yeah, I know. They had to leave in a hurry, but don't hang yourself on it. They didn't say much to me either. What's going on with you, though? Why are you out here?'

Lay gestured her head towards her apartment across the hall.

Alexia nodded, 'Yeah, I heard them earlier. What was it about this time?'

'I don't know. I wish I had my own home like you do. You're lucky.'

Alexia chuckled and walked over to her side, patting her head. 'Do I look lucky?'

'I guess not. Are you going somewhere?'

'Yeah. I need to work. That's how I *can* have my own place.'

'It's so late, though.'

'Well, work doesn't sleep.'

'Or maybe *you* just don't sleep.'

Alexia laughed. 'Oh okay, being a little Miss Observant now, are you?'

'What's the point in having your own place if you can't just sleep whenever you want?'

'Oh, I know, I know, trust me. But I still gotta head off, anyway.'

'Wait, wait, wait! What's *this* word?' she asked, pointing to her picture book.

Alexia leant down and inspected the word. 'Symmetry. That's symmetry.'

'Ohhhh …' She paused with a blank face. 'What's that mean?'

'It's kinda like a … maths thing. When all of the different sides of something are equal, or the same. Something like that.'

'Can you read more with me later? It's really hard.'

'Yeah, I know. We'll see. When I get a chance, maybe we'll get around to it.'

'Thank you.' Lay smiled. 'And be safe, please.'

'Thanks, Lay. You too. Don't be out in this hall too late,' she replied, turning and leaving down the hallway.

Lay returned to her electronic pad, attempting to decipher each word with great concentration.

* * *

A dark smog hung across the city. Old buildings shook from the hovertrains above. Colourful chemicals leaked out of pipes and off neon signs.

With her hands buried in her pockets, Alexia walked through the array of lights and smoke. There was not a car in sight, as the streets were choked with thousands of people. Many of the citizens boasted intense cybernetic augmentations. There were unique metallic, plastic, and neon faces, eyes, hairstyles, and outfits. Some looked like dolls, others like creatures of fantasy. They littered the streets, loitering without cause, smoking, feeling each other's bodies, and eyeing others with suspicious intent. The alleyways were overwhelmed with the homeless, the living indistinguishable from the dead.

Alexia turned into a tall, shadowy club. A long sign ran down its side, reading: *CLUB 24-D.*

The club was doused in mist and lined with holographic, robotic, and human strippers dancing. They were silhouetted by the flashing walls along the edges of the venue. Customers flowed in and out of the building. Some drank, some danced, and others plugged glowing cords into their bodies. Dark, moody electronic music thumped through the air as Alexia sifted through the mist and the partygoers.

Throughout the club were numerous circular tables surrounding tall, thick lava lamp tubes that connected to the ceiling. At one such spot, a skinny man in a dark coat sat alone, drinking from a glass. A blue light shone within one of his pupils while his fingernails glowed neon colours in the dark.

Alexia spotted him and sat down at his side. 'Jed.'

Jed turned, noticing the bruises across her face. 'Jeez, that Myko's doing?'

'What do you think?' she replied, pressing a button on the table. Out of the table, a small compartment slid open, and a fluorescent beverage was lifted out of it. She picked up the glass and took a sip as the compartment closed.

'What happened to your buddies?' Jed asked. 'They do the drop with you?'

Alexia shook her head. 'When it was overdue, they bailed. Probably in a whole different country by now. Or planet.'

'Damn. Looks like it may have been the right call,' he said, gesturing to her bruises.

'Ah, I got it done without them, anyway.' She sculled her glass and pressed the table's button again, replacing her drink.

'Mm, yeah, very successfully it seems.'

Alexia slapped his shoulder. 'I got it done, all right?'

Jed raised his hands, conceding, 'True. True.'

'Do you have another job?'

'You wanna do another one already?'

She grabbed the second glass from the table's compartment. 'Why else would I be here, Jed?'

'Because we're such *great* friends, of course.'

She raised her eyebrows at him, amused and unwavering.

'All right, all right.' He nodded, glancing around with some caution. 'Well, lucky for you, I just heard of one the other day. I've been holding on to it for you.' He pulled out his phone and handed it to her.

Alexia scrolled through the phone, glancing over the job description. 'What's so special about it?'

'Rumour has it, it's a hiring front for *Forward Industries*.'

'You're kidding.'

'That's what I heard.'

'Are you sure?'

'Only one way to find out, right? The details are thin, but I mean, it's something.'

Her eyes clung to the screen as she read over every word.

'They're conducting interviews next week,' he continued.

Alexia paused for a moment, processing his words. Eventually, a small smile broke out across her face, 'Thank you, Jed.'

He nodded and lifted his glass. 'If it's really them, you better tell me all about it. I've got a lot of bets riding on our theories about them.'

'Sure. We'll see.' She smirked and lifted her drink as they clinked them together.

* * *

A week had passed by, and the sun struggled to break through the smoke-ridden sky. A hover train sped over endless miles of cityscape as hundreds of citizens were crammed inside, many of them consumed by the visuals on their digital retinas and sunglasses. Some of them wore decorated filtration masks, loaded with fresh oxygen capsules, while breathing materials and tubes were embedded in the mouths and necks of others.

Alexia leant against the wall of the train, her arms crossed and bruises mostly healed. She gazed out of the window, watching the tallest buildings in the city go by. Amongst them was the home of Forward Industries, the tallest of them all.

Nearing the Yarra River, the train came to a stop at a high-level platform. Its doors opened as floods of people poured in and out. Alexia exited the station and trailed the concrete city docks. The blackened, trash-ridden water brushed against the edges of the path as she approached a series of warehouses.

In front of one large warehouse, multiple armed robots stood guard. A scattering of dubious figures also lingered about, awaiting entry. They were each covered in scars, wore torn and tattered clothing, and harboured grim expressions.

Alexia glanced at her phone, checking the address once more.

Yep, this is it.

She slipped the phone back into her pocket and walked towards a small metallic pole with a laser scanner at its head.

'Please scan yourself in at the IDR and await notification before entry,' one of the security bots repeated every few minutes.

Alexia swiped her wrist over the IDR laser, and the device beeped. Glancing down at her wrist, she saw a small red light begin to glow beneath her skin. Looking back towards the warehouse entrance, she watched as another interviewee entered alone.

Finally, she turned and approached a concrete railing at the edge of the docks. Almost instantly, she was entranced by the black water, watching its waves sway back and forth. Nearly an hour blurred by as numerous pieces of scrap metal and forgotten possessions floated by. She remembered a game that she used to play as a child, guessing the weird and wonderful places each belonging had come from.

Gradually, she turned away and leant against the barrier, crossing her arms as she continued to wait. Sighing to herself, she glanced at a young man who sat atop the railing a few metres down from her. He wore a long coat and was writing in a journal.

Is that paper? she asked herself. *Wow.*

The man noticed her gaze and awkwardly smiled and waved at her. She gave a little wave back before her attention returned to the warehouse.

'You heard the rumours?' the man asked. 'Of what this could be?'

She gave him another brief glance. 'Yeah.'

'I just met with them before ... I think it might be true, but ... I don't know ... Hard to say definitively, you know?'

Alexia nodded along with his words.

Please be them, she thought to herself.

Please be them ...

'I hope it's them,' he added, gazing back at the warehouse.

She almost let out a smile as she nodded. 'Yeah. Me too.'

'Hopefully, we're some of the lucky ones who get to find out, I guess.'

'Don't need luck,' she said before a yellow light flashed inside her wrist.

'Why's that?'

'Cause I'll just ask them,' she said before walking towards the warehouse.

The man stuttered for a moment, attempting to find his words. 'I – I'm Kye, by the way!' he called out.

She glanced back at him, a little surprised and confused, before continuing onwards. A security bot blocked the front door as she approached it and lifted her wrist, presenting the glowing yellow light. The robot nodded and stepped aside. The warehouse door unlocked and slid open. Alexia curiously gazed inside, finding only darkness. She straightened her shoulders and held her breath before stepping into the warehouse. The sounds of voices, howling wind, and crashing water were suddenly silenced as the door slid shut behind her.

She stepped through an automatic body-scanner, which beeped and shone a red light.

'Please remove your weapon and place it on the table beside you,' a robotic voice commanded from the scanner's speaker.

Alexia eyed the scanner up and down before pulling her handgun out from her belt and placing it on the metallic bench beside her.

Continuing forward, her footsteps echoed along the polished black floor. The entire warehouse was consumed in a dense shadow except for a single light illuminating a desk in the centre of the room. A robotic female with undefined plastic skin covering her face sat on the opposite side of the desk, waiting.

Alexia watched the darkness around her as she approached the desk with caution. Stepping into the light, she met the electronic eyes of the being across from her. The robot extended her hand, gesturing for her to sit down, to which Alexia did so.

'Good afternoon,' the robot said with an artificially altered female voice. 'Please state your name and date of birth.'

'Alexia Fifeton. Twenty-sixth of April, fifty-five.'

'And your occupation?'

'I do pickups and deliveries. Sometimes security.'

'All off the record?'

'Yes.'

'Are you familiar with firearms?'

'Yeah.'

'And how long have you been in this field?'

'About seven or eight years.'

The robot paused, tilting her head. 'You started when you were sixteen?'

'Yeah, around about.'

The robot nodded. Her fingers dashed up and down above the table as if she were typing, yet nothing was there.

Alexia watched her fingers bounce off the air with suspicion. 'You're not just any client looking for off-the-book work, are you?'

The robot ceased typing. 'What makes you say that?'

'The security, the scanners, even *you:* a puppet.' Alexia shook her head. 'No underground company could afford all of this, and if they could, they wouldn't be spending it on things like you.' She leant forward, staring into the robot's blank eyes. 'You really are Forward Industries, aren't you?'

The robot gave no hint of an expression. 'So, you're a conspiracy theorist too, then?'

'You're not denying it?'

'I am.'

'But we're still talking.'

'What would it matter to you even if we were?'

'A whole lot, actually.'

'And why's that?'

Alexia leant back in her chair again, flashes of her dreams haunting her mind. 'My parents were murdered when I was a kid,' she said in a blunt tone, with only a hint of something more grave behind her voice. 'It was in our home, just a random night of the week, no apparent motive. And all there was, was a single gun left at the scene. Eventually, the police figured out who did it, but they dropped the case because apparently there wasn't anything anyone could do.'

'And who was that?'

'It was Ryder Mason.'

A long silence befell them.

'I'm sorry?'

'Ryder Mason killed my parents.' Alexia repeated, her voice beginning to sharpen.

'I'm afraid I don't know a Ryder Mason.'

'No, you do. You know what he took. And I know about the others too. About Deisy Forder's "accident."'

'Are you referring to rumours and theories that – '

'My parents' murder isn't a theory. It <u>happened</u>. His fingerprints were on the weapon, clear as day.'

The robot fell silent again. 'I am looking at reports. They claim Ryder Mason was the husband of Deisy Forder. Is that correct?'

Alexia huffed and shook her head.

'When are you saying this happened exactly?' the robot asked.

'Twelve years ago.'

'According to any viable reports I can find, Ryder left the planet at least twenty years ago. I'm sorry, but someone else is responsible for that crime.'

'And I guess you're just saying this out of the kindness of your heart?'

'I'm saying this because you confronted me with a serious allegation. I am merely disproving it.'

Alexia gazed at her in disbelief. 'You really don't know about this, do you?'

The robot remained silent.

Alexia leant forward once more. 'Well, even if *you* don't know, then someone else in your company does, and they're keeping it a secret from you. I know they got the police to do the same, and lucky for you, I haven't said a word either. I've kept my mouth shut for *twelve years* because I always thought that one day you'll send people back in time to clean up your mess. I don't know if what you're doing here has to do with that, but either way, that's why *I'm* here … and I *need* to be a part of it.' For the briefest moment, a crack of desperation finally slipped through Alexia's voice.

Another long silence shrouded their conversation.

Gradually, the robot gestured towards the exit. 'I'm sorry. Thank you for your time, Alexia.'

A shadow of defeat swept over Alexia's eyes as her shoulders dropped ever so slightly. At last, she returned to her feet, clinging onto one more shred of hope, 'I know it might be hard for you to hear it, but it's the truth. Go find out … and when you do, you know how to reach me.' She gave one final glance at the robot before returning to the darkness and collecting her handgun.

The warehouse door slid open, shining a faded light across Alexia's face. She strolled out across the concrete docks and came to a stop, closing her eyes.

You've waited this long, girl. Come on. You can wait a little longer.

Nodding to herself, Alexia pushed forward, walking back towards the train station.

Kye continued to write in his journal before he noticed her passing by. 'Oh, hey! Did you ask?'

Alexia paused and glanced back at him.

'You think it's them?' he continued, hopping off the railing.

Alexia took a breath as she thought for a moment longer. 'I guess we'll just have to see if we're lucky, hey?'

'Yeah. Yeah, I guess so … Will I learn your name, or will I need some more luck there too?'

She tilted her head from side to side as she began walking away. 'More luck, I think.'

'Will you *wish* me some good luck, at least?'

'You're pushing your luck there too.'

'Yeah, I really gotta stop doing that, don't I?'

'Yeah.' She smirked before turning around and continuing on her way.

Kye chuckled to himself and shook his head. Sliding his hands into his pockets, he turned and strolled away in the opposite direction.

* * *

In the heart of the city, deep within the offices of Forward Industries, Dr. Alice Locke sat alone in a dimly lit room. She was in her mid-fifties, still wearing her large glasses and shining white lab coat.

A desk sat before her, just like the one in the warehouse, while a screen covered the wall in front of her, projecting the point-of-view of the robot she was neurologically linked with. Small circular devices and cords ran along her fingers, neck, and head, recognising her every movement and translating it to the robot in the warehouse.

She sat in an eerie silence, processing Alexia's words. Her eyes crawled up towards a security camera in the corner of the room as it stared back at her. Watching her. After a time, she returned to her touchpad as it waited for her to type her interviewee report.

Days later, Alice rode an elevator towards the top floor of the Forward Industries skyscraper. She held her touchpad close to her chest, staring into space.

The girl was lying, Alice thought.

She has to be.

The elevator swiftly and gently came to a halt, dinging as it opened. Alice walked into a hallway before entering a long, clean office. The back wall was constructed of a tall, grand set of windows, looking out across the night sky and the city below it.

A woman in her late thirties, wearing a perfectly clean and smooth business suit, sat behind a desk in front of the city view, working away at her computer. A silver plaque sat before her, reading:

ELODIE WELLS
CEO

Elodie glanced up from her computer as the doctor entered. 'Alice. Good evening.'

'Good evening,' Alice replied with a nod, approaching Elodie's desk.

'What can I do you for? Is the interview process proceeding smoothly?'

'It is. And while it is yet to be finalised, we have a selection of candidates.'

'Excellent, let's see them.'

The pair sat down on a couch before a glass screen that hung on the office wall. Alice wirelessly connected her touchpad to the television. The screen revealed the faces of seven different interviewees, each with their own profile.

1. *Able Louis*
2. *Kingston Roux*
3. *Dax Shanes*
4. *Kye Penson*
5. *Ember Silvas*
6. *Cato Thompson*
7. *Hayes Lee*

'Out of the thousands we've talked to,' Alice began to explain, 'and alongside your specialist's help, I feel rather confident on these seven subjects.'

Elodie read over their brief biographies. 'Why these seven?'

'While there were numerous, more typical militaristic choices, we found that many of those subjects still had a family or strong social standing, which could not only jeopardise the secrecy of the mission but also hinder them from going as far as we may need them to go. So, we decided to pick subjects not necessarily based on their occupation.'

'And instead?'

'Instead, we selected those who, of course, not only have the potential for physical strength and skill, but also those that have … lost something. Whether they've lost family, friends, or are just looking for a purpose, these seven have, for lack of a better term, a *void* within them. A void that *we* can fill for them with the need to complete this mission.'

Elodie nodded, continuing to read the screen, 'So, you're saying they'll be soldiers and nothing but?'

'That's the idea, yes. If trained right, we can mould every one of them so that, when the time comes, they will be willing to die for this mission if need be. And for something as dangerous and risky as this is going to be, that lack of hesitation is exactly what we'll need.'

'I see. You're not concerned with some of their more unsavoury backgrounds? They might not take kindly to orders.'

'Well, that's exactly what our training program should iron out. Two years of our instruction and good care should be enough time to redefine their purpose. We can strip them of any doubt on the matter and create a kind of codependent relationship between them and the company. And considering they don't have much of anything back home, it shouldn't be too difficult to make them want anything *but* to train. *We* will be their home.'

'Okay … and any idea who may be a suitable leader amongst them?'

'Well, incidentally, Able Louis *is* an ex-marine. One of the only candidates to have held a military position *and* a leadership position. He's the oldest of them too. I think he'll be a likely choice. He lost his wife and son some time ago in a train accident. He's got nothing else but his skill set.'

Elodie stared at the screen for a moment, steadily nodding. 'I appreciate the time and discretion you've put into this, Alice. I am wary of how some of these candidates will respond to our training, but this approach sounds like it may be what we need regardless.'

'It is. I promise you, I'll ensure that they do what they need to.'

'I know.' Elodie replied, speaking with conviction and understanding. 'Well, what left is there to do?'

'I'll need to run basic blood and fitness tests to make sure they're in a healthy enough state for this, then I can confirm their positions.'

'Excellent. See to it, then.'

'Thank you.' Alice replied as they stood up and nodded to one another. 'Good night.'

'Good night.'

Alice turned and walked towards the office door as Elodie returned to her desk. Gradually, Alice stopped before the exit.

But what about Alexia? she thought. *Ryder. The gun. Everything she was saying* …

No. It couldn't be true. It couldn't.

Alice reached out for the door handle before hesitating again.

But what harm would it do to mention it? There's probably nothing to it, anyway.

With that, Alice pulled her hand away from the door and turned around. 'Ms. Wells …'

'Yes?'

Alice swallowed, taking a moment to gather her words. 'I did have an interviewee … a young woman, who … made some unsettling claims.'

'What did she say?'

'She said she knew about what happened to Deisy. And she also said that … Ryder had killed her parents, some twelve years ago. She said that it was … covered up?' Alice almost chuckled at her own words.

Elodie's expression remained steadfast. 'Why are you telling me this, Alice?'

'Well … I don't know. I just – '

'Was her last name Fifeton?'

Alice froze. 'You know about this?'

Elodie straightened her suit and posture. 'About twelve years ago sounds right. Somewhere in the outer city, I believe. Not too bad of a neighbourhood. One day the police report came in: two people shot dead, their daughter left alive, and Ryder's gun left at the scene.'

'You know it was his gun?' she asked in disbelief.

'His fingerprints were all over it. And looking over the footage from when he took the device from here, it looked to be the same one. And the fact that he disappeared without a single trace after the incident led us to believe that … it *could* have been him.'

'Ryder came back to the present … and I wasn't *told*?'

Elodie stood up and walked towards her with care. 'I know, *I know* … but you remember what those days were like, Alice. *Everyone* was asking questions about Deisy and "the accident". The public, the press, the government, all of them, they were *this close* to tearing *your* inventions away from you. And just like Mr. Forder did, the board at the time made the conscientious decision to keep *everything* out of the public eye. Ryder moved off-planet, and that was the end of it as far as anyone else was concerned. If the public had learnt he was potentially jumping in and out of the present, indiscriminately *killing* people, then none of us would be here right now. They would've taken everything you built and destroyed it.'

'That doesn't explain why you didn't tell *me*.'

Elodie's shoulders dropped. 'It was never a secret kept out of malice. The board just didn't know enough. We didn't even have a motive as to why he would ever do such a thing. And considering nothing like that ever happened again, we could never be sure what *actually* happened that night. And the board knew you had a personal relationship with Ryder. They didn't want to involve you in something that was so … dubious … but now, with the board gone and me in charge, we're making a stand. We're *fixing* this, once and for all. I'm not even supposed to be telling you about this, but I am because I trust you. And you *know* that. If I didn't, you wouldn't be the one organising this operation.'

Alice's eyes remained fixated on the floor. 'Who were they? The victims.'

Elodie shrugged. 'Just a couple of teachers at some public school, I think.'

'Did Ryder know them?'

'No. No ties. Nothing. That's what I mean when I say we couldn't jump to conclusions. It just doesn't make sense.'

'And the police? They just dropped the case? They didn't say a word?'

'Of course. How else did you think we got things to quiet down all those years ago? What we say goes.' Elodie looked at Alice with sympathy. 'Look, I'm so sorry you're hearing this now, Alice. I know it's a lot, and I wish I told you sooner, but you know *now*. And soon, when this operation is done, we'll have all the answers we need, and we can be done with this whole ordeal. We can *move on*. These secrets won't have to weigh us down anymore.'

'And what about the girl? Alexia?'

'Well, I certainly am surprised she showed up. After her parents were killed, she was shipped off to an orphanage and then, well, she ran away. Fell off our radar. Lived her own life, I suppose. I didn't expect to ever hear about her again if I'm honest.'

'She said she never told anyone about what happened.'

'*Good.* I like her already.'

'She said she wants to be a part of this …'

'Well, from what you say, she must already be good at keeping a secret, and she *certainly* has the motivation. Maybe she'll fit in well. But I'll leave that up to you,' Elodie said with a smile, patting Alice's shoulder before walking back to her desk. 'Get a good night's rest, Alice. And thank you for telling me about all of this. I do appreciate it.'

Alice nodded in bewilderment, looking down at her touchpad where the selection of candidates stared back at her.

* * *

Rain dripped off Alexia's hair as she sat on the outside of her apartment window. She held her knees close to her chest as she felt the cold breeze brush against her skin. The distant city lights reflected in her tearful eyes as her mind drifted.

In her small bed, thirteen-year-old Alexia slept soundly in her bedroom. A soft purple light circled beside her, projecting stars and planets across the walls. The air was calm as she slowly fell into her dreams.

Then, her peace was shattered. A sudden scream erupted from somewhere inside the house. Alexia's eyes shot open as a series of silenced gunshots followed. Then, a loud thud.

Alexia lay in silence, confused and unsure of what she had just heard.

A man's voice yelled out in a panic. It was her father's voice.

Alexia immediately sat up and stared at her bedroom door as her heart raced with fear. A few more gunshots rang out from within the house. Another thud followed.

In an instant, everything fell silent.

Alexia's eyes remained fixed on the door.

She was completely frozen.

Ever so carefully, she slipped out of bed and placed her feet on the floor. She swallowed as she approached the bedroom door, keeping her feet as light as feathers. Her lips tightened as she reached out for the door handle and steadily turned the knob.

She pulled open the door and peeked her head into the hallway. Down the end of the hallway, partially concealed behind a wall, was an arm lying on the floor. Alexia let out a frightened whimper before heavy footsteps walked through the house. She hurriedly pulled her head back into her room.

The footsteps paused.

A moment later, they left the house and faded into the distance.

Holding her breath, Alexia peered back into the hallway. There was not a sound of life left. She poked her foot into the hallway and edged towards the front of the house.

'Mum? Dad?' she whispered.

As she neared the corner of the hallway, the arm became clearer, and the body of her mother with it. Alexia's lips trembled, and the air left her lungs as she turned more of the corner.

Blood soaked the carpet as the bodies of both of her parents became visible; Morgan and Leslie, riddled with a handful of bullets across their chests and necks. Between the bodies sat a familiar handgun.

Alexia opened her mouth to scream.

The cold wind whistled by as twenty-four-year-old Alexia continued watching the distant city from her balcony. Alone, she twisted around and climbed back into her apartment. She glanced at the digital clock sitting beside her bed; it was 12:34 a.m.

The lights flickered above her. A loud, powering-down noise boomed from above before all the lights in the building shut off. Alexia sighed as the glowing lights outside her window danced across her face.

Finally, she grabbed her jacket, slid it on, and picked up her handgun, checking its magazine was loaded. With a solemn breath, she slid the magazine back into the gun and walked towards the front door.

Just as she grabbed the handle, her phone buzzed in her pocket. She paused and pulled it out, seeing the call was coming from an *Unknown ID*.

Her heart froze as she answered the phone and brought it to her ear. '… Hello?'

'Hello, is this Alexia Fifeton?' Alice's voice asked over the phone.

'It is.'

'We'd like you to come in tomorrow for some tests. Will you be available?'

Alexia's eyes immediately flooded with tears as she closed them, feeling her heart bloom. After taking a short moment to regain her lost breath, she opened her eyes. 'What time do you need me?'

Chapter 14

Water poured over Alexia's collection of plants. Drops splashed across their leaves, and little waves rustled over their roots. Through the window, brief glimmers of the sun broke through the smoke and shone upon them.

As the jug emptied, Alexia smiled. She reached out and gently touched one of the leaves. Her hand then trailed down to another leaf, one which was frail and weak, only for it to break off and float to the base of the plant. Sighing, she picked up the dead leaf and tossed it out of the window.

Turning around, she lifted a duffel bag onto her small dining table and packed it with a few more belongings. After leaving her apartment and shutting the door behind her, she found Lay sitting on a lone windowsill at the end of the hallway. Lay's touchpad rested on her lap as she stared out the window, paying no notice to anything else.

Alexia tilted her head and approached her side, resting her hand on her back. 'Hey, Lay.'

'Oh, hey, A.' Lay replied in a dour tone, glancing at Alexia before returning to the outside view.

'What are you looking at?' Alexia asked, bending down and looking out the window. Across the street, on top of another apartment complex, a handful of teenagers played a game of basketball – dunking shots into a hoop that exploded with lights and sounds after every point. The children laughed and joked with one another as they dodged and ran around one another. 'Oh.' Alexia sighed as she realised what Lay was missing. 'Do you want me to take you over there? I'm sure they'd be happy for you to join in, you know?'

'No, it's okay,' Lay said, shaking her head. 'They're too old. They wouldn't want me to. Besides, I have my book. Do you want to do some reading with me?'

'Oh, I'm sorry, Lay, I can't right now. I was just heading off.'

'To work?'

'Yeah. I've actually got a new job, which is going to be taking me away for a little while.'

'Oh … can I come with you?'

'Believe me, you wouldn't want to.'

'But I can do work! You just show me what to do.'

'When you're old enough, I'm sure you'll prove that,' Alexia replied with a chuckle, bending down to her eye level. 'But I tell you what, I'll give you access to my apartment, so if you ever need some time to get away from your parents or anything, just scan yourself in and make yourself at home, okay?'

'Okay … thanks, A,' she said with a small smile before opening her arms for a hug. 'Will you be back soon?'

'I think I'm able to come back on weekends, so I'll try and visit when I can.' Alexia replied, embracing her in a hug. 'But you keep trying to read by yourself in the meantime though, okay? Can you do that for me?'

'Uh-huh.' Lay nodded with determination.

Alexia reached out and rested her hand on Lay's chin, smiling. 'Good girl.'

* * *

After commuting across the city, Alexia trekked through the industrial sector with her duffel bag slung over her shoulder. The wide streets were lined with nothing but warehouses and factories, each of them crowded with humanoid robots constructing materials, packing large metal boxes, and carrying them to and fro.

One warehouse was in the midst of shutting down. Electronic signs were activated, indicating that the workplace was *DECOMMISSIONED*. A collection of robots marched themselves out of the factory and into a shipping container, closely guarded by armed security-bots. Once inside, the robot workers powered down, and the lights in their eyes faded.

After passing countless factories, Alexia came upon an enormous Forward Industries hangar where a handful of security-bots stood guard.

'ID, please,' one bot requested in a monotone voice.

Alexia lifted her wrist.

Beneath the robot's face-shield, its eyes scanned her identification chip. 'Cleared. Follow me,' it said, turning and escorting her inside the facility.

Beyond the front doors, Alexia slowed down as she examined the wide and expansive hangar. Its air was cool and clean, and the bright white floors and walls were pristine. On every side of the facility were numerous rooms dedicated to all manner of teaching and training. Alexia gazed at the floor, finding a polished reflection of herself staring right back at her.

Soon, the robot escorted her towards the facility's primary interview room and stood aside. Alexia stepped inside, alone, finding a single table in the centre of the room with Dr. Alice sitting behind it.

The doctor immediately rose to her feet and outstretched her hand as the door closed behind her. 'Good morning, Alexia. I'm Dr. Alice Locke. I'm pleased to meet you.'

Alexia nodded, feeling a sickness in her stomach as she shook her hand. 'I know who you are.'

'Yes, of course. Please, take a seat.'

The two of them sat down on opposite sides of the electronic table. The time and date were digitally encoded into its corner as Alice stared at Alexia for a long moment. The soft hum of the air conditioner filled their silence.

Eventually, Alice regained her focus and awkwardly shifted her hands above and below the table, attempting to find a comfortable position. 'Before anything else, I – um … I wanted to formally apologise. On the behalf of all of us at Forward Industries. What happened to you and your parents never should have happened.'

A glimmer of hope came over Alexia. 'Do you have any idea why he did it?'

'I don't … I'm sorry.'

The hope retreated from Alexia's eyes as she nodded, painfully unsurprised. 'Well, you're far from the first.'

Another moment of silence overcame them.

'While we're on the matter, though,' Alice continued, 'you may have already worked out that you won't be working alone. You'll be paired with a team of people, and while they will be taught every other necessary piece of information regarding our company's past, we have thought it best *not* to inform them of your particular case. Only as a safety precaution, of course. Considering it's something we understand so little about, involving more people would only be involving more complication and worry on our end. Is that something you would be okay with?'

'Honestly, I wouldn't really want to tell them anyway. I'm not here for them,' Alexia said with a nod, leaning forward in her chair. 'But if I do find Ryder, I'd want to talk to him first. Before anything else. So, if the time comes, I might not have a choice *but* to tell them.'

'Oh, yes – of course. That sounds … I understand.' Alice sat upright and readjusted her coat. 'Do you like the look of the facility?'

Alexia eyed the doctor up and down, curious, as she leant back in her chair. 'It's definitely big.'

'Well, yes, it is a big operation. Forward Industries is taking all of this very seriously. They just need to know that you will too.' Alice tapped the glass table, enlarging a document. She swiped it across to Alexia. At the end of it was a blank space awaiting her signature.

'You don't think I will?'

'No, I know you will. But the company wants assurance. I'm not hiding who we are from you because of your history. There was no point in that. But everyone else won't know until they sign this document. This operation, for as big as it is, needs to be kept an absolute secret from anyone outside of it. Anything you do or learn with us is strictly classified. You can't say a word.'

'Is that the only thing this document says?'

'No. If you are injured in any way, you are not to be treated anywhere else but here. If you are killed in this operation, no one will know the truth behind it. Your records will be wiped. If you jeopardise the operation in any way, there will be severe consequences. To put it plainly, you will be subject to Forward Industries' rule and nothing else. Think of it as moving to a new country or planet. You're adopting a different set of laws in here, all of which are made to ensure, as much as we can, that this mission is a success. Of course, all of this will be taught to you as part of your training, as well.'

'And I'm guessing your "consequences" aren't exactly going to be by the book?'

'I can't say I'm in charge of those security measures, but I imagine you're already used to such parameters in your line of work.'

Alexia nodded, reading over the document. Reaching its end, she returned to the blank spot that awaited her signature.

'Do you have any questions?' Alice asked.

Alexia looked back at her as her lips wavered. 'If I … if I were to want to travel back and stop what happened to my parents, you wouldn't let me, would you?'

Alice shook her head. 'I know it'll be a hard thing to accept when having such a device in your possession, but given that's an event we know has already happened, going back and changing it … well, we just don't know what would happen. It's the same reason we're not sending you and your team to stop any of the other crimes before *they* happened. It could very well create a paradox in which, if you somehow saved your parents, you never would've come here, and then, well … you never would've saved them. It's simply a string of events with consequences too unknowable and too dangerous to play with. This matter will be taken out of your hands, though. All your devices will be locked to the specific times we have predetermined for you. You won't be able to go anywhere else.'

Alexia returned to the document, hesitating.

Alice leant forward in her chair. 'But just because you can't go back to then doesn't mean you can't find the answers you're looking for. If you find Ryder and all the others, you can not only find the truth behind all of this, but you can serve the justice that so many have deemed impossible to give. All we need is to know how willing you are to do this.'

Alexia stared at the blank space.

Memories of her parents' lifeless bodies flashed in her mind.

The blood beneath them. The gun between them.

Finally, she nodded to herself and signed the document. With the flick of her fingers, she swiped the document back to Alice.

* * *

As afternoon arrived that same day, the selected team of eight sat themselves across a series of desks spread about the facility's briefing room, each wearing a black shirt with their names printed on the corner of their chest. Alexia inspected each of those sitting around her with a subtle eye. Of them, there was only one other female member on the team. Meanwhile, the oldest among them appeared only a few years shy of fifty.

Great. I'm probably going to be the youngest here, aren't I? she thought to herself.

Well, yeah, what were you expecting, girl? They didn't exactly hire you for your years of experience ... I just hope they won't get in my way, is all.

As her thoughts drifted, Alexia glanced behind her, locking eyes with the only face she recognised. It was Kye, who gave her a smile and a wave. She smiled back with some surprise before a door opened and her attention returned to the front of the room.

A tall, muscular man with black hair shaved down to a buzzcut and a jet-black military uniform marched inside. Without a glance in their direction, he tapped on a thin glass screen that rested on the wall behind him, enlarging the photos and IDs of seven individuals.

1. *Connor Lavire*
2. *Ryder Mason*
3. *Grey Pines*
4. *Hughes Avil*
5. *Issa Lionel*
6. *Ode Scarlett*
7. *Ian Russ*

'I am Sergeant Clay Desser,' the man began in a firm voice, 'and from this moment forward, I will be your physical and tactical trainer. Everything you're about to see and hear is never to be spoken of outside of these walls.' Clay let his words sink in for a moment before continuing. 'You may have already heard rumours and conspiracy theories over the years regarding the accident that resulted in Dr. Deisy Forder's unfortunate death. Well, in this case, the rumours are true.'

As Clay went on, Alexia felt her breath beginning to slip away, only truly processing the occasional sentence. His words echoed in and out of her head as all that she had believed to be true for so many years was finally spoken aloud.

Eventually, the lights in the room dimmed into darkness as Clay tapped on Connor Lavire's ID, blowing up footage from inside Forward Industries's central laboratory on June 19, 2257 CE. The footage revealed Connor and his masked followers holding Deisy hostage as they made their way into the central laboratory.

Clay's echoing voice went on in pieces. 'The front man, Connor Lavire, the leader of this initial group of six, ... was a security guard in the company's headquarters ... how he infiltrated the laboratory undetected, disabled some of the security footage. As you can see, though, he didn't disable *all* of it.'

Alexia's eyes were completely entranced by the screen as she watched Connor and his assailants gun down Deisy and escape the laboratory.

Next, Clay tapped on Ryder's ID, revealing footage from February 14, 2259 CE. 'Then there's Mr. Mason, Dr. Forder's widowed husband ...'

A tremor rumbled inside Alexia as she sat upright and remained helplessly glued to the screen. The footage revealed Ryder, wearing his thick green coat and backpack, being led inside the central laboratory by Alice.

'Two years after Dr. Forder's murder,' Clay continued, 'Dr. Locke ... giving him a tour ... some kind of closure ... once considered friends ... clearly, Ryder betrayed that friendship ...'

Ryder stood before the Core for a short moment, staring into the heart of its floating lights. Alexia watched him on the screen, unable to stop her hands from shaking and her heart from pounding. Once Alice had turned her back on him, Ryder swiftly removed his handgun and smacked the handle across her head. She collapsed to the floor as he grabbed hold of one of the time gauntlets. Alexia flinched at the sight of his face, his gun, his violence. Ryder gave Alice a final look goodbye before activating the device and disappearing before her eyes.

As the light in the room turned back on, so returned all of its sounds. Alexia immediately looked down at her desk, clenching her fists and suppressing her erratic breath as her eyes turned bloodshot.

Stop it, she told herself. *Come on, just stop it. You're fine. You're okay. Don't let them see you like this.*

'From there, it's not too difficult to posit that Ryder did this in an attempt to track down and kill Connor and his assailants,' Clay continued, his voice finally clear and complete. 'Unfortunately for him, he's only made himself another target, for all eight of you will make up a special unit to be sent back in time. Your objective is to hunt down and exterminate the seven fugitives that have hidden themselves across hundreds and thousands of years of history. And yes, after them, you will be the first people to ever travel back in time. I won't bother asking if you have any questions. I know you'll have them, but trust me, we're going to cover *everything*.'

The team members were at a loss for words as Clay went on, tapping the screen again and revealing an animated timeline of their program.

'Without exactly being at the mercy of a clock anymore, we will be using the next two years to train you in every necessary aspect for this mission. This includes weapons training, hand-to-hand combat, and tactical education. You will learn how to operate as a team, as an individual operator, and how to use your equipment in as precise a manner as possible. You are going to be some of the fittest, fastest, and toughest killers on the planet by the time we're done with you.'

Another team member, Hayes Lee, spoke up with a question. At thirty-one years old, Hayes was most distinguished by his artificial, pale-coloured eyes. 'Sir, if I may … if – if this Ryder is trying to do the same thing as us, why aren't we just bringing him back alive?'

'I'm glad you asked that,' Clay replied, taking a step closer to Hayes. 'Just like with Connor and his own motives, what they are trying to do only matters to us if it helps us find them. Otherwise, who they are, what they want, what they're doing, is not our concern. Ryder had a choice. A choice to work with the company and play it smart or be impatient and betray the trust of all those who trusted him. At the end of the day, between Connor and Ryder, they stole two devices of immense power. Probably the most powerful pieces of technology in all of our worlds, and they have been reckless enough to risk it falling into all manner of hands in all manner of ways. Let alone risked putting everything we know into disarray by playing with something as complex as time itself. And that isn't even to mention the murder of Dr. Forder and the assault on Dr. Locke. Simply put, the matter has already gone far enough. The quickest, easiest, and most surefire way of resolving it is to kill them all and retrieve the devices before they can do any more damage. Is that understood?'

'It is,' Alexia replied, unwavering, drawing everyone's attention.

Upon meeting her stern gaze, Clay nodded. 'Good.'

* * *

As night fell on their first day, the team lined up in a long cafeteria aisle for more food than they had ever seen before. There were copious amounts of freshly cooked proteins, drug-enhanced foods, and pure, clean water. After filling her plate and glass, Alexia glanced at the dining hall across the room, where the others were gathering upon a handful of tables, introducing themselves to one another.

Biting her lip, Alexia looked elsewhere and spotted an exit. Without lingering any longer, she fled the room with her head held low. After exploring a handful of gleaming white corridors, she found herself a quiet spot on a balcony at the top of the hangar. There, she sat down at a high table and ate by herself, looking at a vast view of the neon-drenched city beyond.

Before long, Kye also found his way onto the balcony, holding his own plate of food. 'Oh, here you are,' he said, before pausing as the lights of the distant city caught his eye. 'Wow. You found yourself a nice spot up here. Were you trying to keep this a secret or something?'

'Tried and failed, apparently.'

'Oh, sorry. Don't worry, I won't tell anybody. Do you mind if I sit with you?'

Alexia shook her head and gestured to another stool at the opposite end of the table.

'Thank you,' he said with a nod and a smile, taking a seat beside her. 'Speaking of secrets, actually, I think I know your name now.'

'Oh yeah?'

'Yep. The shirts help a little,' he admitted, gesturing to the imprinted name on her shirt. 'Alexia Fifeton.'

'Well, congratulations, *Kye Penson*,' she said with a small bow, reading his own shirt's name. 'I guess you got lucky.'

'Seems like we all did. It's pretty crazy stuff, hey?'

'That's one word for it.'

'What do you think about it all?'

Alexia took a slow breath, staring at the shifting lights of the city. At last, after a long silence, she spoke in a quiet yet firm tone. 'I think it's ... absurd, and sick, and unjust ... and probably the most important thing I'll ever do ...'

'... That distils it pretty nicely, actually.' Kye nodded with surprise, joining her in watching the view. 'I hope you're right, though. That something really comes of it ... Because otherwise, it just feels pretty lonely knowing all of this when no one else does ... you know what I mean?'

'Yeah ... I do.'

'Do you think the government doesn't know either?'

'Would it matter if they did? If this place can let all of this happen, hurt all of the people that they have, and *still* avoid any of the consequences after this long, I don't think they're going to face them anytime soon. Or ever, probably.'

'Yeah, it does seem that way,' Kye agreed, falling into a quiet reflection. 'You really think we can do it?'

Alexia thought for a moment, nodding to herself. 'I know I can. As for the rest of you, though, we'll just have to wait and see.'

'Ooh, okay, okay, that's some comforting confidence. I'll just have to follow your lead then, ma'am.'

'*Ma'am*?' she replied, raising her eyebrows at him.

'Hey, just because we're contract killers doesn't mean chivalry is dead.'

Alexia resisted the urge for a moment before breaking out into a small laugh. 'Oh, doesn't it, now?'

'Absolutely,' Kye replied with a chuckle. 'But maybe ask me again when we're done. This is only my first gig doing this sort of thing, so I could turn into a real monster by the end of this.'

'Only your first gig? What'd you do before this?'

'Something a little more official. I served with the Earth Defence Force. Stationed up there somewhere,' he explained, pointing up at the night sky.

'Wait, you actually got to go to space, but you chose to come *back?*'

'Yeah, I know, I've heard it all before.'

'So, why did you?'

Kye looked at Alexia, meeting her eyes as he spoke with a softer tone. 'I just … felt like I wasn't done here yet, you know? It probably sounds strange, but it just felt like the planet didn't want me to go yet. Or maybe it was the people … or me … or just some … I don't know. I think I belong here … I just need to find out why, is all.' His eyes lingered on her for another moment before he gazed back up at the night sky.

Alexia looked at him a little while longer as she pondered his words.

He doesn't seem like a killer, she thought to herself. *He has a heart.*

He shouldn't be here. He's only going to find death.

'And what about you, then?' he asked after a time, returning to her gaze. 'What brings you here? Surely you've got a better reason than me.'

Alexia stared back at him, silent, as her mind began to flicker. 'I – uh … I … it just pays a lot better than anywhere else,' she finally explained, quickly looking back towards the city.

'Well, yeah, I can't argue with that. It's definitely more money than …'

As Kye went on, his voice became lost amongst the sounds of familiar gunshots and screams. Alexia stared into the distance, feeling her body begin to shake as the noises overwhelmed her.

What are you doing up here, Lex? she asked herself. *Why are you talking to him? You can't tell him why you're really here, so you should be keeping a distance anyway. You're not here for him, or them, or anyone else, just you. You're only distracting yourself. You just ... you just need to concentrate. So ...*

'Kye,' she found herself saying, interrupting him. He looked at her with concern, noticing her urgent tone. 'I – uh – I'm not feeling great,' she explained, standing up and almost forgetting to grab her plate. 'I'm going to head back to my room.'

'Oh, do you need me to get anything for you? Do you want me to – '

'No, no, I'll be okay. I just need some rest.'

'Okay, yeah, of course.'

Alexia stared at him for a long, quiet moment, hesitating and wavering, before opening her mouth. 'It's probably best I just keep to myself from here on out too. It's nothing to do with you, I just ... this is all a lot, and I just want to focus on myself going forward.'

'Oh ... okay, yeah, sure. I'm sorry I – '

'No, don't – don't be. *I'm* sorry ... I'll see you around.'

With a final look of pain and embarrassment, Alexia turned and walked away, leaving Kye sitting alone on the balcony. He turned back to face the city in total confusion, attempting to piece together what had just happened.

Deep in the training facility, Alexia hurried down a bright hallway and into her new bedroom. It was a narrow, tight space with walls and a floor made of thick white tiles that, upon nightfall, illuminated a warm orange light. The door slid shut behind her as she dropped her plate onto a small desk and leant against the glowing wall, attempting to regain her breath.

Come on, girl, get a grip. Get a grip! What's wrong with you?

You just ... you just need to ...

Gradually, as her breath began to slow down and her thoughts wandered, she noticed a digital pulsating button on the wall across from her. Curious and cautious, she reached out and pressed the button. Seven photos and profiles, one for each of her targets, appeared on the wall before her. All of them staring at her.

Her breath fell short as she looked at each one of them, until landing upon Ryder. With a trembling hand, she clicked on his profile, expanding a litany of information about him. Amongst these details was the video file Clay had shown them earlier. Opening the file, Alexia watched Alice bring Ryder inside the central laboratory before he struck her down. Without thinking, she paused the video, finding her eyes transfixed by the pistol in his hand.

It was just as she remembered it, lying in her parents' blood.

The longer she stared at it, the more her heart shattered.

Why? she pleaded. *Why them?*

With a wave of confusion, anger, and shame, her eyes fell to the floor.

Mum. Dad. I will find out, I promise.

I will.

Alexia's eyes returned to Ryder's profile image, staring at him face to face.

Her and him, all alone.

* * *

One by one, as all of the members of the team fell asleep that night, the first day of their training program had finished, and the following two years were ignited. In the first few days and weeks of the program, Clay remained true to his word, instructing the group in all manner of tactical knowledge necessary for the operation. Meanwhile, Alice taught the group about matters of temporal technology and the nature of time itself. Grandfather paradoxes, splitting timelines, and the potential risks involved in the operation were scrutinised for hours at a time.

'However, regardless of all of these theories,' Alice would often reiterate, 'whether a timeline can be erased or altogether created anew, it's not your mission to find out which one is true; it's only to complete it and return with as little change to the past as possible. I only want you to know about these potentialities so that you know what's at stake. So you know that you *have* to be careful.'

Kye, who would often sit by himself at the end of the room, wrote down these teachings in his own personal journal without fail. After one particular class and another lonely dinner on the facility balcony, he passed by Alexia's room, catching a glimpse of her inside. She had begun sliding the glowing profiles on her wall-screens into their own separate tiles around the room, and was so consumed by her study that she did not even notice his presence.

Before he could speak a word, he restrained himself.

You know what she said, he told himself. *Leave her be.*

She's just here for a mission, and you are too, so get your head straight.

Without another thought, Kye returned to his room.

* * *

Outside of the classroom, the team's physicality was rigorously tested. Every week they ran on treadmills, lifted weights, and partook in core exercises that began shaping their bodies into the perfect weapons that they needed to be.

On one such day, Alexia picked up a pair of boxing gloves for one of the very first times in her life. After sliding them on, she began thrusting her fists into a robot that held up two pads with perfect stillness. Barely two minutes had gone by when her arms began to sting and burn. She stepped back and attempted to shake the pain out of her hand, before noticing the biggest and strongest member of the team, Cato Thompson, on the opposite side of the gymnasium. Cato's punches held such power and force behind them that even the robot's arms occasionally buckled. With biceps twice as big as anyone else's, Cato soon came to be known simply as "The Muscle".

Before Alexia returned to her routine, laughter drew her attention to another corner of the gym, where Ember Silvas and Dax Shanes entertained one another. Ember, with her wavy brown hair and big green eyes, and Dax, with his pronounced jaw and black stubble, were the first in the team to strike up an especially strong connection. Both at twenty-eight years of age, their frequent laughter and effortless rapport became a common distraction for Alexia, and a point of concern for Sergeant Clay, who maintained a close eye on them both.

Meanwhile, as the team approached the sixth month of the program, Alice and Clay promoted the oldest member of the team, Able Louis, to first in command of the squad.

Able, who never ceased to carry a grim expression, accepted the position with a salute. 'I'm honoured. Thank you both.'

'You've certainly earned it,' Alice assured him with pride. 'We're certain you'll lead this mission to success and bring the rest of the team along with you.'

'I will do everything in my power to ensure so, ma'am.'

* * *

Over these early months of the program, Alexia maintained significant distance between herself and everyone else in the facility. Outside of their team exercises, she would roam the many long, white corridors alone, fleeing to her room or seeking a quiet space where she could train her body in one manner or another.

Meanwhile, she returned home almost every second weekend to visit Lay and water her plants. They would often spend their time together atop the rooftop of the apartment complex, doused in the lights of the city, catching up on all that had happened in each other's absence. Yet, despite everything they said to one another, Alexia never dared tell her any specifics regarding what she was doing or where she was going.

In the second half of their first year, Sergeant Clay personally introduced the team to the weaponry and equipment they will be using during the operation, including assault rifles, handguns, firearm attachments, knives, distraction balls, compact med-kits, and cylindrical grenade-sized D-R89 devices – more commonly known as Disintegrators.

On one particular day, Clay presented them, as he would explain it, 'the most important part of their arsenal.'

The team stood at attention in the facility's central hangar, watching in confusion as Clay nodded to an empty space beside him. Then, like an invisible blanket being pulled away, a soldier in a slick, glossy, armoured black tactical suit appeared beside Clay.

The team were awestruck and unable to take their eyes off the suit.

'So, I *could* tell you everything that this suit does. Or you could try it on and see it for yourself. Which would you prefer?' Clay asked with a grin.

Shortly thereafter, a group of Forward Industries scientists assisted each member of the team in slipping into their suits for the first time. After pulling it over her shoulders, Alexia's suit sat loosely on her body.

One scientist pointed down to a button on the touchpad built into her suit's wrist, 'And just press this here.'

Alexia pressed the button with a light touch. Immediately, the suit tightened around her and locked into place, perfectly fitting her frame. Her eyes widened as she smiled and extended her arms, testing its flexibility. Even underneath its armour plating, the jet-black bodysuit allowed her to move with absolute ease.

The scientist handed her the suit's helmet, which was fronted by a curved, tinted visor. She peered inside it before glancing back at him, unsure. After receiving a nod of encouragement, Alexia slid the helmet over her head, seeing through the darkened visor. After a locking sound, the visor brightened and began projecting the time, date, map, her heartbeat, temperature, and other data at the edges of her vision. She quietly chuckled before looking at the other team members, watching them turn invisible. Her visor revealed a yellow outline around each of them so that she could still make them out.

The scientist pointed to another button on her wristpad. 'Use this one to activate the cloaking.'

Alexia held her breath and pressed the button.

In a heartbeat, her arms and body disappeared from sight.

'Holy shit', she said to herself under her breath.

A split second later, the yellow outline of her arms appeared through her visor. She lifted her hands up before her eyes, looking right through them to the other side of the room. A sudden wave of dizziness overcame her.

Gradually, she gazed back at the scientist and began to circle him. The scientist lost sight of her as she stopped behind him. He turned around and peered through her, still uncertain of her whereabouts. Shaking her head in disbelief, Alexia fashioned her fingers into a gun and aimed her hand at his head. With a smile, she pretended to fire a bullet right between his eyes.

* * *

In the months following the acquisition of their new equipment, the team's accuracy and speed with firearms were tested and honed on the facility's firing ranges.

It was during this time that Hayes was given the name "The Eyes" after not only his pale, artificial eyes, but also after proving himself to be the best marksman on the team – regularly hitting bullseyes from up to three virtual kilometres away.

Elsewhere, in entirely virtual environments, fighting against 3-D holographic combatants, Kingston Roux proved himself far and away the fastest shooter on the team. With skin shredded and torn by old scars, a once-handsome face was now almost impossible to see underneath it, but every time he picked up a weapon, he seemed to enter a world entirely absent from our own – one without doubt or concern. In this familiarity, he frequently cleared timed training grounds of all of their hostiles almost a dozen seconds faster than anyone else. Alexia paid especially close attention to him, learning and memorising his movements and habits.

Meanwhile, when it came to their teleportation devices, which were also built into their wristpads, Dax, Cato, and Hayes created their own game that they came to call "Port Catch". Considering most of them were less than familiar with the devices, these few determined that such a fast-paced, competitive manner of training would assist them in becoming as proficient as they could be, as fast as it could be done. Wearing their tactical suits and helmets, which could rapidly calculate the coordinates of where they had to teleport to, the game involved tossing a basketball into an empty space and calling out another team member's name; that member then had to port to said space and catch the ball before it hit the ground. If they failed to catch the ball in time, they would be eliminated from the round, all until one player was left standing.

However, this was not a "Forward Industries–approved" training exercise, a fact Clay made clear to them when eventually catching them in the act. 'These are incredibly powerful tools,' he explained, 'They are *not* toys. By all means, play sports with each other if you want to, but I don't want *any* of you wasting all of your potential and our time by doing something as stupid as porting yourself right into a ball and destroying your innards. Believe me, none of you want that sort of mess on your hands. Let alone the shame of dying from a basketball, of all things.'

However, when Alexia was found and charged with locking up the basketball for them, she instead kept it for herself, and on the occasional night, would sneak into the gymnasium to play Port Catch all by herself.

On other days, traditional methods of tracking were taught to the team, alongside how to operate and read their wristpad technology scanners, which could trace a gauntlet to its precise location. However, as Alice would explain to them, 'The gauntlets were built in secrecy and with secrecy in mind. So, unfortunately for us, that means that any signal it gives off is limited to somewhere between a thirty-to-fifty-metre radius. It's a short distance, I know, but when you are close enough, it *will* help.'

At last, the team also partook in exercises concerning their cloaking and distraction capabilities. It was during these sessions, when they were tasked with sneaking past holographic hostiles and stealing belongings from one another undetected, that the group finally earned their title: *The Ghosts.*

* * *

As the first year passed into the second, Alice interviewed each member of the team on a fortnightly basis, allowing them to explore their thoughts and feelings on how they were progressing. Since they had begun, their confidence in themselves and the mission had grown tenfold.

Meanwhile, back home, Lay would sit on the windowsill at the end of her apartment hallway, watching the street below, waiting hours on end for Alexia to appear. The weeks between her visits soon became months, and eventually, Alexia had forgotten almost entirely about anything and anyone back home.

In the final few months of the program, Alexia was left dripping with sweat after another day of intense physical training. With a towel hanging over her shoulder, she approached her bedroom before catching a glimpse of Kye inside his own quarters. She came to a quiet stop, watching him from behind as he wrote in his journal.

I hope you're okay, she thought to herself. *I hope you've come to understand ... I really hope.*

Gradually, the white walls around her faded into a gentle orange glow. After lingering a little while longer, fighting the distant urge to say even a simple "hello" to him, she sighed and forced herself to continue onwards. As she walked down the hallway, she caught a glimpse of Dax and Ember chatting with one another outside of Ember's bedroom door. When Ember laughed at something Dax had said, she rested her hand on his chest. Alexia slowed down as she came to her own bedroom door, watching them closely.

After saying good night to one another, Ember returned to her room and Dax walked down the hallway, passing Alexia by.

'Lex,' he said with a smile and a nod, 'good night.'

Alexia nodded and lowered her head, concealing her face. 'Good night.'

Without another word, Alexia stepped into her bedroom and pressed a button, sliding the door shut behind her. Leaning her head back, she closed her eyes and shook her head.

They have no idea what they're doing, do they? Or maybe they do, and they just don't care. After all, it's just a job for them, isn't it? Of course, it is. You know that. You know they don't understand ...

After throwing her towel aside, she approached her bedroom wall and pressed its central glowing button. In an instant, almost every tile on the wall before her lit up with images, videos, files, statistics, bloodlines, and digital notes concerning all aspects of her mission. Thousands of hours of knowledge spanning two years of research, all organised to her liking, all resting at her fingertips, towering before her.

Suddenly, nothing but the mission ruled her thoughts.

* * *

Melbourne, Australia, 2281 CE

A set of dark black boots marched down a facility hallway. Sergeant Clay, holding his hands behind his back, approached the gymnasium as the sound of echoing punches grew louder and faster. Upon his arrival, the door slid open before him, and stepping inside, he found Alexia at the opposite end of the room.

There, alone, she fired her fists into a pad-wielding robot. With her back turned, she was entirely immersed in her exercise, groaning and panting as the robot shifted the pads above and below her. In swift, smooth movements, she transitioned between numerous sets of high and low punches, knees, elbows, and kicks.

'Lex,' Clay called out.

With one final punch into the robot, its arm shook, and the sound of her impact echoed into the distance. Finally, Alexia turned around to face her instructor with black tape wrapped around her hands, no longer wearing boxing gloves. Since she had begun, almost two years ago, her body had been hacked down into almost nothing but pure lean muscle, with visible abs, thick biceps, and bulging veins. In silence, she caught her breath and stared at Clay, waiting.

'Ms. Elodie Wells has come to visit us,' he explained, eyeing her up and down, 'and she has requested to meet you. There's no need to change. Just follow me.'

Shortly thereafter, Clay and Alexia stood beside one another in a facility elevator. In their silence, Alexia unwrapped the black tape from one of her shaking hands. Clay glanced at them, seeing her knuckles drip with blood, before meeting her stern gaze. He almost smirked before the elevator dinged and its doors slid open.

Entering a cool, carpeted hallway, Clay escorted Alexia towards a pair of glass doors leading into Elodie's office. As they entered, Able approached them after having concluded his own meeting with Elodie. They nodded to each other before Alexia and Clay stopped partway through the office.

'Thank you, Clay,' Elodie said, standing behind her desk at the opposite end of the room. 'Please excuse us.'

'Yes, ma'am,' Clay said with a nod, joining Able as they exited the room and returned to the elevator.

Alexia glanced about the quiet office, finding it decorated with minimalist, soft-edged furniture. Meanwhile, atop Elodie's desk sat a small holographic image of a peculiar black circle. It seemed to move ever so slightly, with small particles washing back and forth inside of it, almost as if it were alive.

'Do you know what that is?' Elodie asked.

Alexia shook her head, struggling to look away from it.

'It's the Core. A live feed of it, anyway.' Elodie explained with a smile, joining Alexia in her admiration. 'Fascinating, isn't it? Something so powerful, so law-bending, it could've taken *any* shape it wanted, but ultimately it chose its utter power to be encapsulated by a perfect, singular circle. Totally complete and resolute. From beginning to end, confident and formidable in itself and the paths it creates. I like to keep it on my desk as a reminder. To be humbled *and* inspired.'

After a little while longer of being caught in the Core's gaze, Alexia's eyes returned to Elodie's, who met her with great care.

'Thank you for coming to visit me on such short notice,' Elodie continued, gesturing for her to sit down across the desk. 'Please, take a seat. You look like you need it.'

Alexia approached the chair and looked upon it, before standing firm with her hands by her side. 'I'm okay, thank you. I prefer to stand.'

Elodie smiled and nodded, unsurprised. 'Of course. Well, Alexia, I won't waste your time. I don't expect you to speak either. You just have to listen. Firstly, I wanted to apologise that we are only meeting now, so late into your training. I know I haven't been very present throughout the last two years, but that doesn't mean I haven't been watching your progress very closely. And out of everyone here, you have impressed me the most. Not just in your physical capabilities and your dedication to our training, of course,' she said with a gesture towards Alexia's red-stained hands, 'but in the sheer fact that you are still here at all. Now, yes, it's no secret that you are very quiet and isolated. You've been quite careful to put a lot of space between yourself and everyone else here. But I want you to know that I understand it. After all, I'd be more than a fool to think you were anywhere close to being our biggest fan. And after what happened to you under our watch and how long it has taken us to do something about it, I would never blame you for that … *but* … I also think you understand *us*.'

Alexia squinted at Elodie's words and lifted her head, listening with scepticism.

'Because, Alexia, you've kept a painful past close to your chest for a long time now,' Elodie continued. 'And I *know* that it isn't easy. I know because I've had to do it every day for a long time too. So has Alice. And so have many others in this company. But we've all done it because we know, at the end of the day, it's the only way we were ever going to get *here*, to *this* very moment.'

'I didn't tell anyone else because that's what *you* were doing,' Alexia said, shaking her head. 'That's the game you were playing, and I couldn't beat that. I didn't have a choice.'

'Mm, I don't think you quite believe that, Alexia.' Elodie began circling the desk, approaching Alexia. 'Certainly, what we were doing to keep all of this under wraps would've made it difficult for you, and perhaps your attempts would have been in vain, but you still *could* have tried. After all, someone clearly slipped up and told you things that *they* weren't supposed to.' Elodie sat on the edge of her desk beside Alexia. 'No matter what we do, there's always going to be cracks. And you strike me as the kind of person that will take whatever risk you have to, no matter how great, if you truly believed it was the right way to do it. You *could* have tried. But instead, deep down, I think you knew that wasn't going to get you here. So instead, you waited for us. You *believed* in us. And you were right to, because as I'm sure you've figured out by now, if we simply rolled over the truth to the public and the governments as to what's happened here, none of us would be here right now. These magnificent inventions would either be destroyed or fall into the hands of who-knows-who for who-knows-what, and the justice and answers that you and I seek, the responsibility I feel towards you and everyone else hurt by this, the personal connection I have to this company and our past, would be lost with it.' Elodie leant in closer to Alexia, catching her eyes. '*We're both here, Alexia, because we can't trust anyone else to do this for us. We can't trust them to go to the lengths that we know <u>we</u> will.* And thankfully, in that, we have found each other, and we no longer have to do this alone. I know you might not trust me, or even like me, but I give you my word, we're going to get to the bottom of this travesty once and for all. We're going to find out what happened to your parents, and we're going to serve the justice that these criminals deserve. I promise you.'

Alexia stared back into Elodie's eyes without words.

Eventually, Elodie lowered her head and sighed. 'But unfortunately, not everyone thinks like us. And that's another reason why I wanted to speak to you today … Ember and Dax. I've heard reports regarding a certain closeness between them for some time. A kind of bond that, as I'm sure you know, can be very detrimental to a mission as important as this one. Now, I already spoke to Able about the matter, but he was adamant their relationship was strictly platonic.' Elodie looked at Alexia, reading her expression. 'But like I said, I'm no fool. To be clear, though, I wouldn't expect any different from Able. His mission is just as much to ensure the safety of his team as it is to complete it. But that's why I also need someone else, a *second* in command, to ensure that the team itself does not sabotage this operation. To ensure that they do what needs to be done and don't get in the way. You may need to be a little louder and a little more involved, but I believe that person is *you*.'

An even greater surprise came over Alexia as she continued to listen in silence.

'Now, tonight is your last night off, and you have one more week until the operation begins,' Elodie clarified. 'So, don't tell me now what it is you think of this proposal. But please, think on it, and before the week is over, let me know if we're on the same page. If it's a *yes,* or a *no* … Now, go and enjoy your night. You've certainly earned it.' Elodie rested her hand on Alexia's arm before standing up and walking back around to the opposite side of the desk.

Alexia gradually turned and walked towards the office's glass door. Upon reaching its handle, she turned and glanced back at the desk, finding the hologram of the Core staring back at her once more.

With a heavy breath, Alexia closed her eyes before looking back at Elodie. 'I think you already know my answer … but it's a yes. No one will get in the way. And they were never going to. Not with me here.'

Elodie smiled at her words. 'I'm glad to hear that, Alexia. Thank you.'

Alexia nodded as her eyes fell to the floor and she gripped the handlebar. After a long, quiet moment, she returned to Elodie's gaze one last time. 'Thank *you*.'

Chapter 15

Neon blues, purples, and greens flashed across an ocean of nightclub dancers. Techno trance music pulsated through the air as bodies leapt up and down, throwing their hands and drinks into the air. Long walls of glass divided the crowds and shattered the pulsating lights into thousands of shapes. Amongst them, Dax and Ember danced together. He rested his hands on her hips as she swayed them side to side and closed her eyes, letting the purple and blue lights drip down her skin.

Dax watched her as if he were overcome by a spell. After opening her eyes, Dax grasped her waist and turned her around, pressing her against a window at the end of the club. The lights turned green as they both overlooked the shining city below. He slid his hands over her stomach and upon her breasts, kissing her neck as she pressed herself into him, moaning and running her fingers through his hair.

'Do you really think we should do this?' Ember asked breathlessly. 'If one of us doesn't make it …'

Dax shook his head and whispered into her ear, 'If we're going to die, I'd rather this be real … wouldn't you?'

Ember gripped the back of his head and lost herself in his eyes. *'Yes.'* With a smile, she urged him closer, and kissed him under the slow lights. For a time, they only felt the warmth of each other's lips, before resting their foreheads together. 'Let's get out of here.'

Meanwhile, Hayes and Cato sat at the nightclub bar two floors below, almost drooling onto the counter as numerous empty drinks laid about before them.

Hayes, with his cheek resting on the glowing counter, pushed another half-finished glass of neon blue liquid towards Cato. 'Come on, man, you gotta do it. You gotta finish this one.'

'Oh, give me a minute, bro, *please*,' Cato begged, wobbling back and forth in his seat.

'We only got this one last night to let loose, man. What are you waiting for?'

'I'm waiting for the chances of me throwing up to go *down*.'

Hayes groaned and waved away his words. 'Ehhh, what's the point in having all those muscles if you can't even handle a few drinks?'

'You haven't figured it out already? These muscles,' Cato gestured to his thick biceps. 'These are nothing but a shallow disguise to conceal my true fragile, self-conscious state of being.'

In his daze, Hayes fell silent and stared into the distance. 'Shit, man ... that's deep.'

Cato almost rolled his eyes as Ember and Dax approached them from amongst the crowds, amused by their intoxication.

'Oh boy, what are you up to now?' Dax asked.

'Don't ask me. He's counting,' Cato said, gesturing to his inebriated friend.

'Oh ... I thought you were,' Hayes replied, staring back at him cluelessly.

'Okay, maybe try not to die *before* the mission,' Ember suggested, patting their shoulders.

'In this state, I honestly cannot promise anything anymore.' Cato said, shaking his head and struggling to sit upright.

Dax chuckled. 'Well, I wish you good luck, boys. We're heading out for a while. We'll see you later.'

'No probs.'

'Have a good niigght!' Ember said as the pair disappeared into the crowds.

'You toooo,' Hayes replied before smirking at Cato. 'I wonder where *they're* going.'

'World's biggest mystery, right there,' Cato agreed, raising his eyebrows before sculling down the last of his drink. 'Ahh, fuck. All right ... what the hell's next?'

* * *

Elsewhere, on the nightclub's rooftop balcony, where the thumping music was muffled and distant, Kye leant against a railing, looking upon the busy streets below.

Eventually, he turned his gaze towards the city beyond, watching the lights of spacecraft float to and fro while 3-D-projected advertisements danced through the sky.

Able strolled up beside him, passing him a fresh drink.

'Thank you.' Kye nodded.

For a time, Able joined him in observing the view as the cool wind brushed across their faces and the city lights reflected in their eyes.

'Are you going to miss all of this?' Able asked.

Kye looked at Able with some surprise. 'You don't think we'll make it back?'

'I think it's too hard to know what's gonna happen …'

'Do you *want* to make it back?'

Able glanced at him, grim and unflinching. Soon, his eyes fell towards the street below, spotting Dax and Ember as they exited the nightclub, holding hands. Able smiled for just a moment, before his pain came flooding back. 'You know, I know they taught us a lot about how to kill these people, and have done even more to motivate us to do it, but honestly, the second I learnt about them, I already hated them.'

'… Why?'

'Because they ran away. They couldn't deal with their lives. They thought it was too … "tough". And then suddenly they think they have the right to do what they did. To steal, to kill, to put everyone else's lives in danger. All because they just couldn't *handle* it. And at the same time, I had to live my life. Every day, I grew to live with it … I grew to live with those I love never being there anymore.' Able's eyes watered, and his breath shook. 'And they think *they* know pain. That they just get to *run* away from their problems.' He clenched his jaw at the thought of them. 'They're selfish cowards. And they deserve everything that's coming to them.'

Kye contemplated his words in silence. After a time, he held out his drink in solidarity.

Able settled his breath and clanked his drink against Kye's, both taking a sip.

'What are you doing up here, anyway?' Able asked. 'Listening to the rambles of the old man of the group. You're young. You should be enjoying yourself down there.'

Kye shook his head and shrugged. 'I'm happy to spend time with any of you, even if it's not for much longer … though, I hope it is.'

'Funny you say that. This is the most I've ever heard you speak. You're always hiding away and buried in that journal of yours.'

'I like my own company too, I suppose.' Kye chuckled. 'And I guess I don't always know when the right time to speak is.'

'Or you know *too* well, and you're up there in your head thinking about this much more than we are. You've got too much of a heart and mind to be in this group if you ask me. I know you served with the EDF, but you've never done anything like this before, have you?'

'Not exactly … but I have killed a man …'

Able turned to him as the wind grew colder.

'On one rotation, a group of pirates boarded our ship,' Kye explained as he stared into space, remembering. 'He was coming through one of the airlocks, had his gun by his side, and … it was either him or me.'

'Mm.' Able nodded, taking another sip of his drink. 'Him or you is one thing, but this isn't fighting for your survival. This is *hunting*. And if you don't find something to make you goddamn hate your prey's existence, then you better start shutting off that compassionate part of your brain, son. Because when you're hunting like we are, only one thing matters.'

* * *

On another side of the city, Alexia trekked through a narrow street alone. Her duffel bag was tied to her back as she gritted her teeth against the cold. After slipping through a tight alleyway, she finally spotted her apartment building in the distance. In front of it, on the opposite side of the street was Lay, sitting on the ground and wearing a puffy jacket. Before her sat a rusty, skinny robot leant against a wall.

Alexia tilted her head, confused at the sight of them as they gently rolled a glowing pink ball back and forth between them.

'Hey, Lay.'

Lay turned to see Alexia walking towards them. 'A! You're back!' she screamed with joy, bouncing to her feet and rushing over to hug her. 'I've missed you!'

Alexia chuckled as she took Lay into her arms and held her tight. 'I missed you too. I'm sorry it's been so long. But what are you doing out here?'

'This is my new friend I made!' she said, gesturing to the depleted robot.

'Your new friend?' Alexia looked at the mechanical being as it gazed up at her with dim yellow eyes. 'Where did you find him?'

'I saw him when I was waiting for you. He was just sitting out here, all alone. How do I get him to talk?' Lay asked, sitting back down across from him. 'I was hoping maybe he could help me read.'

'You can't, Lay. He's a worker-bot. They're not designed to talk.'

'Oh …' Lay gazed at her new friend with pity.

Alexia squatted down between them, curiously inspecting the robot. 'But it's strange. These guys are built for factory work, and when a factory shuts down, they're supposed to just … phase out with them. They're not supposed to be able to even function. He must be losing power as we speak. He'll shut down any day now.'

The robot took in its surroundings, silent and serene.

'Well, I'm not going to let that happen!' Lay declared. 'He's *my* friend!'

Alexia smiled and climbed to her feet. 'Okay, come on. Let's get you inside. Your parents are going to be worried.'

'They won't be,' Lay said, shaking her head.

'Hey, of course they will be, Lay. Why do you say that?'

'My mum's too sick to even notice, and my dad's always out working. I barely even see him, and even when I do, he's just fighting with Mum …' Before Lay's sadness lingered too long, she beamed back at Alexia, 'But that's okay! I have you and my new friend!'

Alexia forced another smile as she took Lay's hand and helped her up. 'Come on now, it's cold out, and you know you shouldn't be breathing in this air too much. It's not good for you.'

'Can we take Bot inside with us?' Lay asked.

'Bot? Is that his name now?'

'Yep!'

'Did you just come up with that?'

'Yep!'

Alexia laughed as she walked her back towards the building, 'Well, no, I'm afraid not. Bot can stay out here.'

'But he'll get cold too!'

'Robots don't get cold, Lay.'

Lay's shoulders fell as she looked back at her new friend. 'I'll see you tomorrow, Bot!' she cried out, waving goodbye.

Alexia glanced back at the robot as it remained motionless, staring back at them. As the pair reached the front door of their building, a homeless man stumbled up beside them, violently coughing through his ventilator mask.

'Do you have a spare breather I could borrow? I'm all out,' the man explained, showing his tattered and worn-out oxygen capsule.

'I don't, sorry,' Alexia replied, turning away with shame before busting the door open with her shoulder.

Lay slid inside as the man waddled away, continuing to cough. Alexia kicked the door shut behind her and sighed, leading Lay up the stairs.

Across the street, one of Bot's fingers twitched. Its pumping mechanisms and wiring strained as it used all of its strength to lift its hand towards the apartment building's door, waving goodbye.

Inside, Alexia walked Lay back towards her apartment door.

'A, why didn't that man have any more oxy-caps?' Lay asked in a curious and quiet voice.

Alexia looked at Lay with regret. 'Because they're hard to come by, Lay. So, that's why I say, you don't want to have to need them, and you shouldn't go running around out there – *especially* at night.'

'I know. It's just there's not much else I *can* do. I wish I got to go to school.'

'I know you do, I know you do.'

'Will you read with me tonight?' Lay asked with some hope. 'I have some new readings! I think they're some of the new ones they teach in schools, from the last ten years or so, because they're really hard.'

Alexia looked down at Lay as her heart began to sink. 'I don't think that's a great idea, Lay. I need to get some sleep, and I think you should spend some time with your mum,' Alexia said, opening Lay's apartment door.

Lay dragged her feet inside the small, untidy apartment. Its window was obstructed by another building, blocking any natural light from shining inside and causing shadows to infest everywhere. Meanwhile, Lay's mother, Atee, lay asleep in her bedroom. She had cords running from her nose and lungs into an oxygen container resting beside her bed.

'See?' Lay whispered. 'She doesn't even know when I'm gone.'

Alexia gazed at Atee with sorrow before following Lay into her own tiny bedroom. 'That doesn't mean she doesn't care if you're going out there.'

'But *you* go out there all the time,' Lay replied as she sat down at the edge of her bed, frowning.

Alexia knelt down and rested her hand on Lay's knee. 'Hey, you don't want to be like me, okay? You can do *so much* better than that. You've got your *whole* life ahead of you. And you're lucky you've got two parents here at all. That means *a lot*. Don't forget that.'

Lay stared at the floor, silent and sorrowful.

Alexia reached out and stroked her black, braided hair. 'You hold on to them tight, okay? For me?'

Lay nodded. 'But what about you? You're not leaving again, are you?'

Alexia closed her eyes with a sigh. 'I am. I actually came here to say goodbye, Lay.'

'You're coming back though, right?'

Alexia shook her head as she hesitated. 'I don't want you waiting up for me. You've got your parents, and you can always use my apartment if you want to escape everything for a bit, but please, don't wait for me.'

Lay's lips trembled as her eyes welled with tears. 'But I'm gonna miss you.'

'Oh, I'm gonna miss you too, Lay.' Alexia pulled Lay into her chest for another hug as tears rolled down Lay's cheeks. 'It's gonna be okay.' Alexia assured her, rubbing her back. 'You're a smart girl. I know you'll be okay.'

'Why can't you come back?' Lay pleaded.

'Because … because I have to do something very important,' Alexia explained as she began to feel an unrelenting pain of longing enshroud her heart. 'Because a long time ago, some very bad people did some very bad things. They hurt people, and they took them away from those that loved them. They did that to me too. So, I'm going to stop them and make sure they never hurt anyone ever again. But to do that, I have to follow them somewhere that will take me very far away … so far away that I don't think I can come back.'

'Can't somebody else do it?'

'No, I have to do it myself, Lay. I have to make sure it's done because sometimes … sometimes you just have to do things yourself … and I've been looking for them for a long, *long* time.'

'But you know, if you leave, Bot's going to replace you as my new best friend?' Lay said through her tears.

Alexia chuckled and nodded, sniffling away her own tears. 'Well, Bot is very lucky to have you, then. But I guess if you *are* going to see him again, you know what you should do first?'

'What?'

'Go to bed at a reasonable time, which you can start getting used to right now.'

'*Oh, but I'm not tired, A!*'

'Hey, I'm just telling you the truth.' Alexia shrugged, returning to her feet and walking over to a small shelf. She picked out a soft teddy bear and tucked it into Lay's arms. 'Here, this little guy is nice and fluffy. He'll help you sleep.'

'I like Bot more.'

'Trust me, this guy's much nicer to cuddle. Now, you get a good night's sleep, okay?'

Lay's eyes fell to the floor as she sat in silence.

Alexia almost shattered at the sight of her, just barely holding herself together as she returned to the bedroom door.

Lay looked back at Alexia with worry, speaking up once more. 'A, wherever you're going … will you be okay?'

Alexia rested her hand on the door handle before glancing back at her small friend with a shaking smile. 'You don't have to worry about me, Lay. What's important is that *you'll* be okay. And you *will* be ... Good night. I love you.'

Lay clutched her teddy bear and bowed her head, saying nothing in return as Alexia stepped outside and shut the door behind her. Closing her eyes, she rested her hand over her heart, feeling as though a blade had stabbed right through it.

How can you leave her like this? she asked herself. *Why don't you just stay with her a little while longer?*

Alexia buried her head in her hand as she finally caught a long, deep breath.

Because you know why ...

It's for the best. And doing it now will only make it easier for everyone...

'Alexia ...' a weak voice called out.

Alexia opened her eyes as another wave of misery struck her. With light steps, she approached Atee's bedroom. Inside, she found Lay's mother – frail, skinny, and barely able to lift her head off the pillow.

'Please. Come here,' Atee asked, tapping the empty space beside her.

Alexia walked over to her side. 'Hey, Atee. How are you doing?'

'I've certainly been better,' she said, struggling to maintain her breath. 'But thank you ... for bringing her back in. I ... I can barely stand.'

'That's okay. Don't worry. I've told her to stay close to you.'

Atee took Alexia's hand and smiled up at her. 'Thank you. You're a good girl. I'm glad she has you.'

Alexia struggled to smile as her eyes welled with tears again and she patted Atee's bony hand. Atee sighed a heavy breath and rested her eyes again, falling into another deep sleep.

Alexia watched over her for a little while longer before wiping away her tears and sneaking out of the room. Stepping into the hallway, she carefully shut the door behind her and approached her own apartment. At the same time, Lay's father, Sherwin, climbed the stairwell and entered the hallway. His face was gaunt, facial hair unkempt, and had his work bag slung over his shoulder as he wandered up to his apartment opposite Alexia.

'Didn't know you were back.' He yawned.

'Just for the night,' Alexia explained, glancing back at him as she unlocked her door.

'Lay told me you've been going away more and more often. That true?'

'It is.'

'You moving? Going off-world?'

'Something like that.'

'Yeah … that's looking more and more like an option these days. I've actually been talking with some people who, you know, can help make that sort of thing easier.'

'You're thinking of leaving? Do you think Atee could make a trip like that?'

'No … she couldn't.'

A heavy silence befell them both.

'Well, maybe when the time's right, you can talk to Lay about it,' Alexia said. 'I'm sure you'll figure something out. Good night, Sherwin,' she finished, opening her door and stepping inside her apartment.

'Hey, do you know of any good homes, by any chance?' Sherwin asked. 'Somewhere that would be good for Lay?'

Alexia stopped dead in her tracks.

'I mean, you grew up in one, didn't you?' he clarified.

Alexia half-turned around to face him. *'What are you saying?'*

'Well, you know, I can't – I just can't stick around here forever, you know? I'm just looking out for Lay.'

'You're looking out for her, are you?' Alexia glared at him in disbelief, gradually walking towards him, closer and closer. 'Your wife is *dying*, your daughter *needs* you, and you're thinking of *leaving her?*'

Sherwin backed up against his door as Alexia continued to approach him. 'What the hell are you doing?' he whimpered.

'No, what the hell are *you* doing? You're just going to *abandon them?!*'

'I can barely feed myself, and when Atee goes … Lay's gonna need a better place than here.'

A fire raged inside Alexia's eyes. 'Her better place *is* with you. If you try and run off on her, *like a fucking coward,* I'll find you and drag you right back here myself. *Okay?*'

'You can't talk to me like that.'

'I just did. So, go on, *try something ... Try it!'*

Sherwin's entire body froze.

Alexia eyed him up and down in disgust, before stepping away. Without another word, she entered her apartment and slammed the door shut.

Sherwin let out a sigh of relief as he leant his head back against the wall behind him.

Inside her apartment, Alexia panted and clenched her fists. She shook her head at herself before noticing her plants. Instinctively, she walked towards her tap and filled up a jug of water, watering each of them with care. She placed the jug down at their side and watched as the water dripped off their dying leaves.

Before long, a loud, distant boom echoed outside her window, drawing her attention. Alexia pressed her forehead against the glass, looking out across the city. In the distance, a huge, planet-colonising spacecraft was taking off. Red and yellow flames burst out from its massive thrusters, pushing the ship off into the night sky before it disappeared into the smoke and smog.

* * *

Ember opened her eyes as the morning light poured in through her bedroom window. She looked upon Dax, who lay naked and fast asleep beside her. Smiling, she ran her fingers along his arm and shoulder.

Eventually, his eyes opened, seeing her smiling at him. 'Mm, good morning,' he mumbled, still half asleep.

'Good morning. You slept very deeply.'

'Mmmm-hmmm.'

Ember laughed. 'We should go soon. Don't want to get back too late.'

'Mm, let's just stay a little longer,' he said, sliding his arm around her and pulling her closer. They kissed and pressed their heads together, smiling at each other.

'What is it?' she asked.

'What do you mean?'

'You're thinking something. You've got your thinking face.'

'Mm, do I?'

'Yeah. One of your rarest faces.'

Dax chuckled and nodded. 'Yeah, yeah. You know, you were in my dream last night?'

'Really?' Ember asked with excitement. 'What happened?'

'I can't remember.' He broke into a laugh.

Ember rolled her eyes and laughed with him.

Eventually, as their laughs faded, they returned to one another's gaze.

'I don't think I've had enough time with you,' Dax whispered. 'I don't want this to be the end.'

'Me neither.'

'Okay … well … how about we kill everyone we have to, do it as quick as we can, both get back alive, and then we get the hell away from here. You and I. How's that sound?'

'That's the best plan I've heard yet,' Ember agreed, embracing him in another kiss.

* * *

In the midst of a cloud of steam, Alexia stood under her showerhead. She closed her eyes and dipped her head back, letting the water flow through her short hair and trickle over the many scars that marred her body.

Eventually, she reached for the shower's valve, gradually turning it from hot to cold. The water's temperature dropped until her skin felt as though it was being pierced by thousands of tiny needles. She clenched her teeth as her entire body shook. With a sharp inhale, she pressed her hand against the wall beside her.

After a steady exhale, her body loosened and she embraced the cold.

A short time later, Alexia slipped into her boots and purple leather jacket. With her duffel bag ready and waiting on the table, she returned to her plants. She picked up her jug before pausing, staring down at the decrepit flowers. In the time that she had been gone, many of them had lost their colour and fallen away, while others barely clung on to life.

With reluctance, Alexia placed the jug back down on the bench. For one final lingering moment, she looked upon them with a regret that soon turned into frustration.

Just leave them, already, she told herself. *You can't do anything for them anymore.*

At last, Alexia picked up her bag and left the room.

* * *

Operation Day

Inside the Forward Industries armoury, surrounded by walls of firearms and equipment, each member of the ghost team strapped on their gear and loaded their weapons.

With a long stretch, Hayes turned to the team with a smile. 'Hey, do you think they'd let us stay longer if we said we needed some more time? Cause I don't know about you guys, but I don't think I'm ready to leave behind all of the precious food and drinks we've been getting here.'

'I hear you there,' Cato agreed, checking the straps and belts around his suit.

'I think they've waited long enough for us,' Able said, turning to them both as he picked up his helmet. 'It's about time we do what we're here for. And if they're looking for more roles afterwards, do this well and maybe they'll have you stick around.'

'That's true, that's true.' Hayes nodded with confidence, picking his assault rifle off the wall. 'I just have to make them miss me, then they'll never want me to leave again.'

'Good luck waiting for that to happen,' Dax replied with a smirk.

'Hey! Forward Industries and I have a very personal relationship that you just wouldn't understand, okay? They love me. They just don't say it out loud because they don't want to make all of you jealous.'

Cato, Ember, and Dax sighed and shook their heads, and as Hayes continued to bicker and laugh with them, Alexia stood beside Kingston on the opposite side of the armoury. Kingston, beneath his many scars, glanced in her direction, watching her as she picked out various pieces of equipment from the wall.

'I was surprised not to find you training the other night,' he said, bearing an English upper-class inflection in his voice as he loaded a rifle magazine with one bullet at a time. 'You actually took the night off.'

Alexia looked back at him before continuing to slot grenades and disintegrators into her vest. 'Yeah. I had some goodbyes to make.'

'Goodbyes, eh? Well, that sounds just wonderful.'

'You didn't have any?'

'Oh no, I made my goodbyes a *long* time ago,' Kingston explained, locking the magazine into his assault rifle. 'Now we just get to have fun.'

'... Fun?'

'Absolutely.' He smirked back at her with a wild glimmer in his eye.

Before long, the team began filing out of the armoury, kitted out with every piece of armour and weaponry that they had been trained with. Alexia and Kye were the last to leave, stopping before the door as they caught each other's eye. For a moment, they stood in silence, unsure of what to say.

'… Good luck,' Kye said, at last, giving her a small smile.

Alexia smiled and nodded in return. 'You too.'

Soon, in the centre of the facility hangar, the team of eight stood in a line with their assault rifles slung across their chests and their helmets under their arms. Sergeant Clay, Alice, Elodie, and a handful of scientists stood before them.

'Your two years of training is finally complete,' Alice said, 'and you're in the best state we ever could've imagined. I'm proud of you.'

'We know you'll do what you were trained for,' Elodie added.

'That's right,' Clay said, stepping forth, 'but I want to hear it from your *own* mouths. *Why are you here?*'

'To save history!' the team roared.

'What is your mission?' Clay cried, even louder.

'To terminate all targets and retrieve the gauntlets!'

'What are you willing to do to finish the mission?'

'Anything!'

'Who are you?'

'Ghosts!'

'Then go kill these sons of bitches once and for all!'

Without a second's hesitation, the ghosts turned and marched down a series of hallways. Upon reaching their designated port room, a metallic door slid open before them. As the team entered the small concrete room, Alexia stopped behind them and turned to Alice.

'Are you okay, Lex?' Alice asked.

'Yeah. I just … I just wanted to say I'm sorry. For what happened to you. For what they did to you. I know how you feel … so, I won't let you down. I promise.'

Alice's lips hesitated before she forced a smile and a nod. 'I just hope you find your answers.'

'Thank you … Goodbye,' Alexia finally said, turning and entering the port room. The door automatically closed and locked behind her, sealing the team off from the outside world.

A one-way mirror stretched across one of the port room walls. Clay, Elodie, Alice, and a number of scientists watched from their control room on the opposite side. They sat and stood before a long control panel as the ghosts slid on their helmets.

Alice pressed down on one of the desk's buttons, speaking to them through their helmets. 'Remember, the times and destinations might not be exact. Some of them are strictly educated guesses, so don't panic if you have to spend some time looking for them. They're all preset for you, anyway. All you need to do is synchronise and go to each time coded into your devices, and then when the mission is complete, you will return to this room, thirty seconds after you left.'

Cato glanced at the window, speaking through his helmet. 'Man, you guys are lucky. You get to skip all of the hard stuff.'

Elodie smiled and pressed the communications button. 'We know you can do it. We'll be right here for you when you get back. Good luck, soldiers.'

'Sync up!' Able ordered.

The team connected their wrist gauntlets to one another, making each of their devices pulsate a yellow light.

'Synched!' Alexia replied.

'Cloak!' Able shouted.

In unison, all eight ghosts activated their cloaking devices, disappearing from sight.

'Cloaked!' Alexia confirmed.

'On "Go", we port! Three. Two. One. *Go!*'

Chapter 16

London, England, 1864 CE

Grass swayed to and fro in the midnight wind. Fields upon fields rested in darkness as the soft breeze howled and moaned.

In the midst of one such lonely field, the invisible ghosts suddenly materialised. A cold brush of air followed, pushing the low-hanging fog outwards. They aimed their rifles into the darkness, covering and surveying their surroundings.

For a moment, they remained silent and still.

Ember squatted down, outstretching her gloved hand into the flowing grass. 'I've never seen so much grass.'

'It's so quiet too,' Cato added, just as taken as the rest of them.

Alexia lost her breath as she swung her boot side to side through the grass, watching it bend around her feet. Eventually, her gaze lifted towards the moon. Hundreds of thousands of stars lit up the sky, free from smog and spacecraft and artificial light. It was as though the entire universe glowed inside her eyes, and she could not help but be in awe of its cosmic beauty.

Kye's jaw had almost dropped before he spotted a large house consumed by shadow in the distance.

'Eyes on the Dumphree estate,' Dax said.

Able turned, attaining his own visual on the house. 'All right. Focus, team. Let's make this quick and clean. Activate voice isolators and follow me.' With a firm hand signal, the ghosts turned on their helmets' interior soundproofing, silencing their voices from the outside world, and advanced towards the sleeping estate.

They gripped their rifles tight and quietened their step as they crossed a dirt road, fading into the house's heavy shadow. Without a word needed to be said, they broke off into two groups, moving along both sides of the house.

'Picking up five sets of heat signatures and a potential electronic reading,' Dax informed them.

A silenced gunshot pierced the night air before the smash of glass sounded shortly after.

'Activity. Rear of the house,' Able said.

The ghosts picked up their pace, nearing the back of the house. Their temperature readers gave off a sudden, short burst of two beeps. A new wave of cold air brushed past them.

'Picking up a temperature drop!' Hayes exclaimed. 'Someone's here!'

Alexia rested her finger on the trigger and gritted her teeth, rushing ahead. Both squads turned the furthest corners of the estate, finding themselves at the base of a porch. At its centre laid the body of Hughes Avil with a bullet through his head. Broken shards from his glass were soaked in a pool of blood and water.

Kye froze at the sight of him.

'Only picking up three signatures now. No more electronics either,' Dax reported.

'Shit,' Alexia muttered under her breath, scanning the fields around them.

'Must have just missed him,' Cato said.

'All right, I'll confirm the body,' Able replied.

'Wait — people approaching,' Ember interrupted.

Worried voices approached from inside the estate. The ghosts remained in their place, watching as Flavel Dumphree walked towards the back door. He was overcome with dread at the growing sight of Hughes' body. With great caution, he stepped outside, scrutinising his surroundings. His breath was visible in the cold night air as he peered right through the ghosts, oblivious to their presence.

'Hold, team,' Able ordered. 'No sudden movements.'

Mary Dumphree and Stella Lockhurt approached the door a moment later.

'Hughes?' Stella asked as she neared the body. Suddenly, her knees buckled, and she screamed in horror. *'Hughes!'*

Kye lowered his rifle, overwhelmed by what was transpiring before him.

'Oh, God, no,' Mary whimpered, barely able to look at his body as she wrapped her arms around herself.

Stella rushed out the back door and collapsed to her knees beside Hughes' body. Her hands shook as she felt his cold body. She burst into tears and shook her head in disbelief, 'No, *no, no, Hughes, no ... What happened? Don't ... don't leave me. Please. What happened?'*

Confused and unsettled, Flavel glanced around for any sign of the culprit.

There was nothing but darkness.

Finally, he turned back to Stella, unable to find his words. Before long, he took a hold of her arm. 'Stella, we need to get inside.'

'What happened?' she cried.

'I don't know! But whoever did this couldn't be far – we need to get inside, now! Come!' he said, pulling Stella to her feet and ushering her back inside as she cried uncontrollably. Flavel shut the door behind them before handing Stella over to Mary. 'Take her upstairs. I'll get a rifle.'

'Okay, okay.' Mary nodded through her own tears, taking Stella into her arms.

'How long has this guy been living here?' Hayes asked the team outside.

Stella's cries rang in Alexia's ears as she stared at the body and the blood, feeling her nerves begin to shudder.

Able listened to the emotional voices as they descended deeper into the house. Once they were far enough away, his eyes returned to Hughes' lonely body. 'Hold position. I'll dispose of the body.'

With a swift vigilance, Able crept up the porch steps and slung his rifle around his chest. As he knelt down beside Hughes' body, he pulled out a disintegrator from his belt. He peered back through the glass doors and into the house. No one was in sight.

Gazing back at the body, his electronic visor scanned Hughes' face, confirming his identity. Within each of their helmets, Hughes Avil's recorded status changed from **Active** to **Deceased.**

Able clicked a button at the top of the disintegrator, projecting a small needle from the bottom of the device before he stabbed it into Hughes' shoulder. A grey bubbling fluid was immediately injected into his body. Within seconds, Hughes' body began to dissolve into nothing but specks of skin and dust.

The ghosts watched in silence as the small particles of Hughes floated up into the night sky. Kye felt all of his life and energy fading away with them. After a short time, the corpse had disappeared forever, as if it had never even been there.

Only a moment later, frantic footsteps approached from within the house. Able's eyes darted back to the door as Flavel walked out of the hallway, holding a Victorian rifle by his side, nearing the rear of the house.

'Civ is coming back. Let's get out of here,' Able said, sneaking off the porch and returning to the cover of shadow. Both squads of ghosts began synchronising their gauntlets.

Upon noticing Hughes' body was missing, Flavel picked up his pace towards the back door and swung it open, desperately searching for any sign of him. 'Hughes? *Hughes! … Who goes there?*'

'Everyone's synched up except Kye,' Hayes said.

Kye was entirely distant from them all, watching Flavel as he stood alone, helpless and lost.

'Kye, are you ready?' Able asked.

In an instant, Kye's attention returned to the ghosts, nodding to Able. 'Yeah – yes, sorry. I'm ready.'

'All right, then. Let's go.'

After synching his gauntlet, the ghosts disappeared. Flavel felt a wave of cold wind whisk by him as his gaze fell upon the pool of blood that laid beside his feet, beginning to stain the porch's floorboards. His eyes watered and his jaw clenched. With a spark of determination, he wrapped his hands around the rifle and jogged off the porch, beginning his search of the surrounding property.

* * *

Twigs and sticks snapped beneath pairs of invisible boots. Surrounding trees distorted as the ghosts slid past, marching down a tall, hillside forest.

'One down. Six to go,' Dax reported.

Eventually, they came upon a clearing in the woods, overlooking a red, walled, bustling city in the distance.

'There it is … Fuckin' hell,' Cato said, taking in the sight of it.

'Amazing,' Hayes added with a shake of his head, stopping beside him.

'Sun should be down in three hours,' Dax continued, relaying the information from inside his helmet's visor.

'Good,' Able replied with a nod. 'Crowds should be dying down soon then. We'll split into our two squads again, cover the east and west sides of the city, then push inwards. Everyone got that?'

'Copy,' Alexia said.

'All right, let's get ourselves a little closer.'

Synching up their gauntlets, the team ported away, leaving only silence and numerous tiny shards of ice on the many fallen leaves below.

Chapter 17

Beijing, China, 1410 CE

In a field outside the city walls, the tall grass bent backwards, and small pools of water rippled as the ghosts materialised. The invisible hunters jogged through the wet fields, straight towards Beijing's looming gates.

Upon reaching the edge of a road, Able lifted his fist. 'Hold here.'

The ghosts knelt down at the end of the field, watching as citizens passed by on the dirt track before them, strolling in and out of the city. Hayes stared at the towering walls, feeling an excitement rising within him. Meanwhile, Kingston maintained a keen eye on the armed guards at the gates.

Able spotted an oncoming group of citizens walking and riding their horses out of the city. 'There, that group,' he said, pointing them out. 'Slip in between them, then disperse to the left and right once we're beyond the gates. Let's go.'

The ghosts crept onto the dirt track and spread themselves amongst the passing horses and citizens. Holding their weapons close, they slowed down to the same pace as those around them. Alexia watched every movement of those passing her by, making sure to stay out of their way. One citizen amongst them noticed a glint pass him by. He glanced at his side, mildly curious, before continuing on his way.

Finally, the ghosts entered the city gates and broke off into two halves. Able, Dax, Kingston, and Kye in one group; Alexia, Cato, Ember, and Hayes in the other.

The looming, half-constructed Temple of Heaven gazed down upon them as they swept by in silence. Soon enough, they found themselves in the central district of the outer city. Countless citizens filled the streets, scurrying to finish their errands for the day. The ghosts sneaked by at the edges of the streets, where no one was quite paying attention. Before entering anywhere too densely populated, the squads diverted into the surrounding alleyways.

The red of the sun intensified as it fell towards the horizon. As the hours passed, Able's squad eventually came upon a quiet, barren street on the far eastern side of the outer city, where most of the houses and buildings were only half constructed. Workers were in the midst of packing and leaving for the day.

'Stack up on the right side,' Able ordered.

The four ghosts lined up along the right side of the street, scanning each building and alleyway they passed for any sign of their targets.

'Hold,' Able ordered again.

They paused as a handful of construction workers strolled out of a house before them. The ghosts waited and watched them pass by. The workers chatted and laughed with one another, completely blind to the presence beside them. Kingston smirked at their obliviousness as they exited the street.

'All right, keep moving,' Able said, leading them forward.

'Picking up some more heat signatures ahead,' Dax reported.

'Copy,' Able replied, keeping a firm eye in front of them.

Soon, a trail of blood became clear, running from an alleyway on the left side of the street across to a half-constructed house on the right side.

'I got a visual on blood,' Kingston noted.

'I see it. It – *hold!*' Able exclaimed, holding up his fist again.

Ahead of them, a handful of red-robed Jinyiwei exited the incomplete house. With them, they dragged a helpless construction worker whose face was bleeding and swollen. The ghosts remained still as they watched the soldiers pull the workman further and further away. A moment later, their captain exited the house, following them towards the inner city walls.

'I'm still picking up one more signature within that house,' Dax said, waiting to see if anyone else was going to leave the building.

'All right, we'll check it out. Move with caution,' Able replied, gesturing them forward.

The Jinyiwei disappeared from sight as the ghosts arrived at the quiet house. Able stopped and peeked inside, seeing and hearing nothing.

'Still got that signature,' Dax repeated.

'Scanners are picking up electronics now too.' Kingston added.

'Dax, Kingston, upstairs. Kye, you're with me, ground floor,' Able instructed.

'Yes, sir,' Kye replied.

Able held up his rifle as he turned and entered the house. The others crept in behind him as he neared the rear of the house, following the trail of blood. As he edged his foot forward, the floorboards let out a slight creak.

Meanwhile, Dax carefully took the first step up the stairs, with Kingston following close behind.

Able and Kye entered the back room of the house. They cleared each obstruction in their way before finding a splattering of blood where the workman had been beaten.

The floorboards creaked and groaned again as Dax neared the top of the stairs. 'I'm getting a stronger reading. Whoever it is, they're right up here.' Upon hearing a slight rustle of clothes from the room above, Dax paused, catching a fleeting glimpse of Ryder's face pulling back behind a pile of construction materials. 'It's Ryder! *He's here!*' Dax yelled as he sprinted up the remaining steps.

Ryder rushed to his feet and fired multiple rounds in Dax's direction. Dax halted and unloaded his rifle in return. Ryder rushed for the back window before one of Dax's bullets struck his lower back. The rest of Dax's bullets ripped up the wall around him as he vaulted out of the window.

'He's out the back window, he's out the back window!' Dax repeated.

Able and Kye heard Ryder's feet thump onto the ground outside the rear of the house. Able ran towards another window, hurdling over it and into the back alleyway. He lifted his rifle and fired multiple shots at Ryder, each of them missing just as he broke off into another alleyway. 'He's heading back to the main street!'

Kingston ran back down the stairs and straight out the front door, spotting Ryder as he sprinted towards another alleyway across the street. Kingston lifted his rifle, firing a quick shot in his direction. The bullet hit the ground beside Ryder's feet, flinging up dirt and disintegrating without a trace. Kingston took a split second to pause and take a deep breath before firing a second shot. The bullet narrowly missed Ryder's neck, clipping the top of his backpack just as he disappeared into the alleyway.

Able, Dax, and Kye ran out of the house and towards the alleyway. As they reached its entrance, Ryder was nowhere to be seen. He had disappeared into the dense crowds on the opposite side.

'He's gone,' Able said. 'Too deep into the crowds.'

Dax clenched his fists and gritted his teeth. *'Shit!'*

'We know he's here,' Kingston added. 'Don't let it get to you.'

'I tagged him in his back, but I should've had him.' Dax replied, pacing back and forth in frustration.

'Kingston is right,' Able agreed. 'He won't be far. And if he's here, then at least one of the other targets is too.' Pressing a button on his gauntlet's touchpad, Able opened his communications to Alexia's half of the team. 'Lex, we found Ryder. Dax managed to get a shot on him, but he averted us.'

On the opposite side of the city, Alexia, Hayes, Ember, and Cato knelt down in another alleyway.

'How?' Alexia asked, feeling her heart skip a beat. *'What happened?'*

'It was my fault. I'm sorry,' Dax replied.

'He slipped into the crowds,' Able explained. 'They're too heavy for us to move through right now.'

Kingston strolled down the alleyway and knelt beside a fresh trail of blood. 'Your shot on him has left him bleeding. He'll be leaving a trail for us.'

'Good.' Able nodded. 'Once the crowds die down, we'll follow it.'

'All right, we'll port to your position,' Alexia said over the comms.

'No,' Able replied. 'Keep to your side of the city. The more spread out we are, the better chance we have of finding them. Don't forget, he's not the only target here.'

Alexia closed her eyes, fearing and expecting such a response, before reluctantly replying, 'Copy.' She switched off their communications with Able's team and sighed under her breath. *'Shit.'*

'I doubt it'll take him long to close up his wound,' Hayes added. 'He's not going to be leaving a trail that easy.'

'That's why we gotta keep moving,' Alexia replied. 'And if we find whoever else is hiding here before he does, that'll lead him right to us. Let's move.'

* * *

Night fell across the city as the streets emptied of all life. In the corners and the shadows, the ghosts crept by without a whisper. Ryder's blood glowed through the visors of Able's squad as they followed its trail.

'Come on. Come on. *Come on*,' Dax repeated to himself, eagerly scanning his surroundings.

Elsewhere in the city, Alexia's squad entered another street. The moonlight shone upon them as they scoured every house they passed.

'You see that ahead?' Ember asked, pointing out a small group of Jinyiwei further down the street.

'Copy. I got eyes on them,' Alexia replied. 'Slow down.'

The ghosts relaxed into a walking pace, maintaining a sharp visual on the soldiers as they chatted with one another. Soon, another Jinyiwei appeared in the distance, rushing towards his comrades.

'Hold,' Alexia ordered, lifting her fist.

The squad halted and knelt as they watched the soldier hastily approach the others. With a brief exchange between them, all of the Jinyiwei hurried off together, back the way he came.

'They're in a rush,' Hayes said.

'Should we follow?' Cato asked.

'Yeah, could be something.' Alexia nodded. 'Let's go.'

The squad rose to their feet and ran after the Jinyiwei.

Meanwhile, Able's group continued tracking Ryder's trail of blood. Eventually, the trail led them to the edge of a building before it abruptly ceased with no continuation in sight.

'Blood ends here,' Able said.

'Dammit!' Dax grunted, leaning his head back.

'He was bound to close up the wound at some point,' Kingston acknowledged. 'At least we know he's close.'

'Exactly,' Able agreed. 'It's likely he's still in the outer city. That narrows down a lot.' Able opened his comms to Alexia's squad. 'Lex, we reached the end of Ryder's trail. It hasn't led anywhere, but he's got to be close.'

Alexia and her squad continued following the Jinyiwei through the city streets. Their shouting grew louder and increasingly fraught.

'We're following some of the city's soldiers. Looks like some sort of situation is going on. It could be a lead,' Alexia reported through her helmet as she and her squad slipped through another alleyway.

'Good,' Able replied, 'keep on it, then. Update us on any findings. We'll continue searching our vicinity.'

As Alexia's squad exited the alleyway, they paused and watched as more soldiers rushed towards Lu Zhi's brothel down the street, scattering around the building.

'Looks like that's –' Alexia was interrupted when their temperature scanners beeped twice again, recording an immediate shift in temperature to -14° C.

'Oh shit! That's gotta be him!' Cato exclaimed.

Alexia's helmet determined the source of the temperature to be coming from another alleyway three blocks away. Without a second's hesitation, she sprinted towards the temperature's coordinates.

'Shit!' Hayes blurted out, rushing after Alexia alongside Ember and Cato.

'We've just picked up a temperature drop!' Ember declared over their comms. 'We're closing in on its position!'

Able and his squad immediately turned and headed in their direction. 'We're on our way!'

Alexia bolted to the entrance of the alleyway. Just as she reached it, she turned and lifted her rifle, aiming it into the darkness.

There was no one.

He was gone.

'*No, no, no,*' she muttered under her breath, moving through the alleyway and back out the other end. Still, there was no one. 'Shit. *Shit!*'

The rest of her squad arrived moments later, discovering Ryder's absence.

'We missed him. He's gone,' Ember reported over the comms.

Alexia clenched her teeth and gripped her rifle tighter. Turning back down the alleyway, she spotted the Jinyiwei captain exiting the rear of the brothel and heading straight towards them. *'Back up, back up! Civ approaching!'* Alexia ordered.

The squad hurriedly exited the alleyway as the captain entered through the opposite street and rushed out the other side, looking for any sign of Ryder. The ghosts were stacked up on the walls beside him as he peered right through them.

Eventually, the captain groaned, rubbed his jaw, and turned back down the alleyway. Alexia and her squad relaxed their nerves, watching the captain re-enter the brothel. A short time later, Able and his own squad arrived.

'What happened?' Able asked as he approached Alexia.

'He was gone before we even saw him,' Alexia replied with a dejected breath.

'And with temperatures this cold, he didn't just port,' Hayes added. 'He's gone back in time again.'

Able peered down the alleyway at the busy brothel. 'He must've gotten his target then.'

'Yeah, I'm guessing that's what all of the fuss is about,' Kingston said, watching the numerous Jinyiwei spreading out across the surrounding streets, searching.

'The body must be in there,' Able deduced. 'There's too many of those soldiers for all of us to go in, though.'

'Let's just jump ahead an hour,' Dax suggested.

'They could've moved the body by then,' Kingston rebutted.

'I'll go in myself,' Alexia said, at last. 'Slip in and out. Make sure it's gone.'

'I'll come with you,' Kye added.

Everyone looked at him in silent surprise.

Kye nodded to himself and Alexia with reassurance. 'You shouldn't go alone. There should be two of us, at least.'

'Are you sure?' Able asked.

'Yes, sir. I want to do my part …'

Alexia shook her head. 'I don't need – '

'No, he's right, Lex,' Able interrupted. 'You need the backup, just in case. If anything goes south, though, you get out of there, all right?'

'We will … thank you, sir,' Kye replied with a short nod.

Alexia tilted her head and conceded. 'All right, let's go. Follow me.'

Without lingering any longer, Alexia and Kye slipped back into the alleyway and towards the brothel.

'Huh. Will you look at that?' Dax said to the others. 'The two quiet ones are finally starting to speak up.'

'Well, you can't say they don't know how to go by unnoticed,' Hayes remarked with a smirk.

'What do we even know about them, anyway?' Dax asked. 'I have no idea how Lex of all people got placed as second in command. I swear their names are probably the most personal things I know about them.'

'I'm sure they have their reasons,' Ember replied with a shrug.

Able rested his shoulder on the corner of the alleyway, maintaining a firm eye on the brothel, 'Quiet or otherwise, they've both done all of the same training we have. And while I can't speak for Lex, I know Kye's a good kid. So, if he wants to do his part, then we let him do it.'

Meanwhile, Alexia and Kye approached the back door of the brothel. Peeking inside, they spotted numerous soldiers patrolling the halls. With a nervous breath, Kye pulled himself back behind cover.

'Okay, it's probably going to be pretty tight in here,' Alexia began, paying close attention to the movements of the soldiers inside. 'So, we'll move in single file and keep some distance between us. We don't want to bunch up. Got it?'

Kye remained silent for a moment, nodding to himself before returning to her. 'Got it … I'll follow your lead.'

'Let's move.'

With one last glance at the surrounding street, ensuring the coast was clear, the pair sneaked inside. With light steps, they slipped through the hallway, passing by a paper wall that had been torn through. The faintest outline of their bodies drifted through the darkness as they inspected each hallway with caution.

Eventually, they came upon the central open-roofed courtyard of the brothel. Hiding at its side, they spotted the captain as he ordered more soldiers to search the area. Alexia turned her gaze up to the second-floor hallway, where more soldiers walked out of a bedroom consumed by cries of grief.

'Second floor,' Alexia said. 'Lots of activity there. That must be it.'

Kye looked to the second floor, hearing the heartbroken moans and sobs. 'Yeah …'

Hugging the walls of the courtyard, the two ghosts closed in on a staircase leading to the second story. As they reached the steps, multiple Jinyiwei walked down before them. The pair ducked beside the stairs, letting the soldiers narrowly pass them by. Once they had gone, the ghosts remained low and quiet as they climbed up the staircase. Upon reaching the top, another pair of soldiers encroached on him. They stepped out of their way just as they walked past them and down the stairs.

Continuing along the hallway a little further, the pair finally came to the open bedroom. The sounds of crying and sobbing were almost deafening. Peering inside, Alexia found a dozen courtesans surrounding a bed. They were weeping over the body of Issa, who lay on blood-soaked sheets with a puncture wound in her throat. Lu Zhi stood by the devastated girls, comforting them all.

'Definitely a body in here,' Alexia said. 'We'll need to get closer, though. I'll take the far-right corner of the room, you take the left.'

'Copy.'

In the midst of the courtesans' mourning, Alexia and Kye slid into the room and towards both of the furthest corners, shrouding themselves in shadow. Lu Zhi felt a cold chill sweep through the room. She rubbed her arms for warmth as her eyes fell upon the left corner of the room.

From the darkness, Kye stopped and stared right back at her.

Can she see me? he asked himself.

No. Of course, she can't. No one else has noticed.

Maybe she just ... feels it.

As more girls collapsed into tears, Lu Zhi's attention returned to the bed. Kye let out a sigh of relief.

'We've found the target. It looks like Issa,' Alexia reported over the comms.

'Can you get a confirmation?' Able replied.

'Not yet. The body is surrounded, but if we give it some time, it should clear. Then I'll move in.'

'Copy that. Take your time.'

Alexia and Kye settled themselves into their corners, watching the girls wailing over Issa. Their faces grew dreary as the minutes ticked by. Over and over their pain drifted before crashing back again with even greater strength.

After enough time, Lu Zhi began to usher the girls out of the room. 'Come on now. Get some rest and sleep for tomorrow. I'll take care of this. Go on.' She walked them all out of the room before turning back to the bed and approaching its side.

The ghosts watched as Lu Zhi sat down beside Issa's body and stroked her cheek. Gradually, she noticed a subtle distortion in one of Issa's eyes. She squinted and leant closer, edging her finger towards Issa's eye. As she touched it, she found herself moving aside a contact lens and uncovering a distinct yellow eye beneath it.

Lu Zhi shot to her feet and lifted her hand, finding the translucent lens sitting on the tip of her finger. She inspected it in disbelief before her eyes returned to the left corner of the room. 'Who's there?' she asked in her native tongue.

Kye froze in place.

Alexia's eyes suddenly widened as she stood upright. 'Just stay still, Kye. She doesn't know ...'

The lens fell from Lu Zhi's finger as she lowered her arms and clenched her fists. Step by step, she circled the bed and approached the shadows that concealed him. The closer she grew, the colder the air became, and the more goosebumps dotted her skin.

Please stop, Kye begged. *Please.*

Alexia opened her mouth to speak but did not know what to say, only watching her grow closer and closer.

Kye attempted to step back, but there was nowhere to go. His heart froze as Lu Zhi stopped in front of him. With a shaking hand, her fingers stretched into the deepest, darkest shadow of the corner. Before long, her hand disappeared in the blackness and touched something cold and metallic. She gasped and pulled her hand away, unknowingly staring at Kye as he stared right back at her.

Alexia's mouth remained agape as she watched in disbelief, holding her breath.

With great caution and her eyes fixed on the shadows, Lu Zhi reached her hand back towards Kye. At last, her fingers touched his frozen helmet. Each passing moment saw her terror becoming a quiet wonder. Tears overwhelmed her eyes and streamed down her cheeks. 'Please … *tell me what is happening here …*' she begged.

Kye felt his heart beating again as he lifted his own hand towards her cheek. Lu Zhi noticed the glint of his invisible fingers nearing her skin. Her breath shook as she closed her eyes, awaiting his touch …

Alexia thought of making a noise to distract her before they were all interrupted by a set of marching footsteps that quickly approached the room. Lu Zhi retracted her hand and turned towards the door as one of the Jinyiwei appeared.

'The captain will see you now,' the soldier informed her.

Lu Zhi sniffled and nodded, wiping away her tears. With one last glance at Kye, she followed the soldier out of the room, leaving the ghosts in a lonely silence. Kye rested his fingers on his helmet in the same manner that she did.

Alexia stared at him for a time, blinking and unable to find her words, before her gaze fell upon Issa's body. Hurrying over to the bed, she pulled a disintegrator out from her vest, 'We need to get rid of this body *now*. Keep watch for me – at the door.'

'On it!' Kye replied without hesitation, rushing to the bedroom door.

Looking back at Issa, Alexia's helmet scanned her cold face and confirmed her identity. Her status changed from **Active** to **Deceased** as Alexia clicked the disintegrator's top button. For a moment, she hesitated, before lifting the device and stabbing the needle into Issa's chest. The grey liquid flooded her body and began its process of decay. Within seconds, Issa's body had melted away, leaving only specks of dust, flesh, and blood.

With a bite of her lip, Alexia returned to Kye in the hallway, speaking over the comms, 'Target is confirmed and disintegrated. We're ready to move.'

'Copy. Are you in a good position to sync with us?' Able asked.

'We are.'

'Good. Sync up, and let's get out of here.'

Alexia and Kye synchronised their gauntlets to the others before they heard a commanding voice speak from the central garden below. Kye stepped forward and peered over the railing, where he spotted Lu Zhi standing before the captain as he struck her across the cheek. She yelped and collapsed to her knees.

'You were housing an enemy of the emperor and his city!' the captain shouted.

'I didn't know! Please!' Lu Zhi cried back.

The captain gestured to the surrounding soldiers. 'Take them away! All of them!'

'No! *Please, no!*' Lu Zhi screamed as two soldiers grabbed her arms and dragged her out of the courtyard.

Slowly, Alexia joined Kye's side as they watched the Jinyiwei force their way into every room of the brothel. Girls were pulled from their beds, thrown to the ground, and thrust into the arms of soldiers. Screams of fear and panic pervaded the hallways.

Alexia's heart was overwhelmed with pain as Kye shook his head.

I can't just watch this, he thought to himself. *I can't …*

Kye lifted his rifle and rested his fingers on the trigger before their gauntlets activated and they disappeared into thin air.

A wave of cold air swept past the surrounding trees and grass as the ghosts materialised under the cover of moonlight, finding themselves in yet another empty field.

Kye stared into space as the screams of the courtesans faded with the fog.

'You okay, Kye?' Able asked.

Kye slowly lowered his rifle as he regained his attention and nodded. 'Yes, sir.'

'Don't worry. You did good.'

Alexia and Kye shared a grim look in silence.

'Got visual of the castle,' Dax interrupted, turning all of their attention towards a distant glow emanating from within Warwick Castle.

Chapter 18

The trees creaked and groaned as faint shadows glided past. Light footsteps were masked by the heavy wind and thunder that rumbled overhead.

With Able at their lead, the ghosts climbed to the summit of a grassy hill. After lifting his fist, the team knelt along the hillside, acquiring a perfect view of Warwick Castle and its nearby village below.

'Hayes. Sniper.' Able ordered.

'Copy,' Hayes replied, removing a collection of weapon attachments from his vest's pouches. He snapped an extended barrel, scope, and stock onto his rifle before lying down on his stomach. He flipped open the rifle's bipod and rested it on the ground. As he pressed the stock against his shoulder, he peered through the scope. Alternating to heat vision, he scanned his eye over Warwickshire. Lastly, he pressed a button on the side of the rectangular scope.

After a brief glitch, a small screen of the scope's vision appeared within each of the ghosts' helmets. Everything visible to the scope was projected at the edge of their visors.

Hayes' reticle drifted towards the castle gates as they creaked open. 'Movement at the gates.'

The scope watched as Arnest and Lena said their goodbyes to Terric and the knights on duty. Arm in arm, the couple left the castle and strolled back towards the village.

'Not one of ours,' Kingston said.

Hayes retained a visual on the gates as the knights closed them.

Cato noticed a candle flickering to life within one of the castle windows. 'Third story to the right. Looks like movement in there.'

Hayes turned his aim to the window, zooming in. He turned off the heat vision, attaining a clear visual inside the royal bedroom. The scope watched as Margaret finished lighting a candle atop a bench and stepped out of view. 'Doesn't look like ours either,' Hayes noted, moving his aim elsewhere.

'Hold on, there's someone else,' Ember said as another figure stepped into view of the window.

Hayes directed his scope back towards the room, spotting Grey as he changed his shirt and spoke to Margaret.

'Shit, is that him?' Dax asked.

Hayes zoomed in closer. 'I think that's Grey.'

Able nodded. 'Yeah, that's him.'

'What the fuck is he doing in there?' Dax said, completely taken aback.

'All right, Kingston, Kye, and Dax, you're with me again,' Able ordered. 'We'll move in, get a good position by his room, then when he's alone, we hit him. The rest of you, keep alert. Hayes, don't lose sight of him.'

'Yes, sir,' Hayes replied.

'How are you going to get in there?' Ember asked.

'We're going to have to port. We've learnt the layout, though, so we'll be fine. And seeing through those gates, there's a lot of empty space in that centre courtyard,' he explained before turning to his squad. 'All right, let's move.'

With a nod between them, Able's squad returned to their feet and made their way back down the hill. Alexia, Ember, and Cato remained beside Hayes as he held a firm visual on the castle window.

The thunder grew louder as Able's squad whisked towards the castle with quiet haste, passing by the empty jousting arena and numerous festival tents. Then, a raindrop bounced off one of the tents beside them, and then another, and another, and another.

With each step closer towards the looming castle, the rainfall grew heavier. Within seconds, the thick layer of rainfall became impossible to see through beyond a few feet.

Hayes continued to focus his aim on the window as the pouring rain bombarded their helmets and armour. Their temperature readers steadily dropped, nearing 4° C.

Cato held out his hand and watched as the rain assaulted his palm. 'Thank hell our armour's warm.'

Finally, Able's squad reached the castle walls and stacked up beside the gates. Able lifted his wrist gauntlet, revealing a 3-D map of the castle on his touchscreen before he selected an open space within the walls. 'All right, coordinates are locked in,' he said. 'I'll port in first, make sure it's clear.'

'Good luck,' Kingston said with a nod.

Able activated his device and disappeared. For a moment, the spot where he stood was free of rain, before it was filled again in an instant. The thump of air was masked by the storm as Able ported into the centre of Warwick Castle. The violent wind battered the surrounding garden as he knelt down, scanning the area. Sparse candlelights glowed inside the castle, while only a handful of knights stood guard atop the walls and behind the gate.

'All right, coordinates clear. You can port in.'

'Copy,' Dax replied, before syncing up his gauntlet with the others.

After another moment, the rest of Able's squad ported into the castle grounds. Without delay, Able signalled towards one of the castle doors. 'This door. Follow me.'

The knights on duty scattered about, attempting to find cover from the furious storm. Meanwhile, the ghosts reached an entrance to the castle below. Able took a hold of the handle and edged it open, inch by inch. The howling wind and rain slipped inside the stone hallway, snuffing out the candles as Able entered.

The rest of the squad quietly followed before Kye shut the door behind them, muzzling the wails of the wind. Water dripped off their see-through silhouettes as they continued forth, creeping through the shadows.

'We're inside the walls now. Moving for the stairs,' Able informed the others.

'Copy that,' Hayes replied. 'Don't have a visual on Grey anymore, but no one's left the room. He's still in there.'

'Starting to pick up a tech reading too,' Dax reported, looking at a pulsating signal on his wristpad. 'Looks like it's coming from his room.'

Before long, Able reached the base of a tight spiral staircase. Keeping his aim firmly on the corners ahead, he led the squad up the stairs. Drops of water trickled down the steps as they left a trail of wet bootprints. Coming to the third floor, Able peeked into a narrow hallway, spotting Grey's bedroom door.

'Got sights on entry,' Able said, aiming at the door as his squad stacked up on the wall beside it.

Kye watched the opposite end of the hallway, covering their rear.

All of them maintained half an eye on Hayes' scope feed, watching the window through the torrential rain.

Inside the bedroom, Margaret lay in bed as Grey sat down on the opposite end.

'Even still, I just don't think he *trusts* me,' Grey muttered, shaking his head at the floor. 'I know how to handle this, and I want him to see that, but I can't prove myself if he doesn't even give me the chance.' He sat in silence for a time, expecting a reply.

There was none.

Grey turned and looked at Margaret as she stared into space, absent and worried. 'Margaret, are you even listening to me?'

Margaret snapped out of her daze and looked at her husband. 'Sorry, darling, I was just … What did Arnest say to you tonight? I saw you speaking with him.'

'Arnest? You think *he's* got something to do with our prisoner?'

'No, no, I was just curious. His wife, Lena, spoke to me tonight. She said some things that were … terribly worrying.'

'About what?'

'About *the Black Death*,' Margaret said with a frightened whisper. 'She fears it is coming *here*. She told me of the suffering it wrought upon her homeland. She's seen all of it firsthand.'

'Oh no, dear, do not listen to such paranoia. If anyone's going to be safe from such a thing, it's us. Don't worry. We have stores of food in our walls that will last us months.'

'But what of the townsfolk? Lena says they are already struggling.'

'They *always* say that, darling. They'll be *fine*. And I'll always make sure you're safe, which is why what *really* matters at present is our prisoner. Unlike that plague, this man is *here and now*. And I really do think he's dangerous, Margaret. The sooner we get rid of him, the better.' Grey rested his hand on her thigh. 'The sooner *you'll* be safe.'

Margaret smiled at his words. 'I'm here with you. I'm *already* safe.'

Grey turned away with a sigh. 'I just hope your father does the right thing.'

'I'm sure he will. Now, come to bed. Let's forget about all of that,' she said, patting the empty space beside her.

At last, Grey nodded, sliding the blanket aside as he crawled into bed. He kissed Margaret's lips with a growing passion until she put her hands on his chest, stopping him. 'Do you hear that?'

Grey paused, listening out. 'I don't –'

'Listen – listen!' she interrupted.

Grey tightened his lips in annoyance, before he continued to listen for any noise.

After they allowed their silence to linger for a time, the faint sound of dripping water could be heard echoing in the hall just outside their door.

'It must be a leak,' Grey said with a shrug.

'Can you go see what it is?'

With a roll of his eyes, Grey slid off the bed and walked towards the door. Opening it and stepping outside, he surveyed both ends of the hallway. There was nothing.

Yet, the dripping continued.

Grey gazed down at the source of the sound, finding drops of water bouncing onto the stone floor beside him. He squinted, noticing wet bootprints amongst them. Slowly, his eyes traced up for the source of the droplets. Then he froze, discovering that the water was dripping from thin air. His eyes widened as he began to make out a slight distortion of the hallway before him.

'What is it, darling?' Margaret asked from the bedroom. 'Is it okay?'

Grey stared into the invisible barrel of Able's rifle. His finger rested on the trigger.

Watching through his scope, Hayes could see Grey frozen outside the bedroom door. 'Have you got eyes on target?'

'He's right in front of us!' Dax replied.

Margaret climbed out of bed, nearing the door with caution. 'Darling?'

'Take the shot!' Alexia called out through their comms.

Able stared into Grey's fearful eyes. He tightened his grip and began placing pressure on the trigger.

'Darling, what is it?' Margaret asked, walking up behind Grey and resting her hand on his shoulder.

Able paused, hesitating.

'Able!' Alexia repeated.

'I can't. There's someone right here with him.'

Grey gathered his breath and called out, *'G – guards – guards! Intruders are here! Intruders!'*

'Shit!' Dax exclaimed.

Margaret gasped and darted back inside the bedroom.

Hayes turned his scope towards a series of windows on the right side of the castle, spotting a handful of armoured knights running towards them. 'You've got multiple targets closing fast!'

'Back out, back out!' Able ordered, retreating down the hallway with his squad.

'Fuck.' Alexia grunted under her breath.

Hayes shifted his scope to the left side of the castle, finding more knights running up the spiral stairs. 'More targets coming up the stairs! They're closing in from both sides!'

Kye halted before the stairwell, hearing the clanking of armour nearing them from below.

'We've got to sync up now.' Kingston said, flicking his coordinates to the rest of the team's location.

Hayes' scope darted between each window of the castle, watching as dozens of knights hurried to surround them. All of Able's squad synched their devices.

Sir Terric rounded the corner, catching a glimpse of the strange distortions. Without hesitation, Able activated his device, teleporting the squad out of the hallway in an instant. Grey and Terric watched in disbelief as the spectres disappeared and a wave of cold air whipped past them. Finally, the battalion of knights arrived.

Terric turned to Grey, his hand ready on his hilt. 'Lord Guy, *what was that?*'

Grey shook with fear. Gradually, he lifted his hand and pointed to the wet bootprints. *'Intruders.'*

Terric knelt beside the watery tracks, tracing them to the spot where they disappeared, before glancing back at Grey. 'Wherever did they come from?'

'I don't know … but you saw them disappear, didn't you? Right before our eyes.'

Terric looked back at the bootprints, perplexed.

Grey's fear began to dissipate as determination rose in its place. *'Wake up the earl.'*

* * *

Able's squad ported onto the hill behind the rest of the ghosts. Hayes glanced at them before looking back through his scope, watching more and more knights fill the hallways of the castle.

Alexia approached Able's squad, lifting her hands. *'What was that?'*

'It was a bloody close call, that's what,' Dax replied.

'You didn't take the shot?' Alexia asked Able.

Without a word, Able marched straight past her and stopped beside Hayes, surveying the distant castle.

'It looks like those soldiers are lining every hallway now,' Hayes reported.

'Well, there goes the element of surprise,' Kingston joked.

'*Able,*' Alexia repeated.

'What is it, Alexia?' Able finally snapped back, shooting her an impatient glare. 'You think you would've done differently?'

'Yeah, I would've. I would've taken the shot then or grabbed him and taken him. Port him out if I had to. *Then* kill him.'

'*The civilian would've seen. I couldn't risk that.*'

'And where's that gotten us? *The whole damn castle knows now!*'

Able shook his head and turned away.

'Am I going to have to be the one to say what we're all thinking, then?' Dax asked.

The others looked at him, silent.

Kingston nodded. 'Yeah. This mission's fucked.'

'*Hell yeah, it is,*' Dax agreed. 'First, we show up in London, and Hughes has been there long enough to have people *crying* over him. Then there were soldiers *everywhere* for Issa. Then we show up so late here that Grey is in a *fucking castle!* He was *ordering* those knights around! I mean, how bloody long has he been here? And this isn't even mentioning Ryder, who's already been one step ahead of us the whole time.'

'You're right,' Ember said. 'Ryder must've gotten to each destination much earlier than us. Beijing, London. In cities *that* big, he had to have been looking for them for at least a while. Longer than us, anyway. I wouldn't be surprised if he's already here too.'

'And what are you trying to say?' Able asked.

Dax stepped forward, 'We're trying to say something's *wrong* with the mission. How can Ryder have better intel than us? How are we *this* late when *he* isn't?'

Cato nodded. 'Yeah. We were supposed to be here to *stop* their interference with time. It's no damn good if they've already interfered this much.'

Hayes' shoulders dropped as he glanced up at Able. 'They're right. With everything we've seen, we might already be returning to a future that's different from the one we left.'

'The mission may as well have failed already,' Dax said, shaking his head.

'That's not true,' Able countered, turning to them all, unshaken. 'Yeah, I know. I've noticed all of these things too. I've thought about it … but at the end of the day, we were trained for *any* scenario to come our way. We were *trained* to improvise when necessary. And regardless of how much interference there has been along the way, regardless of what future we come back to, this mission's purpose is *still* to eliminate each and every target we have. That's where it begins and ends. I made a call that I thought was right in the moment. Maybe it wasn't, but I didn't spend the last two years training for this mission just to *give up* because it's not easy and it's not going the way we thought it was going to. Even if the future we come back to is *completely* different, that doesn't change *our* pasts. We can't have *any* expectations anymore. We *can't* predict what's going to happen, so don't let your mistaken preconceptions rid you of *all* of the skills and training we have been given. That is *all* we have. If we have to adapt, then we adapt. If we have to wait, then we will wait. We are here to do a mission, and I'm going to see it through until I'm dead.' Able turned back around, watching as the castle and village were consumed by the storm. 'So, for now, we *wait*. And when the time is right, and that time will come, in whatever way we need to, we *strike*.'

VOLUME FOUR

THE PLAGUE

Chapter 19

The light of a small candle flickered across the hunter's pale face. He lifted his gaze from the shadows of his cell, revealing a pair of dark rings hanging under his eyes. 'My name is Ryder,' he said with faded breath.

'And where have you come from, Ryder?' Arnest asked from beyond the cell bars.

'Far away from here. You wouldn't know it.'

'Hm … Seems we are both that way, then.'

'Well, we definitely don't *sound* like we fit in.'

Arnest smiled in amusement. 'Why is it you are here?'

Ryder paused for a moment, his eyes trailing off before he looked back beyond the bars, 'That lord, the tall one from the crowds, do you know him?'

'That I do. That is Lord Guy de Montfort.'

Ryder shook his head. 'What do you know about him? When did he show up here?'

'How does his business concern you?'

'*Please* … what do you know?' the hunter asked, fighting to retain his strength.

Arnest wavered for a time, sceptical. 'I'd say he arrived … almost half a year ago. Maybe longer. When he first came, he lived with us in the village. Both being strangers to this land, we became friends … but then he caught the eye of the earl's daughter, Lady Margaret. It seemed barely a month or two before they were in love and wed.'

'And now he's a "lord"?'

'Indeed. Although he says he was already of much importance from whence he came.'

'And did he say where that was?'

'I cannot recall the name … I had never heard of such a land.'

'And nor should you have. He and I come from the same place.'

'So, you *do* know him then. I saw you conversing with him at the arena.'

'I know him as best I can. But *you* don't. He isn't who he says he is.'

Arnest squinted at his words. He shot a glance down the dungeon hall, ensuring no one else was present. Satisfied, the jouster dragged across a wooden stool and sat down before the cell, leaning in close. 'Explain.'

'His real name is Grey Pines, and he is a *murderer*. He fled from his home a criminal and came here to hide. He's lying to all of you.'

Arnest leant back as his expression remained unchanged.

'You don't look surprised,' Ryder noted.

'I cannot say I am, unfortunately. When he made his way into the earl's family, his intentions became … much clearer to me. He used to appear as though he actually cared for us. But ever since he's been in this castle, he's only grown more and more distant. Even as we struggle.'

'That's all he came here for. If this place didn't offer him the power and wealth he wanted, then I'm sure he'd be somewhere else right now.'

'What did he do to bring you searching so far?'

'He …' Ryder felt his breath slip away before he could finish his sentence, taking a moment to gather himself. '… he helped kill my wife …'

Arnest's tone softened as he looked at Ryder with pity. 'Whatever for?'

'To escape …'

Arnest sighed as he shook his head. 'I am sorry for your loss … So, it is justice you are here for, then?'

Ryder nodded. 'Can you help me?'

Arnest surveyed the dungeon hall once more. 'You are set to be executed tomorrow morning. And you look as though you are half in the grave already.'

'My wounds won't matter if I get my belongings back. I have medicines that will heal me. And I have weapons too, but the longer they are in his possession, the more power he will hold over all of you. I can help you, if you help me.'

'Why should I believe you?'

'Did you ever really believe in him to begin with? And if you don't, can you really trust him to hold that power?'

Arnest bowed his head, contemplating as a heavy silence lingered between them.

'Australia,' Ryder continued. 'That's where he told you he was from, wasn't it? Melbourne, Australia.'

Arnest's head lifted at his words, recognising the names. At last, he nodded. 'If what you say is true, and if I can find a way, then I shall help you find your justice and keep my family and village safe.'

'Thank you.'

Arnest gave him a nod before standing up and placing the stool back where he found it. Before leaving, he turned to face the prisoner again. 'Also … I do apologise about the jousting match. If I knew you would be a friend, I wouldn't have hit you so hard.'

Ryder smiled through the pain. 'Oh … thanks.'

Without another word, Arnest left the dungeon and climbed the stairway out of sight.

Meanwhile, concealed by shadows, Hamo the jester hid behind a wall at the opposite end of the hallway, having listened in on every word.

* * *

Thunder rumbled overhead as the gates of Warwick Castle opened before Arnest and Lena.

Terric bowed to them graciously. 'Thank you for joining us. We pray you enjoyed the feast.'

'We very much did, thank you,' Arnest said with a nod.

'It was wonderful. Thank you,' Lena agreed.

Terric smiled and gestured them outside. 'Good night.'

Arm in arm, Arnest and Lena left the castle and strolled back towards their village. Their worn shoes squelched on the muddy road as the dark clouds growled, growing ever more restless. The couple passed by the village pub, where many voices and candles glowed from within.

'I thought I was full a moment ago,' Lena sighed, 'but honestly, I think I could eat even more.'

Arnest smiled as they walked over the small green hill before their home. 'Shall I open the gates for you, milady?'

'Mm, thank you, my lord.'

Arnest removed their wobbly door off its hinges, stepping aside so she could enter. 'After you.'

'Why, thank you.'

After stepping inside, Arnest placed the door back on its frame, balancing it so it remained in its place.

Lena sat down at their small circular table, relaxing as Arnest retrieved a tinderbox from one of their drawers. He sat on the opposite chair, clinking flint and steel together before the miniature container.

Lena glanced at him, gathering the strength to ask, 'So … how did it go? Did you speak with him?'

Arnest nodded, continuing his attempts to spark a flame. 'I did.'

'And?'

'Well, apparently they know each other. They travelled here from the same land. And … and he said Guy isn't who he says he is. That his real name is Grey, and that … he is a criminal who fled here. That he's hiding. And lying.'

Lena squirmed in her seat. 'Do you believe him?'

A harsh gust of wind knocked their front door onto its side. The cold and the rain swept inside, killing any sparks that had formed between Arnest's flint and steel. Dropping his tools, he rushed over to the door and pushed it back into place. The wails of the wind were muffled once more as he rested his forehead against the door. 'I'll fix this tomorrow.'

'But do you *believe* him? This stranger?'

Gradually, Arnest returned to their table, picking up the flint and steel as he shook his head. 'I do not see why he would lie. And either way, Guy wants him dead. He plans to execute him tomorrow morning.'

'Oh, God ...'

'The man's name is Ryder. As far as I can tell, he only wants justice. And for that, he needs help.'

Lena noticed the solemnity in her husband's eyes. 'What are you thinking, Arnest?'

'I'm thinking Guy, or Grey, or whoever he is ... he has already lied to all of us. He once said he cared about us, but when I spoke to him tonight, it was clear he has no intention of helping our village. Is it such a stretch to think he is lying about his past too?'

'But at least he is not *harming us*.'

'He will be if the plague finds its way here. *He'll be killing us all. He may as well already be with how little time we have left.*'

'No, I spoke to Lady Margaret; she *said* she would help us. I know things are not perfect, but we still live good lives here, despite everything. At some hour, we must trust them. *They* are in charge. We should know our place, Arnest,' Lena pleaded, resting her hand on her husband's knee. 'This is our home.'

'And what kind of home will it be if it is ruled by a man that has told us nothing but lies? If he does not help us withstand the plague? We trusted our leaders once, and we saw how that ended.'

'If it comes to that, then we can find somewhere else. We've done that before and we can do that again.'

Arnest shook his head as the tinderbox finally caught alight. 'We cannot run anymore, Lena. You are right, this *is* our home. A *real* home. And a real home should not be one we run from or give up on so easily. I am tired of losing them, and I do not want to lose another, and I certainly do not want us on the road when our child arrives. It *needs* a home which is safe and secure. I cannot bear for him or her to lead the same life we did. Are you not the same?'

'I *am*, but I also want it to grow up with a father.' Lena's eyes welled with tears. *'Please. Do not fight this.'*

Arnest held a leaf before the tinderbox, setting it on fire and using it to light their candle. As thunder and rain clashed outside, a warm orange light consumed the sombre couple. 'This is our home, my dear. And I will make sure, in every way I can, that it stays that way … I promise.' Arnest leant forward and kissed Lena's forehead as she sat helpless and without words.

Soon, Arnest trekked through the pouring rain, approaching the village pub as he donned his hooded coat. Pushing the door open, a rush of wind swept inside the busy tavern. Dozens of patrons turned and looked at him before he removed his hood and gave them a nod. 'Sorry to interrupt.'

A handful of the villagers called out to him.

'Good to see you, Arnest!'

'Aye, congratulations!'

'Good show today, good show!'

'No apologies needed from our champion,' the barman said, passing him a pint of ale.

'How was your feast with the earl, then?' Hopkin asked, sitting at one of the tables with his own drink.

'Tell us all about it!' another villager exclaimed.

Arnest walked into the centre of the pub, speaking to them all. 'There was more food than you could ever imagine. More than even at the fair today.'

'Got any scraps for us?' a villager slyly remarked.

Others in the pub chuckled and laughed.

Arnest smiled a little, shaking his head. 'No, no. Though, I did learn some things … some unfortunate, disturbing things.' His tone turned grave as the pub fell silent. 'The last man you saw me joust today is not just any stranger wandering through our village. I spoke to him … and you would think that after his valiant efforts today, he would have been rewarded, but no. He was instead locked away in the castle dungeons because he knows the truth of something. Because he claims to have come from the same land Lord Guy has. He tells me that Guy is a murderer, and a thief, and a man running from justice. He tells me his name is not even Guy. It's Grey Pines.'

'You believe all that?' Osbert asked with a snort.

'Don't you?' Arnest asked in return. 'How much do you truly know about Guy? I know many of us considered him a friend, but when I talked to this so-called "friend" tonight to help us with our diminishing food and livelihood, *he dismissed us.* I wish it weren't so, but it seems to me he has no intention of helping us. It seems to me he'd sooner let us all starve before giving up what he's attained. And if there's one thing I know for certain in this life, it is that our gracious leaders are more than capable of such an indifference. I've seen it before. I have not spoken much of my old home to all of you because of what happened to it. Though, I'm sure you've heard the rumours. Of the so-called Black Death … and unfortunately, it is true. It took hold of my homeland and *destroyed* it. I had never seen so much death.' Arnest shook his head as he remembered those dark days. 'And what do you think our trusted leaders did to help us during such a time? … *Nothing.* And as terrible as it is, I believe it is now only a matter of days or weeks before this plague catches up to us, and when it does, we mustn't be at the mercy of Guy and those in that castle.'

'What are you suggesting we do?' Hopkin asked.

'I'm suggesting we walk up to those gates and show them what we want. What we *need* for our families. Otherwise, we will be doomed to the same fate as my homeland.' Arnest relented for a moment, steadying his nerves. 'And then there is Ryder. The man locked away in that castle. With no trial, no questions, Guy has sentenced him to be executed tomorrow morning because he *knows the truth.* Because *he* can help us, and I fear that if we don't do something now, all of our hope for answers and salvation and justice will be *gone.* I don't expect all of you to act on this, or even believe me, but we have little time left for debate. And quite frankly, I am tired of fearing that I will not be able to feed my wife and child come the next sunrise. I am tired of living under the shadow of a place that shows no care for us. A place that would sooner harbour liars and criminals than take care of us hard-working folk. So, tomorrow, with or without your support, *I* will be going into that castle and fighting for

Ryder's life and fighting for our future. I will fight with words, and if that does not work, then I will fight with my blade. So … who is with me?'

The pub remained deathly silent as the villagers looked at one another, uncertain and hesitant. Thunder roared outside as the rain only grew fiercer.

Without a word of support from anyone around him, Arnest's expression dimmed.

All right then, he thought to himself. *I will do it alone.*

Accepting their silence, Arnest gave them one last thankful nod and turned towards the door. Yet, before he could take another step, Osbert climbed to his feet. 'I'll be with ye, Arnest.'

'And I.' Hopkin nodded, standing up.

'And I,' said another.

'And I.'

'And I!'

'And I!'

'AND I!'

Soon, the entire tavern was engulfed in cries of courage.

* * *

Lightning crackled above Warwick Castle. Rain trickled down the windows of the earl's hall as dozens of knights lined the walls, curiously waiting. Grey held Ryder's handgun by his side, standing with Terric in the heart of the room.

Before long, the front doors opened, and the earl entered the hall alongside Margaret, Hamo, and two more knights.

'What is the meaning of this?' the earl asked with haste.

Terric approached him. 'We have had an intrusion, my lord.'

'An *intrusion?'* he replied, his patience thinning.

'Yes, my lord,' Grey interrupted. 'There were imposters in our halls tonight. And I believe it has something to do with our prisoner.'

The displeasure in the earl's tone only worsened. 'And how is that *so?'*

Grey turned to Margaret. 'My dear, I do not want you to see this.' He gestured his hand towards the door. 'Please.'

Margaret looked at the earl, reluctant and uncertain. Without so much as a glance in her direction, her father nodded in agreement. Margaret bowed her head in disappointment and exited the room.

At last, Grey lifted Ryder's handgun for all to see. '*This* is how I know. I have come to discover that this is no ordinary piece of equipment. No, *this* is the most deadly and technically superior weapon you have ever *seen*. Watch.' Grey turned to face the opposite end of the hall, where a silver chest plate sat atop a post. He clicked back the pistol's hammer and fired.

A bullet ripped clean through the armour as everyone jumped back in fright. The knights glanced at one another, puzzled and alarmed.

Terric approached the armour, inspecting the bullet hole in disbelief. 'My God. It's gone right through.'

Even the earl struggled to comprehend the sight. 'It's some kind of … miniaturised cannon?'

'*Exactly.*' Grey agreed with an eager nod. 'It's smaller, faster, and *far* more precise. Nothing we have can compare.'

'What does this have to do with the intruders?' Hamo interjected.

Grey almost rolled his eyes at having to address the jester. 'These intruders swept in and out of here in the blink of an *eye*. They were quick and they were capable, as if the devil himself commanded them. It is no coincidence that the same day we arrest this stranger that there are such cunning intruders lurking within our walls.'

'And you suggest what?' Terric asked.

'I suggest we find out what we can from our prisoner, execute him, and then prepare ourselves for whatever is coming next.'

The earl maintained a firm eye on Grey as he began to pace the hall. 'And what do you make of this, Sir Terric? Did you see these "imposters"?'

Terric hesitated for a moment, 'Well … I did not exactly see them, no. But there were curious footprints throughout the halls.'

The earl paused, glancing around the room. 'Did *anyone* here see these imposters?'

Silence followed.

'Hm?' the lord questioned, eyeing each of his knights as he continued to circle the room. 'And if there *were* imposters in our walls, then is that to say that you men were not fulfilling your duties? That you just *allowed* these intruders to slip into our home so easily? That you are *that foolish?!*' The earl turned back towards Terric. 'Is that true?'

Terric shook his head with a sigh. 'No, my lord.'

'My lord, you must have faith in me,' Grey pleaded, his voice almost cracking. 'There is something sinister about. Something our churches and priests warn us about. You cannot deny what you have seen. What this weapon can do.'

'If this prisoner is so important, as you say,' Hamo added, almost with a smirk, 'then why jump to the conclusion that he must be executed so soon?'

'Because he is a *threat. He brought weapons into our home!* You've *just* seen them!' Grey turned back to the earl with a chuckle, 'My lord, when it comes to such grave matters, you cannot listen to a *clown* of all people. Just *look* at him!'

'Appearances can be deceiving, Lord Guy,' Hamo said.

Grey's gaze snapped back towards him with fury. '*What are you – ?*'

'*All right*, that's enough of this,' the earl interrupted. 'Sir Terric, as a precaution, double the guards on the perimeter. Everyone else, leave us.'

Terric, Hamo and all of the surrounding knights filed out of the hall, leaving only Grey and the earl.

The earl took a long, deep breath. Gradually, he approached his son-in-law with an unrelenting gaze, even as Grey towered over him. 'I see the danger of this weapon you have shown us, Lord Guy. It *is* remarkable. But do you know what I have also seen? Thousands of men dying in battle. Crawling over one another in fields of mud and their own innards. I have seen how much it takes to win such battles. I have *made* such sacrifices. They do not call me the Devil of Warwick without cause.' The earl stopped before Grey's feet. 'Quite honestly, I don't know what my daughter sees in you, but I think you're smart enough to know when enough is enough. I thank you for your efforts, but *I* will be taking charge of the prisoner and *all* manners surrounding him from here on out. I will discover the truth of this *myself*, and you are *not* to intervene. Is that clear?'

Grey restrained a shivering anger. 'It is clear, my lord.'

'Good,' the earl replied, holding out his hand for the weapon. Grey looked away as he placed the handgun in his palm. 'Now, I am going to get a good night's rest. There shall be *no* disturbances.' Without another word, the earl left the room.

Alone in his defeat, Grey turned and looked back down the end of the hall, to the clean bullet hole that penetrated the knight's armour so effortlessly …

* * *

In her quiet bedroom, Margaret sat on the edge of her bed, hunched over and consumed in thought. She glanced at Ryder's backpack as it rested on the wooden bench across the room. The foreign makings of it disturbed her until she could no longer bear the sight of it.

Hamo passed by the open bedroom and stopped in his tracks as he noticed the lonely Margaret. 'Are you all right, milady?' he asked with care.

Margaret lifted her head with some surprise. 'Oh, Hamo. I just … I know not what is happening. I am awfully confused is all.'

'It has certainly been a strange day.'

'*So* strange. Ever since that odd man arrived in the arena today, things have been … not right.'

'Why do you think he's brought about such change?'

'I do not know.'

'Have you spoken to him?'

'To who? The prisoner?'

'Yes,' Hamo said with a confident nod.

'Oh no, I couldn't go down there. That is not my business.'

'But it is affecting your home, your father, your husband, and even your mind, it seems. If that is not your business, then what is, milady?'

Margaret's gaze fell towards the floor as her mind ticked over. She bit her lip, deliberating over his words, before nodding to herself. 'You're right. I should know … I *should* know.' She stood up and approached the door, gifting the jester a small smile. 'Thank you, Hamo.'

'A pleasure, milady,' he replied with a bow.

After ensuring the hallway was clear, Margaret hurriedly sneaked away, leaving Hamo alone by the bedroom door. With a smile, he peered back inside her room, finding Ryder's bag sitting unattended.

Meanwhile, Margaret crept through the castle halls, inspecting her surroundings before coming upon the indoor entrance to the dungeon. Beside it sat a candle rested atop a bench. After gently picking it up, she opened the door, revealing dozens of stairs leading down into darkness.

Perhaps I should go back, she thought to herself. *Guy will not be happy.*

The voices of knights echoed from the halls behind her. Margaret glanced in their direction, hearing them draw closer. Turning back towards the stairs, she dithered for a moment longer.

If you are going to go, you must do it now, she told herself. *You must.*

With the clenching of her fist, Lady Margaret finally stepped into the shadows and shut the door behind her.

Chapter 20

An electronic crosshair scanned across the castle walls. The greenish tint of its night vision switched to thermal imaging, revealing an abundance of yellow and orange figures gathering atop the lookouts.

'Looks like they're upping their security,' Hayes said, peering through the scope of his rifle.

Able knelt beside him amidst the cover of rain. 'Any more movement from the bedroom?'

Hayes' reticle turned back towards Grey's bedroom window. 'No, sir. Nothing.'

Alexia stood on the right side of the hilltop, overlooking the village below. She switched her visor to thermal imaging, revealing dozens of figures rushing back and forth in the muddy streets. 'There's a lot of movement down here in the town too.'

Able walked over to her side.

'A lot of movement considering it's pouring rain,' Dax added as he knelt down beside them.

Able nodded. 'It is.'

'Could be signs of Ryder,' Alexia continued. 'We should look.'

'Yeah. We'll do that,' Able agreed. 'Hayes, you stay posted here, let us know if there's any more movement. The rest of us will split into our usual formations. I'll cover the south side. Alexia, you take the north.'

'Got it,' she replied, checking her rifle was combat-ready, 'and if you do see him again, let us know. We'll be there.'

Able eyed her with a subtle vigilance before Kingston, Kye, and Dax joined his side. Meanwhile, Cato and Ember followed Alexia as both squads jogged down the hill, gliding through the thick fog and torrential rain. The only thing visible through the darkness was the orange glow of the village candles. Upon reaching the border of the village, the two squads separated onto opposing sides, halting before entry.

'We're at the town's edge.' Alexia reported over the comms.

'Copy. We are too,' Able replied. 'Keep a keen eye out. Let's move.'

With a swift hand signal from Able and Alexia, both squads entered the shadowy streets of Warwick village. They peered through the windows of each small house and cottage they passed. Lightning struck beyond the nearby hills, briefly illuminating the translucent outlines of the ghosts.

Alexia maintained a close eye on the villagers who ran through the main street. They held their jackets over their heads, shielding themselves from the rain as they carried stacks of weaponry and armour to and fro. As her squad neared the end of one house, another villager appeared before them. Alexia lifted her fist, stopping her squad in their tracks as the villager narrowly passed by, holding an axe over his shoulder and hurrying off towards the opposite side of the street.

Meanwhile, Able's squad approached the rear of a house that emitted an intense heat and glow. As they drew closer, their temperature readings rose by a few degrees. Rain dripped off their armour as Able watched numerous villagers moving in and out of the building, carrying stacks of tools and armour.

'Lot of civ movement here,' Able reported.

'What are they all up to?' Dax asked, meeting him at his side.

'Don't know.' Able crept up to a window at the back side of the busy house. Peeking inside, he found a blacksmith hard at work, smashing away at a sword atop an anvil. The forge was alight with flames as smoke and embers floated out of the windows. Arnest stood nearby, directing the villagers in moving the weaponry.

'Looks like they're gearing up for something major,' Dax suggested.

Elsewhere, Alexia's squad sneaked over a small hill at the end of the village, approaching Arnest and Lena's quaint abode.

'This looks like the last one,' Ember said.

Alexia held her breath as they closed in on the house. Holding her rifle close and cautioning her steps, she crept towards the back window of the house. Stepping in front of it, she peered inside, spotting Lena on the opposite side, washing cups in a barrel of water.

Ember and Cato stacked up against the wall next to her, covering her sides.

'Any sign of him?' Cato asked.

Alexia's eyes scanned through the window. There was no other movement. Only Lena, alone. Alexia shook her head before lightning struck again in the distance.

The translucent outline of Alexia lit up for a split second. Seeing it in the corner of her eye, Lena's head darted up towards the darkness outside her window. She stared outside, right at Alexia, and Alexia back at her.

'Lex?' Cato asked once more.

Alexia was frozen for a moment, caught in Lena's eyes.

Gradually, she let herself breathe and shook her head again. 'Nothing. There's nothing.'

'Damn,' Cato muttered.

'We'll see what the others found,' Alexia continued, carefully stepping away from the window.

Lena continued to stare outside, curious and unsettled. After some time, her nerves settled, and she returned to scrubbing another cup. After a few more scrubs, she dropped the utensils and gasped, fighting to hold back her tears. She buried her head into her hand as her heart ached.

A short time later, amidst the raging storm, both squads reconvened at the end of the village.

'Found anything?' Alexia asked with haste.

Able shook his head. 'No.'

'But there is a lot of movement from the villagers,' Dax added. 'There's definitely something going on here.'

'You think it's to do with us? With what happened in the castle?' Cato asked.

'There's been no movement from here and the castle since then, so I doubt it,' Able replied.

'There was that tall one in the workshop,' Kingston said. 'He looks like he's in charge of all of this. Held himself as if he were a knight. There could be more relation than it seems.'

'Either way, if Ryder's not here, then he's got to be in that castle,' Alexia deduced.

'Or he's dead,' Kingston countered. 'He already took a bullet. He's lucky to have made it as far as he has.'

'Especially with no help,' Ember agreed.

Alexia's jaw tensed at the thought. 'Well, if he *is* in there, we'll need to make a move eventually.'

'We will,' Dax assured her.

Able eyed Alexia up and down with an air of disapproval. 'Regardless of what we *want*, we're still going to wait for any further movement from Grey. The right time will come. But for now, let's pull back.' With a final nod, Able turned and walked back towards their hillside camp, circling around the outside of the village.

As the other ghosts began trailing behind him, Alexia remained still, staring at the distant castle.

Kingston noticed her and paused. 'You all right there?'

'Huh? … Yeah. I'm fine.'

Kingston chuckled at her response, unconvinced. 'Don't worry. We'll kill them all, in time. We're too good not to,' he said with a smirk.

'I just know he's here. I'm *sure* of it.'

'And we'll get him. No one gets away with everything forever.' Kingston replied, thinking on his own words before turning around and following the others.

Alexia watched the castle for a little while longer, biting her lip. Eventually, she pulled her gaze and returned to the fog and the shadows.

* * *

Deep within the halls of the castle, inside his stone-grey bedroom, Sir Terric removed his silver breastplate. A knock at the door drew half of his attention. 'Yes?'

'It's Lord Guy,' Grey announced from behind the door.

'You may come in.'

Grey opened the door and entered the small room, seeing the armour in his hands. He turned a critical eye towards Terric.

'I'm getting some sleep,' Terric said. 'We have enough people on guard.'

Grey shook his head. 'You're just going to give in like this? Leave us vulnerable?'

'We're not vulnerable,' Terric rebutted without conviction, placing his armour on its wooden stand.

'You know what you saw, Terric. You can't tell me you didn't see *exactly* what I saw.'

'I saw *nothing.*'

'No, you saw something you can't explain. Something *dangerous in our very walls.* Something *we need* to prepare for. And just because we can't explain it doesn't mean we should ignore it.'

Terric bowed his head, taking a quiet breath. 'I can't disobey the earl's orders.'

Grey took a step closer and softened his tone. 'I know the earl has seen much. Fought in who knows how many battles. He has earned our respect; I'm well aware of that. But everyone, sooner or later, makes the *wrong* decision. He doesn't want to believe his own home is in such uncontrollable peril, and frankly, I don't either, but *we* know the truth. *We* know a strange foreigner came to our land with dangerous weapons; *we* know someone was skulking our halls tonight; *we know* we are under attack. And with that knowledge, we *have* to protect the earl and our home.'

'We don't know enough.'

'That's why we must talk to the prisoner. *Torture him* if need be …'

Terric stared into space, saying nothing.

Grey relented for a moment, settling his tone again. 'Well, let me just ask you this then. Would you rather follow the earl's orders and let all of us die? Or disobey him and save us all?' Without another word, Grey left the room.

Terric stood in silence as his gaze gradually returned to his armour.

Grey's footsteps echoed throughout the castle halls as thunder and lightning crackled in the distance. A royal butler stood beside one of the windows, watching the rainfall outside. Without hesitation, he stood at attention as Grey approached him.

'My lord,' the butler said before noticing his tension. 'Is there anything I can do for you?'

'Yes, actually. I am hungry. Fetch me more food. I will wait in the dining hall.'

'Of course, my lord,' the butler replied, leaving for the kitchen immediately.

Almost an hour later, Grey sat at the end of the long dining table, alone. Sparse candles flickered before him as he stared into their flames. Rain pelted against the windows as his eyes shifted about the hall. The ceiling was high, the table was made of finely carved wood, the chairs were tall, and the carpeting was decorated with crowns and swords. He casually reached for his silver cup, taking a sip of wine grown from the earl's very own vineyard.

After another crash of distant thunder, the butler returned, placing down plates of meat and vegetables before him. 'Is there anything else you require, my lord?'

'No. Thank you.'

'Please enjoy, my lord,' the butler said with a smile.

As the butler left the hall, his footsteps faded into the distance, leaving only Grey. His cutlery tinked and clanked as he ate his feast in pure, uninterrupted peace.

* * *

Midnight drew ever closer when Grey returned to his bedroom. Stepping inside, he noticed Margaret's absence, before glancing upon Ryder's bag, which was seemingly untouched. Eventually, his eyes turned towards the window opposite him. It peered beyond the castle walls and into the pure darkness of the night. The longer he looked at it, the darker it seemed to grow, and the harder it became to breathe.

I'm being watched, he thought to himself.

Abruptly, Grey rushed towards the window and pulled the curtains over it. A small relief came over him as he backed away and sat down at the end of his bed. As the seconds ticked by, his gaze was helplessly drawn towards Ryder's bag and the curtain-covered window.

Back and forth he looked.

Stop it, he told himself. *You can't keep thinking of it. Just sleep.*

His eyes returned to Ryder's bag.

But what will Ryder say when the earl questions him? He'll surely tell him everything. It'll give him the perfect excuse to get rid of me.

No, no. The earl won't believe him. He won't.

But what if he does? Ryder will take everything from me. I can't let him find out. The earl can't ...

Grey turned and glanced at the wooden drawer beside his bed. After listening for any sounds of life outside his room, he stood up and approached the drawer, gently sliding it open. The warm candlelight illuminated a sharpened dagger inside.

I can't kill Ryder yet. They would obviously all suspect me ... but the earl? What if he was struck in the night? Margaret would never believe I would do such a thing. Most wouldn't. They'll think it the intruders. Then that will leave the knights at my command. Everything at my command. And even better, they will have all the more motivation to defend this place from whoever else is out there waiting for me. I can just point them right where I need them.

Grey's hand reached into the drawer and pulled out the blade. He held it before his eyes, inspecting its razor-sharp edges.

Then they'll all realise the true threat that is upon them. They'll all realise I was right. They'll all realise that they need me.

The wind howled and lightning crashed as Grey stalked the cold castle halls. Lightning flashed outside the windows, casting glimpses of his disfigured shadow across the walls as he approached the earl's bedroom. His eyes remained fixated on the door as he tightened his grip around the dagger's handle. With each step closer, his eyes became more distant.

At last, Grey outstretched his hand towards the doorknob. Lightning flashed the dark shadow of his long, extending arm across the hall. He gripped the dagger firmly behind his back as his fingers wrapped around the doorknob, beginning to twist it open.

'Guy?'

Grey turned to find Margaret standing at the top of the stairs behind him.

'What are you doing?' she asked, her eyes filled with fear.

Grey stuttered for a moment, pulling his hand away from the door. 'Margaret, I ... I was just going to see if your father was all right,' he explained with a smile. 'With all of the worrying things we've seen tonight, I wanted to make sure he was safe.'

Margaret's lips quivered. '… Is your real name Guy?'

'What?'

'Tell me the truth. Are you really Guy de Montfort?' She pushed harder, her eyes beginning to water.

'Of course I am, darling. What are you saying?'

Margaret stared at him for a time, fighting to maintain her composure. 'You're not telling me the truth.'

'Darling, please, I would *never* lie to you. What has you saying this?' Grey asked with care, stepping towards her.

Margaret backed away from him. He reached out his hand to touch her cheek before she pulled out her sharp, pointy hairpin and pressed it against his throat. *'Don't touch me!'* she cried out as her hair fell across her shoulders.

Grey froze at the poke of the hairpin. *'Darling, what are you doing?'*

'He told me everything! He told me you know who he is! That you're a liar! A *murderer!'* she exclaimed through her tears.

'Who told you this? The *prisoner?'*

'You know who he is!'

'Darling, please, you're really going to believe some *stranger* over *me?* He's *trying* to separate us. He's *trying* to cause this dissent. That's what he *wants.* Don't listen to him.'

Margaret's hand shook as she refused to budge. *'You have a knife in your hand.'*

'Here,' he said, handing the knife out to her. 'Take it.'

Margaret looked down upon the knife in his hand. Her eyes darted back to him.

'I told you, it was just for protection,' Grey reiterated. 'Just to make sure he's okay.'

Margaret refused to look away from him as she took the knife from his hand.

'Now, will you please lower this?' he asked.

Margaret swallowed, blinking away some of her tears as she continued holding the pin against his throat. 'You have to tell me the truth.'

Grey's expression began to turn into something sinister.

At that moment, a brigade of clanking footsteps approached them from down the hall. Margaret and Grey turned to see Terric and a handful of his armoured knights marching towards them.

Margaret's chest fell with relief. 'Terric! Please help me! It's Guy, he's –'

Terric stopped before them, placing his hand on the hilt of his sword, 'Lower the weapon, milady.'

'What? Sir Terric …'

Terric only strengthened his gaze towards her. Margaret eyed her husband with caution before finally lowering the hairpin.

'What is the meaning of this?' Terric asked Grey.

'I was on my way to see if the earl was all right when she came on me. She refuses to believe what is happening here. Fear has overwhelmed her.'

'What?!' Margaret shouted. 'He is lying, Sir Terric! We must –'

'What do you wish us to do, my lord?' Terric interrupted.

Grey gently straightened his posture, standing tall with confidence. 'For their safety, I suggest we place both of them in the dungeon under heavy protection. It's the only way we can do what we must. Then I will have a word with our prisoner.'

'Sir Terric, you cannot listen to him! Do you not trust me?' Margaret pleaded.

Terric looked at her with reluctance before he nodded to the knights behind him.

Following his order, the soldiers marched towards the earl's bedroom. Margaret turned for the stairs, only to see more knights blocking her path. One knight bashed open the earl's bedroom door, waking him with a fright.

'No!' Margaret screamed, running for the bedroom. More knights grabbed her arms and restrained her. 'No! You can't do this!'

Terric marched into the earl's bedroom as he stood up out of bed. *'What is this, Sir Terric?'*

'My lord, for your own safety, we are taking you to the dungeons until the threat of evil has been extinguished,' he explained.

The earl's gaze fell bitter as he shook his head. 'You will suffer for this.'

Terric nodded in agreement. 'Once this is over, my punishment is yours to decide, my lord.' With another gesture towards two of the knights, they escorted the earl out of the room.

'Father!' Margaret cried, breaking free from the knights and rushing into his arms.

The earl held her close. 'It's all right, my girl. It's all right.' He comforted her before noticing his son-in-law.

Grey bowed in his presence. 'My lord.'

The earl scowled at him before he was ushered down the stairs by a handful of knights. Terric approached Grey's side, watching them disappear down the stairwell.

'Thank you for seeing sense, Sir Terric,' Grey said.

'Do not thank me yet, my lord. I can only hope we are a match for whatever evil lurks here.'

'We will be,' Grey assured him, patting his shoulder. 'With God in our hearts, we will be.'

'How shall we proceed?'

'Ensure all of our soldiers are at the ready. I have ideas for certain measures we can take if we are attacked again. But firstly, fetch our other prisoner. Bring him to me in the dining hall. We have much to discuss.'

'Yes, my lord,' Terric replied with a nod before following the others down the stairs.

Once more, Grey was left standing alone in the cold castle hallway. The rain poured, the thunder rumbled, the lightning crashed.

And out he let a smile.

Chapter 21

Lines of shadow sliced across Ryder's pale face. Resting his head against the wall of the cell, his breath turned to mist. His eyes opened and closed until, at last, he succumbed to his fatigue.

The dungeon was silent and still. Drops of water echoed. The wind screamed.

Then, a crooked voice whispered from another cell, *'I'll find you.'*

Ryder's eyes cracked open. He leant aside and looked beyond the cell bars. There was nothing but darkness.

Then another whisper came. This time closer. *'You're still here?'*

Ryder's breath shook as he scanned the surrounding cells, still seeing nothing.

Another voice whispered from the cell directly across from his. *'Too late.'*

Ryder's bloodshot eyes widened as he peered into the darkness shrouding the opposite cell.

'I'm here,' a quick whisper said right behind his ear.

Ryder turned around with a fright, seeing only the shadows of his own cell. He stared into the dark, daring not to turn away as his chest heaved.

Gradually, more voices approached.

Heavier voices.

Real voices.

'This way,' a knight ordered.

Ryder gazed beyond his cell bars again, finding a group of knights directing the earl and Margaret down the dungeon stairs. They were escorted towards the cell beside his own.

A knight opened the cell door as Terric gestured for the father and daughter to enter. 'My lord.'

The earl stopped before the cell and glared at Terric with grave disappointment. 'You have lost your mind.'

'I am merely doing this for your protection, my lord,' Terric replied with the shake of his head, desperate for his master to understand. 'Is that not why we are rebuilding St. Mary's Church? To strengthen the power of the Lord and to repel demonic forces? They are forces that I fear are among us now. They are *written* of. Do you deny them?'

'The only true forces of evil are the forces of men, Terric. *That* I do know for certain.' Comforting Margaret under his arm, the earl entered the dungeon cell. The metal clanked as the gate was shut and locked behind them.

Terric watched as the earl and Margaret sat down in the cold cell alone. He sighed a solemn breath, before marching to the next cell over. Ryder glanced up at him, his face a ghostly white and the rings around his eyes turning darker by the hour.

At Terric's signal, another knight unlocked Ryder's cell and opened the door for him. 'You are to come with me,' Terric said.

In the candlelit dining hall, Grey sat at the end of the long table, waiting. Ryder's bag rested before him as he inspected the silenced pistol in his hand. After a short time, the wooden door creaked open, and Terric entered. Behind him, a slow and weak Ryder followed, still struggling to keep his eyes open before he paused at the sight of Grey.

The butler pulled back an empty chair at the opposite end of the table for him. Ryder glanced at the chair, then back at Grey with great caution. Eventually, he limped over and sat down before a plate of freshly cooked meat and vegetables.

'Thank you, Sir Terric,' Grey said with a nod. 'We will discuss our next actions once I have spoken to the prisoner.'

Terric nodded before exiting the hall alongside everyone else, leaving only Ryder and Grey. Between them, the candle flames flickered while the pelting rain filled their silence.

Ryder's eyes fell upon his bag sitting at the opposite end of the table.

Upon noticing the desperation in his gaze, Grey finally let out a grand smile. 'Well, you just look better and better, don't you?'

Ryder's eyes returned to his captor with displeasure.

Grey extended his hand and gestured towards the food. 'Please. Eat.'

Ryder held his gaze for a moment longer before he looked down upon the food. His hand shook as he reached for his fork, quietly wincing in pain as he lifted the cutlery. With one small bite at a time, he began to eat.

'Nice, isn't it?' Grey said.

Ryder only gave him a scowl in return.

Grey leant back and relaxed into his chair. 'I'm sure you're wondering how I did all of this.'

'Not really,' Ryder replied with a tired voice. 'But I'm guessing you want to tell me all about it, anyway.'

Grey chuckled under his breath. 'Well, if you insist, of course. It was easier than I expected, you know? It's impressive how far our knowledge and strength goes in a time like this. It's just on a whole other level than they have here. I still find it quite amusing, to be honest.' As he spoke, Grey was unable to hide his gleeful excitement. 'Until you arrived and sped up this whole process, though, I was actually just waiting until the plague hit. That way, I could just let it wipe out anyone in my way. I brought *stores* of medicine to survive the ordeal, myself. I had everything I needed. Well, I still do, I suppose. When the time comes, they'll probably even see me as some sort of god for having survived it so easily. Not that I wouldn't have already achieved the status that I've been working towards by then, thanks to you, of course.'

'You think they'll protect you?'

'Protect me? No, *I'm* the one protecting them. I mean, have you seen how *small* some of them are?'

'They only need protection from problems *you've* brought them.'

'No, no, no, they're problems *Connor* brought them. And besides, I'm here now. May as well make the best of it.'

'You're using history as your own damn playground.'

'Oh, come on, Ryder. Don't act like you're here for anything other than killing me. You couldn't care less about what I do here. Or even what you do, apparently. Getting yourself thrown into a jousting match? *Now* who's in the playground?'

Ryder continued to eat in silence.

'I must say though, it *was* pretty entertaining,' he playfully acknowledged, sipping from his cup of wine. 'But while you're rather easy to work out, the others outside these walls are a little more subtle than us two.'

'Then maybe we can work out some sort of deal.'

'Ah, see, we *are* on the same page, then! You help me, I help you.'

'How will you help me?'

'You tell me everything you know about who else is coming for me, and then I'll let you free. We go our separate ways.'

'You'll give me back my things?'

'Oh no, I can't do *that.*'

'Why *not?*'

'Because that'll make it all too easy for you to just come and kill me later, *obviously.* And I assume you'd want to. I mean, you've come *this* far. I imagine it would be a tad anticlimactic for you to just *let* me *go.*'

'So, you're proposing I get *nothing?*'

'No, of course not. I'm proposing you get a *fresh start.* There's a *whole world* out here, Ryder. You should see it. It's beautiful. *Really.* The freedom we have now. You want to travel the world? Go! You want to teach people whatever *you* want? You can! You want to change history for the better? For the worse? There's *nothing* stopping us. This isn't a world tainted by everyone else anymore. It's teeming with possibility, ready to be moulded into whatever *we* want it to be. Think about it. We're smarter, faster, stronger. We're *different*, Ryder, *we're better*, and people see that. They *want* to follow us. If all of that isn't an opportunity worth taking, then I don't know what is.'

'And how can I be sure you won't just kill me after this conversation?'

Grey nodded and reached into his bag, pulling out a small capsule. After inspecting its label, he poured two pills into the palm of his hand and stood up. His footsteps echoed throughout the hall as he strolled towards Ryder and placed the pills on the table before him. 'This won't heal you entirely, of course, but it's a start.' He turned and walked back towards his end of the table. 'And if you help me here, I will give you what remaining medication you need, and I'll see to it that you walk out of this place alive and well.'

As he sat back down, Ryder swallowed the two pills with a scull of water. Immediately, he began to feel the drugs rejuvenating his body. Gazing down at his food, he began to contemplate.

Are you really going to trust him? You know you can't.

He's got no reason at all to let you live ...

But what other option do I have? I have nothing else to offer.

It's either this or ... or no chance at all ...

As his nerves settled, Ryder finally nodded to himself. 'I know that they use cloaking. And that there's more than one.'

'How many?'

'I don't know, but I'd gather there'd be *at least* three or four.'

'What else?'

'From what I can tell, they're trying to stay hidden. When they attacked me, it was in an isolated area, no one else around. They used suppressed weapons, and they moved quietly.'

'How did you escape them?'

'I got myself into a crowd, covered my tracks, and then I didn't see them again. So, if they're going to try and hit you, it's going to be when they're sure there's no one else around to see it.'

Grey nodded, staring into space as he processed his words. 'I'm guessing they're from Forward Industries, then?'

'That's what I assume.'

'And is that everything?'

'It is.'

Grey sat in silence for a moment. After a long sigh, he took another sip of wine. 'Well, it's not a lot, but it'll do. Thank you, Ryder. I really do appreciate it ... *Guards!*'

Without a second's delay, Terric and a handful of his knights pushed open the doors and surrounded the prisoner.

'Escort our prisoner back to his cell,' Grey ordered. 'We will execute him in the morning.'

Yeah. Of course you will, Ryder thought to himself.

The knights grabbed Ryder's arms and pulled him up from his chair. He gave Grey one last cold gaze before he was pushed out of the hall. Terric joined Grey's side as they approached the dining hall's exit.

'Did you discover much, my lord?' Terric asked.

'Enough. But for now, ensure that any guests of the castle depart early in the morning before the execution. We needn't complicate matters with their presence. And most importantly, I want you to gather as much oil and black dye as you can. I will direct you once that has been done.'

'Yes, my lord,' Terric replied with a nod, beginning to step away.

'Oh, and Terric,' Grey continued, stopping him in his tracks. 'Find the jester and take him to the dungeon too. I'm sure his loyalty to the earl would prove to be another thorn in our plans.'

'I agree. I will see to it,' he said with a nod before continuing out of the hall.

Meanwhile, Ryder was escorted into the castle courtyard, stepping into the torrential rain and directed towards the dungeon. Thunder crashed overhead as Ryder glanced behind him. There were two knights at his rear and two at his front.

I can't go back down there, he thought. *It's now or never.*

Without hesitation, Ryder clenched his fists and barged his shoulder into a knight behind him, using all of his strength to knock him off his feet. The front two knights swiftly turned around as Ryder kicked the second rear knight backwards onto the ground.

He twisted around to face the front two knights before one of them smacked their sword's hilt into his face. Blood spurted out from Ryder's nose just as the other knight grabbed him and punched his gut. Collapsing to his knees, the hunter groaned in pain.

The other two knights climbed up and off the muddy ground. 'Bloody hell, come on,' one of them said as he grabbed Ryder's shoulders and dragged him back to his feet.

Ryder gasped for air as the rain dripped off his face and drenched his hair. In a daze, he looked off to one corner of the courtyard, spotting Hamo concealed behind a pillar. The jester watched as Ryder was forced down the stairs and back into the dungeon, disappearing from sight.

Hamo surveyed the rest of his surroundings, spotting more knights searching the castle for his whereabouts. Without a whisper of noise, he slipped back into the shadows.

* * *

At the farthest edge of the village, in their quiet home, Lena caught another flame from the tinderbox. Relighting their small candle, its orange light glowed across her face, acting as the only comfort on this cold, dark night.

'Can you help me with this?' Arnest asked.

Lena turned towards her husband as he sat beside their small dining table, needing his breastplate tightened. She nodded and knelt beside him, beginning to tie each leather strap together.

'Thank you,' he said with a soft smile.

Reluctantly, she tied off the last piece of leather. 'How's that?'

Arnest returned to his feet, twisting and stretching his armour. 'It's perfect,' he said with a nod before picking up his horned helmet.

Lena wrapped her arms around him from behind, both looking down upon his helmet. 'Promise me you'll be safe.'

Arnest placed his hand over hers. 'I promise *you'll* be safe.'

Lena fought to withhold her tears. 'I need *you* to be safe.'

Arnest turned to face her, placing his hand on her cheek. 'I will do everything I can to come back to you. I *will*. After all, I still have that damn door to fix.'

Lena let out a small laugh amidst her aching breath before he gently pulled her into his chest and held her close. She squeezed her arms around him.

'*I love you,*' he said.

'*I love you.*'

Arnest rested his cheek atop her head as they closed their eyes.

I'll be back, he told himself. *I'll be back.*

Finally, he let go of his wife and rested his hands upon her shoulders. 'I must go. I must prepare everyone for the morning.'

Lena nodded as her eyes glistened. 'Will you please go to the church before you do? Say a prayer so that you have the Lord's protection.'

Arnest hesitated.

'Please. For me,' she implored.

With a deep sigh, Arnest nodded. 'I will,' he relented before kissing her lips.

For one final moment, they embraced again.

Then, at last, Arnest journeyed out into the storm.

The rain ran down his cheeks and bounced off his silver armour as he passed the colossal church. He glanced at its dark spirals and looming towers, continuing to walk past it, further and further away, until he stopped, and with a slow turn, he looked back at the cross that hung above its front doors.

Ah, Lena, he thought with another heavy sigh. *For you, then ...*

Wind and rain swept inside the church as Arnest pushed open one of the doors. With rain dripping from his armour, he stepped inside and shut the door behind him. In an instant, the storm was silenced. Only a sparse few candles were lit inside. The ceiling seemed as high as the sky itself, while numerous windows stretched along both sides of the church. He took a moment to bask in the breathless sight.

Eventually, he gazed ahead, spotting a lone figure sitting in the front row. Squinting, he rested his hand on his hilt. His armour clanked and echoed along the stone floor, passing by row after row of empty seats. As he came to the front row, the man turned.

It was Hamo, his hands clasped together in prayer.

Arnest concealed his surprise as he stopped beside him. 'What are you doing here?'

'I am praying,' Hamo replied simply.

'At this hour?'

'Yes. At this hour,' he said, turning towards the largest cross in the church.

'Is there good reason for this?' Arnest asked.

'Does there need to be good reason to pray?'

'I wouldn't know.'

Hamo looked back at Arnest, eyeing him up and down. 'Is there good reason for wearing your armour at this hour?'

'Yes. There is.'

'Good … take a seat with me. Let there be no secrets in God's house tonight. The Lord knows there has been enough treachery on this day.'

Arnest glanced at his surroundings before carefully sitting down beside the jester.

Finally, Hamo turned to him with a smile. 'So, how can I help?'

Chapter 22

'That time will come.'

Ryder's eyes snapped open, hearing yet another broken whisper from the shadows. He stared at the stone ceiling for a time, catching his breath before he slowly forced himself to sit upright.

More colour had returned to his face as he pulled aside his collar, inspecting the wound on his chest. The bruising had lessened overnight. Meanwhile, blood had dried around his nose and lips, and a new bruise marked his forehead. He sat up against the wall behind him, wincing upon the touch of his forehead.

Before long, quiet voices and sobbing arose from the cell next door.

'I'm so sorry,' Margaret said amidst her tears. 'I should've known. I shouldn't have been so *foolish.*'

Ryder pulled himself over to the wall between them, listening in on their conversation.

'It's all right, darling. It's all right,' the earl assured her. 'He is a deceitful one. And from this, you will learn. You will know when you see one now … I am only sorry I did not act sooner.'

'Will Sir Terric truly leave us here? Will he not let us free?' she asked, sniffling.

'I do not know. But I promise you, they will pay for what they have done here. They will pay for this treachery.'

Margaret, her eyes bloodshot with tears, looked at the wall connecting their cells. 'Ryder, are you there?' she asked, crawling up beside it.

'Yeah,' Ryder replied, nodding to himself. 'I'm here,'

'Everything you said … it seems to be true.'

'If you truly know of him, sir,' the earl proposed, 'then do you know how we may overcome him?'

Ryder shook his head in despair. 'Not from here.'

'Does anyone else know of him?' Margaret asked. 'Of who he truly is?'

'I spoke to your jouster, Arnest … but I don't know if he'll do anything.'

'He has a wife, and a child on the way,' she said with a glimmer of hope. 'If he knows anything of what is happening here, surely he will help.'

The earl bowed and shook his head in doubt, before turning back to the cell wall. 'What exactly are those weapons you brought? That gauntlet with the strange symbols. Surely it is not sorcery?'

Ryder paused.

How do I explain? … Should I explain?

I may not have long to live anyway.

'Just … think of it as a map,' he finally said with a tired voice. 'It helps me get to where I'm going.'

'And how far *did* you travel?' Margaret asked.

'A long way. Longer than you can imagine.'

'How long did it take you to get here, then?'

'I'm not even sure … I've lost track of that.'

'Why, is there no one waiting for you back home?'

Ryder opened his mouth before he hesitated. After another moment of silence, he shook his head again. 'No … There's no one.'

'No one at all?' Margaret said with surprise. 'Really?'

Instinctively, Ryder felt the chain around his neck as he closed his eyes. Without any fight left in him, he pulled the seashell necklace out from under his shirt and gently caressed it in his palm. Memories of Rose flooded his thoughts, and for just a moment, he felt unburdened by all that was happening around him. 'Well, I do have a daughter.'

Margaret sat up against the opposite side of the wall, speaking with care, 'What is her name?'

'Rose …'

'Oh, that's a lovely name.'

Ryder let out a smile for just a moment.

'She must be waiting a long time for you,' Margaret continued. 'Is there no way to get back sooner?'

'Only the gauntlet. My map … that's the only way.' Ryder gripped the necklace tighter as his heartache returned. 'But she won't wait for me … she shouldn't.'

'But I'm sure she will anyway. You're still her father, after all … I pray that Arnest or somebody does help us, and that you can get back to her. I'm sure she misses you very much,' Margaret said as she looked at her own father with a small, solemn smile.

Ryder held back any tears as he broke away, unable to bear his memories any longer.

The clank and crash of a loud metal door sounded from above. A beam of sunlight shone down into the dungeon hall. Margaret and the earl looked at the stairs as metal footsteps marched down towards them. Meanwhile, Ryder stared only at the ground beneath his feet.

'Good morning, good morning!' Grey's jolly voice called out. Soon, a handful of knights entered the dungeon as their new lord skipped down the steps, wearing fur-coated robes and a bright smile. 'I hope your sleep was not too unpleasant,' he continued, approaching the earl and Margaret's cell.

'I hope you never know peace,' Margaret replied with a scowl.

'Oh, don't you see? That's *why* I'm doing this, my darling. Once all of this mayhem has been dealt with, peace *will* come. I promise you.'

'You are a *monster*.'

'My dear, please do not break my heart like that. You'll see the truth soon enough.' He patted the cell bars before strolling over to Ryder's cell, smiling down upon him. 'Today's the big day, Ryder. Put on a smile. Your suffering is over.'

Ryder slowly climbed to his feet and glared at him through the cell bars. 'Only someone as stupid as you could think this'll last.'

'Says the man about to be executed at my command. How cute.' Grey gestured for his knights to open the cell door.

As one knight unlocked it, another grabbed Ryder's arm and directed him out of the cell. Ryder gave a final glance to Margaret and the earl as he passed by their cell. Margaret's shoulders fell in defeat, while the earl gifted him a nod, out of respect.

Surrounded by knights, Ryder was escorted up the dungeon stairs and pushed into the castle courtyard. The bright sunlight blinded him for a moment as he squinted and covered his eyes.

As his vision returned, he found dozens upon dozens of knights surrounding the courtyard and lining the walls above. In the centre of the courtyard sat a long wooden platform, a few steps high, where a wooden stump sat atop it.

Grey walked ahead, meeting Terric before the platform. 'Still no word on Hamo?'

'No, my lord. He seems to have fled the castle.'

'Of course, he has. Anyway, let us continue. Once this is over with, we shall turn our attention towards him.'

Terric nodded before directing the knights to escort Ryder onto the platform.

Outside of the castle, rays of sunlight beamed down upon a dirt path leading towards its towering gates. The dewy grass shimmered, the birds chirped, and the flies buzzed about as Arnest strolled up to the castle's entrance. Alone.

The reticle of Hayes' sniper scope tracked the armoured jouster from a distance. 'He's moving towards the castle.'

The rest of the invisible ghosts knelt beside him, atop the hill's edge.

'That's the one from the blacksmith last night,' Kingston said.

'He's all armoured up. You might be right,' Dax admitted. 'Maybe he *is* one of them.'

With his helmet under his arm, Arnest knocked on the castle gate.

After a moment, a knight slid open a square peephole and smiled at the sight of him, 'Hello there, Arnest. What brings you here today?'

'I heard my opponent from yesterday is seeing his final moments. I was hoping I could be there to witness it. If it's not too much trouble, of course.'

'I don't see why not. You're just in time, in fact.'

'How perfect.'

The knight pulled back a large circular lever, opening the tall castle gates.

Grey watched as Ryder was pushed along the platform and forced to his knees before the wooden stump. Upon hearing the groan of the gates, the lord turned to see

Arnest strolling inside the courtyard. 'Arnest! What a pleasant surprise. You've come to see the execution?'

'That I have,' he replied with a nod, surveying the courtyard and the walls above, noting the dozens of soldiers watching. 'He fought so valiantly in the joust yesterday that I thought I'd best show my respect.'

'How noble of you. Please, make yourself comfortable.'

Arnest bowed in return.

Grey approached Ryder, kneeling at his side as he quietened his voice. 'I wish we had more time together, Ryder. But of course, I didn't come here to reminisce about the past ... or should I say the future? I never quite know how to put it.'

Ryder, bruised and dishevelled, only gave him an exhausted, hateful stare in return.

Grey nodded and patted him on the back before standing up, turning to face all of his surrounding knights, 'Today is a day we shall not forget, gentlemen! Today is the day we were brave enough to say, "No more!" No more will we allow foreign evils to corrupt our lands and threaten our homes! No more will we allow the word of the Lord to be trampled upon! No more will we allow our futures to be guided by uncontrolled chaos! Today is the day we fight back, no matter the cost! And it all begins here, executing the first of many traitors who will try to weave their devilish ways into our lives. This shall be a message to them.'

Hayes' scope watched as the castle gates began to close again. 'No, no, don't do that. Leave it open, please.'

'It looks like there's a *lot* of soldiers in there,' Cato said.

'I know, that's why I want to get a good ...' Finally, the gates closed, obscuring Hayes' view. 'Dammit.'

In the castle courtyard, Grey gave a final nod towards Terric. Placing himself beside Ryder, Terric unsheathed his long and sharpened sword. Ryder's hands dripped with sweat as his breath shook. A knight grabbed the back of his head and forced his neck onto the wooden stump.

Terric pressed the edge of his blade against the back of Ryder's neck, lining up his aim. Arnest watched closely, clenching his fists, while a small smile broke out across Grey's face.

Ryder felt nauseous and dizzy, helplessly staring at the ground. Terric lifted his sword, ready to bring it down upon his neck. Ryder closed his eyes and remembered lying in bed with Rose. She slept soundly, her little breaths making the gentlest of sounds. Ryder smiled back at her.

'*Where are you?*' a voice whispered to him.

'*I'm here,*' he softly said back. '*I'm right here.*'

Terric's blade lifted high above his head, shimmering as the sun bounced off it. Ryder closed his eyes tighter, a few tears breaking through. Terric tightened his grip on the blade, about to bring it down, when …

'*Grey Pines!*' Arnest's voice yelled out, cutting through the courtyard's silence.

Terric held back his sword, turning around to see Arnest taking a step closer towards the platform. Ryder opened his eyes with relief, gasping for air. Grey slowly turned towards Arnest, completely stunned.

'That is your real name, is it not?' Arnest asked in front of everyone. 'Or have you not told them?'

Grey scoffed, resisting the urge to gaze upon everyone else's reactions. 'What is this, Arnest?'

Terric looked back and forth between the two of them, curious.

'Have you not told them that you personally know this man that you are about to execute?' Arnest continued. 'That you and he come from the same land? That *you* are a wanted criminal who fled here to avoid justice?' The jouster met the eyes of Terric and every other knight watching. 'Has he not told you any of this?' Arnest pointed at Grey. '*He* has been lying to all of you, twisting the truth for his own gain. *That* is why this man is to be executed without question or trial, and *that* is why he has locked away your very own earl. He has stripped all of us of the truth and abuses his power –'

'*Enough of this!*' Grey called out. 'All I hear is fantasies! A man attempting to win favour with an earl who has failed to see the real threats that are upon us. You have not *seen* what I have seen. What Sir Terric has. There are greater forces upon us, and we are merely doing what we must to defend ourselves. Your lies are just another advent of evil working to stop our service of the Lord. And I know you, Arnest … I *know* you are not a man of God. Isn't that right? Or did you fail to mention that part? How convenient.'

Arnest shook his head. 'You cannot hide your lies forever, Grey.' He turned his focus towards Terric, taking another step closer. 'Sir Terric, I implore you, question the man you are about to execute yourself. You *will* learn the truth.'

Terric looked at Grey with uncertainty for a time, before he returned to Arnest and shook his head. 'I have seen the dangers that Lord Guy speaks of. I know it to be true.'

Arnest sighed in defeat. 'You are making a grave mistake.'

Grey signalled a handful of his knights, 'Take him to the dungeon! We will not hear any more of this devil-speak today.'

'I'm afraid I must agree with Sir Arnest on this matter,' a confident voice pronounced from the opposite side of the courtyard.

Grey's eyes widened, immediately recognising the voice as he turned to find Hamo walking into the courtyard from within the castle walls. Casually, he tossed one of Ryder's circular, silver grenades up and down in his hand. A smile of amazement broke out across Ryder's face.

'Your actions here have been most disrespectful, Lord Grey.' Hamo continued, raising his eyebrows at him.

'Bloody clown,' Grey mumbled to himself before signalling more of his knights, 'Arrest them both!'

Multiple knights approached Arnest and Hamo. Arnest backed away and slid on his helmet.

'As a loyal servant of the earl, I'm afraid I must disagree,' Hamo said before clicking a button on the grenade, turning it red.

Grey's eyes filled with fear as he took a step back.

Hamo used all his strength to throw the grenade into the opposite corner of the courtyard, landing right in front of the knights approaching Arnest. With a small, quick beep, the grenade exploded into a fiery blaze.

The knights were thrown backwards as dirt, dust, and smoke flung into the air. Grey, Terric, and the rest of the knights ducked in terror as the explosion sent a shockwave throughout the courtyard.

Amidst the flying dust and debris, Arnest turned and walked straight towards the castle gates, unsheathing his sword. The knight at the gate yelled out and charged towards him. The knight swung his sword at his chest. Arnest stepped aside, dodging the blade and slicing his own sword across the knight's neck. The knight gurgled and choked on his blood, grabbing his throat and collapsing to the ground.

Arnest continued walking straight towards the gate as a second knight charged at him. He blocked his incoming blade before punching the knight's helmet, disorienting him. Before he could recover, Arnest shoved his blade through the knight's throat and pulled it out, kicking him to the ground. He immediately turned towards the gate's circular lever.

Grey coughed and waved away the surrounding smoke before spotting Arnest pulling the wheel and beginning to open the gate. *'Stop him! Stop him!'* he cried out.

Hayes' scope scanned along the top of the castle walls, watching knights fire crossbow bolts down within their own courtyard. 'What the hell is going on?'

'The gate's opening!' Ember exclaimed.

A crossbow bolt struck Arnest's shoulder guard and bounced off it. He growled in pain as he continued pulling the wheel. Dozens of knights stumbled to their feet and ran towards him.

Atop the hillside, the ghosts heard a growing rumble emanate from within the village. As they looked towards it, they spotted a small army of townspeople appearing from behind the houses, sprinting straight towards the castle gates. They wore makeshift armour, held their swords and spears high in the air, and screamed at the top of their lungs.

'Oh, shit,' Cato said.

Dax chuckled in equal astonishment.

Knights atop the castle walls turned around to face the village, spotting the army of townspeople sprinting towards them.

'Fire! *Fire!*' one knight called out.

Aiming their crossbows and arrows down below, the knights opened fire upon the townspeople.

With the gate firmly open, Arnest finally let go of the wheel and stood before the gate. He turned around to face an army of knights charging towards him. Alone, he lifted his sword, gripped it tightly, and held his breath.

You can do this.

For Lena.

For everyone ...

Suddenly, the approaching knights froze in place as they spotted the army of townspeople behind him, charging straight towards them. Arnest's heart skipped a beat as the people arrived. Alongside them, he gloriously cried out and joined them in their charge. The knights cried back and held their swords at the ready.

With a vicious crack, the lines of townspeople and knights clashed against each other. The fighters were scattered amongst each other's ranks, swinging, stabbing, slicing, kicking, punching, and biting. Metal tinked and clanked as flesh tore and bled. The courtyard erupted into a frantic battle.

The knights above struggled to get an aim on the townspeople below as they mindlessly fired their bolts into the crowds.

Atop the platform, Grey watched the chaos in disbelief. Ryder turned and looked at him before gritting his teeth and running straight towards him. Grey turned to face him just as the hunter tackled him to the floor. Ryder repeatedly punched him across the face as Grey attempted to grab at his mouth and eyes.

Terric swung and sliced at any villagers attempting to climb onto the platform, knocking them back. Arnest, in the midst of battle, cut down another knight before locking eyes with Terric atop the platform, staring at one another through the mayhem. Arnest lifted his sword and ran straight towards the platform. Terric slid one foot back and pointed his blade towards him. Arnest rushed up the platform steps and swung at his throat. Terric swiftly blocked the blade before Arnest furiously swung again, and again, and again, as Terric continually blocked each swing.

Hayes' scope looked beyond the gates, watching the raging conflict inside. 'This is insane … it's amazing!'

'We need to go in,' Alexia said.

'In there? Do you *see* all of those people?' Cato replied, gesturing to the ongoing battle.

'I see all of those people *distracted,*' she explained, looking at Able. 'Now's our chance. Slip in, slip out. No one will notice us amongst all of that.'

Able watched the battle closely.

'You can't be serious,' Cato muttered, shaking his head.

Finally, Able nodded. 'She's right. It's as good a chance as ever. We just have to watch our step. Kingston, Kye, come with me. Dax, I want you to stay here; you're a better shot from a long distance. Cato, you come with me and take his place. The rest of you stay put.'

'Are you sure, sir?' Dax asked.

'I am. Set yourself up beside Hayes.'

Dax nodded, beginning to snap several long-range attachments onto his rifle.

'Let me come with you,' Alexia said, turning to Able.

'No, we're keeping to these squads.'

'Able, plea –'

'I said no!' Able snapped, leaning in close to her. 'I don't know what sort of personal investment you've got going on here, but you're still under *my* command. You're not going to abandon your squad just because of your feelings. Besides, if Grey tries to flee, I need you out here to make sure he doesn't get away. *Is that clear?*'

Alexia could no longer look him in the eyes, nodding in defeat. 'Yes, sir.'

'Good. My squad, with me, *let's go!*' Able ordered, swiftly standing up and rushing down the hill with his squad following closely behind.

Atop the platform in the castle courtyard, Ryder sat on Grey's chest, holding back his arms as Grey fought to scratch at his face. Amidst their commotion, Grey's sleeve slid down his arm, revealing the time gauntlet clamped around his wrist.

Immediately, Ryder lunged for the device before Grey stuck his finger into Ryder's chest wound. Ryder yelled in pain before throwing another furious punch into Grey's face.

Further behind them, Terric dodged another swing from Arnest's blade before he threw his fist into the jouster's stomach. As he bent over in pain, Terric thrust his knee into Arnest's helmet. Arnest fell to the floor as his helmet rolled off and blood streamed out of his nose.

Without hesitation, Terric lifted his sword and swung it down towards him. Arnest rolled aside as the blade smacked into the wooden floor, narrowly missing him. While laying on his back, Arnest kicked Terric away, giving him a chance to scramble to his feet, pick up his sword, and charge straight back towards him.

Meanwhile, Able's squad of ghosts sprinted across the open field, straight towards the castle gates. They jumped over and skidded around the bodies of townspeople who had been struck by bolts and arrows before ever reaching the courtyard.

'Keep your guns up and at the ready! Watch your surroundings!' Able ordered, slowing down and leading them through the tall, open gates.

Atop the distant hill, Hayes watched them through his scope. 'They're in.'

Alexia bit her lip as she anxiously watched.

The battling townspeople and knights became more desperate in their swings, punches, and kicks. They were exhausted. Blood dripped from their faces as dirt and dust stuck to their skin. Able, Kingston, Kye, and Cato moved in amongst the gaps of the fighting crowd.

Cato halted in place as Osbert fell to the ground in his path. Before he could recover, a knight ran over to him and drove a sword into his chest. Osbert yelled in pain as blood spurted out of his mouth. The knight yanked the sword out and charged off into another engagement. Cato forced himself to look away as he moved around the body. 'God damn, this is *fucking* crazy.'

Kingston paused as he spotted Ryder and Grey fighting atop the wooden platform. 'I have visual! Ryder's here too! Him and Grey, both!'

Moving through the surrounding conflict, Able aimed his rifle up at the platform. 'Got it!'

'Trying to get a clean shot!' Kingston replied.

Alexia listened in over the comms, gripping her rifle tighter as she stared at the castle gates.

Grey smacked his gauntlet across Ryder's face, disorienting him. With the upper hand, Grey pushed Ryder onto his side and climbed on top of him, throwing a punch across his face.

'Taking a shot!' Kingston called out, firing a silenced bullet at the platform and hitting Grey's shoulder.

Grey yelped in pain as he fell to his side and gripped his bleeding shoulder. He and Ryder suddenly froze as they noticed the bullet wound. Their eyes turned towards the crowds, noticing several distortions gliding through the chaos towards them.

'Shit!' Grey shouted, clambering to his feet.

Ryder followed him as they both ran for the opposite end of the platform.

'They know we're here!' Able exclaimed, firing multiple rounds at the two targets.

All of the ghosts unloaded silenced shots at them. Bullets whizzed past and ripped up the wooden floor behind Grey and Ryder as they jumped off the end of the platform and crashed onto the dirt ground below. Arnest and Terric ceased their fighting, witnessing the bullets ripping into the wooden planks beside them.

Grey groaned as he rolled onto his side, yelling at Terric, *'The oil! Drop the oil!'*

Terric's eyes widened before he turned towards the knights atop the castle walls. *'Pour the oil! Pour the oil!'* he ordered at the top of his lungs.

The ghosts halted in place.

'What the hell is going on?' Cato asked, looking around in a panic.

The squad turned and looked up at the castle walls as numerous knights poured buckets upon buckets of thick, black oil down across the entire battlefield. The fighting was interrupted as the townspeople, knights, and ghosts were all drenched in oil and a gust of steam arose from the ground. The townsfolk covered their eyes and faces, feeling their skin beginning to lightly burn, while the ghosts attempted to wipe the liquid off their visors.

On the outside hill, Alexia's head perked up at the sudden silence that overtook the castle. *'Able, what's going on in there?'*

As their temperature readers repeatedly beeped, Cato flung some of the oil off his arms, barely able to make out his surroundings through his visor, 'What the fuck is this?'

'I think it's oil,' Kye guessed, inspecting the black liquid as it dripped off his arms and melted through a thin layer of his armour. Before long, portions of their armour had distorted, and their cloaking began to stutter. "Temperature Stabilising" and "Cloaking Stabilising" messages appeared within each of their helmets, automatically recalibrating their cloaking systems into a working state again.

A handful of knights and townsfolk moaned in pain as their skin bubbled and melted, while the rest of them backed away from any oil and regained their bearings. As the steam cleared, Terric and Arnest looked upon the battlefield below and froze in shock.

Able wiped enough of the oil off his visor to find Terric and Arnest standing atop the platform, staring directly at him. One by one, more and more knights and townspeople began to notice too.

Kingston, Kye, and Cato's breath left their lungs as the entire castle had grown silent. Drenched in black oil, an outline had formed around the ghosts, and the entire castle could see them.

'Oh …' Cato uttered.

'What the hell's going on?' Alexia's voice repeated over the comms. *'Report!'*

'Able, are you there?' Hayes' voice followed.

Townspeople and knights alike all stepped back in astonishment, their eyes glued to the dark spectres standing before them, surrounded by the bodies of the fallen. Arnest stepped forth, his mouth agape as he attempted to comprehend the sight.

Able swallowed. 'They see us.'

'What?!' Alexia replied.

Terric almost shook with dread as he stared at the dark, supernatural figures. He turned towards Grey as he climbed to his knees, holding his bleeding shoulder. At last, Terric looked back at the ghosts with resolve and pointed his sword towards them. *'The demons are upon us, men! Kill them!'*

'Uhhh…' Cato groaned, his eyes darting between the surrounding soldiers.

'For the Lord Almighty!' a lone knight cried out, charging straight towards Able with his sword held high.

Able froze as the knight sprinted towards him.

'Ah, fuck it,' Kingston said, walking towards the knight and firing multiple rounds into his chest. The bullets ripped through the knight's armour, throwing him backwards onto the ground.

Able looked at Kingston in disbelief.

Kingston stood beside him, unblinking. 'Mission's fucked anyway.'

At last, the remaining army of knights lifted their swords, cried out, and charged towards the black spectres.

'Shit! Defend yourselves!' Able ordered, lifting his rifle alongside the other three ghosts.

In unison, all four of them unloaded silenced bullets into the enclosing knights. The rounds sliced through their silver armour, dropping each of them to the ground.

'Fire!' Terric cried out to the knights above.

The knights atop the walls fired their projectiles down upon the spectres. Bolts and arrows struck the ghosts' armour and bounced off of it.

'Cover me!' Able said. 'I'll set our coordinates!'

'Copy!' Kingston replied, spraying his machine gun into the knights charging towards him.

Able backed away behind the three ghosts, typing the coordinates into his gauntlet.

Two knights charged at Kye. He stood his ground, gunning down one knight just as the other reached him. He ducked and dodged the knight's sword before firing a bullet up through his helmet.

As another charged at Kingston, he knelt at the last second, flipping the knight over his back. The knight crashed onto the ground as Kingston stood up and fired two bullets into the knight's head.

More knights, covering themselves with shields, ran towards Cato. His heart pounded as he opened fire, breaking their shields in half and cutting right through several of them. As his clip ran out of ammo, he swiftly pulled out a grenade and tossed it towards the remaining knights, blowing their legs out from under them.

'Coordinates set!' Able said. 'Kye, you sync up first. We'll cover you!'

'Yes, sir!' Kye replied, retreating behind the squad as Able took his place, gunning down any approaching soldiers.

On the opposite side of the courtyard, Grey stumbled to his feet just before Ryder tackled him back to the ground.

'You idiot! They're gonna kill us!' Grey cried, struggling to hold him back.

Ryder punched Grey in the nose, breaking it with a crack. Grey moaned in pain before Ryder wrapped his hands around his neck, strangling him. Grey tried to grab at his face before Ryder trapped his arms beneath his knees. As he desperately fought to catch a breath, Grey's face began to turn purple. Ryder only tightened his grip as he glared down at him, unrelenting.

Meanwhile, Arnest and Terric continued clashing swords atop the execution platform. In the midst of their fighting, Terric glanced across the courtyard, spotting Ryder suffocating Grey. Returning to the duel, he knelt and dodged another swing from Arnest. Standing back up, he thrust his shoulder into Arnest's chest and ran him off the edge of the platform.

Arnest's back crashed onto the ground below as bullets whizzed past and more knights fell to their deaths around him. Spinning around onto his chest, he looked about with vigilance, staying low as more and more knights surrounded the spectres.

Grey's breath became shorter and shorter as his eyes rolled back into his head. Just as he fell silent, Terric ran up to Ryder and swung his sword upwards. The blade sliced across Ryder's chest and face, and with a cry of pain, he fell to the ground. Grey immediately gasped for air as he sat upright.

'Come, my lord!' Terric said, grabbing Grey's arm and pulling him to his feet. After placing his arm around his shoulder, Terric escorted Grey out of the courtyard with haste.

Ryder rolled onto his side, groaning in pain as blood poured out of his chest and face.

From the surrounding chaos, Hamo rushed over and knelt by his side. 'Oh, God. Here, let me help.' The jester allowed Ryder to lean on him as he assisted him to his feet.

Before they could properly stand, a knight charged at them and kicked the pair back to the ground. *'You brought this evil upon us!'* the knight screamed, lifting his sword to strike Ryder.

Another blade suddenly impaled the knight's back. Blood squirted out of his chest before he was pushed aside and slid off the blade, revealing Arnest standing behind him.

Hamo and Arnest both hurried back to Ryder's aid, helping him to his feet again.

'My things. I need my bag – my things,' Ryder mumbled through his bleeding mouth.

'I know where it is!' Hamo replied with a nod, guiding them towards the inside of the castle.

Atop the outside hill, Alexia impatiently listened to the distant gunfire and battle cries. Finally, she stood up, *'I'm coming in!'*

'No! Don't!' Able repeated over the comms. *'We're gonna port out! We're almost ready!'* he assured her, picking off more knights as they helplessly howled and whined in pain, his bullets ripping and tearing through their armour.

'I'm synched up!' Kye confirmed, running back to the front line.

'Cato, your turn! *Now!*' Able ordered.

'On it, on it!' Cato replied, backing behind the three ghosts.

Hayes' scope only caught glimpses of their oil-drenched figures through the gate. 'I can't get a good visual on them!'

Cato hastily synched his gauntlet to the others. Just as he was about to finish, a crossbow bolt flew into his forearm, ripping straight through his gauntlet. He stared at the bolt in utter shock, letting out a sob of pain.

'Cato! *What's happening?*' Able asked, preoccupied with gunning down the knights who were almost upon him.

Kingston twisted around to find Cato frozen in place and his cloaking malfunctioning, still staring at the bolt in his arm, 'Ah, shit!' Before he could run over, another crossbow bolt struck his own helmet, cracking it before bouncing off. Kingston grunted and fell to his knees. Through gritted teeth, he turned and opened fire at the castle walls above. *'Hayes, give us some cover from up top!'*

'Copy!' Hayes replied. He and Dax aimed their rifles at the knights along the distant walls and began firing rounds into their heads, picking them off one by one. Before long, the knights ducked for cover.

Another knight charged up beside Kingston, swinging his sword into his shoulder guard and knocking him to the ground. The knight repeatedly bashed him with his sword before Kingston held up his rifle to block the blade. A second knight charged past them and straight towards Cato. Stumbling backwards in fear, Cato reached for his pistol with his left hand before the knight jumped towards him and slashed the edge of Cato's neck.

Still lying on the ground, Kingston used his rifle to push the knight's sword away from him. He immediately pointed his rifle up towards the knight, unloading dozens of bullets into his chest. The knight stumbled backwards as his armour was shredded to pieces.

Cato grabbed a hold of his neck as blood squirted out of it. He mindlessly staggered through the battlefield, feeling his skin turn cold and his breath fade. His legs gave out beneath him as he collapsed to his knees. The same knight rushed up behind him and lined up his sword, ready to strike his neck again before another spray of bullets riddled his body.

The knight collapsed to the ground as Kingston reloaded his rifle. Before he could turn around, yet another knight ran up behind him and shoved his sword into Kingston's lower back. He cried out before turning and smacking the stock of his rifle into the knight's helmet. Immediately, he lifted his rifle and fired a handful of bullets through the soldier.

'Cato, can you hear me?' Able called out, glancing back at him before continuing to fight off more knights. 'Are you with me, Cato? Cato!'

Kingston bit his tongue and ignored his pain as he steadily jogged over to Cato, kneeling beside him. 'Cato?'

Cato stared into the distance as blood oozed out of his neck. Black dots overwhelmed his vision as he gave his last breath, staring at the bodies and carnage before him. His shoulders slumped down by his sides, and his vital signs beeped. His status shifted from **Active** to **Deceased**.

'Shit, Cato's down!' Able called out, kneeling beside Kye as he continued shooting any approaching knights.

Hayes lifted his gaze over his sniper scope, staring at the castle in shock. Beside him, Ember gasped, instinctively raising her hand towards her mouth.

'Kingston, you got him?' Able continued.

'Yeah.' Kingston said as he pulled out his disintegrator. 'Sorry, mate.' Without another word, Kingston stabbed the device into Cato's chest. His armour and weapons began to disintegrate, fizzling away like acid.

'All right, we need to go!' Able shouted. 'Kingston, sync up!'

Kingston looked down at the sword sticking out of his stomach. His cloaking glitched off and on as his cracked visor repeatedly malfunctioned. Slowly, he shook his head as more arrows and bolts pierced the ground around him.

'Kingston?' Able repeated.

A new line of knights ran into the courtyard with shields, spears, and spinning flails. They approached Kingston with caution, catching glimpses of his true form beneath his cloaking systems.

'Just go,' Kingston replied before another arrow flew into his waist and he grunted in pain.

'Just sync up, Kingston! Now!' Able ordered him.

Kingston's breath fell thin as he watched the approaching knights, 'Nah. I've had enough. Just get out of here and finish it. I'll handle myself.'

Alexia, still atop the outer hill, stood up as she listened to Kingston over the comms.

'Are you sure?' Kye asked, hesitating.

'Yes, I'm bloody sure. *Go,*' he replied, waving them away as he stood up and snapped the arrow out from his waist.

Able turned and nodded to Kye. 'All right, come on, let's go!'

Kingston pulled out his handgun as the approaching knights hid behind a wall of shields.

Kye watched him for another reluctant moment before Able activated his gauntlet. They both ported out of the castle courtyard and back onto the hill behind the others.

Alexia glanced their way before looking back at the castle gates.

'Hey, Lex.' Kingston's voice spoke through the comms. 'I told you it'd be fun, didn't I?' he reminded her with a chuckle.

Alexia's shoulders fell as she watched the gates with sorrow.

'Well … good luck,' he added, taking off his helmet and dropping it into the disintegrating pile of Cato's remains. His cloaking turned off entirely, revealing himself to the approaching knights.

'Witchcraft!' one knight shouted.

'Demon!' another cried.

Kingston smiled to himself and nodded. 'Yeah … I know.'

'Charge!' the leading knight ordered.

The knights ran towards him. Kingston pulled out another disintegrator from his vest as he lifted his handgun. Walking towards the small army, he gunned down each knight in quick succession.

His bullets ripped through their armour as they yelled and cried in pain, collapsing to the ground. Each knight that fell, another drew closer. Kingston continued pressing forward, steadying his breath. Numerous arrows and bolts were fired down upon him, striking his armour and the ground around him. He pressed the button atop the disintegrator, ejecting its small needle as his eyes welled with tears. A knight almost reached him before he fired a bullet right through his helmet. The knight was swept off his feet and crashed backwards onto the ground.

The others were almost upon him when Kingston swallowed, held his breath, and stabbed the disintegrator into his own chest. He suddenly felt an intense wave of heat flow through him as the liquid invaded his body. With a thud, he collapsed to his knees and dropped his gun. The knights surrounded him as the skin on his chest began to melt away. His teeth clamped down, fighting the pain. He looked upon the knights standing before him as they watched in fear. A few tears ran down Kingston's cheek. Before he could scream, the air had left his lungs, and as the acid burned through his heart, his eyes glazed over. At last, he collapsed onto the blood and oil-soaked ground.

His vital signs changed to **Deceased.**

The knights hastily stepped back as his body began to break apart into clumps of grey, acidic liquid. Before long, he had disintegrated into nothing but bubbles and ash. The courtyard fell silent as the knights stared at the remains in total horror.

On the outer hill, Alexia sighed a solemn breath as she watched smoke pour out of the castle's courtyard.

Able clenched his jaw and shook his head in frustration.

'Over there!' Ember pointed towards a field on the left side of the castle.

The ghosts gazed at the field, spotting a battalion of knights riding on horseback straight towards the surrounding forest. Terric was at their lead and Grey in their centre — all of them making for an escape.

Alexia's eyes sharpened as the battalion disappeared from sight.

Chapter 23

Explosions and battle cries echoed throughout the empty castle halls.

Soon, stumbling footsteps followed, drawing closer.

'This way, this way!' a voice exclaimed.

Hamo and Arnest, with Ryder's arms around their shoulders, rushed into the hallway towards Grey's bedroom. Hamo opened the door as Arnest stood guard.

Blood dripped out of Ryder's face and chest as he staggered towards the small wooden bench where his bag rested.

Hamo watched with concern as Ryder rummaged through his bag. Before long, he pulled out a bottle of pills and sculled half a dozen of them. With a hefty swallow, he grunted and took a deep breath, feeling an overwhelming sense of energy burn inside his chest. Afterwards, he immediately reached back into his bag, pulling out an adrenaline shot.

Arnest turned and watched him, curious and confused, as Ryder stabbed the needle into his arm. He gritted his teeth and closed his eyes as he felt the pain of his wound subside.

'Are you going to be okay?' Hamo asked.

'Yeah. Just fine.' He said as he shoved the needle back into the bag and ripped open a concealed back pocket. Reaching inside, he pulled out a small black device and began unfolding it at both ends.

'What is that?' Arnest asked.

'A weapon,' he explained as he flipped open a reticle, extended a small barrel, and pulled back the stock, revealing it to be a compact submachine gun.

'What lies outside, Ryder?' Hamo asked with fear. 'Are they truly demons?'

'No. They're just people. From my home.'

'Sounds like quite a home,' Arnest remarked.

'Are you going to go back there? To your home?' Hamo asked.

Ryder paused for a moment, glancing at them both. 'I can't go anywhere without my gauntlet. And Grey has it.'

'I'm certain he has already fled the castle,' Hamo said, shaking his head.

Ryder's hands steadied as he loaded a magazine into his gun and pulled back its slider, cocking it. 'Yeah. He won't get far.'

'I will join you,' Arnest replied. 'It seems that the rest of his forces are distracted for the time being.'

'I will see to the earl and Lady Margaret, then,' Hamo added. 'I will ensure they are freed.'

Ryder grimaced as he slung his bag onto his back and nodded to them. 'All right. Let's finish this.'

* * *

With Terric at their lead, Grey and his battalion of knights rode through the forest of Warwick. Their horses' hooves trampled over the dirt as they swerved around trees and ducked under branches.

Once the castle was far from sight, Terric halted and turned his horse around. 'My lord, the rest of my men will escort you north. Continuing in this direction, you will eventually find refuge at Kenilworth.'

'What?' Grey replied, squinting at him in disbelief. 'You're going *back* there?'

'I must, my lord. I took an oath to protect that castle and our land. I cannot abandon it in such an hour.'

'Did you not see what is *happening* back there? I need you to escort me out of *here*, not get yourself killed going back *there!'*

'My men will take care of you in the meantime, I promise you.'

'Sir Terric,' one knight interrupted, fear tainting his voice, 'with all due respect, I do not understand what we saw back there.'

'Is it not obvious?' another knight interjected. 'They are demons who have come to plague our lands!'

'We are surely doomed, then!' a third knight shouted.

Grey gazed at the surrounding soldiers with disgust as they continued to cower in thought, each of them voicing their unease, one after the other.

'How can we fight such forces?'

'I do not think we can.'

'Sir, I wish to return to my family. I cannot stay here.'

'Aye, I agree.'

'So do I.'

'No, no, no – NO!' Grey snapped. *'Will you all just shut your fucking mouths! This isn't about you! Can't you see that? It's about me! I'm your lord, and I'm in charge!'*

At last, Terric was overcome with regret as he watched Grey's outburst.

'I'm the one you need to protect!' Grey continued. *'I've already been shot once, for Christ's sake! We cannot allow this – this madness! I'm your lord, and I say –!'*

A silenced bullet struck Grey's chest mid-sentence, sending him flying off his horse and crashing onto the dirt ground. All their horses neighed and panicked as the knights attempted to regain control of them.

Terric unsheathed his sword and watched for any movement around them. *'Watch between the trees, men! The demons are in our midst!'*

All the knights readied their weapons as they shook with terror, hearing the sporadic snaps of twigs closing in from every direction.

Grey groaned in pain as he rolled onto his back, finding blood oozing out of his chest. His eyes watered in pain as he climbed to his knees and reached into his coat pocket, pulling out Ryder's handgun.

The knights remained quiet, nervously eyeing every angle of their surroundings. Amidst their silence, a small silver ball came flying through the air. It softly bounced right before the battalion. The knights and Grey paused at the sight of it, all of them holding their breath before the device beeped. A second later, the silver grenade detonated, exploding at their feet. The knights and horses were blown backwards as dirt and flames engulfed their surroundings.

Grey's ears rang as his vision blurred. He looked around in a daze, watching as the knights attempted to regain their bearings. Silent gunfire erupted around them, picking off each helpless knight as they stood up.

'Close in! Close in!' Able repeated to the other ghosts as they surrounded the doomed battalion.

Terric gripped a tree and pulled himself to his feet. 'Hold your ground, men!'

A handful of knights who remained atop their horses charged towards the source of the gunfire, holding their swords high. Ember knelt down as one horse galloped towards her. She lifted her rifle and fired multiple rounds into the animal, causing it to trip and collapse onto the ground before reaching her.

Dax, using a tree as cover, spotted another knight riding in his direction. With the steady aim of his rifle, he fired a single round into the knight's chest. The knight slid off the side of his horse before his foot was caught in the stirrup. The horse continued riding off, dragging his body with it.

In the distance, Hayes watched the battle through the scope of his sniper. He turned his aim towards another knight as he crawled out of cover. Steadying his breath, he fired a bullet straight into the knight's helmet, flinging him backwards. His scope scanned over the rest of the panicked knights. 'I've lost sight of Grey.'

Deeper in the forest, Grey tripped and stumbled between the trees and over their roots as he fled for his life. He panted for air as he continually glanced behind him, ensuring no one was following.

Meanwhile, the ghosts continued their attack. Another knight climbed to his feet as Alexia sneaked up behind him, swiping his feet and knocking him to the ground before unloading multiple rounds into his chest.

Terric took cover behind a tree, attempting to catch his breath as he held his sword close to his chest. He scanned his surroundings, witnessing his remaining few knights scattering. Those who fled were gunned down in their backs, while others hopelessly charged at their invisible attackers. Terric focused his hearing, pinpointing the slight sounds of silenced gunfire and footsteps nearby. With a careful peek beyond his tree, he spotted the remnants of oil dripping off Able's invisible suit.

Able was in the midst of gunning down yet another fleeing knight. The knight collapsed to the ground as Able continued firing, endlessly riddling his body with bullets. Even when the knight was long dead, he continued to mutilate his body with lead, staring at him with broken, rageful eyes.

Terric, meanwhile, quietly bent down and picked up a handful of dirt. With his other hand, he gripped his sword tight and closed his eyes. *'Lord above, please guide my hand and forgive me.'* Standing up, Terric ran out from behind the tree and tossed his fistful of dirt towards Able, revealing more of his invisible exterior.

Able twisted around and fired two bullets into Terric's chest just before he ran his sword straight through Able's stomach and collapsed on top of him.

* * *

In the heart of the forest, Grey tripped and fell to his knees. His breath faded as blood seeped out of his chest and shoulder. His skin was turning pale and his surroundings increasingly distorted. With a painful grunt, he forced himself back to his feet and continued running through the forest.

Suddenly, an array of silenced bullets ripped up the ground behind him and struck his legs. He yelped in pain and collapsed onto the dirt. After dropping his handgun, he dug his fingers into the earth and attempted to drag his limp body away.

Slow and steady footsteps approached him from behind.

Blood dribbled out from Grey's mouth as he ran out of breath. Unable to pull himself any further, he tugged back his sleeve and pressed any button he could on the gauntlet.

A hand reached down and picked up the silenced handgun he had dropped.

Grey continued dragging his fingers across each button, not knowing what he was pressing, before a boot came down and stepped on his arm. Hopeless, Grey rolled onto his back. His entire chest had become soaked in his own blood.

Above him stood Ryder, looking down upon Grey without an ounce of sympathy. He bent over and unclipped the gauntlet from his wrist, sliding it off and locking it onto his own. Grey merely watched him, waiting. Ryder looked back down at him and aimed his handgun at his head. Grey closed his eyes, bracing himself.

Ryder's finger hovered over the trigger as he slowly, in the ensuing silence, looked upon Grey's ravaged body.

He's already dead, isn't he? Ryder thought to himself. *You could just let him bleed out here. Alone. It's not like he deserves anything better.*

And ... and you just don't need to, do you?

The boom of another explosion echoed in the distance, drawing Ryder's attention, before his gaze fell to the gauntlet on his wrist, its glowing dates and coordinates awaiting his touch once more.

You don't even need to keep going either. This has all gotten so out of hand, and you just barely made it out this time ... But you've got the gauntlet back now. You've got this chance, so, maybe ... maybe it is time to just go back home. Time to go see Rose again ... at least just to check on her. To make sure she's all right ...

But you have to do it now, Ryder. Before the others catch up.

Gradually, Ryder's face dropped, and with a long breath, he lowered his gun. With the nod of his head, he forced himself to turn around and walk away.

Grey opened his eyes, perplexed. 'Wh – what are you doing?'

Ryder continued walking away as he slid back his coat's sleeve and began typing on the gauntlet.

'Aren't you going to kill me?' Grey asked. '*Ryder! Aren't you going to kill me?!*'

Ryder shook his head as he deleted Grey's fiddlings on the device.

'Oh, come on, you're not leaving now, are you? You know it was Connor who orchestrated everything. It was all *his* idea.' Beneath his cracked lips, Grey let out a devious smile. 'And you wanna know what – what he said right after he killed your wife?'

Ryder came to a sudden stop.

'He said – he said he *had* to. He said she *had* to die.' Grey smirked and chuckled with what little breath he had left, spitting blood out from his mouth. 'And he was right. That *bitch* was always gonna get it. 'Cause she caused all of this. *This is all her fault.*'

Ryder slowly turned and looked back at Grey in shock. Suddenly, Deisy's smiling face overwhelmed his thoughts. Ryder forced himself to look away, clenching his fists and beginning to hyperventilate as he stared at the ground. Then came all of Deisy's hopes and dreams for the good that her invention could achieve, everything that the rest of the world never truly understood. Ryder tried to blink away his tears, before he finally glanced back at Grey's arrogant, blood-soaked smirk one more time, and remembered Deisy's final words.

A dark shadow came over Ryder's face as he turned and walked straight back towards Grey, turning the handgun around in his hand. In an instant, he knelt before Grey, grabbed his collar and smacked the grip of his handgun into his forehead. Over and over, he beat his handgun across Grey's head until it caved in and blood poured out.

Ryder's teeth ground together as his rage intensified and blood splattered across his face. Eventually, the top of Grey's head was nothing but blood and bones.

Arnest appeared through the trees, running towards them before he froze at the sight of the relentless beating. With one final blow, Ryder let go of Grey. His disfigured, crimson body slumped to the dirt ground.

Ryder panted as he stared at the ground, blood dripping off his hands and face. His eyes filled with tears as they fell upon his hands. Not a dot of his skin was visible beneath the blood. After hearing the dirt rustle beside him, he noticed Arnest standing and watching him with a grim sympathy. Ryder stood up, no longer able to meet his gaze. Without anything said, he turned around and began to stumble away.

'You're leaving?' Arnest asked.

Ryder paused, blinking to see through the blood as he turned around, still unable to look him in the eye. 'I'm finished here.'

'Will you return home?'

Ryder fell into another long silence. 'There's still more out there. Just like him … I have to find them … I — I — I have to stop them.'

Arnest sighed and walked before him. 'Come back with me.'

'I can't … The rest of them'll be looking for me.'

'Just for a night. We can help you, and you can help us. Many good people have died today. Many families torn. If you could … help make sense of some of it, make clear what has happened here today, it would mean everything.'

Ryder shook his head as he continued to stare at the ground. 'I'm sorry. I have to go.'

Arnest sighed once more and nodded in return. 'Well, I wish you well on your path, Ryder. I can only hope that something good will come of all that we have seen today. With Hamo on our side and Grey dead, I think there may be a chance. Either way, though, I hope you find what you are looking for in the end.'

At last, Ryder looked his friend in the eye. 'Thank you.'

Arnest stepped forward and extended his hand. Ryder reached out his own hand before a series of bullets struck the ground around them and ripped through Arnest's back.

Arnest froze in place, confused, as blood dripped out of his chest and mouth. Ryder stared at him in disbelief before more bullets whizzed by, one of them cutting his shoulder. He fumbled backwards and ran between the trees. Arnest dropped to his knees as he stared at the bullet wounds that so easily pierced his armour.

Alexia sprinted down the forest after Ryder, holding her rifle close. Ryder scurried behind a tree, frantically lifting his gauntlet and selecting his next destination. Alexia ran past Arnest and lifted her rifle as she neared the tree. Her temperature reader beeped just as she turned the tree's corner.

He was gone.

Alexia gripped her rifle tighter, pacing back and forth as she shook with rage, restraining a primal scream.

Arnest collapsed onto his back. With a steady motion, he lifted his hands, watching his own blood dripping off them. As his breath began to stutter, he laid his arm by his side and gazed up at the blue sky above.

Come on, Arnest, he thought to himself. *Just … just stay awake. You'll be okay.*

Soon, a set of footsteps grew closer, before the distorted, invisible figure of Alexia stood over him. As their eyes met, she watched as a palpable fear came over him.

With his last breaths, he pleaded to the glistening spirit. 'Please don't … don't hurt … don't hurt my family.' After holding on for as long as he could, his voice faded and his head fell back onto the dirt, lifeless.

Alexia stared at him as her expression fell sombre and his words lingered in her head. After a short, quiet time, she turned away and approached Grey's mutilated body, pulling out her disintegrator. She knelt down before him, inspecting his broken skull with disgust. Lifting his hand, her visor scanned his fingerprints, confirming his identity. Finally, she dropped his hand and stabbed the disintegrator into his chest. Returning to her feet, she watched as his body melted away, feeling an exhaustive, endless weight beginning to drag her down into the darkest of depths.

* * *

'Able's wounded!' Dax shouted, covering Ember and Kye as they rushed over to their captain's aid.

The two ghosts pulled Terric off Able, revealing the sword still lodged in Able's stomach.

'Pull him back, let's pull him back,' Ember ordered.

They grabbed a hold of Able's shoulders and dragged him away from the site of their attack.

Dax carefully scanned the area, searching for any remaining knights. 'Hayes, you see any more?'

Hayes continued to survey the area through his scope. 'Getting no movement. I think we got them all.'

Ember and Kye pulled Able to a quiet, shaded spot amongst the trees. They knelt beside him as his cloaking repeatedly glitched.

'Okay, we've got to pull out the blade and then seal the wound,' Ember explained. 'We've got to be quick.'

Able lazily turned off his cloaking device.

Dax ran over to Ember's side. 'How is he?'

Blood continuously flowed out of Able's stomach as Kye wrapped his hand around the grip of the sword, ready to pull it out.

Ember removed a small skin-tissue-sealing device from her vest. 'Ready?'

Kye nodded. 'Yeah – yep.'

'Don't,' Able said as he placed his hand on Kye's chest, his voice raspy and weak. 'Don't.'

'*What?*' Ember interjected, 'We have to take it out, Able. It's the only way to – '

'I know ... but just leave it. The damage is done. I can't do anymore,' he said in between his fading breaths. After pulling off his black gloves, he removed his helmet, allowing the warmth of the sun to touch his skin. He inhaled the fresh air, watching the sunlight flicker and shine through the bright green trees above.

Hayes jogged over as they all watched Able in silence. Kye continued gripping the handle of the sword, hesitating.

Able gently placed his hand over Kye's. 'Let go, soldier.'

Ember shook her head as tears overwhelmed her eyes.

'We can still help you,' Kye said. 'This doesn't – '

'Kye,' Able interrupted, patting his hand, 'just let me be with them. I just want to be with them.'

Kye's eyes watered and his lips quivered as he let go of the sword's grip.

Able rested his hands by his side, letting his fingers run through the dirt and tingle against his skin. He lifted his gaze back towards the bright sky as his vision began to blur and distort. 'He would've loved all of this. The castles, and the horses ... he would've ... loved it.' A few small tears ran down his cheeks as he smiled and let out one last breath.

Ember rested her head on his chest. Dax held her shoulder, comfortingly.

Hayes bowed his head in mourning.

Kye patted Able's hand.

Alexia returned through the trees, approaching Terric as he lay on the ground. He struggled to catch his breath as blood seeped out of his chest. Glancing to his left, he spotted a dagger lying on the ground. He reached out for the blade, and just as his hand touched the grip, Alexia passed him by and fired a single bullet through his head. His head flung back as a burst of blood splattered the ground beneath him.

Alexia slowed down upon reaching the others, watching as Kye closed Able's eyes. She quietly walked beside them all, looking over the body with a tired sorrow. For a time, they all remained in silence. The cold wind whispered and rustled the leaves and branches above.

'Grey's dead. Ryder's gone,' Alexia eventually explained. 'It's time to move on.'

'What about all of the bodies?' Hayes asked. 'We're just leaving them?'

'We don't have enough disintegrators for all of them. Besides, there'll be no trace of the bullets. Everything tied to us will be gone.'

Hayes looked around at the countless bodies, unconvinced.

'Hayes, everything was tampered with before we even got here,' Dax added. 'There's nothing we can do about it now.'

'Yeah … I know.'

Alexia knelt beside Able's body and rested her hand on his chest. In time, she pulled out another disintegrator and carefully injected it into his stomach.

Limb by limb, his body began to deteriorate into the soil. Everyone watched as he eroded and the tip of Terric's sword melted away with him. Before long, its bottom half fell to the ground, and there the blade remained, lying alone beside the black and burning earth.

Chapter 24

Rome, Italy, 47 BCE

An ocean of orange clouds swept across the sky. Below, a busy market bustled with life. Doric columns marked the sides of temples. Small white houses were open with tradesmen selling everything from food to clothes to everyday tools. The citizens wore tunics, big and small. The white, red, and orange robes blurred together as flocks of people strolled to and fro.

At the edge of the street, beyond the crowds, stood a lonely figure. Ryder. The shadow of his hood concealed his face as his dark eyes peered through the masses.

He looked on as if in a trance. His beard had only grown since his time in England, and the wound across his chest and face had healed into a long scar. His frame was smaller and his cheekbones and jawline more defined as he stared at the stall across the street, watching a tradesman converse with his customers, handing off fresh loaves of bread. His eyes fixated on their crusted edges and soft innards. Ryder's stomach grumbled as he swallowed.

A wave of cold air brushed against his skin. Night was falling and the temperature with it. He blinked, forcing himself to look away.

You've still got pills in your bag, he reminded himself. *They're not all gone yet. Come on, the sooner you find them, the sooner you can move on.*

Ryder's gaze shifted towards the rest of the street. More places he had yet to scour. Rolling his shoulders and forcing his legs forward, he entered the crowd and continued on his way.

High above, the sun fell beyond the horizon. Candles began to light the many orange-roofed houses, marble streets, and grand temples.

Darkness had long enveloped the sky when Ryder descended a set of white marble steps, approaching the sleepy docks of the River Tiber. Before getting too close, he veered off the path and moved through the trees that lined the riverside. His foot slipped on the curve of the hill, making him stumble a little before he regained his balance and continued onwards.

After some time, he happened upon a spot of cover amidst several trees. He bent down and scanned his surroundings. A small fishing boat rowed by, illuminated by the moonlight and a candle sitting inside it. Three men were aboard, casually chatting as they drifted into the night.

Finally, Ryder relaxed his shoulders and slid his bag off his back. He sat down against one of the trees as a stark pain burned inside his stomach. With little energy, he pulled his bag onto his lap and unzipped it. He dug through numerous empty bottles before finding one with fewer than a dozen pills inside. Popping open the lid, he poured two of them into his palm and stared at them.

Eventually, he dropped one pill back into the container. Throwing his head back, he swallowed the other. He drank the last drops of his water bottle before sliding it back into his bag. Zipping open the front pocket, he pulled out a handful of pictures, one of each of his six targets. He sifted through the pictures of Hughes, Issa, and Grey, before focusing on the photographs of Ode Scarlett and Ian Russ.

Ode was twenty-three years of age. The photo was from her university profile. Her eyes were green, her hair brown with blonde streaks, and her face bright and innocent as she smiled with excitement.

Ian was in his early thirties. An independent artist with a gaunt face, grey hair, and a gloomy, introspective look about him. It was a portrait taken from his personal website.

Ryder's eyes scanned over the pictures, memorising every one of their facial features. Next, he brought forth the photo of Connor Mavire. Forty-two, stubble, dark hair turning grey, and an indifferent expression on his face, taken from his Forward Industries security ID. After only a brief moment, Ryder buried the photo amongst the others and slipped them back into his bag. At last, he rested his head back against the tree and closed his eyes.

The little waves of the river trickled back and forth. The wind grazed against the leaves above. Ryder's head began to lower as he fell into an exhausted sleep.

'He has to be here,' a sudden voice whispered through the wind.

Ryder's eyes shot open as he peered through the surrounding darkness.

'Keep looking,' another whisper said over his shoulder.

Ryder twisted around and looked behind the tree. There was no one there.

After settling his breath, Ryder pulled his seashell necklace out from under his shirt. He inspected its rusted curves as he held it close to his chest.

I am looking, he told himself. *I am* ...

I will find them.

I will find them.

I will find them.

* * *

The following days and weeks blended together as Ryder walked from street to street. The glaring sun beat down upon him as he dragged his feet through another street on the outskirts of the city.

Under the shadow of his hood, sweat dripped from his brow as he surveyed the street around him. A beggar approached his side, speaking a language he struggled to decipher. Ryder shook his head and held up his hand, stepping away. The deeper he trekked, the more the homeless marred his surroundings. Numerous men, women, and children begged those who passed by, while others merely stared into space, all of them looking as though they were as light as a feather.

Amidst the hunter's daze, a bony hand grabbed his ankle. Snapping out of his trance, he yanked his leg away and looked down to find a young boy, his lips crusted, eyes sunken, and his breath wheezing. The boy rested one hand on his stomach and another out to Ryder, pleading without words. Ryder stared back at him with a surprise that soon faded into misery.

I only have so many pills left, he thought.

I can't ... I can't spare any.

With a painful turn, Ryder pulled himself away from the boy and continued onwards, leaving him behind. He felt a sickness rise in his throat as he passed endless lines of starving plebeians. Among them, a group of women in bright red togas caught his eye. They moved between the homeless, feeding them bowls of bread and water.

At least someone's doing something, he thought.

Passing by an alleyway between two houses, Ryder glanced inside. He noticed another woman knelt before some of the citizens, offering them water from her bowl. Ryder continued onwards before stopping himself. The woman in the alleyway had brown hair with faint blonde streaks in it. Her face was bright and youthful. The hunter returned to the alleyway, watching as the young woman stood up. Upon noticing the hooded figure, she froze.

It's her, he thought. *It's Ode.*

The two of them stared at each other for a quiet moment.

Steadily, Ryder rested his hand on his belt, gesturing to his holstered handgun.

Go on. Run. Let's just get this over with.

Ode swallowed her fear and took a deep breath. Holding her bowl of water close to her chest, she approached him, attempting to see through the shadows of his hood. As she made out his face, she looked at him with shock. 'Ryder? Ryder Mason?' she whispered.

The hunter stared back at her without a word of reply.

'You're looking for us?' she asked. Her eyes darted away in a panic for just a moment, before returning to him. 'Have you found Ian?'

Ryder shook his head. 'Where is he?'

'I can show you, but you have to wait. I'm helping these people, and I'm not going to leave until I've finished.'

'No. We're leaving now.'

'No,' she replied, shaking her head. 'If you can't wait, then just jump ahead or something. Either that or you can kill me right here in front of everybody.'

Without anything more to say, Ode walked around him and back into the busy street. Ryder turned and watched her as she continued to feed those in need.

If I jump, then she'll just run.

Keeping a close eye on her, the hunter walked to the edge of the street and sat down amongst the homeless. Resting his back against the wall, he settled in and watched Ode from afar. Sneakily, he slipped two distractor balls into his pocket.

Just in case.

The hours crawled by as the sun's strength waned. Ode made her way up and down the street, feeding those that she could with her companions. Every now and then, she would glance at her surroundings, ensuring that Ryder was still there.

One of her friends noticed Ode's worried gaze and approached her side. 'Is everything well, Ode? Who is that man over there?' she quietly asked in Latin.

'Oh, he's just … someone I know. Don't worry.'

'Well, you tell me if you need any help, and we can get some soldiers down here.'

Ode smiled and nodded. 'I know. Thank you, Regina. It's okay, though, I'll take care of it.'

Regina nodded and turned a suspicious eye towards Ryder before continuing to feed others.

Towards the end of the afternoon, the street had quietened, and the breeze turned cool. Ode walked towards Ryder and knelt before him. She handed out a bowl with a final piece of bread for him to pick. He sat up at the sight of it before eyeing her with caution.

'Go on. You can take it,' she encouraged, holding the bowl closer to him.

With a slight shake in his hand, Ryder reached out and took the bread. He maintained a firm eye on her as he took a bite of it. A feeling of relief overwhelmed him as the soft bread filled his mouth and, for a moment, his stomach pain ceased.

'Good?' she asked.

He nodded, still eyeing her with vigilance.

'Come on. I'll show you before it's dark,' she continued, climbing to her feet.

The shadows grew deeper and darker as a blood-red sun consumed the sky. Ode wiped away faint tears from her cheeks as she led Ryder beyond the city walls and up the surrounding hills. With each step closer to the top, a series of symbols became clearer. Rows of crosses lined the hills, silhouetted by the burning sun. Ode held her toga over her feet as she climbed to the summit of the grassy hill. Ryder kept his hand close to his holster as he approached her side. Eventually, he turned his gaze towards a cross that towered before them. Ian, naked and decomposing, hung crucified in the way of the sun.

Ryder's demeanour fell as he stepped closer to the crucifix, inspecting the nails that pierced his hands and feet. His eyes were half open and his head slumped down against his chest. As the sun lowered, the lines across Ian's face darkened, blurring his features. The slits of his white eyes stared down at him.

Ryder sighed.

Now there's only her.

He subtly gripped his handgun.

Ode gazed upon Ian with pain before she forced herself to look away. 'Come on,' she said, turning and walking back down the hill.

Ryder unholstered his handgun and held it by his side, watching her walk away. His finger hovered over the trigger as she almost reached the bottom of the hill. Finally, he softened his grip and tilted his head in frustration, following after her.

* * *

Night fell across Rome as thousands of candles burned. An orange warmth emanated throughout the dark streets as Ode guided Ryder up a series of steps into her small mud-brick apartment. Inside was a single room with a bed on one side and a circular table before it. Ryder stopped at the entrance, inspecting the tiny apartment as Ode put together a small bowl of food scraps.

'You look hungry,' she said, placing a bowl and a cup of water atop the table. 'Sit?' She gestured to the stool across from her.

Ryder remained still for a time, eyeing his target up and down. Ode began to fiddle with her toga as she seated herself at the table. After another long moment, the hunter hobbled over and sat down at the opposite end of the table.

Ode pushed the bowl of bread and fruit towards him. 'Go ahead. It'll be off by tomorrow. Someone should eat it.'

With a steady pace, Ryder rested his handgun on the table, keeping his hand on top of it as he pushed the bowl back towards her. 'You first.'

Steadying her nerves, Ode nodded and picked out a piece of bread. Ryder watched as she took a bite of it, chewed, and swallowed. Satisfied, he pulled the bowl back towards him and began picking away at the food.

'Ian – uh … he said too much, I think,' Ode explained, anxious to fill the silence between them. 'He hated the way things are here. We both did, but he tried to, you know, guide the people along a lot more … directly. He wanted to make things better for them … but they love their Caesar. They wouldn't listen.'

Ryder nodded as he continued to eat.

Ode bit her lip. 'Did you … find the others?'

'Yeah.'

'Did they – How did they manage?'

'It didn't matter in the end.'

Ode rubbed her eyes before any tears broke free. 'Yeah … we were stupid,' she admitted as her voice broke. 'We were so stupid.'

Ryder looked at her with a tired indifference.

'You know it wasn't supposed to go the way it did?' she continued. 'She wasn't supposed to –'

'I know,' he interrupted. 'I've heard it before. And every time, it doesn't matter.'

'Well, it mattered to us,' she said, her lips stuttering. 'The second after it happened, Ian fought Connor to bring us back, but he wouldn't listen. He just left us here … We didn't want this. We didn't want any of it to happen the way it did.'

'What did you think was going to happen? That you'd just take it and everything would be *fine*?'

'We *weren't* thinking … we were just angry, and feeling so desperate.'

'Mm. *I bet.*' Ryder placed his finger on the gun's trigger.

'Will you take me back?' Ode asked through her quiet tears.

'… What?'

'Will you take me back home?'

'Why? You know they'd probably just kill you anyway.'

'I don't care. As long as there's some sort of justice.'

'That's why *I'm* here.'

'Then take me back. *You* can hand me in, and I can give everyone the answers they need. I can help make sense of what happened for them. For everyone.'

'No, no one would even know. The public has no idea about anything that you did … And besides, I'm not going back.'

'You're not going back?'

'Forward Industries is after me too. They're hunting after both of us right now.'

'Well, maybe I can speak to them. I can –'

'They won't listen. They'll just kill us the moment they find us.'

'What if we went back to Forward Industries directly? Or the police? Or the government?'

'I'm not going back.'

'But – but don't you have a daughter?'

'No.'

'But – Rose. That's her name, isn't it? Rose.'

Ryder shook his head, gripping his pistol tighter, 'I told you. *I don't have a daughter.*'

'But – but … I did my research. You *do have* a daughter, don't you?'

'What does it matter to you?'

'I – I just … I've thought about her a lot. And you, and …' Ode's lips trembled as her tears overwhelmed her. 'I'm so sorry, Ryder. I'm *so* sorry.'

Ryder leant back in disbelief. As he processed her words, he forced his gaze elsewhere, fighting to contain himself.

'I want to help,' Ode continued. 'I know I don't deserve anything, but I want to help.'

'If you want to help me, tell me where Connor was going in Greece.'

'I don't know.'

'Anything. Just *anywhere* he might've gone.'

'I don't know. All I know is that he was going to hide somewhere he didn't think anyone would find him. It was going to be remote or something. But otherwise, I don't know anything. But please, just take me back and maybe – maybe Forward Industries will thank you. Maybe it'll make it better for you.'

'It won't.'

'But what about Miles Forder? Won't he –'

'He's dead.'

'But ... but what about Rose? Don't you want to see her again –'

Ryder slammed his fist on the table. *'Of course I do! But I can't, can I?! I can't raise her! I can't look after her! Because of all of you, I don't have that in me anymore!'*

'What did you do with her?'

'She's somewhere safe. *Far away from all of this.'* Ryder pointed his handgun at Ode's head. 'Far away from me.' His lips quivered as his eyes began to glisten.

'It's not too late to go back.'

'It is.'

'It's not! You can go *right* back to the moment you left her. We can find a way to make it work. *I'll* go back with you, and I'll tell everyone what you did to bring me back. Everyone can know and understand, and we can just *end* this. *Then you can be with her again.'*

'She wouldn't even recognise me.' His voice shattered.

'She *will*, Ryder. She *will* know her father when she sees him. I *promise*. She'll be waiting right there where you left her. Please. *Let's just leave this all behind. We don't have to be here anymore.'*

Ryder gritted his teeth as his hands began to shake. Inch by inch, he pulled back the trigger. Ode's devastated eyes stared back into his.

Rose, sleeping soundly in her basket, flashed in his memory. Ryder choked before he released his finger from the trigger. Gradually, he lowered his gun and burst into tears. Leaning forward onto the table, he buried his face into his arms.

Ode eyed the handgun clenched in his hand. With the bite of her lip, she reached out and wrapped her hand around his. 'It's okay. It's gonna be okay.'

At last, the handgun slipped out of Ryder's hand.

'It's okay, it's okay.' She repeated, continuing to stroke his hand.

'I miss them *so* much,' Ryder whimpered.

'I know, I know. I'm so sorry, but it's going to be okay now. It's going to be okay. She'll be right there waiting for you, just as you left her.'

With a sniffle and a nod, Ryder sat upright again. 'Okay … okay.'

'She'll be so happy to see you,' Ode promised, smiling through her heartache.

Ryder took a long, deep breath, deflating into his chair. 'Okay.'

His eyes returned to Ode's soft and sympathetic smile before he noticed a distorted shimmer slip into the corner of the room. Before a word could be spoken, a silenced bullet flew into Ode's forehead. Her blood sprayed across Ryder's face as she collapsed to the floor. Ryder froze in place before he picked up his handgun and jumped to his feet. Just as he turned around, the invisible stock of a rifle was smacked across his face. He stumbled onto his knees as his vision turned hazy. Groaning in pain, he attempted to stand up again before another whack to the head knocked him unconscious.

The five ghosts scattered throughout the room. Dax knelt beside Ode's body. His visor scanned her blood-covered face, registering her identity and updating her status. Without delay, he pulled out his disintegrator and stabbed it into her chest.

Alexia picked up Ryder's gun and grabbed his unconscious body. She grunted as she pulled him over to the bed and laid him down. Dax stood up again as Ember, Kye, and Hayes surrounded the bed.

Alexia depressurised her helmet and removed it as she stared down at Ryder's face. Her cloaking deactivated, revealing her black, armoured suit. Cradling his handgun in her palm, she inspected the weapon with agony.

'Is it him?' Dax asked.

'Yeah, it's him,' Alexia replied.

'All right, then.' Dax lifted his rifle and pointed it at his head, ready to fire.

'Wait! Don't!' she shouted, lifting her hand.

'What?'

'We need to wait until he wakes up.'

'Why?'

The ghosts all looked at Alexia, perplexed.

She hesitated for a moment before clenching her fists and standing her ground. 'Because I need to ask him some questions.'

'*What* questions?' Dax asked.

'About the timings, right?' Hayes presumed. 'About how he was so much earlier than us.'

'No,' Alexia said. 'About my parents.'

'Your *parents*?' Ember repeated.

Alexia nodded. 'When I was just a kid … my parents were murdered. In our own home. Just a random night. And Ryder … he's responsible.'

'What?' Hayes muttered under his breath.

'Are you fucking with us?' Dax asked.

'No. The only thing left at the scene was his gun. *This* gun.' Alexia held up Ryder's handgun for the others to see. 'I saw it myself the night he killed them. It had his prints *all over it.*'

Kye looked back down at Ryder, processing Alexia's words.

'You gotta be kidding me,' Dax scoffed, slowly lowering his rifle.

Ember slid off her own helmet. 'Who else knows about this?'

'Does Forward Industries?' Dax added.

'Yes. They know.'

'What the hell.' Dax stepped back and shook his head.

'What are you saying happened?' Hayes asked. 'Your parents are some of our targets?'

'No. They must've been some of his, though. But … I don't know. That's why I need to ask him.'

'So, hold on, he killed *two* more people?' Dax interjected. 'Why did none of us know about this?'

'It was covered up like everything else. And even if it wasn't, there were no answers, anyway. He killed them and then just disappeared.'

'But how come *we* didn't know?'

'Because it didn't matter to any of you.'

'Kinda feels like it does. Did you know about all of the screw-ups on our arrival too? Why we're so goddamn *late*?'

'No, I didn't. All I came for was him. Forward Industries just gave me the means and pointed me in the right direction.'

'So, you just want the truth out of him?' Kye assumed.

'I wanna know why he did it, yeah.'

'Then what?' Dax asked.

'Then I'll kill him myself. Him and every other target, so nothing like that can *ever* happen again.'

A wave of silence swept across the room.

'I'm sorry, Lex,' Ember said softly.

Alexia met her caring gaze, and with a reserved nod, she thanked her.

'I can't believe this,' Hayes said. 'This whole mission.'

'Yeah, it's fucked,' Dax agreed. 'We've been *lied to* this whole time. How are you second in command when you have *this* personal a tie to the mission?'

'Dax, it's okay,' Ember said.

'No, it's not! We've lost three people already, our timing's been fucked, and one of us has been on a secret vendetta mission the whole damn time! We trained *two years* for this shit?'

While Dax's voice continued to climb, Ryder gradually awoke. Keeping his eyes half shut, he peered at the ghosts around him.

'Yeah, I'm with Dax,' Hayes added. 'This isn't the mission we were trained for.'

Ryder's eyes turned towards his handgun clutched in Alexia's hand.

'We were trained to deal with *any* scenario,' Alexia argued. 'Able was right when he said that there was never any guarantee of how this was going to go.'

'Yeah, but did he know you were here to ask Ryder *questions? Did he know you had a personal stake in this?*' Dax yelled back.

Ember placed her hand on his arm. 'Dax! Be quiet!'

Dax shook her hand off him. 'No, this is bullshit.'

Ryder crept his fingers into his pocket.

'You're gonna talk about personal relationships, Dax?' Alexia asked. *'Really?'*

Dax lifted his shoulders. 'Fuck you.'

'No, fuck you, Dax. I don't give a *shit* what you think. I have my reasons to be here, and you have yours.'

Dax took a step towards her before Ember blocked him with her arm. 'She's right, Dax! Why care about the rules when everything's fucked, anyway?'

Dax turned and looked at Ember, panting.

'We still have each other,' she continued, her eyes locked with his. 'Right?'

Dax looked back and forth between the two ghosts, biting his tongue. Finally, he stepped back with the shake of his head.

A small *ting* sound bounced by Alexia's feet. Her eyes darted to the floor, spotting a distractor ball rolling up beside her feet. *'Get d – !'*

The ball exploded with a flash, bombarding them with a blinding light. Their ears rang from the bang as Ryder leapt off the bed. He slammed Alexia against the wall amidst the sparks and flashes. Tearing his gun out from her hand, he turned and fired an array of bullets throughout the room. The ghosts ducked as the silenced bullets whizzed by. Ryder smacked the handgun across Alexia's face. She stumbled over with a cry of pain, still half-blinded from the flashes.

Ryder bolted for the door, pushing past the disoriented Kye and Hayes. Alexia growled through the chaos as she lifted her rifle, firing multiple rounds at Ryder as he disappeared out the door. Without a second's hesitation, she sprinted outside after him. She reached the top of the stairs and spotted him rushing towards an alleyway across the street. Lifting her rifle, she fired two more shots, ripping apart the wall behind him as he fled into the alleyway. Just as he fell from sight, she sped down the steps and began her pursuit.

'What the hell!' Dax shouted, attempting to recover his vision and balance.

'She ran out after him!' Hayes explained, gesturing to the door as he bent over himself, still hearing a perpetual ringing in his ears.

'Fuck, we gotta go,' Dax said, cocking his rifle and walking towards the door.

Kye caught his breath before looking across the room. 'Dax!'

Dax stopped before the door, 'What?'

'Ember!'

Dax spun around, finding Ember leant against the wall. A bullet had gone through her throat. Deep red blood poured out profusely as she tried to cover the wound with her hand.

'Oh sh – Emy! Emy!' Dax called out as he ran over to her. He took a hold of her shoulders, helping her slide down to a sitting position, 'Come on, come on, sit down, sit down.'

'You have to cover the wound!' Hayes exclaimed.

'I know!' Dax replied, pulling out his skin-repairing gel.

Ember's eyes were frozen in shock as blood continued flowing out of her throat.

Dax tried to hold her steady as he aimed the gel dispenser at her neck, 'Stay still, baby, stay still.' He gritted his teeth as he sprayed the gel onto her neck.

Kye and Hayes watched with worry as the gel began to seal her wound. Steadily, Ember's hands fell to the floor. Her skin turned pale, and her frightened eyes gazed upon Dax one last time. Before long, her head drooped onto her chest.

'Hey – *hey! Stay awake! Stay with me!*' Dax continued, lifting her head back up. As soon as the wound was sealed, he dropped the container and gently slapped her cheek. 'Emy, Emy, come on, wake up. Wake up, you're gonna be okay. Come on, you're gonna be okay … Emy? *Emy?!*'

* * *

Ryder sprinted through the candlelit Roman streets. He repeatedly stumbled over himself, barely maintaining the strength to run. Alexia followed only a street's distance behind him, gripping her rifle tight.

Buildings and houses blurred by as they neared the outer walls of the city. Ryder skidded into another street and continued towards the opposite side. Alexia turned the corner moments after him and lifted her rifle, firing a handful of rounds at him. The bullets whizzed past Ryder and struck the ground beside his feet. Dirt and dust flicked up around him as he manoeuvred his feet out of the way. In the panic, he lost his footing and collapsed to the ground. Dragging himself away, he lifted his gauntlet and pressed down on the T-Port button. The red lights began their five-second countdown.

One.

Alexia fired another two shots at him, tearing into the dirt around him.

Two.

She steadied her aim, pulling the trigger once more. Her rifle clicked. She was out of ammo.

Three.

Alexia swiftly ejected the magazine as she continued walking towards him.

Four.

Ryder watched the red light flick by each second in terror as Alexia loaded in a second clip.

Five.

Ryder's gauntlet light turned blue. Alexia aimed and fired a single bullet straight towards him. With a thump, Ryder evaporated.

Athens, Greece, 591 BCE

A large, full moon shone upon numerous hills of grass and rock. Ryder suddenly materialised on one such hill. He gasped and climbed to his knees, catching his breath as he looked around him, finding no sign of Alexia. Straightening his posture, he gazed out beyond the hills, spotting the walls of Athens in the distance. He scanned its entrances and exits before shaking his head and forcing himself to look away.

No, I need to go, he told himself. *I need to get out of here. I need to get back to Rose.*

Ryder looked at his wrist gauntlet, finding one of Alexia's bullets had ripped through the top of it. Wires hung out of it while the digital screen repeatedly glitched on and off.

His heart almost stopped.

With a shaking hand, he ran his fingers over the gauntlet, trying to press any button he could. Nothing worked. They were all destroyed and ceased to function.

'No, no, no, no …' he repeated as his fingers became more and more desperate to find a working button. Flipping his wrist back and forth, he took in the sight of his mangled device. *'No, no, no, come on, come – come on,'* he begged as his eyes began to water. Over and over, he pressed every button he could. The screen continued to glitch, and small sparks shot out from the broken wires. *'No, no, no – no – NO!'* he furiously shouted, throwing his arm aside and clenching his fists. Gazing up at the night sky, his rage, pain, and fear consumed him as he screamed at the stars. Then, with a long moan, he collapsed onto the ground, breaking down into tears.

* * *

Rome, Italy, 47 BCE

Alexia fell to her knees with a scream, staring at the empty street before her.

Before long, concerned voices arose in the distance, and Alexia retraced her steps through the dark, Roman streets. Without her helmet, she hid in the shadows of an alleyway as two citizens passed by. When the window arrived, she slid out and hurried back to Ode's apartment. She climbed the stairs and entered the room, finding Dax knelt beside Ember. Her skin was pale, her eyes lifeless, and the wall stained in her blood.

Kye and Hayes turned to Alexia without words.

Dax's hand rested on Ember's shoulder as he stared at her face, his eyes red and tired.

Yet another wave of anguish overwhelmed Alexia as she swallowed in pain. 'Dax … I'm so sorry.'

Dax continued to stare at his love in silence.

'You can take her back,' she continued. 'You don't have to keep going anymore.'

'We were both supposed to come back,' he finally said, his voice quiet and broken. 'Together.'

Alexia bowed her head.

'But you ... *you* had to keep him alive, didn't you?' he continued, his tone turning sour.

Alexia opened her mouth before she stopped herself, thinking before speaking. 'I did ... I'm sorry, Dax ... but I *promise* you, I *will* kill him.'

Dax shook his head, clutching his rifle as it slung across his shoulder. 'No ... *I'll* kill him ... *And you're not gonna lead this team anymore.*'

Alexia rested her hand on her holstered pistol. 'Dax, we both have reason to kill him.'

'But you haven't *done it, have you?* You *let him* get away. *You lied to every one of us.*' Dax placed his finger on his rifle's trigger, his back still facing her.

'Dax. Don't.'

'Or *what? You gonna kill me too?'*

'Only if you make me.' She unholstered her handgun and held it by her side.

Dax looked into Ember's cold, dim eyes as they stared at the floor. His own expression began to dissipate before he gritted his teeth, gripped his rifle and twisted around.

Alexia lifted her pistol and fired a silent bullet through his forehead. His blood sprayed across Ember's face and the wall behind her as his head flung back. With a thud, he collapsed onto her lap, dead.

Hayes froze in disbelief, while Kye eased his rifle down, having been ready to fire.

Alexia stared at the two lovers lying together. Gradually, she lowered her handgun and holstered it. Walking over to them, she pulled out a disintegrator and knelt down. She lifted the device over Dax, pausing. Her hand shook as it resisted. Tears overcame her as she looked away from them and let out a long, shaking breath.

Once her tears had settled, she looked back at them with distant eyes and stabbed the disintegrator into Dax's chest. Following suit, she pulled out another one and injected it into Ember's neck. As the two ghosts melted away into flakes of skin and acidic bubbles, Alexia returned to her feet.

Next to the bodies, Dax's helmet caught her eye. Picking it up, she found only her cold reflection staring back at her through the visor. Her lip almost trembled before she dropped the helmet in amongst their disintegrating bodies. Without lingering any longer, she retrieved her own helmet and slid it back on, reactivating her cloaking. 'Let's sync up.'

Hayes looked back and forth between Kye and Alexia, still processing what had transpired. 'Wh – what about Connor? Or Ian? Do you think one of them's here?'

'We'll ask whoever we find next,' she replied bluntly, selecting their next destination on her gauntlet.

Kye and Hayes glanced at one another before doing the same.

'Synched.'

'… Synched.'

The air thumped and sucked inwards as the three ghosts disappeared.

Eventually, the bubbling acid fizzled away, and the remaining flakes of skin and black armour gently floated to the floor, resting in silence.

VOLUME FIVE

THE FLOWER

Chapter 25

Athens, Greece, 591 BCE

Birds chirped and danced out of a thick, mountainous forest and into the sunlight. A short time later, three invisible spectres marched out of the forest, one by one.

Hayes, at the back of the trio, bowed his head as he followed, barely lifting his feet each step of the way.

After climbing to the peak of a small hill, Alexia stopped for a moment, spotting the distant city of Athens. In its centre sat a tall, rocky outcrop that overlooked all of the surrounding land. Kye and Hayes stopped behind her, soaking in the view as the cool wind brushed against their reflective suits.

Soon, amidst the tranquil silence, Hayes' eyes began to water, and his lips quivered. He held his breath for as long as he could, fighting to remain quiet as Alexia and Kye continued down the hill and towards the ancient city.

Hayes stayed on the hill, aimlessly pacing back and forth as he reckoned with himself. Eventually, however, tears overwhelmed him as he gasped for air and buried his helmet into his hand. After a short sniffle, he shook his head and looked back down at Alexia and Kye. 'I can't keep going.'

Alexia and Kye stopped and turned around to face him.

'I – … I can't, I just can't,' Hayes continued in shame, dropping his head as tears fell onto his visor. 'I just … I signed up to see – '

'You don't have to explain yourself,' Alexia interrupted. 'You can go.'

Hayes looked back at her with surprise, struggling to find his words.

'I'm still going to finish this,' she continued, 'but I don't expect either of you to keep going.'

At last, Hayes felt as though he could breathe again. '*Thank you.*'

'We should arrive back at the same time as you, anyway,' Kye said, walking towards him.

'And if you don't?'

'Then tell them what happened,' Alexia replied.

'They're not going to like it.'

Kye stood before him with a reassuring voice. 'We'll finish it and make it back. Don't worry.'

Hayes nodded through his tears, gathering his nerves again as Kye stepped away. 'I'll see you in a moment, then.' He paused for a short time, resisting more tears. 'Seriously, you guys better make it, okay? I don't want to be showing back up there alone, especially if everything's different.'

'We will,' Kye said before holding up his gauntlet. 'Besides, if these still work, the Core probably still works. I'd say that's a good sign.'

'Yeah. Yeah … you're right.' Hayes' breath stuttered as he nodded to them both and reluctantly waved goodbye. Alexia and Kye waved back as he selected their final destination: thirty seconds after they had first left the Forward Industries port room. After sharing a final look of sorrow, he activated his device and disappeared.

Their temperature readers beeped as Kye turned back to Alexia, who gestured towards Athens. 'Come on. Let's keep going,' she said, turning and continuing off towards the city.

Kye nodded and rested his rifle on his shoulder, following closely behind.

* * *

Dust and grass fluttered by as a gust of wind blew through the outskirts of Athens. Soon, a pair of invisible footsteps followed, entering the city.

Alexia and Kye scanned their surroundings as they passed by numerous mud-brick homes, tall and pointed cypress trees, and small, rocky creeks. They clung to the edges of the street as Athenian citizens, all wearing tunics, walked to and fro beside them. The deeper they trekked, the more they were consumed by the shadow of the

Acropolis. The huge, mountainous rock formation was surrounded by thick stone walls, shading anyone and anything below it.

Alexia gripped her rifle tight as she repeatedly checked her temperature reader and electronic scanner. Following the curved street, the pair soon spotted a collection of citizens entering the busy agora ahead. With caution, they followed, steering clear of any large groups as they entered the public centre.

Under the bright blue sky, and despite the relentless heat of the sun, the Athenians debated politics, loudly traded with one another, and laughed and danced to public singers and the plucks of their lyres. Meanwhile, others cooked, ate, painted, and simply relaxed.

In the midst of the agora, Kye stopped beside a stall where numerous pots cluttered the ground. He squatted down beside them, inspecting their red and black artwork. There were tales of battles, gods, and monsters carefully strewn across their exteriors. He smiled and shook his head in amazement. Gazing upwards, he noticed the stall's owner, an older man who sat alone under the cover of shade, staring at his sandalled feet, solemn and tired.

You're not alone, Kye thought. *And you have some truly amazing art here. I'm sure you know so much ... I wish I could tell you even more. If you could understand me ...*

Kye lingered a little while longer, dreaming of what he could say, before he sighed and returned to his feet, continuing on his way.

Further ahead, Alexia turned to notice Kye had fallen behind. 'You see something?'

'Just some pottery. That's all.'

Alexia nodded, turning and surveying the busy agora once more before moving into the next city street.

After circling most of the city without any luck, the orange glow of the afternoon sun had arrived. The humming buzz of cicadas filled the air as the ghosts approached the end of another street at the base of the Acropolis. They concealed themselves in the shadow of a tree, scanning the path behind them, seeing citizens strolling home after the long day.

As the wind took a cool turn, Alexia peered up at the towering Acropolis. 'I think we get to the top of the Acropolis. Get an overview and see if we've missed anything, then we move to whatever town is closest.'

'All right. Sounds good.'

'We're going to have to walk, though. Can't port this.'

'No complaints from me.'

With swift caution, the pair carried on around the edge of the Acropolis and began their trek up the hundreds of steps. The path was quiet and lonely, with only the wind singing a soft breeze. Meanwhile, shades of purple and pink swept across the sky above.

At the end of their climb, the ghosts reached the top of the rocky mountain and strolled past an ancient Mycenaean palace. Its once-bright red and orange paint had faded and chipped away, illuminated only by a handful of flickering candles that surrounded the building.

Eventually, the duo stopped at the very edge of the outcrop, overlooking the city and the surrounding lands below. They quietly embraced the immense view as it stretched as far as the eye could see. On one side sat the distant, shimmering blue Aegean Sea, and on the other the great green fields and mountains from which they had come. Meanwhile, distant villages, with their warm, orange candles dotted the horizon.

Kye looked at Alexia as the purple sun shone through her. For a moment, he even thought he could see her face inside the helmet, illuminated by the glow of the sun. The urge to say something rose within him, yet, with a reluctant swallow, he returned to the view.

As the sun set and the moon rose, Alexia glanced at Kye, wondering if she, too, should say something. Before he could notice, though, her eyes darted back to the ground. After an awkward shuffle, she looked back at the view and pointed to the nearest village outside of Athens. 'That light source. We'll try there next.'

Kye turned around with a nod, readying his gauntlet before spotting something behind them. With the tilt of his head, he tried to grasp a better glimpse of it.

Meanwhile, Alexia selected their new coordinates. 'We'll port into the field nearby.'

'Hold on just a sec,' he said, walking off towards the northern edge of the outcrop.

Alexia lowered her gauntlet and followed, readying her rifle. 'What do you see?' she asked, walking behind him as he reached a small ledge and jumped down, out of sight. 'Kye?' She picked up her pace and jumped down after him.

After a rough landing, she found herself standing underneath a tall, vast olive tree.

Kye stood before it, admiring its curved trunk, its long branches, and its thin green leaves as rays of moonlight shone between them. 'You know what this is?' he asked, resting his gloved hand on its trunk.

'Yeah. It's a tree.'

'Well, yeah, but it's not just any tree. '

'It's an *olive* tree.'

Kye looked at Alexia with surprise, 'Yeah! Exactly! Did you know about this one in particular?'

Alexia shook her head. 'No.'

'Well, what they say is,' Kye explained, turning back to face the tree, overwhelmed by the sight of it, 'that in this one spot, this tree has been replanted over and over again for *thousands* of years. This must be one of its earliest forms.' Kye reached his hand up to its leaves and felt them between his fingers. 'The story goes that Athena herself gifted it to the city.'

'Does it still stand?'

'No. It's long gone now. I only know about it through some books.'

Another quiet gloom washed over Alexia as she stared at the ancient tree. In time, she pulled her eyes away from it. 'Well, come on. Let's keep moving,' she said, walking over to the edge of the outcrop and readjusting her gauntlet's coordinates again.

Kye glanced at their surroundings, ensuring they were clear, before he unlocked his helmet and took it off.

Alexia turned to see his cloaking deactivate. *'Kye, what are you doing?!'* she cried before realising he could no longer hear her. Quickly, she switched off her helmet's soundproofing and hushed her voice. *'Kye!'*

'I know, I know!' he replied with a nod, reaching up to one of the branches. From it, he plucked a small sprig and brought it to his nose. The leaves touched his skin as he closed his eyes, breathing in its pure, fresh, bitter smell, after which he sighed with relief.

Alexia anxiously watched their surroundings, listening for any sounds of life nearby.

Kye attempted to hand the sprig out to her, unsure of where exactly she was standing. 'Here, you should smell it!'

Alexia looked at the sprig in his hand, waiting just for her.

Maybe you should, she thought to herself. *Just for a moment.*

Alexia began to remove one hand off her rifle, before she pulled it back and shook her head, 'No, no, just – just get rid of it and sync up, Kye. We need to leave.'

Kye lowered the sprig and nodded with embarrassment. As he slid his helmet back on, Alexia returned to the edge of the outcrop and readjusted her gauntlet once more.

* * *

Another day passed as Alexia and Kye exited a small village outside of Athens without any sign of their targets. They traversed over sun-kissed hills, ported from farmland to farmland, and scoured the streets of villages. Yet, still, there was nothing.

One night, the two of them discovered a clear spot at the edge of a forest. They sat down against a pair of trees, looking out across the green fields before them. The sky alighted with millions upon millions of stars, all of them clustered together, sparkling and twinkling.

Kye, with his helmet removed, wrote in his journal as it rested atop his lap.

Meanwhile, Alexia pulled out a small, cubed piece of food from one of her pockets and unwrapped it. They sat in silence as she chewed on the compressed meal.

Soon, the slight itching and scratching of Kye's pen drew Alexia's attention.

You should just ask him, she thought to herself.

I mean, now's a better time than ever, isn't it?

Alexia hesitated for a moment longer, until …

'Why are you still here?' she finally asked.

Kye ceased his writing and looked up at her, taken aback by her words. '… Why wouldn't I be?'

'Because you don't have to be anymore. You can just leave.'

'But I … I want to help you …'

'Why?' she asked, almost breathless.

'Because you're here for a good reason … and after everything that's happened, it's probably the *best* reason. And I don't think I'm the only one who thinks so. A while before we left, Dr. Alice actually asked me to help look out for you too.'

'Dr. Alice?' Alexia squinted and leant forward. 'What do you mean?'

'I mean, she didn't tell me exactly why you were here, obviously, but she told me that you needed to talk to one of the targets about something … and that it was important.'

'Why would she tell you that?'

'I think she just wanted someone here to help you if you needed it. To back you up if the others wouldn't. In hindsight, I suppose you didn't *really* need it, but I guess she must've noticed we got along at the start or something, so she picked me, anyway. Just in case.'

Alexia leant back against the tree in silent thought, processing his words.

Gradually, Kye smiled a little. 'You know at first, when you told me you didn't want to talk much anymore, I thought it was because of the whole calling you "ma'am" thing. Made you feel *old* or something.'

Alexia looked at Kye, struggling to hide a smile beneath her dreary eyes.

'I didn't really know what was going on,' he continued with a shrug, 'but I get it … I'm here now, though, and if there's two of us, maybe there's that bit more chance we can both make it out of this.'

Alexia's eyes returned to the dark, rolling hills. 'Thank you, Kye ... but I'm not going back.'

'You're *staying*?'

Alexia shook her head.

Kye inspected her grim expression and exhausted eyes, gradually realising her meaning. *'Why?'*

'Because there's no point.'

'No point? Where's the point in going all of this way just to end it all afterwards, anyway?'

'Because at least then I will have done something *good* for once. And whether the future is entirely different or the same as we left it, there's nothing left for me back there. And that's okay,' she said with a small smile. 'That was my choice. I gave up my chance at living a normal life a *long* time ago ... and, honestly, all I've done since then is hurt people. And cheat them. And disappoint them, and ... I mean, you've seen it yourself. The things I've done ...' Alexia's eyes began to glisten as she shook her head at herself. 'But I did that so I could get *here*, and do the *last* good thing I can. And that's make sure these people can never hurt anyone else *ever* again ... and that includes me.'

Kye shook his head as he looked at her with care. 'But you're a *good* person, Lex. I've seen that too.'

'What? When I was ignoring you for two years?'

'Well, you know, the *other* couple times we talked ...'

Alexia almost smiled again before her lips trembled.

'I *do* mean it, though,' Kye continued. 'You *are* here for a good reason, and you yourself just told me that, at the end of the day, you do *want* to do good. That *says* something, doesn't it?'

Alexia shook her head, scowling at herself as she remembered all of the blood and tears at her hands. 'It doesn't change anything I've done.'

'But it changes everything you *can* do. And Lex, if you're a bad person, then so am I. I was right there with you in England, and I gunned down so many of those knights I *lost count*. I've got *a lot* of blood on my hands too.' Kye sighed a shaking breath at the thought of them. 'But I'm just saying it doesn't *all* have to keep being bad.'

With every bone in her body, Alexia fought to withhold her tears. 'And I'm just saying the longer you stay for me, the more you're risking your life for nothing ... because, at the end of the day, I'm just ... I'm just tired, Kye ... I'm just *so* tired ...' Alexia closed her eyes as she rested her head back against the tree behind her, yearning for the moment she could fall into a deep, peaceful sleep. 'It's only going to go one way,' she said with a quiet voice, 'and I just don't want you to be another person that gets dragged down into it all for no good reason ... So, you should just leave, sooner or later, before it's too late.'

The gentle rustling of the grass in the wind filled the silence between them.

Kye nodded with pity before looking out at the stars above. 'I'm sorry you feel that way, Lex. And I *am* sorry for what happened to you ... but I still don't think you should die. You're right that a lot of people have that shouldn't have ... and I only think *you'd* be another one of them.' As another silence followed, Kye looked down upon the soft, elegant motion of the grass before them. '... Did you know your parents very well?'

Alexia looked at Kye, taken aback by his question. 'I'm sorry?'

'I mean, personally, who they were, as their own people, did you know them well?'

'Um ... not as well as I would've liked to, no. But I ... I knew them enough.'

'What were they like?'

'They were ...' Alexia trailed off for a time as distant memories began to bloom in her mind. 'They were both teachers ... and ... well, you could tell. They were smart, and caring, and helpful. Also pretty firm when they needed to be.' She smirked for a glimmer of a moment, gently running her fingers along her hand. 'And they were very much in love ... I could tell that too.'

'They sound like good parents.'

'They were.' Alexia stared across the fields, remembering, before she regained her concentration. 'Okay ... well, I guess if you're staying for now, you should get some rest. I'll keep first watch.'

'Okay. Thank you.' With a nod, Kye reached into one of his pockets. 'And I guess if the end really is near, you might as well enjoy a little bit of the time we have left,' he said, pulling out the olive tree sprig and handing it out to her.

'I told you to get rid of that,' she said, raising her eyebrows at him.

'I know, but come on, when else are you going to have this chance?'

With a roll of her eyes, Alexia took the sprig from his hand.

Kye laid down and turned over. 'Good night.'

Alexia looked down at the sprig, twirling it between her fingers. 'Good night.'

For a long, quiet time, as the cool wind sang and the fields of grass continued to dance, Alexia stared at the sprig, hesitating. With the bite of her lip, she finally closed her eyes and brought it up to her nose, breathing in its fresh, natural odour.

After a long yawn, thirteen-year-old Alexia opened her eyes, sitting atop her blankets on her small purple bed. A pillow rested upon her lap with a laptop on top of that, as she continued typing away with great concentration. The glow of the screen doused her face in white as her eyes followed along with each new word that she entered.

After pressing Enter and venturing into a new paragraph, a soft knock came from behind her bedroom door. A moment later, her mother, Leslie, poked her head inside with a smile. 'Hey,' she said with a soft voice.

'Hey, mum.' Alexia replied, giving her mother a quick glance before returning to her work.

'How's it going?' Leslie asked, sitting down beside her.

'Good. I'm almost done.'

'Almost done? Which one is this for again?'

While keeping her eyes on the screen and one hand on the keyboard, Alexia picked up and showed off an old copy of a novel that rested beside her, titled *Bunny Things*.

Leslie's face lit up at the sight of it, taking a hold of the book and flipping through its worn, discoloured pages. 'Oh, yeah. This is my copy, isn't it?'

'Yep, I hope you don't mind. I found it in your study.'

'Not at all. Much better reading from something you can actually feel, isn't it?'

'Oh, so much better!'

Alexia and Leslie met each other's eyes for another brief moment, sharing another knowing smile before Alexia returned to her screen.

'Annnndddd … done!' Alexia entered the final full stop of her essay and let out a grand sigh of relief.

Leslie offered her hand and high-fived Alexia's, 'Nice work. I thought this wasn't due for another few weeks?'

'Oh, it is. I was just getting it done now, though, so I don't have to worry about it.'

Before Leslie could reply, Alexia's father, Morgan, walked up to the bedroom door in the midst of a great, long yawn. 'Oh, what are you still doing up at this hour, little miss?'

'Our daughter was just finishing her English essay three weeks before it's due,' Leslie explained with raised eyebrows.

'Three weeks?' Morgan chuckled as he strolled towards the bed. 'Where's this coming from, huh? I'm never this on top of my work. This is all from your mother, isn't it? She's to blame for this.'

'Nuh uh, not even *I'm* this ahead of the curve,' Leslie said before patting her daughter's head. 'Our daughter's just a very smart girl.'

Alexia shook her head and shrugged, 'It's just so I don't have to worry about it, is all. I don't want to be behind.'

'And that's *exactly* the right attitude to have,' Morgan replied, pointing at her.

'Do you want me to read over it for you tomorrow?' Leslie asked.

'Yes, please. If you have time,' Alexia said with a quiet voice.

'Of course, I will. I'll always have time for you.'

Morgan reached forward and picked up the book from Leslie's lap. 'I can't believe how long they've had this book in the curriculum. We were reading this back when *we* were at school, five billion years ago. Does have a great title, though. Very punny … You get it? Like … it's *funny. Punny.* No?'

Alexia and Leslie looked at each other, groaning and rolling their eyes.

'Daaddddd,' Alexia moaned, shaking her head.

Morgan handed the book back to Leslie and lifted his hands in surrender, 'I'm just doing my job. That's not an offence, is it?'

'It *should* be,' Leslie replied before looking back down at the book. 'But I think it's a good book. I'm glad we're still teaching it. I'll *always* remember that last line … "Even after everything, all was well … and there were *many* carrots."' Leslie turned back to Alexia with a smile before kissing her forehead. 'Okay. Now, I think you've earned a good sleep.'

'No doubt about that,' Morgan added.

Alexia yawned again as she shut her laptop screen and handed it to Leslie, who placed it on the floor beside the bed.

Turning back to her daughter, Leslie stroked her hair and looked into her eyes once more, 'Good night, baby. I love you.'

'Good night. I love you, Mum. I love you, Dad,' Alexia replied as she climbed underneath her bedsheets.

'I love you too, sweetie. You sleep well,' Morgan replied, stepping forward and bending down, planting another kiss on Alexia's forehead.

As Leslie and Morgan returned to the bedroom door, Alexia twisted around and switched on the twirling purple light beside her bed, shining its flowing aura across her walls and the ceiling above. Together, her parents turned and looked back at Alexia, smiling and waving good night before they shut the door one last time.

* * *

The light of the sun touched Alexia's face as she slept soundly against the tree. Her eyes scrunched up as she awoke. With a soft groan, she raised her hand to block the light before her eyes shot open.

Shit, how long have I been asleep for?!

She glanced beside her, seeing no sign of Kye.

Jumping to her feet, she looked for him in every direction.

Did he … did he leave?

He must've …

Alexia's expression fell sombre before she bent down and picked up her helmet. As she slid it on, her visor revealed Kye's position deeper within the forest. She picked up her rifle and activated her cloaking as she slid into the forest. Holding her rifle close, she stepped over roots and curved around bushes, closing in on his position.

'Kye, are you there?' she asked over their comms.

Gripping her rifle with purpose, she rounded a series of trees. As she moved between them, a small opening within the forest revealed itself. Stepping through it, Alexia found Kye standing in a clearing without his helmet. Gradually, she lowered her rifle as she watched him inspecting each and every plant and flower before him with wonder. A hint of curiosity came over her before she felt the weight of her armour grow upon her shoulders. After stifling her thoughts, she turned off her cloaking.

Kye turned to her with surprise, 'Oh, good morning! How'd you sleep?'

'Way too long. You should've woken me,' she replied, walking towards him.

'You looked so peaceful, though. I didn't have the heart to interrupt. Besides, you probably needed it.'

'Sleep is the least of our concerns right now. What are you doing?'

Kye picked a dark berry off a bush and smelt it. 'Well, it was *going* to be a surprise, but I was actually looking for something that isn't processed for us. Because, I don't know about you, but walking past so much fresh food all of the time has given me a craving for something real. I think this berry's okay to eat,' he said, lifting it towards his mouth.

In an instant, Alexia grabbed his wrist and stopped him before he could eat it, 'Wait – don't! That's a nightshade berry. It's *poisonous*.'

'Shit, are you serious?'

'Yep.'

'Oh wow, thank you … That – uh – that would've been embarrassing.'

'Yeah. Just a *little*.'

'I guess my stomach's getting the better of me here.'

Alexia wavered for a moment, uncertain, before she finally unlocked her helmet and removed it. Suddenly, with perfect clarity, she could hear the humming of bugs and the singing of birds, and could see all of the blooming flowers that swayed around them, and the rays of sunlight that broke through the branches above. The fresh air filled her lungs as she almost gasped at the sensation.

Soon, she turned and walked deeper into the forest with purpose, scanning every tree and bush around her. Kye followed her until she came upon a family of vines wrapped around a tree, each with a small cluster of berries growing out of them.

Reaching up, she pulled out a handful, sniffed them, and passed them to him. 'Here, these are blackberries. You can eat these.'

Kye took them with surprise before a group of flowers also caught Alexia's attention. She strolled over to them and bent down, picking out a couple from the ground.

'You can eat some of these too if you want. They're violas, I think. Not really filling or anything but they're good for you in moderation.'

Kye stared at her in disbelief. 'How do you know all of this?'

'I used to have a lot of plants and flowers back home.'

'No kidding.' Kye spotted another thin purple flower and pointed to it. 'You know what that one is?'

Alexia nodded as she thought for a moment. 'Um … yeah. That's aconite, I think.'

Kye raised his eyebrows before he pointed to a pink set of flowers. 'And those?'

'Uh … asters … Yeah. Asters.'

Kye slowly began pointing to another flower. Alexia smirked and gently slapped his hand back down. 'All right, that's enough, you've had your fun. Let's go.'

'Okay, okay, sorry. I just didn't realise I had an expert on my hands here,' he said, picking up his helmet and following her through the forest. 'You could've been a botanist or something in the past.'

Alexia looked at Kye with a flash of excitement. '*You* know what a botanist is?'

'Yeah! I know, not many people do anymore, do they?'

'No, I've never met *anyone* that does! How do you know about it?'

'My grandma, actually. She's got a garden of her own in her front yard that she'd seriously die for. So much so, sometimes I wonder if she cares about it more than *me*,' Kye said with a chuckle. 'But anyway, she's got like a *million* books on every kind of plant and flower and tree you could imagine.'

'Just not berries?'

'Yes, I unfortunately did *not* read the book on berries. But I did read about the olive tree on the Acropolis, so I wasn't entirely ignorant. Wait up a minute,' he said, stopping Alexia as he tried one of the berries. Upon tasting it, he let out an amazed breath and outstretched his hand. 'Oh, you gotta try this.'

Alexia paused, looking back and forth between Kye and the berries. After a quiet moment, she stepped closer and took a berry from his palm. 'Okay, just one,' she said, trying the berry and tasting its fresh and natural sweetness.

Oh my God, she thought to herself, *this is the best thing I've ever eaten.*

Before long, her eyes nervously darted back to Kye. 'Okay, maybe *one* more,' she said again, picking out another berry and eating it.

Kye joined her in picking out another berry and revelling in its taste. 'Well, you know, we probably don't want to have to *carry* this around or anything, so … we really should just eat it all now and get it off our hands.'

'Mm … I agree, I agree.' Alexia nodded.

For the next few minutes, the pair simply ate in silence, enjoying every bite of every berry. Before long, she and Kye had eaten all but one. Yet, before it could be finished, something rustled within the grass behind Alexia.

'Shit!' she said under her breath as the pair immediately slid on their helmets, activated their cloaking, twisted around, and lifted their rifles. They fell completely silent as Alexia knelt on one knee, carefully watching as something moved behind a tree ahead of them.

The pair gripped their rifles tight and held their aim steady, waiting as the rustling grew closer and closer. Then, at last, a small, hazel-coloured bunny rabbit hopped out from behind the tree, sniffing and blinking at its surroundings. Alexia and Kye sighed with relief and laughed under their breath, watching as the rabbit gradually hopped its way towards them.

Over and over, the small animal would stop and sniff the air around it, before hopping closer. Glancing at his feet, Kye noticed the last berry he had dropped.

Kneeling and picking it up, he carefully outstretched his invisible hand towards the rabbit. The animal noticed the berry and, with quiet caution, hopped towards it.

Alexia knelt in a nervous silence as the rabbit hopped right past her and up to Kye. For a time, it stared at the berry, curious and wary.

'Come on, little fella,' Kye whispered. 'It's all yours.'

Finally, the rabbit leant forward and took the berry from his fingers. A smile broke out across Alexia's face before she laughed in astonishment. Kye smiled with her as they both watched the animal in total peace, enjoying the berry without another worry in the world. Then, once it was done, it hopped past Kye and continued on its way.

Alexia shook her head, entirely without words, before looking back at Kye. He met her gaze as the many trees above them gently shifted back and forth in the wind. After another quiet moment, Alexia returned to her feet and looked ahead, spotting the distant edges of the forest, where the rising sun grew brighter by the hour.

* * *

The days rolled on as the pair scoured more rural towns.

Sitting atop mountains of rock, they surveyed vast landscapes, picking their next destination. Kye gazed up at the endless blue sky, spotting an eagle soaring high above them.

Trekking through more forests, Alexia frequently pointed out a variety of plants to Kye, teaching him about each one and studying them together.

Zooming in through their scopes, they spied on distant farmhouses, watching their inhabitants for any recognisable faces.

Trailing riverbeds, the pair attempted to spot different fish swimming through the shimmering water. They cheered and laughed as one occasionally jumped in and out of the stream with a great splash.

At the edges of busy crowds, the ghosts spent hours scanning each townsperson who passed them by. Still, there was no sign of their targets.

Deep in another forest, Alexia and Kye knelt behind a thick array of moss-covered trees. Peering between them, they found a group of young, naked pagans dancing, singing, and swimming together in a small pond, all gathered underneath the shade of a low-hanging willow tree.

Another sun fell as the two ghosts rested atop a forested hill. Under the moonlight, the hill overlooked the distant Aegean Sea and the Cyclades Islands, silhouetted against the horizon.

Kye's pen scratched away in his journal again as Alexia sat down, eating another handful of berries. 'I guess we got lucky the first few times,' she said. 'We were bound to run out of it eventually. I wouldn't be surprised if it's still a while before we find anything.'

'It does seem like we've been later and later the further we've gone back,' Kye replied, looking up from his journal. 'Connor and Ian really could've settled somewhere far from here by now.'

Alexia sighed, staring out at the large, glowing moon.

They're still out here somewhere, she thought to herself. *They've got to be.*

As Kye flipped through a handful of pages in his journal, Alexia glanced back at him, curious. 'You know, I've never seen someone write as much as you do. Let alone on *paper*. What are you always writing in there?'

'Oh, just everything, really,' he replied with amusement. 'My thoughts, experiences ...'

'Is it just for you?'

'Kind of. It's also kind of a family tradition. Another thing I learnt from my grandma. So, a lot of this book will be for her.'

'You really think Forward Industries will let you keep that sort of thing?'

'No, no way. That's why I plan to be a little sneaky about it ... but we'll see. Hard to forget a lot of this, anyway, so if I have to pass it on verbally, then so be it.'

Alexia soon fell into a grim silence. 'Is she your only family back home?'

Kye nodded, flipping his pen between his fingers. 'Yeah ... I didn't really know my parents either. Both passed before I could even talk ... pollution poisoning or something. So, it's just her and I left now.'

Alexia's shoulders fell as she listened to his words. 'I'm sorry to hear ... I'm guessing she doesn't know anything about this?'

'Oh, definitely not. I told her it was just work. She'd be *way* too worried otherwise. I mean, I'm sure if she could have it her way, she'd just have me perpetually helping her with her garden. Nothing else, just *all* garden, *all* day.'

'Hey, that doesn't sound too bad.'

'Well, maybe not for *you*, no. But I like my writing much more.'

'Okay, give me an example, then. What was the last thing you were writing about?'

'I was ...' Kye sat up straighter, gathering his words. 'Well, I was actually writing and thinking about something you said the other day. About whether the future will be the same as we left it or not ... Do you think it will be?'

Alexia thought for a moment, picking out a flower beside her and twirling it between her fingers. 'After everything we've done? I don't know how it could be ... You think otherwise?'

'I don't know.' Kye shrugged. 'I guess I think it might be the same, yeah. Or at least, I really hope it is.'

'I think it'd be a little sad if it was, honestly. The world deserves another future.'

'People could still learn a lot in this one, though. From the things we've experienced. From what's happened to you.'

'Yeah, like Forward Industries would ever let *that* happen,' Alexia replied, almost scoffing. 'Besides, you'd only be telling people about all of the things they can't have anymore. It'd just be another thing for them to be hopeless about.'

'But don't you think Forward Industries deserves some justice too? After what they've done to you?'

'Of course. But that doesn't mean it's possible. They practically run the world at this point ... And besides, at least they're doing *something* about all of this. I mean, they trusted *us,* didn't they? They gave us this opportunity. At this point, what else *could* they do?'

'That's true.' Kye nodded, looking back at the ocean as the moonlight bounced off its waves. 'I don't know. It was just a thought.'

Alexia looked back at Kye, seeing the concern on his face. 'I'm sorry. If anything stays the same, I do hope it's your grandma.'

'Thanks, Lex,' he said, looking back at her with a smile before he lifted up his journal, 'but, funnily enough, I actually haven't just been writing. I'm also partial to a little drawing.'

'Oh, are you now? That a family tradition too?'

'No, no, this is my own thing. Been trying to get better.'

'Can I see some?'

'Nope, not yet. I'm working on a little surprise. You can have it when it's ready.'

'A surprise?' Alexia raised her eyebrows. 'Come on, let me see it,' she said, leaning forward to snatch the journal from his hands.

Kye held it away from her, shaking his head, 'Nuh-uh-uh! It's not ready, it's not ready!'

'I don't care! Let me see!' Alexia fought to climb over him as he leant further and further backwards, laughing.

'No-no-no! Trust me!' Kye cried out, falling onto the grass as he held her back. 'You'll see it when it's ready! I promise – I promise!'

Finally, Alexia huffed a sigh and sat back down against her tree. 'It better not be something stupid, okay?! Otherwise, I'll burn it before Forward Industries does.'

Kye chuckled and shook his head. 'No, no, I promise it won't be … I like it. I just hope you do too.'

Alexia rolled her eyes again as she turned her gaze back towards the distant ocean. Yet, the longer she stared into the darkness of the night, the more a thought began to linger inside her head.

She is his only family left.

And soon, Alexia's smile began to fade.

* * *

Night after night, day after day, the two ghosts travelled across Attica, continuing their search without any sign of their targets. And every time Alexia would look upon Kye, her heart would sink further and further.

Early one morning, when a pervasive grey mist surrounded the ghosts, they knelt beside a clear stream of water. The pair washed their faces and drank from their palms. Eventually, as the rippling water beneath Alexia began to settle, she caught her heartbroken reflection staring back at her. She closed her eyes and took a long breath, letting the cold water drip off her face and back into the stream.

Come on. Don't be stupid, girl. You know what you have to do, so just do it.

After refreshing themselves, the pair continued on their way through the hills and fields.

'You ever heard of that "talking to your plants" theory?' Kye asked, strolling through the mist. 'I can't remember where I heard it, but it's that idea that somehow the sound of our voices can help propagate a plant's growth.'

As Kye continued talking, Alexia gradually fell behind until she came to a complete stop.

'Isn't that amazing?' Kye continued, walking ahead without noticing her. 'I wonder how that even works. You probably know, don't you?'

'Kye …' she said, causing him to stop and turn around.

'Is everything okay, Lex?' he asked with concern.

Alexia swallowed and nodded, standing in a cold silence as she tried to find her words. 'That woman in China … the one who spoke to you … you wanted to help her, didn't you?'

Kye fell silent as he thought for a moment. 'Um … Yeah … I did … Hell, I wanted to help a lot of people.'

Alexia closed her eyes before taking a few steps closer to him. 'Kye, I know you came here looking for some kind of … direction … and I *really* do want you to find it,' she said with a bright smile that quickly faded, 'but I also know you're *not* going to find it with me. So, please, *please* just leave now. Go back to your grandmother. Give her your book, tell her your stories, help her with her garden. Just

go be with her *while you still can. Please don't throw that time away, and please ...*
don't make me ask again.'

Kye stared back at Alexia with heartache. 'You really want me to just *leave*
you?'

Alexia only looked at him with desperation in her eyes, unable to speak
anymore.

After a long, quiet moment, Kye bowed his head and forced himself to nod.
'Okay ... I'll give it one more day ... and if we don't find anything by then, then I'll
go.'

Alexia's body shook as she fought to maintain her composure. '... *Thank you.*'

Without another word, Kye turned around and continued on his way.

Alexia's eyes welled with tears as she felt an overwhelming pain pierce her
heart. With a long, heavy breath, she followed after him, and together the two spectres
disappeared into the endless fields of mist.

Chapter 26

The burning sun fled to the horizon, and the pale, glowing moon soon took its place. In time, the moon continued its journey out of sight, and the sun returned. Once more, as it fast approached the horizon, the skies were struck by long, sweeping shades of orange and purple.

With the day drawing to its close, the lone pair of ghosts approached a columned marble temple on the outskirts of a forest. They sneaked around the front of the building, passing by a patch of fragile red and violet flowers growing along the edges of the temple.

With their rifles close, the team climbed up the steps and slid in between the columns. Inside, a single candle flickered before a towering statue of Aphrodite. A young girl in a red tunic knelt at the base of the statue, looking up at the goddess. The ghosts split onto both sides of the temple as they secured each corner of the room.

'Clear.'

'Clear.'

As they lowered their weapons, the girl's quiet voice echoed throughout the room, speaking to the goddess in her native tongue. Standing at her side, Alexia watched the girl in silence, finding hope and heartache in her eyes.

Eventually, the young girl bowed her head, held up her dress, and left the temple undisturbed. Before long, the pair of ghosts also left the temple and stopped beside one another at the top of the marble steps. Without a word between them, they watched as the fiery sun disappeared behind the dense forest before them.

'So, where will you go next?' Kye finally asked.

Alexia looked at him with pain. 'The next closest place is Sounion, further east. If there's nothing there, then I'll double back north and just keep going.'

Kye paused for a moment, trying to find his words. 'Lex … are you really sure about this?'

Alexia slowly nodded. 'I am … and besides, you should be there with Hayes when he returns. So he's not alone.'

Kye's gaze fell to the floor as he nodded in return. 'Okay … I'll tell them what's happened. And I'll tell them that you finished it.'

'Thank you,' she replied, before taking out the olive tree sprig from one of her vest pockets and handing it out to him. 'Here. You take this.'

'Oh, no. I got it for you. It's yours ... but maybe you could tell me what those are, though?' he said, turning and pointing to the red and purple flowers growing at the edges of the temple.

'Oh … they're anemone,' she replied with a small smile.

'You're too good,' he said, smiling back at her. 'I thought you might slip up sometime but no such luck, I guess.'

Alexia's heart burned as she looked at him. '… Goodbye, Kye.'

Kye stood in silence for a time, gathering the strength to speak. 'Goodbye, Lex.'

Alexia began to descend temple steps before she stopped and turned back to him. 'When you get back, I really hope you find what you're looking for.'

'Thank you … you too.'

Alexia forced one more smile before she turned away and continued down the steps.

Kye shook his head as his breath shook. Gradually, he lifted his gauntlet and selected their final destination. The date: *31/08/81,* appeared before him. Staring at the numbers, his finger hovered over the T-PORT button, hesitating. He looked back at Alexia, watching her walk towards the forest, further and further away from him. Soon, his eyes returned to the gauntlet as he held his finger right over the button, ready to push it.

It's what she wants, he told himself.

This is what she wants, so just do it for her.

The tip of his finger pressed down on the button, yet to place enough pressure to activate it. His heart pounded inside his chest as his entire body rattled with hesitation.

What are you doing, man? Are you really going to do this? Just leave her like this? How could you do that? She's still right here, and so are you. You know you'd never forgive yourself if you did this. And even if she doesn't change her mind in the end, you still have to try. You still have to be there for her.

You can't give up now.

There's <u>still</u> a chance.

At last, Kye lifted his finger off the button. Immediately, he felt as though he could breathe again as he turned back to her with excitement. 'Lex, wait!'

Alexia's heart skipped a beat as she stopped and turned around, looking up at him with surprise. Kye smiled with joy as he opened his mouth, about to speak before their temperature readers let off a loud and repetitive beep. Without a second's hesitation, the pair turned towards the forest and lifted their rifles.

'I'm getting a heavy reading!' Kye said.

'Me too! Multiple targets approaching!' she replied, backing up the temple steps.

Both of them met halfway, aiming at the forest. Their heartbeat sensors indicated seven bodies moving towards them from every direction. The duo covered both sides of the front of the temple, searching for any sign of movement between the trees. There was nothing, yet the figures drew closer and closer.

The two ghosts gripped their rifles tighter as the approaching footsteps rustled from within the darkness. Alexia activated her helmet's thermal imaging, revealing seven armoured and invisible figures moving out of the forest before them. The duo squinted at them before their cloaking turned off, revealing seven new ghosts lining the edge of the forest before them.

One of the ghosts stepped forth with a firm announcement. 'Lex. Kye. Lower your weapons.'

Alexia paused, recognising the voice. 'Clay?'

'That's *Sergeant* Clay to you,' he replied with a lighter tone.

Alexia and Kye glanced at each other before lowering their rifles.

'What are you doing here?' Alexia asked. 'You've got a new team?'

'Well, it's not exactly new, no. As I'm sure you'd understand, Forward Industries wasn't just going to invest all of its resources into *one* team. They wanted back-ups.'

'And Hayes, he reported back to you?' Kye asked.

'He did,' Clay replied with a nod. 'And so did you. Both of you.'

'We already came back?'

'You informed us that *we* sent you back, so that's why I'm here, to send you back.'

'But we're not done with the mission yet,' Alexia said, still processing his words.

'You are now. We're going to finish off the rest for you; don't you worry about that.'

Alexia gradually shook her head, gathering her words. 'Sir, with respect, I'm going to finish what I came here to do. You can join in, but I'm not leaving.'

'I already saw you come back, Lex. You *have* to go. Besides, your team has created enough of a mess as it is. We don't need you meddling with anything anymore. *We'll* finish it.'

'If Hayes told you anything, you'll know that I've done *everything* necessary to keep this mission alive. I didn't do that just to drop out before I finish it. *I am not leaving.*'

'Lex, I'm not asking you. *This is an order.* Return to your designated time or *face the consequences.*'

Alexia glared at Clay, refusing to budge.

Clay sighed with frustration before looking at her partner. 'Kye, will *you* at least abide by my order?'

Kye thought for a moment, piecing together everything Clay had told them. 'There's just one thing I'm unsure about, sir. You say we returned to the future because we told you to tell us to come back. If that's the case, then why would we have come back in the first place? When would such a cycle start?'

'You're thinking about this too much, Kye. You *wanted* to come back. You told me yourself. Both of you did.'

Kye and Alexia slowly looked at one another, both sharing the exact same thought.

Yeah. He's lying.

Finally, Kye looked back down at Clay. 'I'm sorry, sir. I just don't believe that.'

Clay, dumbfounded, shook his head at them both. 'Do you know what you're doing? What did I teach you? You're outgunned, you're outmanned, and we can track your suits *anywhere* you go. Assess the situation and *stand down.*'

'That's entirely up to you, Clay,' Alexia replied.

Clay stopped and stared at her in a long silence.

Everyone rested their fingers on their triggers.

Alexia eyed an opening within the forest behind the new team of ghosts.

Gradually, Clay nodded to himself as he straightened his posture and sharpened his tone. 'Well, I guess everything works out after all … *Fire!*'

All seven of the new ghosts raised their rifles, aiming at the pair. Alexia immediately grabbed Kye's shoulder and teleported them into the forest behind the ghosts. They almost stumbled over as they reorientated themselves and lifted their rifles, opening fire.

The new ghosts ducked and twisted around, shooting back through the forest.

'They're behind us!' one of them shouted through his in-helmet communications.

Silenced gunfire erupted throughout the edges of the forest, ripping up dirt, bark and leaves. Bullets whizzed back and forth as Alexia and Kye unloaded their rifles at the squad of ghosts.

A round smacked into Kye's chest-piece. He quickly spun behind the cover of a tree beside him. Alexia rushed behind another tree, tightening her body as a line of bullets pierced the trunk behind her.

Kye peeked out from his tree, spotting several ghosts pushing towards him. A few bullets smacked into the trunk. Pulling his head back behind cover, he unclipped a flash-bang grenade from his belt and pressed its activation button. The device powered up before he tossed it towards them. The grenade landed right before the closest ghost's feet. The soldier tried to turn away just as the grenade exploded with a blinding light and a high-pitched ring. The other ghosts took cover and shielded their visors, all of them momentarily disoriented.

Kye instantly slid out of cover and charged the blinded ghost, unloading his rifle into him. The ghost stumbled onto his knees as Kye fired his entire magazine into his chest. His armour was ripped to pieces as the bullets tore through his skin. Upon reaching him, Kye smacked the stock of his rifle across the ghost's helmet, knocking him to the ground. More bullets whipped past and struck Kye's armour. The other ghosts moved out of cover again and pressed towards him. Kye returned fire as he backed away.

Meanwhile, Alexia remained knelt down behind her own tree, keeping two ghosts pinned down with gunfire. More rounds tore into the tree beside her. Glancing to her left, she spotted two more ghosts entering the edge of the forest.

She noted the coordinates behind them before pulling herself back behind cover. More and more of the tree turned to dust as the approaching ghosts continuously fired on her position. Alexia hurriedly entered the coordinates into her gauntlet with gritted teeth.

Come on. This better work.

Holding her breath, she activated the gauntlet and immediately teleported behind two of the ghosts. Lifting her rifle, she unloaded her entire magazine into one of the ghosts' backs. The bullets tore into his body as he stumbled to his knees and collapsed to the ground, his armour and spine shattering to pieces.

Alexia redirected her aim just as the other ghost turned and sprayed bullets into her chest. Alexia's chest-piece was dented by several bullets before she stumbled backwards and looked towards the head of the temple. In a panic, she activated her gauntlet again and teleported to the top of the temple's stairs.

The ghost froze for a moment, processing her teleportation before seeing her at the top of the temple. 'She's back at the temple! She's porting all over the place!'

Alexia fired down the temple steps before pulling back behind one of the columns. Two ghosts, one male and one female, hurried towards her.

Elsewhere, Kye retreated deeper into the forest as the other ghosts continued their pursuit. He aimed and fired at each of them as more and more bullets struck his armour. His suit began to fall apart as he ran back behind another tree. Panting, he ejected his magazine and loaded in another before noticing a sniper glint amongst the distant trees, aiming right at him.

'*Shi – !*' he cried, throwing himself out of the way. A .50-calibre sniper round whipped past him and tore right through the tree beside him.

Kye scrambled to his feet as more bullets ripped up the dirt around him. Sprinting in between the trees, he was repeatedly knocked about by bullets striking his armour. Amidst the chaos, he pulled out another grenade and threw it towards the three ghosts behind him.

'*Grenade!*' one of them called out.

The trio of ghosts ducked for cover just as the grenade exploded. Dirt and smoke flew into the air as Kye dived behind a fallen tree.

Still hiding behind the temple pillar, Alexia heard the distant explosion. She nervously glanced out of cover and towards the forest. '*Kye, are you okay? What's going on?*' More bullets ripped into the marble pillar behind her as the two approaching ghosts reached the base of the temple steps. Alexia gripped her rifle and stood out from cover, firing back down at them. Bullets struck and dented all of their armour.

'*They've got a sniper holed up somewhere too!*' Kye replied over their comms. '*I've got four of them on me! Where are you?*'

The top corner of Alexia's breastplate broke apart, and her shoulder was pierced by shrapnel. She yelped in pain and backed into the temple. '*I'm in the temple. I've got two on me!*' she said, attempting to catch her breath as she stacked up against the wall beside the entrance.

'*We need to regroup!*'

'*I know!*' she cried, beginning to activate her gauntlet again. Before she could finish, the two pursuing ghosts entered the temple beside her. Alexia grabbed onto the closest rifle, pointing it away from her. The other ghost opened fire just as Alexia kicked her backwards, causing her bullets to fly throughout the temple.

One of the bullets struck Alexia's helmet, indenting itself in her visor. Her helmet's electronics began to glitch as she punched the other ghost's helmet, feeling her fingers crack upon impact. Alexia grunted before the ghost kicked her backwards. She fell onto her back and frantically lifted her rifle towards the two of them. She furiously cried out as she sprayed numerous bullets in their direction. The two ghosts mindlessly fired back at her. Their cloaking continuously eroded as their armour began to break apart piece by piece.

Meanwhile, Kye fired a burst of bullets at the ghosts behind him before he turned and ran deeper into the forest. Another sniper bullet narrowly whizzed past, ripping apart a tree trunk beside him. He ducked and rolled onto his knees, twisting around and unloading more bullets into the forest.

His gunfire struck their armour, knocking one of them back. Another ghost fired more rounds into Kye's breastplate, making him lose his balance and stumble to the ground. The third ghost threw a grenade towards him, landing just a metre beside him. Kye clambered to his feet just as the explosion went off, throwing him off his feet and crashing him onto the dirt ground. Dust and bark filled the air as Kye's vision turned hazy and his mind dizzy. He stood up and stumbled into a run again before a sniper bullet flew right into his chest. Half of his breastplate ripped off as he was flung backwards onto the ground.

Rolling over, he groaned in pain as blood poured out of his chest. He looked ahead, seeing the ghosts fast approaching. Clenching his teeth and pushing through the pain, he forced himself to his feet. The ghosts fired an array of bullets at him as he ran for more cover, his feet tripping over themselves.

Elsewhere, in the temple, Alexia and the two ghosts fired every bullet in their magazines at each other. Once they had exhausted their ammo, they all paused to catch their breath, panting and groaning in pain. Alexia stumbled back to her feet as she ejected her magazine. She went to load in another before one of the ghosts sprinted towards her, crying out and tackling her to the marble floor.

Alexia cried in pain as the ghost sat on top of her, repeatedly smashing the stock of his rifle into her helmet. The other ghost reloaded her rifle as Alexia desperately attempted to unholster her handgun, which was stuck underneath its retention strap. Her visor repeatedly cracked, edging closer and closer to breaking open.

Finally, Alexia unclipped the strap, pulled out her handgun and pressed it against the ghost's neck, unloading multiple rounds right through his jugular. The ghost's neckguard broke apart, and blood burst out of his throat as he fell to her side.

The second ghost aimed down at Alexia just as she aimed her handgun back. They both opened fire, hitting each other's armour before two bullets struck the female ghost's visor. She spun around as the inside of her helmet's electronics sparked into her eyes.

Alexia forced herself to her knees, emptying her handgun's magazine into the ghost. The impact of the bullets knocked the woman onto her hands and knees before she tore off her helmet and glared back at Alexia with ferocity. Her hair was short and black, with numerous cuts scarring her face. Without delay, she pulled out a knife and growled through her teeth.

Alexia removed her own broken helmet and tossed it aside. With a vicious scream, she unsheathed her knife, and the two women ran towards one another. Clashing together, they grabbed each other's arms and held back their knives.

Alexia kicked the ghost's knee backwards. She screamed and fell onto her other knee before freeing her hand from Alexia's grip and slicing her bicep. Alexia drove her knife towards the woman's chest before she dodged it and sliced her blade up across Alexia's mouth and cheek.

Alexia cried in pain before the woman stabbed her knife into her stomach. The blade only just pierced her skin, narrowly restrained by her armour. Grabbing her arm, the ghost then bit into Alexia's hand, digging her teeth down to the bone.

Alexia screamed, dropped her knife, and threw a swift punch into the ghost's face. She freed her hand from the woman's jaw before she picked up the helmet sitting beside her and smashed it across her face. Blood spewed out of the ghost's mouth as she fell to the floor. Alexia immediately dropped the helmet, ripped the knife from her stomach, and sat atop her waist. The ghost grabbed at her face before Alexia slashed the knife across her throat, letting blood pour out of her neck and mouth as she gargled for air.

Drenched with sweat and high on adrenaline, Alexia climbed back to her feet, picked up her firearms, and rushed out the front of the temple. She peered into the forest for any sign of life. There were none, only the distant echo of suppressed gunfire. She twitched at the sounds before she sprinted down the temple steps and into the forest.

Meanwhile, more bullets struck Kye's back as he collapsed behind another tree. Groaning in pain, he sat himself up against the trunk for cover.

One ghost hurried towards the tree, keeping his aim locked on Kye's position. Before he could get any closer, silenced bullets struck him from another direction. He turned and spotted Alexia before shooting back at her as she ducked behind a tree. Kye peeked out from his own cover, unloading more rounds into his armour, redirecting the ghost's attention again.

Amidst his distraction, Alexia sprinted up beside the soldier, pressed her rifle barrel against his neck, and sprayed several bursts of ammo through his throat. He fell to the ground with a thud, helplessly choking on his own blood.

Panting for air, Alexia turned and jogged towards Kye as another sniper round flew past her. More bullets ripped up the surrounding dirt as she fell to her knees behind the tree. Her heart almost froze at the sight of Kye, his armour destroyed and dark red blood oozing out of his chest. Refocusing herself, she scanned the forest for another distant clearing. After spotting one, she pointed towards it. 'What are the coordinates for there?'

Kye winced in pain as he slid off his helmet.

'What are you doing?' Alexia asked.

More bullets bombarded the tree trunk behind them as Kye pulled out his journal from one of his pouches. He took Alexia's hand and firmly placed the journal into her palm. *'Here. You take this,'* he said with fading breath.

Alexia squinted at him. *'No, we're getting out of here!'* She reached for his helmet before he grabbed her hand, stopping her.

'Lex, don't. They'll just track us down and I'm already gone. I'd rather go out …' Kye lost his breath again for a moment. '… I'd rather go out buying you some more time … so, just get yourself out of here and finish this.'

Alexia shook her head. *'No, no, you're coming with m –* ' Another sniper bullet flew into the tree behind them, tearing off more chunks of bark. They both ducked, and as the debris settled, they returned to one another's gaze. Alexia's lips trembled and her voice began to break, *'Kye, I ... I'm so sorry.'*

Kye shook his head and held her hand tighter, fighting to stay awake. 'Don't be ... if I could do it all over again ... I'd still be here with you.'

Alexia's heart shattered as she stared back at him without words.

'Now, go,' he continued, patting her hand. 'I'll do what I can.'

Alexia looked into the forest, hearing the approaching footsteps of more ghosts. Restraining her tears, she entered the coordinates for Sounion into her device.

At last, her eyes returned to him, and as the colour faded from his face, Kye used his remaining strength to smile back at her. Tears overcame Alexia as she leapt forward and hugged him. His eyes began to water as he hugged her back, and for one quiet moment, they held each other tight.

More bullets tore into the tree. Alexia pulled away and looked upon him with anguish, unable to find her words. Finally, on the cusp of breaking down, she activated her gauntlet and disappeared.

And there Kye remained, staring at the empty space before him as he felt the cold wind touch his skin. He let out an upset breath before pulling his rifle up to his chest and grabbing his helmet. *'Okay. Okay ...'* he muttered to himself.

Clay approached the tree with haste, readying his rifle. His temperature reader beeped just as he turned the tree's corner, finding no sign of Kye or Alexia. 'They've ported somewhere again! Keep your eyes sharp.'

Deeper in the forest, another ghost knelt before a collapsed tree. His sniper rifle rested on the trunk as his scope scanned the forest. 'I'm not seeing anything,' he reported. 'What the hell? Where did you go?' he mumbled to himself before his temperature reader beeped.

With his helmet on again, Kye hobbled up to a tree behind the sniper. He lifted his rifle and shot a handful of rounds at him. As the bullets flew into the dirt around him, the ghost spun around and blindly fired his sniper rifle. The bullet struck the edge of Kye's helmet, ripping half of his visor off as he stumbled back behind the tree.

'He's over here! On me – on me!' the sniper shouted over his comms.

Kye tore off his broken helmet as another ghost neared the sniper's position.

'He's behind the tree!' the sniper exclaimed.

'All right, let's finish this!' the ghost replied.

The two hunters crept towards the tree from both sides. Kye bit his tongue as he ripped off one of the loose straps on his vest. His hands shook as he pulled out a grenade and a disintegrator, tying them together with the strap. Holding his breath, he listened to the approaching footsteps. One set was coming from his left, and the other from his right. Before they approached any further, he pressed the grenade's top button and tossed it behind the tree and in between the two ghosts.

'Grenade!' the sniper shouted.

Just as the ghosts went to jump away, Kye stepped out from behind the tree and fired at the sniper. The other ghost paused and aimed at him before Kye pulled back behind cover. The grenade exploded, sending acidic liquid flying everywhere and covering both of the ghosts.

The pair collapsed to the ground as the liquid began to burn through their armour and skin. They grunted and panted as they fought to pull off their armour. Yet, the acid was too quick, dripping and melting onto their faces and through their chests. Their panicked voices soon twisted into screams, then into bubbling gurgles, then finally into silence. Both of their bodies melted away into nothing but black metallic puddles.

Kye's skin was deathly pale as he slid down the tree and onto the ground. His hands let go of his rifle as his head fell into a slump, staring at the ground and feeling his breath slip away. Gradually, his eyes trailed towards a small, lone, yellow flower growing beside him. With the very last of his strength, he reached out and gently felt its petals between his fingers.

Huh ... I wonder what this one is ...

A small smile broke out across his face.

Invisible thumping footsteps approached him as his eyes remained fixated on the flower. Soon, the footsteps stopped and the cloaking deactivated, revealing Clay towering over him.

At last, Kye's eyes began to close, and he gave his final breath.

Clay lifted his handgun and fired a single silent bullet into his head. After lowering his weapon, he looked at the surrounding bodies. All of his soldiers, dead. His jaw clenched at the sight of them. With a rigid motion, he holstered the handgun and pulled out his first disintegrator.

Chapter 27

Melbourne, Australia, 2257 CE

The sound of police sirens spiralled in the distance. Spacecraft rumbled overhead. Construction vehicles beeped and moaned. Gunfire and screams pierced the air. A pair of eyes creaked open.

Connor lay on a rickety bed, staring at his apartment's ceiling. The room was small, unkempt, and grey. A single chair sat in the corner with a Forward Industries security uniform hanging over it. Quietly, he sighed and sat up on the edge of his bed, wearing an old white singlet and a washed-out pair of tracksuit pants. For a short time, he did nothing but stare at the floor. Eventually, after a long yawn, he pulled himself to his feet and filled up a plastic cup with green-tinted water.

His eyes were heavy as he strolled up to the apartment's only window. The view was blocked by another apartment complex across the dividing alleyway. He gazed down at the alley far below, spotting the body of a man lying alone and still. A handful of fresh gunshot wounds riddled his chest. Blood streamed down the damp alleyway as his lifeless eyes stared up at him. Connor stared back before taking a sip of water.

After showering and changing, Connor exited his apartment. A sharp chill tainted the air as an endless wave of dark clouds concealed the morning sun. He turned into the alleyway and walked down towards the lone body, inspecting the scene. Eventually, his eyes landed on the man's cold, pale face. Connor glanced at his surroundings before checking the man's pockets. There was nothing. Next, he felt the soft material of one of his grey coats. Satisfied, he pulled the coat from his body and tried it on for himself.

It's a little big, he thought to himself. *But it should keep me warm enough.*

After a final, apologetic look to the man, Connor rested his hands in his new pockets and strolled out of the alleyway, entering the never-ending city streets.

Elsewhere in the city, numerous conveyor belts rattled through plumes of smoke and heat. The air was bathed in shades of orange as dozens of bagged bodies lined the conveyor belts. One by one, the corpses were pulled into chambers of furious flames. Worn-down, metallic signs plastered all sides of the building, reading *M.C.F. – MASS CREMATION FACTORY*. Meanwhile, the crematorium workers wore large, grey hazmat suits as they moved with slow purpose throughout the factory.

Beside one of the conveyor belts, Hughes Avil watched a body crawl towards its fiery fate. He donned a long coat and a sorrowful expression as he watched the body approach him. Before long, Connor appeared out of the smoke behind him, joining Hughes' side as they both watched the approaching body.

Hughes glanced at his friend. 'You didn't have to come.'

'Of course I did,' Connor replied with resolve.

'Thank you …'

Steam whistled and sobs echoed throughout the facility, consuming the silence between them.

'How were his final days?' Connor asked.

'Mostly quiet. I think he liked me reading to him, so I did a lot of that. Then he just slipped away in the middle of the night. Nothing special … I just hope it was peaceful.'

'I'm sure it was.'

The body passed them by on the conveyor belt. A tag printed on its side read: *FRANK AVIL - 2173–2257*. The pair began walking alongside the body as it continued its crawl.

'Will you keep the apartment?' Connor continued.

'I don't know. It'd at least keep me afloat for a time if I sold it. Same with all of his old books and records and whatnot.'

'You mean your family history? You can't get rid of that, those heirlooms are priceless.'

'Ohh no, there can *definitely* be a price, especially for stuff *that* old. But besides, it's probably not like the family's going to be around for much longer, anyway,' Hughes chuckled. 'Don't think it matters.'

'That's not true. You're *more* than smart enough to get out of this slump.'

'No, *he* was the one with all of the wit and ideas,' Hughes replied, gesturing to his father's body. 'And I certainly can't read and write as well as him either, so that's not an option.'

'Then there'll be something else for you to find. I could even wrangle you a placement at Forward Industries with me. We can work together.'

'I don't know,' Hughes sighed, shrugging his shoulders. 'What's the point, Connor? I'm not going to get anywhere anyway. Even my dad was barely holding on with whatever he was making at the end of his career. How am *I* expected to?'

Connor fell silent and grim for a time, contemplating. 'Well … what if there was *another* way, then?'

'What other way?'

'A whole new opportunity to start over.'

'Oh no, I definitely can't afford to go off-world.'

'No, no, it'd be *here* … it'd just be … a long time ago.'

'I don't understand.'

The two of them stopped before one of the crematory chambers, waiting for the body to catch up.

'I mean an opportunity that only *Forward Industries* could give us.'

Hughes looked at his friend with confusion, shaking his head. 'Are you joking?'

'I'm not. I've been feeling the same way as you have for a long time, Hughes. You're *right*. This *isn't* a life here. It's not fair, it's not healthy, and we can't make something of ourselves in the way we want to … but in the past? There's *endless* possibility. We can go *anywhere* we want and make *anything* of our lives.'

'Is Forward Industries actually offering this sort of thing?'

'… We would have to make this opportunity ourselves.'

'What's that mean? *Stealing it?*'

'Yes, but I know how we can do it.'

'I'm not going that way, Connor. And neither should *you*. You'll just get yourself killed.'

'What's the alternative? You said yourself, what's the *point* in all of this? We haven't got anything else here. We've got *nothing* to lose. At this stage, we either wither away and die here in the same place we've *always* been, or we take a risk and give ourselves a *real* shot at a *proper* life.' Connor took hold of Hughes' shoulders, 'Think about it. We can *breathe* fresh air again, we can *explore* the world, we can have *everything* we can't have here.'

'It's *Forward Industries,*' Hughes replied, quietening his voice. '*How do you expect to get out of that?*'

'They're too afraid to do *anything* with it, Hughes. They wouldn't dare come looking for us, and even if they wanted to, what could they do? We'd be gone in a flash, and before they knew it, we'd be *anywhere* we wanted in *all* of time. They'd *never* find us.' Connor relented for a moment, meeting Hughes eye to eye. 'They've created a *perfect* opportunity for us, Hughes, but they're keeping it for *themselves*. I don't know about you but I find that insulting, and I think it's about time we make something of it … don't you?'

Hughes gently pushed his hand off his shoulder, shaking his head again. 'I told you, I'm not going that way. I'm not a criminal.'

'No one would get hurt. I've got people who I *know* would be interested, and I'll make sure it's as smooth a process as it could be. You wouldn't have to do anything. You'll just get the chance you deserve.'

Hughes bowed his head with a quiet breath. Gazing back at the conveyor belt, he noticed the body was almost upon them. 'Can you please give me a moment?'

'Of course, take your time. I'll be outside.' Connor went to turn around before he stopped and looked back at Hughes once more. 'But you know your family doesn't have to be gone, Hughes … Lunch is on me.' Turning around again, Connor disappeared into the smoke.

Hughes watched his father's body pass him by and enter the fiery blaze. Bit by bit, the body and the bag melted away into ash and smoke. Then, it was gone.

Hughes stared into the empty chamber as another body slid inside. Eventually, he turned and looked at the smoke Connor had left through, before looking back at the flames once more.

* * *

Athens, Greece, 591 BCE

The air was warm and still, the birds and bugs sang, and a soft voice hummed a tranquil tune in the distance. Connor's eyes opened. More lines marred his face, and his hair was greyer. He looked to his side, where his wife, Zoe, lay fast asleep. Her hair was long and black, and a distinct mole marked her cheek.

Connor smiled at her before slipping out of his wooden bed. Walking out of his bedroom and to the front door, he leant against its frame. Outside their mud-brick home was Nyx, his eleven-year-old daughter. She faced the endless fields of green before them, twirling side to side as she hummed a song to herself.

'That's a very beautiful tune,' he said, speaking in Dorian Greek, 'Where did you hear it?'

Nyx turned to him with a worried smile. 'Good morning, patér. I made it up myself. I don't have any words yet, though.'

'It's very good. I look forward to hearing your voice with it.'

'No, I'm singing it to keep the Lamia away.'

'Lamia? What's that?'

'A monster! It takes children away and eats them!'

'Who told you this?' Connor asked with amusement.

'My friends over the hill! I don't want to be taken away from you, patér.' Nyx's eyes watered at the thought.

'Hey, hey, you're not going to be taken away,' Connor assured her, walking over and pulling her into a hug. 'I'll never let anything happen to you, gorgeous, I promise. There are no monsters here.'

'I'm scared it's coming for me,' she continued with quivering lips.

Connor rested his hand on her soft cheek. 'Here, let me show you something.' Standing up, he walked back inside.

Nyx stared at the front door, holding her hands and biting her lip.

Before long, her father returned with a shimmering bronze and silver sword. He knelt by her feet and held out the sword. 'Did you know I made this?'

Nyx shook her head.

'Do you know *why* I made this?' Connor continued.

She shook her head again.

'So I could protect you, *always,*' he told her. 'I made it out of a very special material, the same metal that I used to travel here. That means that I will never be leaving you, and I will always be protecting you. I couldn't have anything more special in my life than you.'

Nyx smiled and bowed her head. 'Thank you, patér.'

'No, you never need to thank me. Besides, I should be thanking *you.* Your beautiful voice will have scared away anything dangerous already.'

Zoe walked out of the front door and joined them. 'Is everything all right?'

'Yes,' Connor replied, standing back up. 'Someone was just a little scared of a monster some certain friends told her about.'

Zoe rolled her eyes, unimpressed, before pulling Nyx close to her and stroking her hair. 'There is no such thing as monsters, my baby. Don't listen to those children.'

'She was humming a song to try and scare it away,' Connor explained.

'Were you now?'

'Yes,' Nyx admitted, wrapping her arms around her mother's waist.

'Better watch out,' Connor said to his wife. 'She might have a better voice than you soon enough.'

Zoe scoffed, 'Oh, I'll be making sure of it! I'll teach her myself.'

'Excellent, then you can both sing me to sleep,' he chuckled, leading them inside for breakfast.

A little while later, Connor was dressed for the day as he climbed atop his horse. Zoe and Nyx waited beside him.

'I'll probably be late tonight, so don't wait up for me. Get a good night's sleep, all right?' he asked Nyx.

'Yes, patér.' She nodded. 'Tell me if you see any more cats and dogs!'

'I will.'

Zoe patted Nyx's shoulder, 'Go along, get started on the washing. I'll be behind you.'

'All righhttt,' she moaned before waving to her father. 'Goodbye, patér!'

'Goodbye, gorgeous.'

Nyx scurried away into the house as Zoe stepped up to the horse, resting her hand on its neck. 'Must you be so late?'

'You know it's an important time. Solon is unveiling his new constitution. I can't miss it.'

'You never say anything there, anyway. Why bother?'

'The only time I'll say something is if I think it'll affect you and Nyx, and thankfully, I haven't had to do that yet.' Connor reached out and stroked her cheek. 'This will be good news, I know it. I'll tell you all about it tomorrow.'

'Okay,' she sighed. 'Do you want me to get started on the olives?'

'No, no, we can do that together tomorrow too. Maybe we can all take a trip into the city to deliver them as well.'

'You *know* Nyx will be wanting to take a cat or a dog back with us again.'

'If she hides it well enough this time, then maybe we'll let her.'

Zoe shook her head and playfully hit his leg. 'Go on. I'll see you soon. I love you.'

'I love you,' he said with a smile, before riding off along the dirt path and disappearing over the nearby hill.

The sun glided across the sky. Midday had passed as Zoe and Nyx worked behind the house, soaking their clothes in wooden buckets. Sweat dripped off Nyx's curly hair as she tensed her small arms, squeezing all of the water out of another shirt.

Zoe smiled at her effort. 'Okay, you can go play now. I'll do the rest.'

'Really?!'

'Yes, really,' she chuckled.

'Thank you, mḗtēr!' Nyx exclaimed, launching into her mother's arms before rushing off towards the front of the house. Zoe smiled to herself, squeezing the water out of another shirt.

Before long, Nyx walked the path by the front of their house, trailing the green field and picking out flowers. As she hummed to herself, a dandelion caught her eye. She bent down and picked it up, inspecting it with curiosity. Blowing on it, she sent all of its bright white seeds flying through the air. She smiled in wonder at the sight of it, watching them float away in all different directions. Then, as the seeds parted, a distant figure became clear behind them.

Nyx narrowed her eyes, attempting to make out the thin silhouette as it lazily trekked over the hill towards her house. After passing the summit of the hill, the figure lost its footing and collapsed to the ground. Nyx dropped her flowers and ran back along the dirt track towards it. As she grew closer, she came to a stop, finding the figure was that of a man. Lying at the edge of the track, his body was skinny and his face gaunt underneath a large, dishevelled beard. He wore a faded grey shirt, long tattered pants, and had a backpack slung over his left shoulder.

What strange clothes he has, Nyx thought to herself. *And he's so tall!*

In a daze, the man lifted his head, revealing a long scar that stretched across his face and neck. The sun glared down upon him as he squinted at her and lifted his bony hand, attempting to block out the sun. 'Rose … Rosy?' he asked, out of breath, before his head fell back and his eyes closed once more.

Nyx froze in fright, lifting her hands up to her mouth. Ever so carefully, she stepped closer to him and tapped his shoe with her foot. 'Hello? … Hello?'

The man remained silent and motionless.

Overwhelmed with worry, Nyx rushed back down the hill towards her house. 'Mḗtēr! Mḗtēr!'

Zoe jogged out from behind their house. 'What is it, Nyx? What's wrong?'

Nyx ran up to her and grabbed her hand, fighting to pull her towards the dirt track. 'There's a man on the hill! I think he needs our help!'

Zoe gazed up at the hill, catching a glimpse of the figure lying on the ground.

'Come on!' Nyx cried, yanking her arm again.

Finally, Zoe gave in and ran towards the hill with her daughter. As they neared the figure, she placed herself in front of Nyx. With careful, quiet steps, Zoe approached the unconscious man and knelt before him. Her eyes filled with sorrow at the sight of his feeble body.

'Is he all right, mḗtēr?'

Zoe swallowed before looking back at her daughter. 'Get a bed ready, I'll help him inside.'

After an awkward struggle, Zoe placed the man's arm around her shoulder and walked him down the hill. They shuffled through the narrow door into her bedroom. His eyes were barely open as his feet dragged along the floor. Nyx placed his backpack down on the bedroom floor as she watched them from the door.

Zoe attempted to hold the man steady and sit him down on the bed before she lost her grip and he collapsed onto the mattress. With a grunt, she pulled off his boots and grabbed his legs, attempting to lift them onto the mattress.

'I'll help!' Nyx offered, stepping towards them.

Zoe held out her hand. 'No! Stay there, Nyx. I don't want you getting too close.'

Nyx stepped back again, watching as her mother rested the man's legs on the bed.

Zoe inspected his scarred face before turning back to Nyx. 'Fetch me some water and a sponge.'

A short time later, Zoe dabbed a wet sponge across the man's dirtied face, neck, and arms. Drops of water trickled down his skin as he slept. She pulled back one of his sleeves, revealing his metallic gauntlet. Pieces of old fabric had been wrapped around it, covering its gaping wound and open wiring. A shiver of fear shot through her as she glanced back at the man.

He was still fast asleep.

With shaking breath, Zoe ran her fingers along the gauntlet, feeling its cold, weathered exterior. Without intending to, her finger pressed a button on its lower side, unclamping the device from his wrist. Her eyes darted back to the man's face.

He remained silent and still.

Steadily, Zoe took a hold of the gauntlet and slid it off his wrist. Lifting it before her, she inspected its strange markings. She wiped a layer of dust off its rectangular screens, finding all of them black and lifeless.

The man took a sudden breath.

Zoe clenched the device and looked back at him in terror.

His eyes remained closed as he merely readjusted his shoulders.

At last, Zoe rested the gauntlet on the wooden table beside the bed, picked up her bucket of water, and backed out of the room.

'Who is he, mḗtēr?' Nyx asked.

Zoe shook her head, staring at the sleeping man. 'I don't know.'

'He looks so strange … What do we do?'

'We … we just have to wait until your patér returns home.'

* * *

The sun had long set when shadowed clouds concealed the moon and a howling wind whisked through the fields. Over the nearby hill, Connor appeared atop his horse.

With a yawn, he rode towards their small stable. After locking the horse behind their stick gate, he strolled towards his home and pushed open the front door to find Zoe sitting at their small dining table.

Nyx sat beside her, leant against her chest, half-asleep. The light of a single candle flickered across her face as she opened her eyes. 'Patér!'

Zoe patted her daughter's hair, holding her close. 'Shhh, keep quiet, baby.'

'Hey, what are you doing awake at this hour?' Connor asked, shutting the door behind him and sliding off his bag. 'I told you not to wait for me. It'd have to be sunrise soon,' he said, walking over to them and kissing their foreheads.

'There's a man here,' Zoe whispered.

'What?'

'A man came over the hill, patér,' Nyx added.

'A man? Where is he?'

'We took him inside. He's asleep in our bedroom,' Zoe explained before gripping his hand and sharpening her tone. 'He wears the same kind of clothes you used to. He has the *same* contraption you came here with. The one that locked around your wrist.'

Connor looked at her in disbelief before a sudden *click* drew all of their attention towards the darkness of their bedroom.

Step by step, Ryder crept out of the shadows and into the candle's orange glow, aiming his silenced handgun at Connor. 'Sit down,' he ordered with a quiet, broken voice.

Connor remained motionless, processing the sight of him.

'Now,' Ryder repeated.

Connor lifted his hands and sat down beside his wife and daughter.

The hunter limped towards the table and sat across from all of them, holding his aim on Connor. The candlelight danced across their faces while the wind knocked on the front door. Zoe held Nyx close to her as she eyed her husband.

All of them sat in long silence, waiting, until …

'Why?' the hunter asked.

'Why did I do it?' Connor replied in English, clinging to his composure. '… It was so I could have a chance. So I could have a family. A *life* … That place was no place for any of that.'

'I had one.'

'Well, not everyone could.'

'But *I did* … So, *why?*'

'Why what?'

Ryder leant back in his chair, staring into Connor's eyes. 'Do you even know who I *am?*'

Ever so slowly, Connor shook his head.

The hunter's gaze fell to the floor, almost with a chuckle. '… You killed my wife. You shot her in the head. Does that jog your memory?'

Connor's breath fell short.

'Still don't know my name?'

'I'm sorry.'

'It's *Ryder*. And I'm *asking you why*.'

Connor glanced at his family before returning to Ryder's tired eyes. 'Because I was scared … When she said she'd find us, it scared me. I … I didn't want to lose this chance, and I thought it was the right thing to do, but it wasn't. I regretted it as soon as I did it, and I've never forgotten it.'

'But you didn't know my name, did you? Did you even know our daughter's name?'

'Ryder, I'm so sorry. I know I made a grave mistake that day, but I promise—'

'Her name was Rose. She was barely three years old when you killed her mother.'

Nyx glanced at her father's sword sitting in the corner of the room.

'What happened to her?' Connor asked.

'Don't ask like you care. You took everything from me because you're a *coward*, and now you just want me to *accept* your apology?'

'I don't want you to forgive me, I just want you to understand that *I know* I made a mistake. And everything I've done since then has been to ensure I *never* hurt anyone like that again.' Connor leant forward, looking into the hunter's eyes. 'I'm sorry I can't take back what I did, Ryder. I wish I could, but all I have is what I have now. And I'm just trying to make that work.'

'These are just *words*,' Ryder said, his voice unravelling. 'All you really are is a man who destroyed so many others' lives just so he could get his own … and you really think you deserve that?'

Connor's lips trembled.

Ryder's finger lingered on the trigger before the wind pounded against the front door. The wind slipped through the cracks, carrying faint whispers with it.

'I will do it,' one of them said.

'Nothing more,' said another.

'The real truth.'

Ryder tightened his grip on the handgun as he scrunched up his eyes and twisted his head back and forth. *'Just stop.'*

'… Stop?' Connor asked, confused.

'The whispers. *They just don't stop.*'

'You're hearing whispers?'

'They're everywhere.'

Connor gradually nodded, watching Ryder with caution. 'I know what you're talking about. When I had travelled between enough times, I heard them too. I don't know what they are, but they stopped eventually. When I stopped travelling.'

Ryder glared at him and opened his mouth before Nyx lunged out of her seat and grabbed Connor's sword. 'Patér!'

Connor flipped the table up towards Ryder, knocking him backwards onto the floor. 'Come on! Outside, outside!' he yelled, directing Nyx and Zoe towards the front door. Swinging it open, he took the sword from his daughter's hands.

Ryder groaned as he pushed the table off himself and fired a shot at Connor. The bullet narrowly missed him, ripping into the wall beside the door as the family fled outside.

Connor stayed behind them as they ran towards the stables. 'Get to the horse!'

Ryder stumbled outside of the house and fired another handful of shots at them. The bullets struck the stable and flew into the ground around them.

Nyx screamed as Connor steered them away from the stable and behind the house. 'No, this way, this way! Hurry!'

They entered a long grass field, running through a thick layer of fog as Ryder limped after them. The clouds parted, and the distant moon shone upon the field. Ryder panted as he lifted his handgun, firing more rounds into the fog.

Nyx stumbled to the ground, crying as the bullets whipped past her. 'Patér, help! Patér! Métēr!'

Zoe stopped and looked back at her daughter. Connor lifted her into his arms and continued sprinting through the field. 'I've got her! Just keep going!'

Ryder tripped over his feet as a series of pains stabbed his chest.

The whispers refused to relent.

'Take us back!'

'What's happened to you?'

'The last beaches and forests.'

Ryder grunted and lifted his handgun again, steadying his aim.

The family neared the end of the field, approaching the edge of a cliffside before a bullet ripped through Connor's back and out of his stomach. He cried in pain and stumbled to the ground with Nyx in his arms.

'Nyx! Connor!' Zoe screamed as she ran back to them.

Nyx scrambled to her knees, tears streaming down her face as Connor groaned in pain. Zoe pulled him back to his feet as they hobbled away. With blood pouring out of Connor's stomach, they only made it a few more steps before he lost his balance and collapsed back to the ground, dropping his sword. Zoe glanced behind them, spotting Ryder fast approaching from out of the fog. She reached for the sword, grabbing it just before Ryder ran towards them and kicked it out of her hand.

Without delay, he picked up the blade, threw it back into the fog and pointed his handgun down at them. *'Don't move!'* he shouted, fighting to catch his breath.

Connor's skin turned pale as blood continuously seeped through his shirt. With what little strength he had left, he climbed to his knees and held Zoe and Nyx behind him. *'Please, you can kill me, but don't hurt my family. Please don't hurt my family.'*

'Why shouldn't I?!' Ryder yelled. *'You took mine away, and you have no idea what that felt like! How can you ever be sorry if you don't know?!'*

'They don't have anything to do with this! Please!'

Ryder paced back and forth as his head twitched. 'They're only here because of *you!* This is all *your* fault!'

'This is all your fault!' another whisper repeated.

'We have a gift now.'

'Your voice.'

'You don't deserve them!' Ryder howled.

'No, no, please.' Connor pleaded.

Ryder clenched his jaw as his breath settled. With the click of his hammer, he turned and pointed the handgun at Zoe. 'This. *This* is what you did.'

'No!' Connor cried, climbing to his feet.

Ryder pressed his finger on the trigger.

A gunshot echoed through the air.

A round struck Ryder's shoulder, throwing off his aim as he accidentally fired a bullet into the ground. Connor lost his footing and collapsed to his knees again.

Ryder growled in pain, finding a gaping gunshot wound in his shoulder. A fierce scream echoed through the night air. Ryder scanned their surroundings for the source of the noise before Alexia charged out from the fog straight towards him, holding Connor's sword.

Ryder lifted his handgun before she came upon him and stabbed the blade through his stomach. He fired another bullet off into the distance as she wrapped her arms around him and held the blade in his stomach. They stepped backwards for a moment, holding each other as Ryder began to lose his breath. His handgun slipped out of his hand before they collapsed to the ground.

Alexia continued gripping the blade as she knelt by his side, staring down at him with ferocity. *'My name is Alexia Fifeton. On the fourteenth of March 2069, you murdered my parents, Morgan and Leslie Fifeton. Why?'*

Ryder stared up at her in complete shock.

'On the fourteenth of March 2069, you murdered Morgan and Leslie Fifeton. Why? Why did you kill them?'

'I – I don't know them,' he said with fading breath.

'Don't lie to me! Your gun was there! You were there! Why?!'

'I – I ...' He paused, staring into Alexia's green, aching eyes. 'Did you ... did you say Alexia?'

'Yes! Alexia Fifeton! You killed my parents, Morgan and Leslie! Why?!' Alexia could not help but cry as she screamed at him. *'Tell me!'*

Ryder noticed her blonde hair, and underneath her shattered armour, numerous familiar scars marked the underside of her forearm. Ryder gasped as his eyes returned to her. *'Rose?... It's you.'*

'What?'

A smile broke out across Ryder's face. 'You ... you found me.' His frail hand lifted to touch her cheek.

Alexia stared down at him in total confusion, moving her head away from his hand.

Ryder's lips trembled as he retracted his hand. 'I'm … I'm sorry. I'm *so* sorry. I'm *so* sorry for everything, Rosy.' Ryder wrapped his bony hand around his seashell necklace, struggling to pull it off his neck. It would not budge. Using the last of his strength, he tightened his grip and ripped it off. His hand shook as he held it up to her chest, 'This – this is *yours*. She wanted you to have it … when the time was right …'

Alexia shook her head at him, speechless.

Ryder broke down into tears. 'Please.' He pressed the necklace against her chest. 'Please take it. Please take it.' Blood trickled out of his mouth as he fought to hold on to his breath. '*Please.*' Ryder held the necklace as long as he could as his hand increasingly shook. Looking at her face one last time, his vision faded, his head fell back to the ground, and his eyes froze in place. His hand, still holding the necklace, collapsed to his side.

'*Hey,*' Alexia said, shaking his body. '*Hey, wake up! What do you mean? What do you mean?! Tell me! You have to tell me! Please tell me!*' she shouted at his cold face, beginning to sob.

Connor held Nyx and Zoe close to him as they sat on the grass, watching Alexia cry alone. Back and forth she rocked, tears streaming down her face. Even as the sky began to brighten, her wails and moans persisted.

Eventually, Alexia inhaled and looked down at the necklace in Ryder's hand. In great pain, she pulled it from his palm and dangled it before her eyes, inspecting the stained seashell. Bloodshot, her eyes returned to Ryder, and with little feeling in her arm, she pulled a disintegrator out of her belt. Holding it above his chest, she paused, squinting at him through her tears.

At last, she stabbed the needle into his chest.

Beyond the cliffside, a great orange sun arose from behind the Aegean Sea. The darkness fled the sky as rays of light shone down upon them. Ryder's body melted into pieces as his ashes floated away with the wind. The top half of Connor's sword disintegrated, and the bottom half fell to his side. Alexia remained knelt beside him until every last piece of him was gone. The sun touched her skin as she stared into space, silent and broken.

After some time, her eyes trailed down towards Ryder's handgun. She clenched her fist around the necklace and grabbed the handgun. Standing up, she turned and aimed at Connor, marching towards his family and steadying her aim. Zoe cried out as Alexia stopped before them. Her chest heaved, and her teeth clamped together.

Come on, she told herself. *Just finish it.*

Resting her finger on the trigger, she stared at Connor's pale face, before a young pair of eyes caught her attention, staring at her from behind Connor's back. Helpless and innocent. Confused and frightened.

Alexia's hand shook as her gaze returned to the familiar weapon in her grasp.

With a long, surrendering breath, she lowered the handgun, relaxed her fingers, and dropped it onto the ground. Noticing Connor's bleeding stomach, she pulled out a tissue-repair tube and tossed it towards him. He caught it and looked up at her, confused. She gestured her hands to the button on the side of the device and mimed spraying it across her stomach.

Unsure of himself, Connor lifted his shirt and pressed its button, spraying the gel over his gunshot wound and sealing it. Nyx and Zoe's jaws almost dropped at the sight of it. After finishing, Connor gifted Alexia a thankful nod.

'Thank you,' Nyx said in her native tongue.

Alexia looked at her in anguish, shuffling in place, before bowing her head with a nod. At that moment, a heavy pair of footsteps sprinted towards Alexia from behind. Hearing the noise, she spun around before an invisible rifle smacked her across the head. Nyx screamed as Alexia collapsed to her knees, disoriented and dizzy. Another crack to the head knocked her onto her back. Connor stood up to help before the invisible figure's cloaking deactivated, revealing Clay in his black, armoured suit, standing over her. Zoe and Nyx screamed in terror at the sight of him as he pointed his rifle at Connor and fired a bullet into his shoulder, flinging him backwards onto the ground.

'Connor!' Zoe cried out, rushing to his side again.

Clay aimed his rifle back down at Alexia's head. 'This all could've been so much easier if *you just listened.*'

'*Fuck you,*' Alexia mumbled, looking around in a daze as she slowly gathered her bearings.

'You're pathetic,' Clay muttered to himself, shaking his head and resting his finger on the trigger.

Alexia closed her eyes and rested her head back on the grass.

'*Nyx! No!*' Zoe screamed.

Clay and Alexia turned to see Nyx picking up the remaining half of Connor's sword and charging at Clay. Without thought, she swung the blade and sliced the back of his leg.

Zoe's eyes darted towards Ryder's handgun. In an instant, she dove towards it and grabbed a hold of the weapon. Clay lifted the back of his hand and smacked it across Nyx's cheek. As she fell to the ground with a yelp, Zoe cried out to Alexia and threw Ryder's handgun towards her. Alexia outstretched her hand and caught the weapon in mid-air before pointing it straight up at Clay. He looked down at her just as she fired four straight bullets into his helmet. The final bullet shattered his visor and ripped through his skull. For a moment, he stood in place, swaying back and forth, before falling onto his back with a thud.

Alexia stared at the orange sky above, catching her breath and lowering her arm.

Soon, little footsteps approached her side. Nyx appeared over her, holding out her hand to help. Alexia forced a smile as she let go of Ryder's handgun and took hold of Nyx's small hand. She pulled herself to her feet and stumbled back towards the others.

Zoe knelt beside Connor as she fiddled with the tissue-repair tube, unsure of how to operate it.

'Here,' Alexia said, holding out her hand and kneeling beside Connor.

Zoe passed her the tube, allowing her to seal up Connor's shoulder wound as he winced in pain.

'Thank you,' he groaned, sitting up beside them.

'It'll take you a while to heal still, but it should make it easier.'

Nyx hugged her father as Zoe rested her hands on both of them. Turning to Alexia, she smiled through her tears. 'Thank you.'

Alexia nodded and returned to her feet, rubbing the back of her head. There was a sting to her touch, and as she looked upon her hand, found blood dripping from her fingers. Her legs almost gave out beneath her before she tensed her muscles and remained steady. Glancing back at Clay's body, she limped towards him with a sigh. Pulling out the last disintegrator from his vest, she stabbed it into his chest, letting him waste away into nothing but dust in the wind.

As Zoe, Nyx, and Connor continued to embrace, Alexia approached the tall cliffside. Her eyes flickered, fighting to remain conscious as she watched the tangerine sun rise above the horizon. The ocean was a deep blue, shining in the light. Birds soared high above, while the warmth of the sun touched Alexia's skin once more. She closed her eyes and filled her lungs with the fresh air.

Before long, Connor noticed her, alone and silent. 'Give me a moment,' he said to Zoe and Nyx, patting them as he struggled to stand up. Zoe took hold of his arm and helped him to his feet. 'Thank you. I'm good, I'm good.' He squeezed her hand and smiled at her before approaching Alexia's side.

Together they watched the beginning of a new day, listening to the distant waves crashing and the singing of birds.

'... He killed your parents?' Connor asked.

Alexia opened her tired eyes. 'I thought so ... but I don't know anymore.'

'What *happened* back there? In the future, I mean.'

'It's complicated ...'

'I figured that ... What will you do now?'

'Go back, I guess. Find out what answers I can until they get me.'

'You know, you could always stay here. Make a new life. Or go somewhere else entirely.'

Alexia shook her head and lifted her gauntlet. 'They've restricted us to certain times and places. And besides, that's not what I'm looking for. You're lucky to be alive as it is, anyway.'

'Do you think there'll be more?'

'No. Not for a while, at least.'

Connor thought for a moment, hesitating. 'Everyone else that came with me too … are they … all dead?'

Alexia nodded.

Connor glanced back at the ocean view with a shivering sigh. Eventually, he returned to her with another nod. 'Well, thank you again … and good luck.'

Alexia gave him one last look before he returned to Zoe and Nyx. She watched as they all hugged one another, feeling a hollow pain in her heart. With the bite of her lip, she gazed back down at her gauntlet, selecting her return destination to the Forward Industries port room, thirty seconds after they left; *31st of August, 2281 CE.* Her finger hovered over the port button before she noticed another destination encoded in her device. She squinted and clicked on the next option, revealing a different set of coordinates for the *5th of September, 2281 CE.*

What the hell? she asked herself. *How long has this been here?*

Confused, Alexia glanced back at Connor's family. They held each other close and watched her, waiting. Her eyes returned to the gauntlet.

Well, there's only one way to find out, girl. What else have you got to lose?

Finally, Alexia selected the destination and held down the port button. As her gauntlet beeped, she looked back at the horizon, watching the great sun reflect off the vast blue ocean one last time, before she evaporated into thin air.

Zoe and Nyx almost jumped backwards with a gasp.

'Patér! How did that happen?!' Nyx exclaimed.

Connor smiled through his tears as he pulled his wife and daughter close to him, embracing them like he never had before.

Chapter 28

Beams of light slipped through cracks in the walls, illuminating particles of dust floating in the bedroom. Zoe outstretched another piece of tanned fabric and wrapped it around Connor's shoulder. Clenching his fists, he looked away and closed his eyes.

After tying it off, Zoe rested her hand on his cheek. 'I'm finished. Are you all right?'

He opened his eyes and nodded, placing his hand over hers. 'I'm sorry … I didn't think they'd ever come here.'

'We're all safe, so it's all right,' she assured him before hesitating. 'Do you think it's over now?'

'I think so … I can't be sure, but I think so …'

Zoe clenched her lips with worry. 'All right … I'll go check on Nyx again. You get rest.' She squeezed his leg and kissed his lips before leaving the room.

Connor sat in silence for a time. Eventually, he turned his gaze to Ryder's gauntlet, sitting on the wooden bench beside him. He reached forward and picked it up, peeling back some of the cloth and inspecting its shattered electronics.

A short while later, Connor entered Nyx's bedroom. Zoe sat on her bed as she held their daughter in her arms and stroked her hair.

Connor hobbled over and sat on the edge of the bed, resting his hand on Nyx's foot. 'How are you doing, gorgeous?'

Nyx stared back at her father with glistening eyes. 'What happened, Patér? I don't understand.'

'I know, and you shouldn't have to. I'm so sorry you had to see it. You never should've been put through that.'

'What did the monster want from you? Why was he so angry?'

'Because of something that happened a long time ago. And he wasn't well because of that. In his mind, he … he just wasn't right. But he's gone now. Do you understand what that means? For someone to die?'

'Like what happened to Pappou?'

'Yeah, like what happened to him. Or to any animal. Eventually, their time comes to an end, and they leave this world.'

'Do they go to the gods?'

Connor looked at Zoe, who continued for him. 'Yes, baby. The bad people, like those men yesterday, they go to Tartarus. But if they were good, like Pappou, or like you, they go to Elysium.'

'What's that?'

'It's a beautiful land where those that pass will live for eternity. It is like a gift from the gods after living a good life here.'

'Does that mean I will get to see Pappou again?'

Zoe smiled. 'I hope so, baby. I hope so … but you mustn't focus on that. You must focus on living your life *now*.'

'That's right,' Connor added. 'You make the most of what you have now.'

Nyx's eyes filled with tears once more. 'I'm sorry I brought the monster to you, Patér. I should've protected you more.'

'No, *no*, don't blame yourself for that. It *wasn't* your fault.' Leaning in closer, Connor looked into her eyes. 'It was mine. And you were very, very brave to do what you did, but I should be the one protecting *you*. And I promise, I will.'

'He won't come back, will he?'

Connor swallowed and shook his head. 'No. He won't … I'll make sure of it.'

* * *

The following day, battling against howling gusts of wind, Connor returned to the cliffside. He wore a few thick layers of clothing as he approached the violent site of the day before. Spots on the grass were soaked in blood and others burnt to ash. He glanced at the edge of the cliff where Alexia had disappeared.

Who was *that girl?* he asked himself.

Shaking his head, Connor kicked around the grass until something caught his eye. Ryder's handgun. He stopped and stared at it for a moment before picking it up with his sleeve and inspecting it.

It was ... Morgan? And Leslie? What was their last name? Iketon? No. Fifeton? Morgan and Leslie Fifeton. That was it. Alexia, Morgan, and Leslie ...

The next night, Connor lay in bed beside Zoe. She was fast asleep as he stared at the ceiling. The wind shrieked and whistled outside. He glanced at his sleeping wife, before gazing back towards the bedside table where Ryder's handgun rested. It stared back at him, waiting ...

Another day passed. Connor sat before a series of clay pots outside their home, pouring handfuls of olives into those containing olive oil. Nyx knelt beside him, humming as she continually handed him portions of the fruit from other pots filled with vinegar. After sneaking a glance at her father, she shot an olive into her mouth.

'I saw that.' Connor smirked.

'Saw what?'

Connor chuckled, shaking his head.

Nyx pulled out another group of olives, becoming lost in thought before turning back to her father. 'Patér, who was that girl the other day?'

'I don't know, darling. I'd never met her before.'

'She was the most amazing person I've ever seen! She was so strong and had magic!'

Connor smiled a little as he took the olives out of her hand. 'I guess she did.'

'Do you think she'd ever come back? Maybe to visit?'

'I don't think so.'

'Oh ...' Nyx bowed her head.

'You should be glad. There was a lot of danger when people like her were around.'

'I know ... but if she didn't come, maybe we would've died too. I'm glad she came. I wish I got to give her a gift. Or even sing her a song to say thank you!'

Connor placed the olives into the pot before looking back at his daughter. After a short pause, he nodded and forced a smile. 'That's very nice of you, Nyx. I'm sure she knows we're thankful.'

'I hope so.'

Connor placed one last handful of olives into the pot before resting a lid over the top and climbing to his feet. 'Okay, that should be enough for now. How about you grab a couple extra for your mother.'

'I will!' Nyx exclaimed, picking a few more olives from one of the pots before her.

The two began walking back towards the front of their house as Connor popped one of the olives into his mouth. 'Mm, pretty good. Wouldn't you agree?'

'Maybe.'

Connor laughed and patted his daughter's head as they approached their front door.

The next morning, Connor sat up on the edge of his bed, rubbing his face with a yawn. He admired the sight of his sleeping wife, quiet and tranquil. Then, before long, his eyes fell upon Ryder's handgun and gauntlet once more.

Entering a small wooden shed, Connor carried the gauntlet over to his makeshift workbench. He knelt and sifted through a series of boxes underneath the bench, pushing aside tools and materials until he found his old journal. Pulling it out, he dusted it off and flipped through the pages where he had written all of his initial plans, times, dates, and coordinates. He placed the journal on the bench before continuing to look through the boxes. After another minute of searching, he found the electronic heart of his old gauntlet, made up of wires and a battery.

Placing it beside Ryder's gauntlet, he began his work, carefully detaching the metal casing of Ryder's gauntlet. Keeping his hands steady, he replugged the wires from his old gauntlet into Ryder's metal exterior. Midday had almost arrived when the gauntlet returned to life with a short, sharp beep. Its red digital screen lit up with dates and coordinates. Connor inspected it in amazement, almost losing his breath. With great care, he slipped the gauntlet around his wrist and locked it in place.

Returning to the house, Connor fiddled through Ryder's backpack. He pulled out his oversized, faded green coat and a pair of gloves. After slipping them both on, he discovered another magazine and reloaded the handgun.

With Ryder's bag on his back, he exited the rear of the house and peeked around the corner, spotting Nyx and Zoe hanging up clothes together. With light steps, he sneaked back through the fields until he returned to the distant cliffside. Pulling out his journal, he turned to the coordinates page. At the end of which, he came upon the *"Emergency Return"* heading. Underneath it lay a specific set of geographical coordinates and times.

Lifting his gauntlet, he copied in the coordinates, one digit at a time. Once entered, he held his finger over the port button.

What if something goes wrong? he asked himself.

Are you just making it easier for them to find you again?

No. You'll come back. You'll come back.

Connor pressed and held down on the button as the gauntlet light flashed red four times. Upon a flash of blue, he disappeared with a thump.

* * *

Melbourne, Australia, 2257 CE

A small shed rattled as Connor ported inside it. A chill stung his skin as his breath turned visible. After a small stumble, he glanced around the cramped shed, finding himself surrounded by tin walls and numerous shelves lined with tools. His eyes landed on the workbench before him.

Where did I put it?

Climbing down onto his hands and knees, Connor peeked underneath the bench, finding a laptop and a mobile phone. Sliding them both out, he pocketed the phone and rested the laptop on the bench. As he opened it, he was greeted by a password lock.

He pulled out his journal once more and scanned through it, finding his password and entering it into the laptop with slow, deliberate typing. The device unlocked. His mind lagged for a moment as his finger landed on the touchpad. After a few moments, as his memories of the technology returned to him, he opened an internet browser and stared at the search bar.

Eventually, he typed in *Forward Industries.*

Numerous articles appeared in the results. At the top of the page: *Renowned Inventor Deisy Forder Killed in Tragic Accident*

The article was published less than twenty-four hours prior. Connor squinted at the headline before clicking on it, reading through the article until finding Forward Industries' official statement on the matter.

Today, we deliver tragic news with the heaviest of hearts. Yesterday, on the 19th of June, 2257, an accident, involving a machinery malfunction, occurred within one of our primary facilities. The incident, which is currently under investigation, fatally wounded Dr Deisy Forder, whose death was confirmed on the scene. Forder was a loving daughter, wife, and mother, and was the world's leading inventor and scientist, skyrocketing humanity's progress further than was ever thought possible. The loss of such a mind will be felt forever. Tomorrow, we will hold a public memorial at the Royal Botanical Gardens, celebrating her life and achievements. The day after, we will strive forward, exploring and transforming the future in the way she would have wanted and has given us the power to do. May her heart and mind be with us always, whether it is the past, present or future.

Connor almost scoffed at the words.

No one knows. No one even knows.

With a shake of his head, Connor typed in the name: *Morgan Fifeton*

Various results appeared, one of them being a schoolteacher's profile page. He clicked on the link, reading his details and scanning over his profile picture. His skin was dark, his hair greying, and he wore thick black spectacles. Connor opened another tab and searched for the name through various social media websites. After a short time, he discovered the same face connected to another profile. Clicking on his photo, he scrolled through his various posts. There were dozens of photos of Morgan with his wife, Leslie, and their young, blonde-haired daughter.

That's her.

Connor scrolled further down the page, discovering a post celebrating the purchasing of their new home. Copying the image of their house and searching for it online, he discovered the property's address. He closed the laptop and slipped it into his backpack. Turning towards the shed door, he slid back its bolt lock and paused. Distant sounds of machinery and electronic droning tainted the air. He sighed and opened the door, finding himself standing in an industrial graveyard. Decommissioned machinery, ruined cargo crates, and techno-junk littered the concrete land before him.

To his left, beyond the metal railings, was the black ocean. Mountains of trash and forgotten belongings floated by. He shook his head at the sight of it. Breathing in the smoke-ridden air, he readjusted his backpack and trekked through the wasteland.

Following the map's directions on his phone, Connor journeyed for hours through the city. Keeping his face concealed under his hood, he glared at the oceans of augmented citizens, crippling infrastructure, and endless neon advertisements.

Night had fallen as he reached the Fifetons' home address. He slipped into an alleyway across the road, where he retreated into the shadows. Lifting his gauntlet, he contemplated.

We'll just take it one year at a time, he told himself. *We'll reach it eventually.*

Marking his current coordinates, Connor set the time and date exactly one year into the future. He took a long, hesitant breath before porting again.

In that same alleyway, one year later, Connor appeared out of thin air. Thin layers of ice had formed atop his shoulders as he sighed with relief. He pulled out his phone, searching Morgan and Leslie's name online. There were no noteworthy results, only their social media profiles.

Okay. Another year, then.

Connor selected the same coordinates, another year ahead. Activating the device, he ported into the future. In that same alleyway, in the dead of night, one year later, he appeared again. After searching his phone to no avail, he ported again. And again. And again. And again.

After several more years, he arrived in the year 2270. His teeth chattered as he pulled out his phone. The screen stuttered a moment before operating as usual. He searched Morgan and Leslie's name, and finally, a new headline appeared: *Police investigating local murder of two.*

Connor clicked on the link, reading the article, which stated:

Police are currently investigating the murder of two local Glen Iris schoolteachers, Morgan and Leslie Fifeton. On May 15th, 2669, at approximately 11:00 pm, an unknown assailant forcefully entered the couple's home via the front door. Police claim a single firearm was used, which was discharged up to ten times between both victims. Police were notified after the couple's thirteen-year-old daughter discovered their bodies and promptly contacted authorities. Police are continuing their investigation and are asking the community to come forward if they hold any information on the matter. If you do know anything, contact 000 or...

Connor's eyes trailed off before he nodded to himself and typed in the date and time: *May 15th, 2669, 10:45 pm.* Porting back in time to that night, he brushed the ice flakes off his coat and walked up to the edge of the alleyway. He gazed at the Fifeton house across the street. Their lights shone through the windows. Morgan walked up to the front lounge room window.

Connor pulled back a little, spying on him as Morgan closed the blind. He glanced around the rest of the street. It was empty and quiet. Only the cold streetlights illuminated the houses below.

Come on, he thought. *There's gotta be somebody.*

Gazing down at his phone, Connor watched as the minutes ticked by, ever approaching 11:00 p.m. His foot tapped the ground and his eyes darted back and forth between both sides of the street, waiting.

Ryder. Somebody. Come on ...

The time was 10:59 p.m., and there was still no one in sight. No movement. No noise. Only the endless hum of the streetlights above.

Soon, a dreadful hopelessness washed over Connor. He swung his bag around to his side and pulled out Ryder's handgun. Lifting his phone again, it was 11:01 p.m. No one else was there, except him. He stared at the phone in his hand with a cold, defeated gaze. Gradually, he closed the phone and slipped it into his pocket. His eyes returned to the handgun.

It's already happened, he told himself.

You don't have a choice.

You don't have a choice ...

Swinging his bag onto his back, Connor stepped out of the shadows. His footsteps echoed throughout the street as he held the handgun by his side. Climbing up the front steps of the Fifetons' house, he stopped before the front door. The soft chatter of a TV sounded from inside. His hand shook as he rested it on the handle. Inch by inch, he twisted it until ... *click.*

It was locked.

Connor sighed.

Come on. Just do it. Then it can all be over.

Connor's eyes welled with tears as he gritted his teeth. Aiming his gun at the door handle, he fired a silenced bullet into it. The handle ripped apart. He fired two more shots through the door, destroying the latch. The door loosened before he pushed it open and stepped inside.

Upon his first step inside, he found Leslie staring at him from down the hall, her eyes struck with fear. *'Morgan!'* she shouted.

Before she could turn and run, Connor lifted the handgun and fired three shots into her chest. She screamed and collapsed to the floor.

'What? Leslie?!' Morgan cried out, stepping out from the lounge room to find her body. He almost jumped at the sight of Connor. *'Hey!'* Without thought, he broke into a charge towards him.

Connor lifted the handgun and pulled the trigger again, firing four shots into Morgan's chest. With a cry of pain, he tripped onto his hands and knees. He coughed up blood across the carpet as he fought to breathe.

Connor looked away as he lifted the handgun and fired one more bullet through Morgan's head. He fell with a thud. Leslie wheezed as she stared at the ceiling in shock, blood soaking her chest and dribbling out of her mouth.

After lifting his handgun again, Connor discharged the remaining two bullets into her chest. Her body rattled, and blood splattered onto the walls. A second later, her head dropped to one side, lifeless. Connor stood in silence for a moment, violently shaking.

A soft whimper came from down another hallway to his right. Connor's heart was flushed with fear before he walked in between Morgan and Leslie's body, dropping the handgun onto the floor.

I'm sorry.

I'm sorry.

Without lingering any longer, he turned and left the house. Morgan and Leslie's bodies lay in silence, their blood soaking the carpet. Before long, Alexia crept out of her bedroom to investigate.

* * *

Athens, Greece, 591 BCE

Grass swayed side to side. The ocean crashed against the cliff face. The wind whispered and whistled over the rolling hills.

With a thump, Connor ported back onto the edge of the cliff. He collapsed to his knees and broke down into tears. Moaning in distress, he almost threw up as he laid his head on the ground.

'Find them,' a twisted whisper said from behind him.

Connor immediately turned and looked behind himself, seeing nothing but the lonely cliffside.

'In our home,' said another whisper.

Connor shook his head as he unclamped the gauntlet. Screaming, he smashed it against a rock over and over until it had shattered into pieces. Next, he pulled out his laptop, dismantling it just the same. And lastly, his phone. Its screen glitched and froze on the time, 11:06 p.m., before shutting off forever. With one last bout of energy, he gathered all the electronics and threw them off the cliffside and into the Aegean. As his legs gave out beneath him, Connor fell onto the grass, wallowing in pain.

In the early hours of the afternoon, Connor wandered back home. With a flower in her hand, Nyx sat alone on the steps outside their house. Upon lifting her gaze, she spotted her father approaching. A bright smile came across her face as she dropped the flower and raced towards him. 'Patér! Patér!'

She ran straight into his arms as he knelt before her. Zoe stepped outside and watched them from a distance, smiling a melancholy smile.

'I was worried about you, Patér!' Nyx exclaimed. 'Where did you go?'

With eyes full of tears, he held her close to his chest. 'I was just making sure you're safe, gorgeous. I was just making sure you're safe.'

Chapter 29

Melbourne, Australia, 2281 CE

'Sync up!' Able ordered.

Inside their control room, Clay, Elodie, Alice, and a handful of Forward Industries scientists watched the ghosts synchronise their gauntlets on the opposite side of a one-way mirror.

'Synched!' Alexia replied.

'Cloak!' Able shouted.

In unison, all eight ghosts activated their cloaking devices.

'Cloaked!' Alexia confirmed.

'On "Go", we port! Three. Two. One. *Go!'*

With a thump in the air, the ghosts disappeared from the port room.

A digital timer on the wall began its thirty-second countdown. Everyone watched and waited in anticipation. Alice held her breath. Elodie crossed her arms. Clay remained steadfast, holding his hands behind his back.

Five ...

Four ...

Three ...

Two ...

One ...

After the final second, a single ghost appeared back inside the port room. He twisted around, attempting to orient himself before looking at the mirror. Elodie and Alice glanced at one another, feeling their hearts skip a beat, before Alice leant towards the control panel, pressing down on the communications button. 'Who is it?'

The ghost scanned the room, finding himself entirely alone, before he removed his helmet, revealing it to be Hayes; his eyes bloodshot and wrought with dismay.

A short time later, Hayes was isolated from any human contact, being promptly tested for diseases, cleaned, and changed into plain black-and-grey clothes. At last, after the quarantine process, he was securely escorted to a private interview room where he sat across a table from Elodie. Clay stood behind them, watching with a detached gaze.

Before long, Alice also entered the room, placing a glass of water down in front of the ghost. 'Water?'

'Yes. Thank you,' he said with an anxious nod.

Alice sat down beside Elodie as Hayes drank the entire glass. With a shaking hand, he rested the empty cup back on the table.

'What happened?' Elodie asked.

Hayes' eyes darted between the one-way mirror and the security camera in the corner of the room. 'It – uh … it didn't go how we thought.'

'The others, are they dead?' Alice asked.

'When I left, Alexia and Kye were still there. They were continuing on.'

'You left them?' Clay clarified.

'I — They were supposed to come back and meet me here. They said they would … but they mustn't have made it …'

Alice's eyes fell to the table in thought.

'And the targets?' Elodie continued.

'We … killed most of them. Or, well, Ryder did. Everywhere we went, he was there much earlier than us. Same with the targets. He killed Hughes, Issa, and Grey. Eventually, we caught up to him. We got Ode, and almost got him too, but he escaped again. So, him, Ian, and Connor were still out there when I left.'

'So, why'd you come back?' Clay asked.

'Things just — so many of us died. So much went wrong, and then … and then Alexia told us why she was here … or there …'

Alice and Elodie looked at one another, concealing their thoughts, before returning to Hayes.

418

'How about you start from the beginning, Hayes,' Elodie suggested.

Hours ticked by before Elodie and Alice entered the opposite room. They stood before a one-way mirror, watching Clay as he continued to speak with Hayes.

Elodie sighed. 'Well, this is a disaster.'

Alice looked back and forth between Elodie and Hayes, still processing all she had heard.

'What do you make of it?' Elodie continued. 'They were so late, *and* Ryder was early. How's that possible?'

'It was always a gamble with how accurate the timings were going to be, especially the further they went back,' she explained, shrugging her shoulders. 'Ryder, just … must've gotten lucky.'

'That's some luck.' Elodie noted, shooting a suspicious eye towards her.

Alice dodged her gaze. 'Well, one thing we can gather is that Hayes still returned to his future. Despite everything that they did, it didn't change our present.'

'That's true,' she replied, staring at Hayes through the mirror. 'And what do you think happened to the others?'

'I don't know … maybe they all died, or maybe a few have managed to live. They just didn't return.'

'Mm.' Elodie thought for a moment, nodding to herself, before turning back to Alice, 'All right, you get some rest, put some more thought into it, and write up a report. I'll handle the rest for now.'

'What are you going to do?'

'Clean up this new mess that's been made,' she explained, walking towards the exit.

'How?'

Elodie paused at the door, looking back at Alice again. 'Your team failed, Alice. I appreciate all of your efforts, and I still need you, but this is a matter of security now. I'll handle it. Don't you worry,' she assured her before gesturing her to leave the room.

Alice wavered for a moment, before forcing herself out of the room. Elodie exited behind her and re-entered the interview room as Alice continued down the hallway. With caution, she glanced over her shoulder at the door to the interview room.

Keeping her head low, the doctor slipped into another hallway and approached an elevator with haste. As she stepped inside, she swiped her wrist on the elevator scanner and typed in a clearance code. The scanner beeped green, and the elevator took her two levels above. As soon as its doors opened, Alice rushed down another hallway.

Glancing at her surroundings and ensuring the coast was clear, she approached the security control room. Using her body to shield the door from the view of any cameras, she typed an elongated code into the keypad. The device flashed yellow: *"CLEARANCE OVERRIDE"*. The door unlocked before she stepped inside and shut the door behind her.

The room was dark and overwhelmed with shelves upon shelves of server boxes. A long series of black-and-white screens lined the wall before an empty desk. Alice crept up to the desk, staring at the security footage. She flipped through the facility's various cameras, eventually landing on the interview room, watching as Elodie and Clay stood across the table from Hayes.

'So, this is the same place I left?' Hayes asked. 'The same future?'

'That seems to be the case,' Elodie replied.

Hayes slunk into his chair with relief.

Alice leant closer to the computer screens.

'And you've told us everything?' Clay asked. 'No missing details?'

'No. That's everything that happened … I'm sorry.'

'Don't be,' Elodie assured him. 'We're glad you told us. We appreciate the honesty,' she said before giving a small nod to an empty space behind him.

'So, what happens now?' Hayes asked. 'Will I get to – ' Before he could finish his sentence, a silenced bullet tore through the back of Hayes' head. He fell face-first onto the desk with a pool of blood forming beneath him.

Alice jolted upright as her jaw dropped.

Three sets of cloaking devices were deactivated, revealing a trio of ghosts standing behind Hayes.

Elodie turned to Clay. 'Dispose of the body, and then I want you to ready your team.'

'Yes, ma'am,' he replied with a nod, gesturing to the other ghosts before exiting the room.

Alice stared at the screen in disbelief, unsure of what to do with her hands. As a ghost stabbed a disintegrator into Hayes' back, she turned off the screen. Only the droning hum of the servers remained. Slowly, the room around her began to spin and blur as she leant over and placed a hand on the desk, fighting to stay upright. Soon, her surroundings steadied.

After another lingering moment, Alice caught her breath, straightened her lab coat, and slipped back out of the room.

Returning to her office, she shoved her laptop and a litany of paperwork into her bag. Her mouth was sealed shut as she rapidly breathed in and out of her nose, clinging to her composure. Footsteps neared her door. She froze and shot a glance towards it, spotting two scientists chatting with one another as they walked past the office.

With a short sigh, she swung the bag around her shoulder and exited the room. Her footsteps echoed throughout the facility as she entered the central hangar and walked towards the front entrance.

'Alice!' a voice called out. 'Alice, wait!'

Alice stopped and turned around to see Elodie approaching her. Her chest tightened and her lips clamoured to find words. 'I was just leaving. Like you said.'

'Of course, of course,' Elodie replied with a nod. 'I just … I know all of this must be hard for you to process. And I hope I wasn't too blunt earlier. I'm still trying to work it all out myself.'

Alice nodded, gripping her bag tighter.

'Anyway,' Elodie continued, 'I just wanted to tell you that I'm glad you've been here to help us work through this. Despite the complications, it's still a good thing we're doing, and I know we'll get through it. I'd like to have another meeting sometime this week to discuss this further. How does that sound?'

'Sure … I can do that.'

'Good. Excellent,' she said with a smile. 'You can finally return to working in your proper office too. Leave this facility behind for a while.'

'Yep.'

'Have a good night, Alice.'

'You too.' Alice forced the words through her teeth as Elodie turned and walked back through the facility. Her nails had almost pierced through her bag as she spun around and left the building once and for all.

* * *

Night had fallen across Melbourne as Alice paced back and forth in her small sky-rise apartment. She fiddled with her fingers, feeling her heart pounding and her breath slipping away. The endless city lights shone through her apartment windows, reflecting off the polished floors and glass decor as she gazed up at the ceiling, feeling sick to her stomach. Finally, she stopped and forced herself to swallow, letting out a gasping breath.

Turning around, her eyes landed upon the laptop on her small desk. Sitting down before it, she opened the laptop and an internet browser, typing in: *Morgan and Leslie Fifeton Murder.* A series of years-old articles appeared. She meticulously scanned through each one. At last, she came upon the name *Marlo Long*, the lead detective behind the homicide investigation. She typed his name into the search bar and clicked *Enter.*

The next morning, a bullet train arrived at Portsea Station, resting beside the Mornington Peninsula coastline. Wearing suit pants and a short jacket, Alice exited the train and walked through the station. She eyed the unfamiliar surroundings with discretion, keeping her hands buried in her pockets as she entered the beachside town. Most of the buildings were small and constructed from rare wooden materials. Old neon lights hung from their windows, flickering on and off.

Almost all of the locals wore oversized, tattered clothing as they strolled to and fro without cause, smoking and drinking the day away. Amongst them, Alice noticed an elderly woman pushing a trolley housing all of her belongings. She wore raggedy clothes and a prosthetic leg that wobbled along the cracked pavement. Strings of paper and plastic tied to the trolley floated in the wind as she limped by, disappearing into a misty haze.

Upon reaching the end of the street, Alice followed a dirt path through the Point Nepean National Park. The trek was quiet and lonesome. Abandoned, half-constructed concrete buildings were left to decay around her. Most of the trees and foliage had withered away, while the many leaves and plants lay dead upon the path.

Alice readjusted her bag and held it close by her side. As she approached the end of the path, she came upon the rocky peak of the peninsula. Over and over, the cold and violent wind smashed waves against the nearby rocks. The defensive bunker of Fort Nepean sat alone before her. Numerous concrete and wooden extensions had been built atop and alongside it. Fighting against the wind, Alice fought her way to the front of the building and buzzed the doorbell. As she waited, she wrapped her jacket around her chest.

After a short time, the intercom clicked, and a voice came through the other side. 'Who is it?'

Alice stepped before the microphone. 'It's Dr Alice Locke, from Forward Industries. Am I speaking with Mr Long?'

There was no reply.

The intercom clicked again, turning off.

Alice stared at the intercom, confused. She waited for a moment, before a series of unlocking sounds bellowed from behind the door. With a heavy yawn, the door was pulled open.

From the darkness, Marlo stepped out before her. Grey stubble distinguished his face as he wore a pair of dark, loose pyjamas. Meanwhile, his eyes were tired and his voice dour. 'You're here alone?'

'I am. No one else knows.'

With a slow nod, his eyes scanned her up and down. 'Okay.' With the tilt of his head, he turned around and shuffled back inside. 'Shut the door behind you, please.'

Alice stepped inside and pushed the heavy door closed before following Marlo into the heart of the refurbished bunker. A dusty electronic control panel sat before an old slit-view window, peering out across the ocean. The rest of the room had been converted into a makeshift lounge. Worn-down couches, carpets, trinkets, drawings, and books were sprawled throughout the place, and a series of candles sat atop a coffee table. The outside wind beat against the concrete walls without remorse.

'What was this place?' Alice asked.

'Well, it used to be a defensive bunker,' Marlo explained, sitting down at his small dining table. A formation of dominoes sat before him, stacked atop one another. He continued placing more on top of them, carefully balancing each one. 'Then it was a control centre for those rigs out there.'

Alice gazed out the narrow window. Beyond the land, a series of old environmental and ocean stabilising rigs stood tall amidst the water, abandoned and covered in rust.

'But once those shutdown,' he continued, 'they were just going to leave this place and let it become another home for junkies. Either that or let the sand swallow it. So now, it's just my home.'

'You worked here after your detective work?'

'Yeah. It was a nice change of scenery. And it's quiet, despite what the wind may tell you.'

Alice nodded, approaching the table and sitting down across from him. 'It's nice.'

He glanced up at her and smirked. 'You don't have to say that. Just cut to it. What are you here for?'

'I wanted to ask you about your investigation into Forward Industries. About the Fifetons' murder.'

'And why would you want to do that?'

'I saw you left your position sometime after it happened. I wanted to hear what you had to say … and I wanted to make sure you were alive.'

Marlo placed another domino on top of his structure before he leant back in his chair. 'What have they done now?'

'A lot … I only learnt about the Fifetons' murder two years ago. What happened?'

'It's pretty simple, really. His gun was left at the scene, his prints were on it, and I tried to track him down. That's when I found out that seemingly *no one* knew where he was or where he had been for the last ten years or so. Him and his daughter had both just disappeared off the face of the planet, and no one even seemed to know or care. So, then I went to Forward Industries, asked some questions, and the next thing I know, they shut down the whole case. They said he had moved "off planet", wanting to start a new life out of the public eye, and that – of course – he had *nothing* to do with it.' Marlo lifted his eyebrows and rolled his shoulders. 'Obviously, as an investigator, and feeling an obligation towards the Fifetons' daughter, I only dug deeper. Stumbled upon a whole lot of "conspiracy theories". Things about how not only Ryder's disappearance, but Deisy Forder's "accident", just didn't quite add up. Eventually, I pestered my superiors so much about it that they caved and told me they knew the truth the whole time. Deisy's murder, Ryder's escape, everything. But I couldn't say anything. I got a few warnings from Forward Industries too, some people following me, leaving me subtle messages, and so I got the idea. I wanted to keep going but … I had an obligation to Alexia. At that point, I thought her safety was a priority over her parents' justice, so I dropped it.'

'You didn't take it to the media?'

'I tried leaking some stuff here and there, but who would believe it? Anything called a "conspiracy theory" is pretty easy for people to roll their eyes at. And besides, do you see the media ever asking Forward Industries the hard questions anymore?'

'You left the force of your own volition, then?'

'Yeah. To nobody's surprise, I don't think they were too comfortable with me being there after that, but I stayed because I had some stupid idea that I could protect Alexia if I kept my ear to the ground. I thought I'd at least have some "power" to protect her.' Marlo chuckled. 'But a bit before she turned eighteen, she cut me off and disappeared on me too. So, I hung up my badge and came out here.'

'You never heard from her again?'

'She wouldn't want to speak to me. I'm the guy who let her parents' murderer get away. I wouldn't want to speak to me either.'

'Well, I've met her too … In fact, I spoke to her just yesterday.'

'*Yesterday?*' Marlo's eyes lit up as he leant forward in his chair.

'Yes. She came to me two years ago. She's the one who told me about her parents.'

'And how is she?'

'I don't know. She wanted to do something about her parents, and so Forward Industries has been helping her …'

'Helping her? *How?*'

'They started an operation. They sent people back in time to hunt down everyone that escaped, Ryder included. And she went with them.'

Marlo scoffed in amazement, retracting in his chair again. 'Of course, she did … And has she come back?'

'Not yet … I'll know in a week's time. You can't tell anybody, though.'

'You think I don't know that?'

'I know, I'm sorry. It's just a habit … I've never told anybody any of this outside of the company.'

'Yeah, well, welcome to the club,' he replied, picking up another domino and placing it atop his sculpture.

'I don't know if she's going to come back or not, but I think she'll be in danger if she does.'

'No shit. She'd know who she's dealing with.'

'I don't know if she does.'

'*She'd know.* She just might not care. And I mean, who can blame her? *Your* friend was murdered over twenty years ago, and *two time machines* were stolen; probably the greatest crimes in history, and it was swept under the rug like it was *nothing*, and *you* certainly didn't say anything. Are you going to tell me you didn't realise until *just now* what you've been doing? That it was an accident that you and your company have been playing with time like it's your toy? The entire human race has *no idea* just how much they're at *your* mercy. The *power*, and the things you have *allowed* to happen … they sicken me.'

Alice stared back at him without words.

'Or have you just been so immersed in your invention that you've forgotten where the hell in time you even are anymore? … I guess that sort of thing would get hard to distinguish for you. But one thing I know for certain is if even *you* can't do anything to stop this, then no one can.'

Alice's eyes fell to the floor.

'So,' he continued, 'why don't you just save yourself a little more time and go back to your office and ignore it for another twenty years? We both know how that's how it's going to go, anyway … and I have things to do.'

Alice looked at him in shame, before standing up and leaving. With a rumble and a heavy echo, the metal door shut behind her.

Piece by piece, Marlo continued placing dominoes atop his sculpture. He balanced them at three different ends, before placing another domino, which slipped off. The sudden movement caused all of them to collapse, splashing across the table. He stared at the wreckage, taking a quiet breath and burying his head into his hand.

* * *

Alice stared into her apartment window as her reflection gazed back at her. The city lights swayed across her face, while her eyes were as heavy as the shadows that consumed her.

Suddenly, a knock at the door cut through the silence. Alice turned and glanced at her digital clock. It was 9:51 p.m.

With quiet steps, she crept up to the door and peered through the peephole. On the opposite side was Elodie, standing and waiting in the complex's hallway.

Alice unlocked and opened the door for her. 'Ms. Wells? What are you doing here?'

'You didn't show for work today. I was a little worried. Can we talk? May I?' she proposed, gesturing to come inside.

'Sure …'

'Thank you.' Elodie stepped inside and surveyed the apartment with a smile. 'It's a nice place.'

'Thank you,' Alice replied, shutting the door.

Elodie noticed two small couch chairs facing one another. 'Can we sit down?'

Alice nodded, flicking on the apartment lights. The city view sparkled beside them as they sat down across from one another.

For a time, only silence filled the air between them.

'Would you … like a drink?' Alice asked.

'No, no, I'm fine, thank you. I don't want to pester you for too long at this hour. I just wanted to … be upfront about things. We don't have to pretend. You and I both know this company has kept things from you. *I've* kept things from you, but honestly, I don't want to have to do that anymore. You've been with us for a long time, and I think I can trust you. Would you say the same?'

'Yes. Of course.'

'Good, good …' Elodie took a long breath, locking eyes with Alice. 'I know you saw what happened to Hayes.'

Alice's expression filled with unease as she shuffled in her seat.

'Don't worry,' Elodie reassured her, 'I completely understand. I'd actually be surprised if you *didn't* want to know. You hand-picked them and taught them for two years, after all. It's *good* that you care about them. And I should've been honest beforehand, but I didn't want to make you worry. Of course, you were going to do that anyway, though, so I'm sorry. And I'm sorry you had to see it happen.'

'Why?' Alice blurted out, almost breathless. *'Why did you do it?'*

'Because we needed to, Alice. You know just as well as I do the scale of the mess we are cleaning up. We can't go through *all of this*, just to let a whole new group of people wander around with this sort of information. *Especially* one who just lost his whole team and is feeling completely *alone*. He would've been a ticking time bomb and created a whole new line of issues, eventually. And I don't think either of us would've wanted that. And we have to remember, they signed a contract. We are perfectly within our rights.'

'No. You didn't have to kill him.'

'Then what *would* we have to do? Try and make friends with him? Send him to years of therapy? Keep an eye on him every day for the rest of his life and hope that he is able to bring a secret of that magnitude to the grave? It's *too much* of an investment and *too much* of a risk, and minimising risks is the entire point of this mission. It's the entire direction I'm trying to push this company in.'

'Killing is not minimising risk.'

'Isn't it? Isn't that what we've been doing already? Hayes *was one of those killers.*' Elodie restrained herself with a sigh, sitting upright. 'But you're right that it's not a sustainable solution. I don't want us to have to kill. We all know there's been more than enough of that. So, things are going to be changing from here on out.'

'How?'

'Well, first, we're going to relocate our headquarters off-world. I know Miles was always very proud of the company being housed on Earth, and I think it's admirable how long we have been able to boast such a fact, but at this point, it's just not practical anymore. The real growth is all happening elsewhere, and if we stay, we'd only be doing ourselves a disservice. Earth is a dying planet. I don't think it's a particularly healthy place for the company, and especially not for my children to grow up in.'

'Where would you go instead?'

'It's not decided, but I wanted to hear your suggestions too. I want *you* to come with us. You are the smartest mind we have, and I want you alongside us as we expand our operations.'

'What expansions?'

Elodie leant forward in her chair. 'If the last day has taught us anything, it's that travelling into the past does not "destroy the world" or "the fabric of reality" or whatever cautionary theories people have posited. We can do it and *be safe.* And now that we know we can do that, I think we can begin issuing travels into the future.'

'*The future?*'

'Yes! Of course, we'll operate under strict protocols, but think about it, we can send personnel into the future and build the company beyond the scale we ever thought possible. Imagine what we could learn from having people report back to us *from* the *future.* Our knowledge will be *endless.* We can discover which off-world colonies will fail, which will succeed, what politicians will win elections, what natural disasters will occur, what conflicts will erupt, we can know *all of it* and tailor ourselves around it completely. We'll know where to invest, where to build, who to support. *Everything, Alice.* And all the while, we'll grow into a position that can help *everybody*. Never will humanity have had such a hopeful, trusted future.'

'We have no idea if any of that would work.'

'*Yes, we do.* I know you're afraid, but at some point, we have to take a leap, and *this is it.* Our mission into the past has already gotten the ball rolling.'

'And what about the people you send into the future? You'll just kill them too?'

'Alice, no, of course not. I told you that's not what I want to do. There'll be no more off-the-street hires. We'll do everything in-house with trusted sources and, despite the inherent risks, we'll do it with as much safety as humanly possible. This is not something I've considered lightly, trust me. We can change *everything* for the better, and I want *you* to be a part of it. You understand this technology more than anyone. I want you to see your invention be used for *good.*'

Alice shook her head. 'I think it's too much.'

'No, it's exactly what your invention is *supposed* to do. Isn't this what you and Deisy dreamed of? Don't you deserve to see that? After everything that's happened, don't you want to see your invention finally live up to its potential?'

Alice felt her throat constricting itself, refusing to let her speak.

'I'm sorry, I know I'm throwing a lot on you,' Elodie admitted, lifting her hands. 'It's just I'm so excited at what we can accomplish. I don't think we should waste this opportunity we have.' After another moment of silence, Elodie climbed to her feet and peered out the window at the glowing city. 'Think of the lives we can change. The people we can save. The impact we can have. So much worry and so much uncertainty will finally be a thing of the past … We need you, Alice. We really need you.'

Alice heard a slight shuffling noise behind her. She looked over her shoulder, seeing nothing out of the ordinary.

'I'll give you some time to think it over, though. There's no rush,' Elodie explained, turning back to face her. 'I know it's a lot, but I hope you make the right decision … Thank you for seeing me, Alice. I really do appreciate it.' With a smile and a nod, Elodie walked back towards the front door.

Alice stood up, watching her open the door. 'Did you send Clay back too?' she asked.

Elodie paused and glanced back at her. 'I did.'

'He had his own team?'

'As a precaution, yes.'

'And has he come back?'

Elodie let out another sigh. 'No. But honestly, I think it makes matters a lot less complicated that way. Whether they're living or dead, we can leave them in the past. We've got a lot more on our horizon. Good night, Alice.'

Alice nodded back as Elodie exited the apartment, shutting the door behind her. For a short time, the doctor remained in total silence again, before she noticed something beside her feet on the grey, polished floor. Bending down and focusing her eyes, she discovered the slightest imprint of a boot. Her heart froze as her eyes darted around the rest of the room, scouring every empty space, doorway, and corner. All was quiet.

With a shaking breath, Alice returned to her feet and backed away towards her bedroom. Without looking, she bumped into a small bench sitting beside her bedroom door, knocking over a framed photo. Glancing back at it, she picked up the frame and turned it over, finding it was a photograph of Miles, Deisy, Ryder, and young baby Rose all sitting together in Deisy's house, smiling. With a soft hand, she stroked the edges of the photo.

Please come back, Rose.

Chapter 30

Tiny yellow stars were sucked into the black hole of the Core, disappearing and reappearing without end. Its glowing violet aura surrounded the endless influx of light. Purple flashes of electricity zapped against its circular cage.

Alice stared deep into its heart, feeling its pull. Its energy. Its power.

She fought to turn away, but its hold was too strong.

Enough, Alice told herself.

At last, she broke its spell, glancing at the central laboratory's digital clock. It was 5:49 p.m. on the fifth of September, 2281 CE.

Looking out of the window and into the facility hallway, she watched the last remaining scientist leaving. He waved good night to her as he entered the distant elevator and the door slid shut behind him. Now alone, Alice turned a subtle eye towards the security camera in the corner of the room.

Straightening her lab coat, the doctor exited the central laboratory through its dual security doors and approached the opposite end of the hallway. There, she stopped before the elevator control panel and scanned her wrist. The panel beeped, allowing her to type in a code. After doing so, the words "EMERGENCY LOCK" appeared on the small screen. The panel beeped again before she approached another panel beside the stairwell exit, locking it in the same manner. At last, she retraced her steps through the hallway and stopped halfway, turning to face an empty space before her.

Glancing down at her watch, she noted it was 5:54 p.m. With a quiet breath, she looked back at the vacant space with nervous anticipation. The minutes ticked by. The UV lights hummed. Her eyes darted between the elevator, the security cameras, and the spot in front of her.

With a nervous swallow, she glanced over her shoulder, inspecting the laboratory for any distortions. Returning to her watch, the time was 5:59 p.m. Alice took a step back and braced herself.

As soon as the clock struck 6 p.m., Alexia appeared before her with a chilling thump of air. Alice's heart lifted inside her chest before Alexia spun around and aimed her rifle at her head.

Alice threw her hands into the air, 'Wait, wait, don't shoot! Don't shoot!'

'Why shouldn't I?' Alexia asked with a wild-eyed glare. *'You sent them back to kill us.'*

'No, I had no idea about that until after it had happened. It was Elodie. She had another team waiting that she never told me about. She killed Hayes when he came back too. I saw it. But I encoded this back-door location and time into your gauntlet in case of such an emergency.'

'Why?'

'Because I wasn't completely sure how any of this was going to go. I didn't know any of *this* would happen, but I took a precaution, and I'm glad that I did.'

Alexia shook her head. 'Kye's dead. They killed him too.'

Alice's expression fell grim. 'And everyone else? Ryder?'

'Dead. All of them.'

Alice's heart sank at her words.

'Before he died,' Alexia continued, 'he said he didn't even know who my parents were. He called me Rose and gave me this instead.' She pulled out the seashell necklace from one of her pockets, dangling it before Alice as she tightened her aim. *'What does it mean?'*

Alice froze at the sight of the silver seashell. Her eyes began to water as she looked back at Alexia, hesitating.

Noticing Alice's lack of surprise, Alexia squinted at her. *'What do you know?'*

Before Alice could speak a word, Alexia noticed two invisible figures approaching them from down the hall. She dropped the necklace and pushed Alice out of the way just as two ghosts sprayed silenced bullets at them. Alexia fired back as gunfire erupted throughout the hallway.

A few rounds struck Alexia's breastplate before she dove into one of the laboratories beside her. The building's emergency systems activated, sounding a howling alarm and dousing the facility in red lights.

Alexia crawled backwards along the floor, trying to spot the ghosts through the glass walls dividing the laboratory and the hallway. There was no sign of them. Her eyes scanned the rest of the room for cover before a fire alarm caught her attention. She stumbled to her feet and smashed the alarm window with the stock of her rifle.

Meanwhile, Alice picked up the necklace and crawled into another laboratory on the opposite side of the hallway. Clambering towards one of the benches, she began turning on every gas tap in the room, one by one.

Alexia pulled the fire alarm, causing sprinklers to spray water throughout every laboratory in the facility. She turned to cover the door just as more silenced bullets struck her armour and shattered the walls around her. After ducking behind another bench, a flash-bang bounced beside her feet. Leaping forward, she grabbed the grenade and tossed it back over the bench before it exploded in the middle of the room.

Amidst the blinding light and deafening ring, Alexia popped out of cover and sprayed dozens of bullets throughout the laboratory. Lights, electronic equipment, and glass tools were smashed to pieces. Debris and water bombarded her skin as she unloaded her entire magazine.

One ghost fired back a string of bullets, ripping up the bench before her and narrowly clipping the back of her head. Alexia collapsed to the floor, feeling a burning pain where a bullet had scraped her skull.

After turning on all of the gas taps, Alice glanced beyond the glass walls to the laboratory across the hall. Through the flashing lights and pouring water, she spotted the shimmering outlines of two ghosts blocking both entrances to the laboratory, keeping Alexia pinned down. Alice ran over to another bench and searched the drawers underneath it, pulling out a fire extinguisher.

Across the hallway, Alexia curled up behind her laboratory bench, unable to move as the two ghosts continued firing upon her position. Piece by piece, the bench shattered, leaving less and less room to hide. Holding the rifle close to her chest, she loaded in her last magazine, waiting for a window of relief.

Alice's hands shook uncontrollably as she tied a rubber band around the fire extinguisher handle. Tossing it across the hallway, the extinguisher landed beside one of the ghosts, covering him in smoke and foam. The ghost twisted around and fired a handful of bullets in Alice's direction, striking her stomach. With a cry of pain, Alice stumbled back to the ground.

Alexia peeked out of cover, catching glimpses of the ghost through the foam. Taking the chance, she bolted out of cover and dived towards another bench, unloading her rifle at the ghost. The bullets struck his armour as she landed on the floor, spraying more bullets at his feet. The ghost's boots tore to pieces, tripping him over onto the floor.

The second ghost rounded the corner behind Alexia, firing multiple rounds into her armour. She yelled in pain as the bullets scraped and pierced her leg armour. Scurrying around to the opposite side of the bench, she pulled out a grenade and tossed it towards him without looking.

The ghost ducked for cover as the grenade beeped and exploded, blowing back every piece of equipment in the room. Alexia shot to her feet and approached the ghost, unloading the rest of her magazine into him. He collapsed to the floor as the bullets assaulted his armour, causing his cloaking to malfunction.

Upon running out of ammunition, Alexia dropped the rifle and pulled out her handgun, firing its remaining bullets into him until the handgun clicked. She panted as she ejected the handgun's magazine. In the moment of respite, the ghost sprang to his feet and charged at Alexia, grabbing her and slamming her against one of the benches.

Alexia grunted and groaned as she held back his hands from wrapping around her throat. His cloaking continued to flicker as water poured down Alexia's bloody face. She reached out one hand and smashed piece after piece of debris against his helmet, all to no avail. At last, one of the ghost's hands found a grip around her throat, pushing her head back and squeezing her airway.

Alexia felt the air leaving her lungs as she tried to push him away. In a panic, her hand flustered along his equipment belt to grab something, *anything*. Her throat began to collapse under the weight of his grip.

As her vision began to blur and her throat started to crack, her hand found his grenade pouch. Pulling it open, she pressed the grenade's detonation button. Black spots consumed her vision as the grenade began to beep. The ghost looked down at his vest, seeing the grenade glowing red in his belt's pouch.

Without a second thought, he let go of Alexia's throat and fumbled to pull the grenade out of his pouch. Alexia gasped for air and used the last of her strength to kick him backwards. The ghost stumbled away and slipped on the floor while Alexia began climbing over the bench for cover. The ghost pulled out the grenade just as it exploded in his hand, blowing off his limbs and throwing Alexia off the opposite side of the bench. She fell to the ground with a thud as smoke, armour, and blood engulfed the room.

Rolling onto her back, Alexia coughed profusely. As the smoke cleared and water continued to drench the laboratory, Alexia pushed herself back to her feet and bent over herself. Eventually, she noticed the other ghost lying on the wet floor, blood pouring out of his boots, his cloaking glitching and body writhing.

Alexia limped over to him and pulled another magazine from his vest. She ejected her empty magazine and loaded the new one into her rifle. Pointing the rifle down at him, she fired a few more shots into his neck and helmet. His body ceased moving as blood seeped out of his broken visor.

With little strength remaining, Alexia stumbled up to the laboratory door for support. Across the hallway, Alice leant against the opposite laboratory door, holding her bleeding stomach. They looked at one another for a long moment, catching their breath. The sprinklers continued to rain down across their faces. The lights flashed crimson shadows over them.

Eventually, the sprinklers shut off, overwhelming the facility with a sudden silence.

Alice glanced down the hallway at the elevator and stairway entrances. 'More will be here soon. Come on.'

Alexia watched as Alice shuffled over to the central laboratory door. She placed her eyes in front of the retina scan. The device beeped, rejecting her identity. She rested her head against the wall for a moment, fighting to maintain her strength before entering an emergency code into the panel. The door beeped and unlocked. As she entered, Alexia pushed herself off the door and followed.

They both filed into the small dividing room between the rest of the facility and the home of the Core. The door slid shut behind them and the air pressurised, sealing them off from the outside. The sound of a loud buzzing saw emitted from down the hallway. Alexia peered through the door's window, watching the stairway entrance begin to heat up from the opposite side.

Alice unlocked the second door into the central laboratory. She almost collapsed as she stepped inside, grabbing the wall to keep her balance. Alexia followed her inside, watching her deadlock the doors before stumbling towards the control panels beside the Core. In an instant, the purple floating lights of the Core took hold of Alexia's gaze. She hobbled towards the mesmerising sight, staring into its black hole as if nothing else existed around it. The stars reflected in her eyes as her pupils dilated.

In an instant, the Core's purple exterior shrank away into nothing, and the yellow lights disappeared. Only the small black hole remained floating at its centre.

Alexia turned back to Alice, watching her sliding dials and pressing buttons. 'What are you doing?'

Alice gripped the control panel for support as her blood dripped across its buttons. 'I'm shutting it off.'

'What?'

Alice pressed another button, ejecting a small lever on a second panel in front of the Core. As her face turned another shade paler, she walked towards the final panel. She almost reached it before her legs gave out beneath her and she fell to the floor.

Alexia stepped backwards, watching her with confusion.

Alice struggled to lift her head again, meeting Alexia's gaze. 'When I – when I tested your blood, when you first came here, that's when I found out who you are.'

'What are you talking about?'

'I found … I found out that your birth parents are Deisy and Ryder. You're Rose Forder.'

'No, my parents are Leslie and Morgan Fifeton. You know that. My name is *Alexia Fifeton.*'

'They were your *adoptive* parents. And that name, that's just the name Ryder gave you when he gave you away. He didn't want you to be a part of any of this, so he tried to hide you.'

'Why are you saying these things?'

'Because it's true.' With a shaking hand, Alice dug the seashell necklace out of her pocket. 'This was from your mother. She bought it for *you*, as a gift. She wanted *you* to have it. That's why Ryder gave it to you. He must've recognised you somehow.'

Alexia shook her head as she took another step back. 'Everything *has* changed. I've come to a different future.'

'If this was a different future, he wouldn't have given this to you in the past.'

'No, it can't be. That's not me. That's not my life.'

'Maybe they would've told you eventually.'

'No – *no!* I'm telling you *that's not me, Alice!* This has changed! This isn't my past or – or my future or my present! None – none of this is *me!*'

'I'm sorry, Lex, but *it is*. The first time you met me, you told me about Morgan and Leslie. And the last time we spoke, you said you were sorry for what had happened. *It's all the same.*' Alice grimaced as she sat up against the Core. 'I tested everything I could to make sure. And it was all a match. I knew all of it before you left.'

Alexia's entire body shivered. 'And – and what? You didn't think to *tell me?*'

'I did ... so many times.'

'So why didn't you?!'

'Because I – I didn't know what I was doing, Lex.' Alice's voice broke as her eyes welled with tears. 'I don't think I've known for a long time now ...' Her chest heaved up and down as her bleeding stomach drenched her shirt in red. 'It was me who helped Ryder escape.'

Alexia stared down at her, speechless.

'I let him in here,' Alice explained. 'I let him take it ... I wanted to do something for Deisy. For what they had done to her and our creation. But then so many years passed that I wanted to find out what happened. I wanted to know if he had succeeded. I still wanted to give him time, though, so I sent all of you back later than he was. And I wanted to help you find the truth about your parents too, but then I found out who you really were, and then I didn't know how any of this had happened and I didn't know how to tell you or if I should and then ... then I just thought it would all work out somehow. I thought the Core would somehow make things right, that it would eventually make everything clear … but it never did … I'm sorry. I'm so sorry for everything.'

Alexia felt her head spin as her heart pounded inside her chest.

'Deisy would be much better at knowing what to say than I am,' Alice continued, fighting to keep her eyes open. 'She's the one who should've been here for you. The last time I spoke to her was in this room. That's when she showed me this.' Alice held up the necklace in her hand. 'She was talking about leaving all of this behind so she could raise you, so you could see the world together … but they killed her before she ever could.'

Alexia paced back and forth, beginning to hyperventilate. 'What's this supposed to make me do, Alice? What am I – what are you – ? I – I didn't *know them*. They were never there. The only ones who were there are *dead because of them.*'

'They're dead because of what we made. And we never should've.'

'But you did.'

'I *know* … I know … and that's why we need to destroy it.'

Alexia stopped in her tracks.

'We're the only ones who can,' Alice continued. 'And then we need to tell everyone what's happened so it never happens again.'

'No,' Alexia said. 'No. You're not doing that. I still don't know what happened to my parents.'

'But you know what happened to everyone else. Do you even know what this is?' Alice asked, gesturing to the floating black hole behind her. *'Neither do I.* So, I can't let you go back again.' Alice reached her hand up towards the control panel.

Alexia pointed her rifle down at her, resting her finger on the trigger. *'Alice. Don't.'*

Alice paused, sliding her hand back down to her side as her breath faded with every passing second.

Finally, the stairway door was broken through. Multiple armed guards poured into the facility hallway and sprinted towards them, with Elodie at their rear. The guards ran up to the first central laboratory security door, attempting to cut through their locks with an electric saw.

Elodie approached the laboratory window, finding the two of them inside. Her eyes lit up at the sight of Alexia. 'Alexia? You made it back!'

Alexia met her gaze with a scowl.

'What happened?' Elodie asked.

'What do you *think?* Your fucking hitmen tried to kill me. They killed *Kye.* And you killed Hayes too, didn't you?'

'No, Clay was never supposed to touch you. I sent him to bring you and Kye back here. I wanted you *alive.*'

'Well, somehow, I don't think he heard you. And neither did the other two lying dead out there with you.'

'Lex, they were operating of their own accord. I had no idea. I told you before you left, I *want* you to succeed. I admire you. I understand you. I'm *glad* to see you. Did you find out what happened to your parents?'

'*No.* Ryder said he didn't know them. And Alice says they weren't even my parents.'

'What do you mean?'

'I mean she's saying Ryder and Deisy are my parents. Did you know about this?'

'Did I know? What are you *talking* about? That's absurd!' Elodie exclaimed, looking at Alice as she continued to lose more and more blood. 'Alice, what *is* all of this?'

'It's the truth,' Alice replied with a fading voice.

'She was going to destroy it,' Alexia explained, keeping her rifle aimed at her.

'Wh – why would you ever do such a thing?' Elodie asked.

Alice could barely lift her head any longer. 'Because I don't want it to hurt anyone else.'

'The only ones hurting each other are *people*, Alice, not your invention.'

'What's the difference?'

'The difference is that things are going to *change*. We will use it for *good*, we'll make the future a *better* one, and I want *you* to be a part of it.'

'Only because I can give you what you want,' Alice mumbled under her breath before dragging her eyes back to Alexia. 'Enough people have been hurt. More than enough.'

Elodie looked back at Alexia. 'Don't listen to her, Lex. She's clearly not in a right state of mind. She's lost a lot, we *all* have, but you know better than anyone that sometimes the truth, and making things better, requires sacrifice.'

The security guards cut through the first central laboratory door, grunting as they pushed it open and moved on to the second one.

Alexia looked back down on Alice as her voice shattered. 'I just want to know why.'

'I know,' Alice said with an understanding nod. 'I wanted to know a lot of things too.'

'Lex, you *will* know what happened,' Elodie interjected. 'If you stay with us, we *will find out*. You can go back and learn the truth. The real truth. And, who knows, maybe you can even *stop it* from happening.'

Alexia looked at Elodie through the window, clinging to her words.

'You can change another thing for the better,' Elodie encouraged her. 'We can do *so much* good together.'

Alexia's lips trembled as she gazed back down at Alice. The electric saw cut through more of the door's mechanical lock, firing sparks throughout the room.

'Don't go back,' Alice muttered, resting her hands over her blood-soaked stomach. 'Please … don't go back …' With a long sigh, Alice's head slumped down onto her chest, her eyes closed, and her hand fell by her side.

'… Alice?' Alexia quietly asked. '*Alice?*'

There was no response.

Gradually, Alexia's heart sank as she lowered her rifle.

Elodie shook her head with pity. 'She didn't deserve this … but she wasn't well. At least she won't have to suffer this burden anymore.' Elodie redirected her focus back to Alexia. 'The control panel for the door is behind you. Let us in, and we can take care of her.'

Alexia looked back down at Alice as she sat quiet and alone against the Core. Her eyes gradually fell upon her open palm, where the seashell necklace lay. She stared at its faded silver and its rusted stains of blood.

With tears welling in her eyes, Alexia let go of her rifle, letting it hang across her chest.

Amidst the lingering silence, Alice's stomach gently rose and fell.

She's still alive! Alexia realised, feeling her heart bloom inside her chest again. Hurrying down by her side, Alexia lifted the doctor's head with care. 'Alice? Alice, are you still there?'

Alice's eyes flickered open, smiling at the sight of her. 'Rose … you're still here.'

'Yeah.' Alexia nodded. 'I'm still here.'

Alice's eyes filled with tears as she smiled even brighter.

Elodie watched through the window, nervous and unsure, as sparks continued to shoot through the cracks in the door.

'How do I shut it off?' Alexia asked.

'You … pull the lever.'

Alexia nodded and returned to her feet, gripping the small black lever on the control panel.

'Alexia, what are you *doing*?' Elodie asked.

Alexia stared at the panel in her grasp for a time, contemplating, before turning her tearful gaze back to Elodie. 'I'm staying.'

Finally, Alexia pulled back the lever. A second later, the black hole fizzled apart into three even smaller black orbs, quietly floating around their circular enclosure. Eventually, they returned to the centre of their space, lining up next to one another and remaining in harmonious alignment.

They're beautiful, Alexia thought to herself, staring at them in awe.

After another breath, her focus returned and she knelt back down before Alice. 'What now?'

'Give me … give me a grenade.'

'No, I'll destroy it.'

'No,' Alice said. 'You … you get out of here. You keep going … and you show the world who you are. Tell them everything. All you know, all you've seen. There's still *so much* you can do.'

Alexia gasped for air as she withheld her tears, hesitating, while the saw cut through one of the last remaining locks on the door.

'Lex, whatever she's saying to you, *don't listen*!' Elodie yelled. 'She's not thinking straight! She's not well!'

Alexia pulled a grenade out from her vest. After taking the necklace from Alice's palm, she rested the grenade in its place.

Elodie's eyes filled with terror before she turned towards the guards. '*Oh God, they've got a bomb! Get in there!*' she shouted before looking back through the window. 'Lex, please wait! Think about this! This is the greatest invention humankind has *ever* created! If you let her do this, everything we've done will have been for nothing! All of your sacrifices, all of the lives, *everything*!'

Alexia took a long, needed breath before standing up and stepping away from Alice.

'You – you won't know what happened!' Elodie pleaded, placing her hand on the window. '*You won't ever be able to go back!*'

After selecting new coordinates outside of the building, Alexia glanced at Elodie one last time. '*Good.*'

As she rested her finger above the T-PORT button, Alexia turned back towards Alice, who met her with a smile.

'It was good to see you again,' Alice said.

Alexia replied only with a small, heartbroken smile, before she activated her gauntlet and disappeared from the room.

Elodie watched in complete dismay. Her head shot back towards a handful of the armed guards, '*Find her!*' she screamed before looking back into the central laboratory. 'Alice, please don't do this. *Please.* This is your life's work. This is *my* life's work. *Don't* take this away from me. From everyone!'

Ignoring Elodie's words, Alice rested her head back against the Core. Her hand shook as she tightened her grip around the grenade.

The remaining guards almost finished sawing through the locks.

Alice hovered her finger over the detonation button.

Elodie gritted her teeth together before she sniffed something in the air. She turned towards the guards with worry. 'Do you smell that? … Is that gas?'

The electric saw sliced through the final mechanical deadlock, and the guards began pulling the door open.

Elodie watched them with terror, *'Wait! Wait!'*

The guards stepped inside just as Alice pressed her finger down on the detonation button. The grenade beeped as Elodie turned around, sprinting back down the hallway.

The grenade exploded, throwing all of the guards back and smashing the Core's circular enclosure to pieces. The floating orbs briefly flashed a purple aura across Alice's face as the explosion engulfed her.

Her eyes shot open with a fright. All was quiet. All was still. Glancing around, she found herself standing in the facility hallway. Everything was clean and untouched. She looked down at her bleeding stomach before looking ahead and seeing a woman walking away.

'Hello?' she asked, confused.

The woman stopped and turned around. It was Deisy, just as Alice remembered her all those years ago. Deisy's mouth dropped, and her eyes filled with horror. *'Alice? What happened? Are you okay?'*

Tears ran down Alice's cheeks as a smile came over her. Unable to speak, she simply nodded.

Down the hall, the elevator dinged, and its doors slid open, revealing Connor and his group of masked assailants inside. Deisy's attention was pulled towards the elevator as Alice closed her eyes one last time.

The explosion ripped through the central laboratory. Once it reached the hallway, the explosion intensified and set the air on fire. Elodie ran towards the stairway exit before the flames completely enraptured her, disintegrating her and every other guard in the facility in an instant. The entire underground laboratory was evaporated.

In the heart of Melbourne City, a single block away from the Forward Industries skyscraper, Alexia ported onto a busy sidewalk.

A handful of citizens jumped out of her way, gasping and staring at her in shock. Alexia, covered in blood and bruises, stared back at them, catching her breath. Before anything could be said, a loud boom sounded from the nearby skyscraper. The entire street shook. Everyone froze and looked around in confusion. Frightened murmurs arose from every corner.

Alexia bit her lip as she glanced at those around her. Amidst their distraction, she slipped into an alleyway behind her. Turning a corner and descending into another connecting alleyway, far from the sight of others, she found a spot of rest against a concrete wall. Blood oozed out of her leg as she gritted her teeth in pain.

Light rain fell upon her as she pulled off each piece of her wrecked armour until she was left wearing only her shredded black bodysuit. She slid down the wall and onto the ground, sitting against it as she sealed her wounds with one of her tissue-repair tubes. As she did so, she remembered the identification chip embedded in her wrist.

Shit ...

Unsheathing her knife from her armoured vest, she held the blade over the underside of her wrist, panting and hesitating. Clenching her teeth and holding her breath, she pierced her skin with the pointy end of the blade, making a small incision. Drops of blood began to trickle out of her as she dug her fingers underneath the skin, carefully moving them back and forth, searching for the chip. She shuddered and whimpered, fighting to not make a sound, before she finally took a hold of the capsule-shaped chip and slid it out from her wrist. Without a moment to waste, she dropped it beside her and crushed it underneath the handle of her knife. Her lips quivered and her eyes watered as she sealed the cut on her wrist. Dropping the container and clenching her fists, she fought back against her tears.

After closing her eyes and lifting her head, she let the rain bounce onto her skin. With a long, shaking breath, her hands relaxed, and her breath settled. Sitting all alone, Alexia let the rain wash over her face. Feeling every drop.

Once the blood had long washed away and her hair was soaked by the rain, Alexia sifted through the nearby dumpster, finding an old, worn-out hoodie. She strapped her rifle across her chest and hid it underneath the black jumper. After dragging all of her armour behind the dumpster, she retrieved Kye's journal and the small olive tree sprig from her vest pouches. Slipping them into her pockets, she pulled the hood over her head and sneaked into the city crowds.

Keeping her head low, Alexia trekked through the city, farther and farther away from the chaos at Forward Industries. As nightfall approached, in a quiet portion of the city, she came upon an old orange-brick high school that had since been converted into an apartment complex. Stopping before the front door, she inspected the various buzzer buttons and their correlating apartment numbers.

Which one was he? she asked herself.

Which one? Which one?

Seventy ... six? I think that was it. Yeah.

Alexia pressed the apartment's buzzer.

As she waited, she scanned the grey street behind her. Only a handful of junkies loitered about, minding their own business.

A few more moments later, Jed's voice came through the microphone speaker. 'Yeah? Who is it?'

'It's Lex.'

'*Lex?* What the hell are you doing here?'

'I'll tell you inside. I just need to lay low for a while. Can I please come in?'

'All right.'

Unlocking the entrance, Alexia climbed to the seventh story of the complex.

Jed opened his apartment door, looking her up and down as she stood before him. 'Uh ... hey?'

'Hey, *thank you* for this,' she replied, grasping his shoulder firmly before stepping inside and approaching the TV with haste.

The old classroom was decorated with eclectic sets of couches, rugs, Lava Lamps, posters, holograms, and alien and paranormal conspiracy memorabilia. The blinds were half shut, while green and blue lights shone across the walls.

Jed tilted his head, processing her intrusion, before closing the door and turning to face her. 'Uh, I thought you were dead, dude. Or long gone, at least. Where the hell have you been? It's been, what? A couple *years?*'

Alexia picked up the remote and turned on the TV, flicking onto a news channel where drone footage captured images of the Forward Industries skyscraper. Numerous emergency services surrounded the building as thick black smoke poured out of the first floor. The headline banner at the bottom of the screen read: TERROR ATTACK AT FORWARD INDUSTRIES.

Jed's eyes widened as he approached her side, staring at the screen. 'Damn … don't tell me *you* have something to do with that,' he chuckled.

Alexia looked at him, nervous and silent.

Jed's smile faded. '*Fuck.* Okay, no, Lex, you need to leave,' he said, shaking his head and walking back to the door. 'I can't have you here. No way, not if you've done that.'

'Jed.'

'Nuh uh, this one's way too much. They're gonna be coming here and they're gonna – '

'Jed!' she snapped.

Jed stopped as he gripped the door handle, looking back at her.

'You remember our theories about Forward Industries?'

'… Yeah …'

'Well, I've got a lot to tell you.'

Chapter 31

Three Months Later

A soft coat of rain fell from the dark sky above. Wearing torn jeans and a black hoodie, Alexia leant against the corner of an alleyway. She peeked out into the connecting street, surveying her apartment complex on the opposite side.

There was no one in sight.

A low-flying spacecraft rumbled overhead. She glanced up at the flying vehicle, watching it pass by. As the sounds of its engines faded away, she noticed a man carrying a handful of shopping bags approaching the entrance to her complex and scanning his wrist at the door. After beeping and unlocking, the door malfunctioned a third of the way open, freezing in place. The man shook his head in frustration and slid through the door.

Come on, Alexia said to herself. *Just leave it. Just leave it open ...*

Without bothering to close it behind him, the man disappeared inside the building.

Alexia sighed with relief before she slipped out of the alleyway and approached the building, keeping her head down and her hands buried in her pockets. Upon reaching the door, she slid inside and jogged up multiple stories until she came to her own. Keeping a keen eye on her surroundings, she approached the apartment opposite hers and knocked on the door. In the proceeding silence, her foot tapped on the floor, waiting.

After a short time, the door opened, and a young man stepped out before her. 'Hi there.'

Alexia was taken aback by his unfamiliar face. 'Oh, hi. Um, you're new here?'

'Yeah, moved in just a few weeks back. You from here too?'

'Yeah, yeah, just across the hall.'

'Oh. Huh. I haven't seen you around before. Must be bad timing, I guess. I'm Devin, anyway,' he introduced himself, shaking her hand with a smile.

'Yeah – uh – do you – do you know what happened to the last tenants of your apartment? I used to be a friend.'

'Oh, I'm not sure exactly. I didn't really meet them. I just heard that one of them passed away, I think. They were sick with something?'

'Oh. Right.'

'I'm sorry if this is the first you're hearing of it.'

'No. No, that's okay. Thank you for telling me.' She forced a nod before turning away towards her apartment door.

'I'll see you around,' he said with an awkward wave, shutting the door.

'Yeah …' With a sigh, she rested her head against her apartment door.

Dammit…

Hopefully, she's just somewhere better now.

Alexia shook her head before she placed her hand on the door handle and found it was unlocked. Confused, she opened the door and stepped inside, pausing at the sight of her room. Her flowers and plants lined the windowsill, freshly watered and blooming. Her belongings were tidied, and Bot sat on a chair beside the window. Noticing her, he lifted his hand and waved to her.

Alexia squinted at him and gave an awkward, little wave back. 'What the hell are you doing here?' she said to herself under her breath.

'Lexi!' Lay shouted with a bright, excited smile, appearing from within the bedroom and sprinting straight towards her.

Alexia immediately knelt down and wrapped her arms around her, laughing as she almost fell backwards. 'Hey! You're still here!'

'Of course! I was waiting for you!'

'Oh, baby.' Alexia gently pulled her back. 'Where's your dad?'

Lay's smile fell away in an instant, 'He left me … right before Mum died,' she explained as her expression shattered and a rush of tears overwhelmed her. 'They're both gone.'

'Oh, hey, it's okay, it's okay.' Alexia pulled her back into her arms, holding her close. 'It's okay, Lay, I'm here now. I'm here.'

'Please don't leave me again,' she wailed in fear.

'Oh, Lay, no, I'm *not* leaving. I promise I'm *never* leaving you again.'

'I miss them so much,' Lay said as she jolted up and down in tears.

'I know, I know … I miss them too. I miss them *so much* too.' Alexia's heart broke and her body shook before she burst into tears with her.

The pair remained inseparable in each other's arms, holding one another as tight as they could and crying together until they no longer had any tears left.

As Alexia gathered her breath, she kissed the top of Lay's head. 'I'm here now. I'm here. We've got each other. We've got each other, okay?'

Lay nodded, sniffling and wiping her nose. 'I kept your plants watered for you.'

Alexia smiled at her. 'I noticed. Thank you, Lay.' She rested her hand on her cheek, before looking up at Bot in the corner of the room. 'And I see you brought your friend.'

'Yeah!' Her voice lifted again. 'Bot's been keeping me company. He helps me around the house. Come see!' Lay exclaimed, hurrying over to his side. 'Bot, meet Lexi. She's a friend.'

Alexia climbed to her feet, curiously watching as Bot stood up, approached her, and outstretched his skinny metallic arm.

'I taught him how to shake!' Lay explained.

Alexia looked at them both in amazement. 'I didn't think they could do that.' With care, she outstretched her hand and shook his. 'Nice to meet you, Bot,' she said with a chuckle.

Bot simply nodded back.

'The only thing is that he can't speak, so he hasn't been able to help me with my reading,' Lay said.

'You've done amazing as it is. I've never seen anything like it, Lay.'

'Could you help me with some reading now?' Lay asked with hope. 'I've got a lot of books I've been wanting to read!'

'Oh, we should probably get packing, Lay. We can't stay here for long.'

Lay's expression faded again as she forced herself to nod. 'Okay.'

Alexia wavered, glancing at the door before shaking her head. 'You know what? I think we have a little time. Not *too* much, just a page or two, and we can do more later, but what do you want to read?'

Lay smiled as she ran back into the bedroom. 'I've got a whole bunch!'

Alexia laughed and walked in after her. 'I bet you do. It's your pick,' she said, climbing to the end of her bed and sitting against the back wall.

'How about this one?! It's about how the world used to look!' Lay explained, climbing up beside her and showing her an old graphic novel titled *The Old Green World*. Its front cover was a cartoon drawing of Earth, perfectly green and blue.

Alexia looked over it and smiled. 'That looks great.'

Lay sat up against her and opened the book as Alexia rested her arm around her. 'You read first!'

'Okay, sure. You ready?'

'Yep!'

'Okay. Well, "Once upon a time, there was a curious planet, and on this planet, a tiny flower grew out of the ground. It was the first flower there *ever* was. If this flower had not grown when it did, more flowers would not have grown after it, and if they had not grown, then neither would the flowers after that, and after that, and after that. Eventually, after all of the flowers that were, all of the flowers that are, and all of the flowers that will be, had grown across *all* of the world, the planet found itself a name. Earth …"'

* * *

One week later, Alexia arrived at the front gate of an old, nineteenth-century home. The white paint of the house gleamed, while a glorious garden adorned the front yard. Numerous plants and flowers rested delicately around the small path leading to the front door.

Wearing her hood and holding Kye's journal by her side, Alexia smiled at the surrounding garden as she approached the front door. After knocking, she looked over the journal once more and ran her fingers along it.

With the click of a lock, the front door opened, revealing an elderly lady with bright white hair and a flowery dress. 'Hello, can I help you?' the lady asked.

'Hi. Florence?'

'Yes. Do I know you?'

'No, no, you don't. I did know your grandson, though. Kye?'

Florence's face lit up at the mere mention of his name. 'Oh, really?'

'Yes. I thought we could talk, if you have the time?'

'Of course. Please, come in,' she said, stepping aside and gesturing her through the door.

'Thank you,' Alexia said with a gracious nod.

A short time later, the pair sat down across from one another at a small, round table in the kitchen. They each had a cup of tea between them, fresh and steaming. The inside of the house was just as well maintained as its garden, barely changed from how it would have been when it was first built.

Alexia quietly pushed the journal across the table, placing it in front of Florence. 'This was his. He was writing in it right up until the end. He explains things a lot better than I can.'

'Oh.' She picked up the journal, handling it with care as her eyes watered. 'I did wonder if he had been writing.'

'He was doing it a lot, actually. He told me you taught him.'

'Oh no, he did a lot of the teaching himself. He enjoyed it so much, regardless of my influence.'

'He definitely did enjoy it. He wrote so much in there about himself that I didn't know. I wish I had more time with him. I wish I got to know him better.'

Florence placed the journal down and looked at her with hope, 'Do you know what he was doing? He was gone for so long before they told me what happened.'

'It was the police, wasn't it? They told you it was an accident?'

'*Yes*. I had to press them and press them to even say that much. Do you know what happened to my boy?'

'I do,' she replied with a solemn nod. 'And it was no accident. I hate to tell you this, Florence, but he was murdered.'

'*What?*' Florence's hand rested upon her chest in disbelief.

'I was there.' Alexia swallowed, her own eyes beginning to glisten. 'I tried to help him, but I couldn't …'

'Who would do such a thing to him? *Why?*'

'It's a long story. But it started two years ago; when he signed up to work for Forward Industries …'

A handful of hours passed before the front door of the house reopened and Alexia stepped outside with Florence behind her.

'I'm sorry it took me so long to come and tell you all of this,' Alexia said, turning back to her with regret.

'No, no, please. I'm thankful that you did at all,' she replied with a melancholy smile. 'What will you do now?'

'I'll tell the world the truth … everything I know.'

'Do you really think that's wise? Won't they come for you?'

'They already are. Besides, people deserve to know what they've done. It might get worse before it gets better, but at least everyone will know the truth. Then they can decide for themselves what to do next.'

Florence nodded, thinking for a moment, before holding up her hand. 'Hold on just one moment.'

'Okay,' she replied as Florence waddled back inside, out of sight. Alexia cautiously glanced back at the grey, suburban street, surveying her surroundings.

After a quiet moment, Florence returned to the door and handed out an incredibly old, weathered journal. 'Here, take this.'

'What is it?' Alexia asked, gently taking the journal and looking over its faded leather. 'Is this …?'

'Read it and you'll see. It dates back a long time. If you have it authenticated, I'm sure you'll find it's genuine. It may just be the extra piece of proof you need to convince others of all that you say.'

Alexia looked at her with gratitude. 'Okay. I will.'

'And if there's ever any help you need, I'm here.'

'Thank you. Keep well, Florence.'

'You too, dear.'

Alexia nodded and walked along the garden path before stopping and turning back to her. 'I love your garden too, by the way.'

'You do?'

'Yes! I wish *I* had one like it.'

'Well, if there's one thing I could use help with, it *is* this garden. Would you be interested sometime?'

Alexia chuckled and nodded. 'Of course. I'd love to. We'll make a date of it.'

'Perfect.'

Alexia looked back across the garden again before noticing a batch of white roses sprouting beside her. Reaching out her hand, she brushed her fingers against their soft petals. At last, in a moment of pure and tranquil silence, she smiled.

Epilogue

Inside Florence's old home, the wooden floorboards creaked beneath her feet as she slowly waddled back to her kitchen table. After taking a seat, she laid Kye's journal down before her, and with great care, opened it and began to read.

JOURNAL
August 18th, 2279

I suppose I'll start the traditional way. My name is Kye Penson, I am twenty-five years old, and this is my seventh journal. In London, England, 1864, a man by the name of Hughes Dumphree was murdered outside the Dumphree estate under mysterious circumstances. His body went missing, as did any trace of the culprit. All that remained was his journal.

Hughes' partner, Stella Lockhurt, discovered the journal sometime after the incident. Written inside was Hughes' entire account of his brief time in Victorian London. Most importantly, he made the fantastical claim that he was, in fact, a time traveller and that he had sought refuge in London after escaping the future.

Despite all common thinking at the time, Stella believed every word he had written. She attempted to reveal such truths to Hughes' relatives, Mary & Flavel Dumphree, but they did not want to, or simply could not, believe the claims. At this time, Stella also discovered she was pregnant with two children. Despite Mary & Flavel's reservations about her mental health, they were kind enough to support her after she was disowned by her father.

Stella lived out the majority of her life in a rural property not far from the Dumphree estate, where she raised her and Hughes' two children. With the little wealth she had, she transformed her home into a refuge for London's poor. Inspired by

Hughes in more ways than one, she also began writing journals, telling her story and keeping his alive.

These journals were passed down from generation to generation, for hundreds of years, until now, when they have been given to me. This is why I am writing now. My grandmother taught me, and her mother before her, and her father before her, and so on and so forth. It has been a tradition to keep this story alive for over four hundred years now.

Some of my ancestors wrote out of sceptical obligation, and others out of true passion. My grandmother was one of those who believed in what Hughes had first written all of those years ago. She has kept every journal, dating right back to Hughes' very first one, in as fine a condition as she can. I suppose her enthusiasm has rubbed off on me. Especially when, only in the last twenty years, the truth behind Hughes' story began to become clear. In 2253, the company known as Forward Industries announced its breakthrough invention: time travel.

Only four years later, an accident was reported to have taken place in Forward Industries' laboratories. This resulted in the unfortunate death of time travel's co-inventor, Deisy Forder. However, in the years since then, conspiracy theories have begun to arise. The theories posit that this "accident" was something more. That it was, in some way, deliberate. For my grandmother and I, we knew something was amiss. After all, in Hughes' original hand-written account, he claimed to have stolen a time machine from the future and assisted in the death of a certain inventor. The stories are too coincidental and surreal to deny.

I, myself, have spent much of my short time on this planet attempting to discover some sort of purpose. Hughes' ambitions to help the world's future, and my ancestors' perseverance to sustain his story over the years, have influenced me from a young age. I can't help but feel an obligation to all of those before me to discover the truth behind this tradition. An obligation to somehow bring this all full circle, to answer the questions so many of my family have had for so many years. In doing so, perhaps I can find my own way forward, just as Hughes once did.

Six months ago, I resigned from my service with the Earth Defence Force. Since then, I have had my ear to the ground, and I recently discovered an underground job listing that has had certain rumours circulating its validity. Whispers say it is a front for Forward Industries, and if it is, perhaps this is their long-awaited response to the laboratory "accident". Perhaps, this is the very event that led to Hughes' death.

Only moments ago, I was interviewed by this supposed Forward Industries front, and it is difficult to tell if any of these theories are true. I spoke to a young woman who has gone in for an interview now, and she seemed to share my intrigue. Maybe she will have more luck deducing the truth than I will?

* * *

Dozens of entries later

July 14th, 591

It's the end of the eighth day in Attica, and there has still been no sign of Connor, Ian, or Ryder. Maybe we really are too late this time. Maybe they're all dead, or they've just travelled too far for us to find them. All I can really think of though, is Alexia's demand that I return home, and my agreement that I will do so by tomorrow's end.

There are many reasons I feel I should, of course. I can be there for Hayes, ensure he has at least one person left to share his experience with and corroborate his story. I have also discovered many truths that my grandmother deserves to hear. After all, she is relying on me to carry our family legacy forward. I can't just leave her.

Yet, I also can't forget about Alexia and why she is here. Her entire life has been driven by a pain and suffering that Forward Industries fostered. I suppose because I knew Forward Industries had been keeping secrets long before they were ever confirmed to me, I never really thought to blame them. With the knowledge my family has always had, it just felt inevitable, in a way. As if they couldn't help it. Yet, in now knowing the extent of the damage that they have caused, the number of people they have harmed, and the lies they have told, I can't ignore it any longer.

Alexia doesn't seem to believe any of that matters much anymore, partially due to their influence over her, and partially due to the belief that the future will have already changed, but I can't help but feel differently. Before this, I thought I may have been able to help Hughes, or at least speak to him somehow, but when I arrived and found him already dead, well, it was just all too fitting. He was still in the past, just as he always was. Ryder was always going to kill him, and we were always going to be here chasing after him.

If all of this is the case, then that means Forward Industries is still there, getting away with everything that they always have. In fact, they'd probably prefer it this way. Us being stuck in a place where we can't change anything. And it's sad to see Alexia accept this. She has such a story to tell, and such a drive for goodness and justice, that it's a shame she doesn't believe she can bring it to a time where things can *truly* change. Maybe I'm just too optimistic, though. Maybe things really are different in the future, and the longer I wait the more I'll miss out on returning home. Or maybe I just don't want to see our time together end.

I can't deny that, despite everything around us, I really have been enjoying this time together. I'm not sure what I will do tomorrow, but if there's anything that I know for certain, it's that I do like her. I suppose, if anyone else ever reads this, they'll discover the decision I will make in the next entry. I wish I knew.

for lex.

THE END

www.ingramcontent.com/pod-product-compliance
Lightning Source LLC
Chambersburg PA
CBHW051521050726
47503CB00014B/318